P9-CCT-196

WITHDRAWN

CHARLOTTE E. HOBBS
MEMORIAL LIBRARY
LOVELL, ME 04051

A FUGITIVE TRUTH

Also by Dana Cameron

SITE UNSEEN
GRAVE CONSEQUENCES
PAST MALICE

DANA
CAMERON

A FUGITIVE TRUTH

AN EMMA FIELDING MYSTERY

AVON BOOKS
An Imprint of HarperCollinsPublishers

This is a work of fiction. Names, characters, places, and incidents are products of the author's imagination or are used fictitiously and are not to be construed as real. Any resemblance to actual events, locales, organizations, or persons, living or dead, is entirely coincidental.

AVON BOOKS
An Imprint of HarperCollins*Publishers*
10 East 53rd Street
New York, New York 10022-5299

Copyright © 2004 by Dana Cameron

ISBN: 0-7394-4320-8

All rights reserved. No part of this book may be used or reproduced in any manner whatsoever without written permission, except in the case of brief quotations embodied in critical articles and reviews. For information address Avon Books, an imprint of HarperCollins Publishers.

Avon Trademark Reg. U.S. Pat. Off. and in Other Countries, Marca Registrada, Hecho en U.S.A.
HarperCollins® is a registered trademark of HarperCollins Publishers Inc.

Printed in the U.S.A.

For J.P.G.,
in the words of R.A.H.:
Semper toujours.

Acknowledgments

As with every book—and endeavor—I've relied on many people for advice and encouragement. These include my own Diego, Ann Barbier, Pam Crane and Peter Morrison, Beth Krueger, the Thursday Morning Ladies (Cathy Bennett, Linda Blackbourn, Mildred Jeffrey, Roberta MacPhee, and Joan Sawyer), my agent Kit Ward, and my editor at Avon, Sarah Durand. My neighbor Pierre A. Walker, Professor of English, Salem State College was more than helpful with his advice on things academic. Detective Sergeant Leonard Campanello of the Saugus Police Department was generous and enthusiastic with his advice, and I thank him for it. I borrowed some of Harry's examples of extreme bibliomania from Nicholas A. Brisbanes' *A Gentle Madness: Bibliophiles, Bibliomanes, and the Eternal Passion for Books*. If anyone's ever accused you of being nutty about books, read his book; you'll feel better about yourself and your harmless, peaceable habit.

A FUGITIVE TRUTH

Chapter 1

I STARED, UNCOMPREHENDING, AT THE BLOOD AS IT welled up into a perfect sphere, balanced precariously on the ball of my thumb. Finally the surface tension broke and the globe turned into a trickle, running down my hand. That transformation also broke the spell on me, and I stuck my thumb into my mouth as the vibrant pain of the slice brought itself to my utmost attention. The excruciating sensation did nothing, however, to mitigate the triumph at hand, and I knew that if I was still capable of making puns like that, I needn't call the undertaker just yet.

It wasn't the paper cut that was causing my good mood to evaporate, however. I was sitting, freezing, in my faithful, though beat-up Civic outside the gates of the Shrewsbury Foundation, and as their newest Fellow, I really hadn't expected the kind of treatment I was receiving. All I wanted to do was get up to my room, unpack, and get ready for the four weeks of research that awaited me, but the supercilious guard who had so thoughtlessly snatched my acceptance letter away was taking his time checking his clipboard.

I sighed while he looked at the letter again suspiciously,

like the barbarian hordes were crouched just behind me, waiting to storm the gates of Shrewsbury. I was tired; at three o'clock in the afternoon it had already been a long day. As excited as I was to be here, it had taken forever to pack, and of course I'd postponed it until the last minute, delaying the moment when I would have to abandon my husband, Brian, to the rigors of solitary household renovation for the next month. As a result, I'd left nearly two hours later than I'd expected, but the drive from our home in Lawton, in northern Massachusetts, out to Monroe in the western part of the state had perked me up immeasurably, perhaps even encouraging me to push the Civic beyond its present capacity and ignore the speed limit.

The views of the Berkshires were wonderful from the highway, vistas of craggy, wind-buffeted trees and steep gray cliffs, and I realized, a little guiltily, at how much I was looking forward to getting away from the never-ending home improvements and escaping into work that was purely my own. Libraries had always been where I'd gone to make sense of the world, and this one had the added lure of primary sources directly related to my work. I even had a chance to visit friends who worked nearby. I was on my own, and it was a good day for driving: clear, cold, and just a little overcast. After a couple of uneventful hours, I found myself in Redfield County, where the hilly terrain made my ears pop regularly and the pines and bare oaks stood out against the empty March sky. There the driving got a little more interesting; I was wrestling for the steering wheel with the wind, resisting the pull to the edge of the road and the cliff.

And then I didn't resist. I pulled over, got out, and considered the vista before me, cataloguing it as would a social scientist and someone with a nodding acquaintance with geology and environmental studies. My stomach contracted even before I reached the guardrail and considered the drop down to the icy river below. I forgot to wonder whether the area had been formed by volcanism or tectonic smashing and forced myself to edge over and look straight down. I craned my neck to see, as if the mere act of moving closer to the cliff meant that I would immediately hurl myself over the side. The black water one hundred feet below me looked as though it sucked all the light and heat from the surroundings, keeping the town on the opposite rocky bank firmly entrenched in late wintry gloom. As if that weren't enough, the little factory town—I didn't even know what its name was—appeared to have seen better days since its founding; there was no smoke coming from the stack and there were no lights in the windows. A lone car moved along the street on the opposite bank, and I shivered. It might have been that the mill or factory was now converted to a high-technology haven, and the light was wrong for me to tell that there was any life inside; it might have been that the town was enjoying a well-earned rest before they geared up for a thriving summer tourist trade, but I had no way of knowing. From this distance, it all seemed as bleak as the cliffs, as scrubby and weather-worn as the firs I saw by the riverbank. I pulled my coat closer and got back into my car. I was surprised that the view should have had that dismal effect on me, but I chalked it up to a too-hectic schedule and fatigue.

Driving another twenty minutes brought me to Monroe, the town closest to the library, and the source of the Shrewsbury family's wealth. At least I could see signs of life here—cars filled the main street, shops were open and busy—and that cheered me again.

The Shrewsbury Foundation was located a short distance outside of Monroe, a tall wrought-iron fence surrounding its grounds. From what I could see of the house from the breaks in the trees along the road—one of the hazards of creating a view for yourself is that it also tends to put *you* on display—the fence suited the place, all Victorian gothic and curlicues.

The real blot on the landscape was this foolish, imposing, and totally inappropriate guardhouse at the main entrance, complete with an orange-and-white-striped hinge barrier—nothing could have been more obvious or obnoxious a bar to the outside world. When I pulled up to it, its occupant was watching a monitor carefully.

That had been nearly two minutes ago. Perhaps he'd forgotten about me, turning into a paper-cut popsicle in the still-cold March air.

I tried again. "Hello there!"

The window slid open slowly, and a blast of warm air rushed out of the house toward me. I only noticed it because, even with the Civic's heater chugging away, I was still wondering about the possibility of hypothermia.

The man—a guard presumably—wasn't wearing a uniform, but a smartly tailored suit and regimental-style tie. There was a posh-looking overcoat hung up at the back of the booth. His iron gray hair was expensively cut and blow-dried in the vertically puffy style that Brian would have derisively described as "'possum head," and he was clean shaven with a tan that bespoke beach vacations or trips to a tanning booth. The whole impact was one of self-indulgence and image consciousness.

When I'd explained who I was, he'd snatched my letter from me—resulting in the paper cut—and then studied the paper like it was a fragment of the Dead Sea Scrolls. When I called out again, he took his time sticking his head out the window, moving with the lassitude of a reptile in a cold climate.

"Is there some problem?" I shouted over my engine. "I was told it was all right to move into the house today, even if it is Sunday."

The guard looked at me with a disapproving frown, then cast a glance at a clipboard with dark, heavy-lidded eyes. "We were expecting you over two hours ago." He finally handed my letter back to me slowly, but then made no move to wave me through.

"Got a late start," I explained, smiling. "Sorry."

"Can I see your license please? Some form of picture identification?"

Usually, this was the part I loved, where I got to say "Open sesame" and enter the secret cavern. I would be initiated into the rites of another institution, become part of another community. When I'd handed over my acceptance letter at his request, I'd at least expected some recognition that, for a while in any case, I was one of them, one of the privileged few who would be allowed to handle the treasures that were kept in the library. Maybe a smile of welcome, even if my credentials didn't impress him the way I thought they should. But this guy was doing his level best to act the literal part of a gatekeeper and was obviously relishing it.

"No one had said a thing about needing extra I.D.," I said, trying to restrain my annoyance; of course they had to be careful around here. He was just being a stickler and for good reason: Shrewsbury held one of the most valuable print collections of Americana in the world. "Here you go."

The man made a real show of comparing me with my license picture. If I had suspected him of having the least sense of humor or a working knowledge of Shakespeare, I would have given him my version of Olivia's inventory: two eyes, indifferent hazel; hair, not so red as to be called carrot but neither so brown as a sparrow; one nose, inoffensive and called by some attractive; one mouth, ditto, etc. The guard was really taking his time; he could have guessed from looking at me that I claim to be five nine and then compared the rest of the information with that on the acceptance letter. I mean, no one's license looks just like them, but he should have at least believed his own eyes. Something was going on here.

"Can I have my key, please?" I asked, a little miffed. I

was tired and my magic word wasn't opening Ali Baba's cave.

Abruptly the guard, or whoever he was, handed me my license and a key on a fancy key chain. "No need to get testy. Here's a key to the house—*please* don't lose it. You'll find a packet waiting for you there with all the information you'll need. Please familiarize yourself with our security protocols. Stop by the main office in the library annex tomorrow morning to get your picture taken for your I.D. I'll expect you at nine." He looked at me shivering, then surveyed the dirt-and-salt-covered Civic and was similarly unimpressed. "Promptly. Ask for me, Mr. Constantino."

"Thanks." I rolled up my window with a hand I could barely feel. The striped barrier rose up hesitantly, as if reluctant to admit me. "Jerk," I muttered, as I got the car into gear and drove up the hill.

I pulled up the long sloping drive, both sides lined with woods. The trees were huge stately things that gradually thinned out into a large, open area near the summit of the hill to reveal the house. "House" seemed too small and too warm a word to describe the structure. What I saw was a three-story stone mansion, built at the very height of the Gothic revival. The main part of the house had arched windows and was fronted by a tall rectangular tower with a castellated roof. It didn't matter that the skinny towers that were on either side of the center-hall tower were only decorative, and it didn't matter that this summer residence wasn't truly on the scale of the Newport cottages: this place was designed to impress. I knew that *I* was blown away.

I pulled off the road to the small parking lot at the back of the house and could see fragments of the road twisting down and around a number of small rises, leading north to the library annex, I figured. It was clear that the house and other buildings were in the southwest corner of the enormous property, because I could see the fence following the stream to the west, and nothing but gently rolling hills, valleys, and woods to the east and south. I noted with some irony that Monroe was obscured, being behind the next hill to the south—nothing to obscure the views of sunrise and sunset, nothing to remind the former—or present—inhabitants of Shrewsbury of the world outside. The stream marked part of the western boundary, then cut across and down the slope on which the house sat, following the road for a while before it cut across that in a culvert and flowed off to the south.

I tried the door near the lot and found that my key opened the lock: at last. That led to a large eat-in kitchen that looked like it might have been scaled down for more limited use after the family and its staff had left. Contrary to the medieval-looking exterior, it was modern with a stainless steel gas range and refrigerator. It was the sort of setup that Brian and I drooled over but could never think of affording; at this point, I was glad to have walls where they were called for in the kitchen, never mind gourmet accoutrements. A small staircase, presumably for the servants, led up from the kitchen. Leaving that room, I passed a small dining room opposite the kitchen on the central hall, and farther down, there was a monstrous staircase suitable for descending debutantes, epic sword fights, and banister sliding. At the bottom of the stairs, a parlor was off to the right, and to the left was a study. Right in front of me was the foyer and front entryway.

In the front hall was a small table with discreet notices left for residents, and I found my packet there. There was also a Victorian coat stand, the sort with a seat, hooks, and an umbrella rack, just like Grandpa Oscar and Grandma Ida used to have in Cambridge. On the table I found a room key marked 3, and so began the trek up the stairs. Number 3 was off to the left and faced the front. Just like downstairs, there were four rooms, two on either side of the hallway, with the bathroom in an addition on the back. The stairs that had led up from the kitchen passed through here, on the way up to the third floor that had been the servants' quarters.

When I opened the door I saw what was to be my home for the next four weeks. The room was large, with a huge carved bed, leather-covered desk, a straight-backed wooden chair, an armoire, and another chair, this one stuffed and more comfortable-looking than the one at the desk. The windows were large, and I was thrilled with the view out the front of the house.

For a moment I was overwhelmed by a sense of luxury that had nothing to do with my opulent surroundings: It was privacy. I was free from worrying about which room was packed with the furniture of the room that was being renovated. I didn't have to think about whether I would have to make a run to the hardware store after dinner to try and get the right-size widget for the third time, so I could have my bathtub back. I figured it was a good thing that I had a superlative husband waiting for me at home, otherwise between the deluxe living quarters and the library, they'd have a hard time getting rid of me.

But then I realized that I was glad to have a break from Brian himself, which took me by surprise. It wasn't that I felt any differently about him—I knew I loved him as much as ever—but lately it seemed as if we were spending all of our energy on everything but us. The work on the house was important, but I didn't like feeling as if it owned us, was driving us, instead of the other way around. Maybe if I had this time to spend on my own research, with no students, no house, no husband to make demands on me, I would be able to get my head into a clearer space to see how better to handle the things that were piling up on top of us.

I walked next door to the central hallway over the foyer and found that it had been made into a small sitting area with an extension phone and had a wonderful view of the south forty, then the mountains in the distance, same as my room.

Back in my room, I chucked my suitcase on the bed and then made several trips for my boxes of books and papers. By the time I was finished I was absolutely pooped, but thought that a walk around would clear my head, show me the grounds, and stretch my tired back. I flicked on my cell phone to see how low the battery was: damn. Plenty of battery charge, but I could get no signal in the house. Leaving my unpacking for later, I grabbed my coat, gloves, and key, and thumped down the stairs, banister sliding postponed for the moment.

The house seemed to be deserted, but as I headed out back through the kitchen I found the first of my colleagues—who'd probably missed me by coming down the back staircase or through the front. He was a small, pudgy man, nearly bald with a wisp of dark hair slicked across the top of his sweaty scalp. He was dressed in a white shirt and dark trousers that were shiny with wear and tight across the seat. I could hear the muted strains of synthetic music coming out of a pair of headphones clamped to his head—the reason he didn't hear me enter. He was replacing a bottle of Cutty Sark in one of the cupboards when I startled him, and he turned around to glare at me owlishly through his thick black glasses, nervously muttering, "ooh, oh dear." It occurred to me that he looked precisely like Morocco Mole without the fez.

"You startled me!" he exclaimed, as he pulled the headphones off. I could hear Kenny G. "You must be the new one, er, ah, Dr.—?"

"Emma Fielding," I said, extending a hand. His hand was small and a little clammy from the ice in the glass.

"I'm John Miner—Jack," he said, transferring his drink back to his right hand and taking a big sip. "Welcome, welcome. What are you researching?"

"Madam Margaret Chandler's diary is here. I did a little survey at the Chandler house last summer, and it has a good eighteenth-century component intact, so I'm going back in a season or two. Then I found out her diary still existed, and here I am."

"Survey? Component?" He screwed up his face in puzzlement, and I realized I'd lapsed into professional jargon.

"I'm excavating the site of her home," I explained. "I'm an archaeologist."

I had been expecting the usual curiosity, even excitement, that comes when I tell people what I do for a living, but Jack only looked doubtful and cleared his throat. "Ah. How interesting."

Clearly, he wasn't about to admit that he'd always wanted to be an archaeologist the way so many people did at cocktail parties. I changed tack. "What is your work? I read the letter describing who else would be here, but I can't recall. You're also doing the eighteenth century, right?"

Jack brightened a bit. "I'm just putting the finishing touches on my book on the economic history of the Connecticut River valley during the Revolution. There are some very important manuscripts regarding the lumbering concerns here."

I tried to look enthusiastic, but economic history bores the pants off me. Fair enough; even folks in related fields couldn't always get excited about the same things. "Well, it seems like this is the place to be then, isn't it? I'm going for a walk, would you like to join me?"

Jack was confused. "Where are you going to walk to? There's nothing out there. Not for miles."

I laughed a little, figuring he was kidding. "I'm not going anywhere, just down to the library and back, have a look at the scenery."

He shook his head violently, scenery apparently not big on his list of priorities. "Oh no, no thank you. It's just trees and cold out there. No, ma'am, not for me."

"Then I guess I'll see you later—"

"The rest of us are driving into Boston tonight for dinner, and if you like you could join us." Jack was doing his best to be kind. He reached over and pulled out the batteries from a charger plugged in by the sink. "You can meet Michael and Faith. Faith's staying in town tonight, doing work there for a couple of days, so you won't get a chance to meet her until she gets back midweek. But perhaps that's just as well, she's er, a bit, um, you know . . ."

I cocked my head and smiled vaguely to encourage him, but apparently Jack thought better of it. He carefully re-placed the batteries in his stereo, placing the old ones in the charger. "But Michael, he's just come in now. He's in the parlor, um, I guess. Will you join us?"

I considered it, then shook my head. "Thanks, but I don't think I'm up to another long drive today. I'll go for my walk, then unpack, get some rest. Maybe next time."

"Maybe next time. We have sort of a bathroom schedule for the morning," he said, rubbing his hands together like a raccoon washing its food. "You could either go before me, about six-thirty, or after Faith, about seven-thirty."

"The later the better, as far as I'm concerned. This is practically a vacation for me, and I'm going to make the most of sleeping in while I don't have to commute too far."

"Well, that's all right then." As I headed for the door, Jack looked concerned for a minute. "You do know it's almost a mile to the library as the road goes, don't you? It's freezing out there."

I smiled: He needn't have worried. I regularly ran five miles. "Thanks, I'll be fine. See you later."

Realizing that Jack was at least right about the outside temperature, I decided to get a scarf. On my way back through the hall, I ran across the second of my three fellow Fellows in the darkened parlor. Or at least, I thought I had. All I could see was a large dark shape off to one side of the couch.

"Hello?" I asked quietly, just so Jack wouldn't hear, in case I was actually greeting a pile of coats or something.

The pile stirred and a voice came mournfully from the depths of the cloth. "Oh God."

I looked around and flicked the light switch. "I didn't mean to disturb you, I wasn't certain if you were a—" A piece of furniture, I almost said. "—asleep."

"I wasn't asleep." The man had an attractive face, chiseled nose, fine lips, and wavy dark hair that was just a little too long in just the right way. His eyes were still closed.

"I'm Emma Fielding."

"Of course you are," came the reply, heavy with weltschmerz.

My eyes adjusted to the light, and I saw that the bulky lump was not a pile of coats, but a tall man wrapped in an enormous greatcoat and scarf. He pulled his hand out of his pocket, and, not getting up or opening his eyes, stuck it out in front of him, presumably for me to shake.

"Michael Glasscock. You're looking at that eighteenth-century diary, right?" His eyes opened on pronunciation of his name, and they were stunning, a deep sapphire blue. He looked the way I always imagined Heathcliff did, and I admit, in spite of his odd behavior, my heart beat a little quicker and my breathing got a little shallower.

Damn it. Why does just the thought of library work always have this effect on me?

"That's right." He knew what I was working on! "Margaret Chandler's husband, Justice Matthew Chandler, was a fairly consequential jurist in the early part of the eighteenth century. He had his finger in every important political pie, and there's been some research done on his life, but no one's ever done a full-scale excavation at the site of their house. And no one's ever tried to see how Madam Chandler might have fit into things, aside from a few little articles from the turn of the century, you know, colonial revival "great lady as helpmeet" stuff. So I'm hoping to look at it all together, write *the* book, a little feminist theory, a little social history . . ." I did a little cha-cha in time with my plans. I really was showing off, but Michael Glasscock didn't notice.

"Oh. Goody," he said in a monotone.

I combed desperately through my memory. "You're doing something on the American Transcendentalists, aren't you?"

"Idealists. God, they just didn't have a clue, did they?" he said. Michael got up and stretched, catlike, then slunk over to prop up the mantelpiece. "I just can't stand how naive they were. Painful."

That floored me; shouldn't he have been acting more the role of the apologist, if he were interested in them? "Sure, naive, but they thought they could change the world with their ideals. Not such a bad thing." Then I couldn't resist asking. "What drew you to them?"

"I study the history of American philosophy, and there was money in them," he said, with a monumental shrug of resignation. "It pays the bills."

He must have seen the unconcealed look of surprise on my face, but Michael just laughed hugely and humorlessly. "Oh, God. You're worried that I'm a cynic. Well, Emma, you don't know the half of it. I take it you met our august colleague already. Jack about half in the bag by now?"

"Uh, he's in the kitchen."

Michael looked as if he expected my polite evasion, and it didn't impress him. "He's wandering from institution to institution on the strength of the book until it's time for him to retire. He told you about the book, right?"

I could only nod. Dr. Glasscock was a decidedly odd duck and getting odder every minute.

"Those 'finishing touches' have been in the works for about seven years now and counting, so I wouldn't hold my breath waiting for it. Why they don't just let him go early so he can finish drinking himself to death in peace is just beyond me."

"Oh." It seemed the only safe thing to say, under the circumstances, but it wasn't safe enough. Michael picked up on my reticence.

"Oh, come off it, Auntie. I'm just being honest." Michael patted himself down, then caught himself. "Shit, no smoking in this crypt. This place is going to be the end of me." He sighed with galactic weariness. "I just thought maybe you would be someone who enjoys the truth as much as I do."

That nettled me—I always fancied myself as more than usually truthful and open-minded. "Yeah, well, facts are one thing, but I think that we of all people could agree that history—or the truth—is never as straightforward as one person's take on it."

Michael was unaffected by my tart response. "Like I said, you don't know the half of it." He slunk back and resumed his place on the couch and once again, closed his eyes. "See you around, probably. If you could turn the light off on your way out, I would consider it a great kindness."

I got my scarf as quickly as I could and shut the heavy door to the house firmly, trying to get a little distance between me and my new housemates. When I found myself hoping that this Faith person would be a little more normal than the other two, I reined in my thoughts. I was just tired and new to the scene, more than a little suggestible and in need of fresh air. Researchers and academics of every stripe have their quirks, and everything would seem a little less enigmatic after I'd had a couple of hours to settle in.

I set out briskly to chase the gloom from my mind and the cold from my veins. Following the road as it snaked away from the house, I moved over the hillocks on the slope on which the house stood, which eventually led out to a flatter stretch, delineated by a small brook. The wind wasn't as bad now as when I'd been driving, and I could just detect the signs of life beginning to peep out of the dead-looking ground. Little pale green shoots reached up through the carpet of muddy brown leaves and small buds appeared on the trees and bushes around me. A little gazebo stood in the middle of an open area some way off the road and I was stopped in my tracks by the view when I climbed up into it. The hill on which the estate was settled dropped away into a plain and I could see the countryside for miles to the east, the rest of the Shrewsbury property with the thin line of the fence in the distance and Monroe's lights nestled in the western Massachusetts hills farther south. The sense of exposure I felt took me unawares; although anyone from out of state might not have noticed the difference, it was unusual for me, accustomed to the crowded seacoast, to see such thinly inhabited expanses to the western horizon.

Farther down the road, I found the library and security offices just beyond the next turn, nested snugly in a little dell surrounded by more of the imposing trees. The library clearly postdated the original house, as the Tudor-revival style in the United States came into vogue closer to the turn of the twentieth century, but the stone-clad walls and low gabled roof line complemented the older house. I remembered from somewhere that the annex had been originally used as a retreat and guesthouse. The building was two stories, with a one-story ell in back, but the low roof and spread-out design made it blend into the surrounding landscape. I decided that it was pretty but nothing special, unusual only for what I knew was locked up inside: one of the best collections of Americana anywhere. I turned around and headed back.

I was halfway home again, really feeling beat now, when I heard the engine of a large car behind me. When I turned and saw that it was a security vehicle, an SUV, I moved a little closer to the side of the road so the driver could get by. The driver made no move to continue, so I waved him on. Nothing. I resumed walking and still he followed me, at a snail's pace, not passing, not falling back. If he wanted something, he should have rolled his window down and asked, rather than trailing me like this. I let him follow for another fifteen steps before I got worried about what was going on, and suddenly cut across his path so that he had to stop again.

I went over to the driver's side window. I couldn't see in because the glass was tinted, but I waited there anyway. Aggressive, for me, but I am learning that sometimes aggression is a good thing.

The window lowered with the smooth whirr of a hidden motor and I found myself staring into the smirking face of a crew-cut blond security guard. This wasn't the middle-aged guy I'd met down front—Constantino—this guy was a twenty-something and pure grade-A beefcake. He didn't say anything, just let his car heater warm the great outdoors for a moment or two longer.

"Is there some particular reason you're following me?" I said.

The guard flushed. "Can I see your I.D.?"

With his jaw clenched as hard as that, I wasn't really surprised that he couldn't get a "please" past his teeth. A little vein pulsed near his shorn temple.

"I haven't got one yet, I just moved in." I showed him my house key with the fancy Shrewsbury key chain. "Can I see yours? I don't think that real security should be harassing people this way."

I knew he was making the most of his uniform and this

flashy car that he didn't own, and bullies never expect confrontation. That became even clearer when he backed off.
"I'll just take your name, for now."

I told him my name. "Emma Fielding. That's Fielding,
as in Samuel Richardson's friend Henry," I explained help-
fully, just in case he was a fan of *Tom Jones*, which I think
is one of the funniest novels in the English language. But I
was starting to believe that he was beefcake between the
ears, too.

"I don't care who your friends are, you're not supposed to
be on the premises without your I.D. badge," he said, ignoring the fact that I'd just told him I didn't have a badge. He
very carefully clicked a pen and wrote my name down.

What an awful lot of clipboards there seemed to be
around here, and all attached to macho idiots. "What's your
name?" With the gate so securely guarded at the front and no
one for miles around, and on top of everything else, presumably, he'd been told to expect me. I was determined to report
this nonsense.

He stared at me another minute. "Officer Gary Conner. I
don't like your attitude."

"I guess we're even then. I don't like yours."

I suppose I shouldn't have been surprised at how immediately hostile he became, but I found myself settling into a
ready stance out of habit. What the heck was going on
around here, that everyone should be so wound up?

Officer Gary Conner suddenly decided to depart from our
little tête-a-tête. I jumped back out of the way, but he didn't,
however, pull away fast enough for me to miss the words
"just like that other dyke" he spat out on the way past. Obviously he had many other calls of a similar nature to make,
possibly kittens that wanted a jack-booted stomping.

I just shook my head and wandered back to the house as
the sunlight finally bled away in the west. Talk about falling

down the rabbit hole; the acquaintances I'd made in the past several hours were no less strange than Alice's. And this wasn't even my first official full day.

I sighed and let myself in the back door. Welcome to Shrewsbury, Emma.

Chapter 2

As I DESCENDED THE STAIRS THE NEXT MORNING I smelled coffee and was grateful that I wouldn't have to figure out the kitchen without benefit of caffeine. One good thing about the Shrewsbury library was that it didn't open until nine in the morning, which meant that I was able to sleep in moderately late. In the field, I was forced to drag my carcass out of bed at the ungodly hour of six, or even earlier, which was anathema to my natural inclination to late nights. As the saying goes, I get more done between 1 and 2 A.M. than most people do all day.

When I got downstairs, I found Michael sitting in the kitchen, staring out the window with a cup on the windowsill. He was wearing his overcoat over pajama bottoms, and it was abundantly obvious that he wasn't wearing the matching top. The *Wall Street Journal* and a copy of the *Weekly World News* were spread out in disarray on the table.

I sat down at a corner of the table and let the coffee have its way with me; I could feel the crenellations in my brain deepening as my mind was resurrected from the chaos of dreaming sleep. After about five minutes of comfortably mind-blank silence, Michael spoke without turning around to face me.

"Would you ever, on pain of your life, buy a mug like this?" He held up his coffee mug as if he were saluting the view outside rather than carrying on a conversation; he was funny about making eye contact sometimes, I was learning, either making too much or too little. I looked at my mug, and it had a row of ducks with bows around their necks, some with little galoshes on. One had a jaunty sailor hat.

"Uh, no."

"Precisely. Made expressly for the aunt market, stocks depleted at Christmas time. Terrifying."

"What is it you have against aunts?"

"Nothing, in principle. It's the auntie attitude that I can't abide."

Michael continued his contemplation of the world outside, and I put another pot on.

"That's some choice reading material you've got there," I said, when I finally felt my spinal cord connect with my brainstem. Houston, we have contact.

"Do you know what the worldwide readership of the *Journal* is? Close to two million a day. Do you know what it is for the *News*? Close to three a week." Michael turned around and I could see that he was wearing his half-rimmed reading glasses. "That means that on any given day for every individual who believes that there is order in the universe and that it can be observed in this world through the laws of economics, history, and geopolitical diplomacy, there are nearly two who believe that a potato chip in the shape of Elvis's head will tell them their lucky lottery numbers. You, my dear, are presumably one of the outnumbered former group, and it behooves you to pay attention to those other patterns."

"So which are you?" I asked, not at all convinced that his math or the numbers he was spouting were accurate, but dying to know what he was up to.

"Neither. I sit back and remark, that is all."

That little beauty was too good to let go unchallenged. "Oh, c'mon, Michael, confess. Are you secretly hoping that pyramid power and garlic will keep you alive till you're a hundred and fifty—?"

Coffee sloshed as he shuddered. "Gods forbid!"

"—Or do you think that true immortality lies in the size of your stock portfolio?"

"If you really are that curious, I will tell you." Michael got up and refilled his cup. "I am—" he took a sip "—a post-post modern, post-Hegelian nihilist."

I set my coffee cup down abruptly. "Excuse me?"

He mopped up the coffee that he had sloshed onto the table with a handkerchief from his raincoat pocket. "I don't believe it matters whether truth is personal or universal, and I don't believe that even if we find out for ourselves, it makes one jot of difference. What I am is merely an ardent admirer of the meaningless cosmic joke."

"What you are is a bullshit artist!"

Michael smiled beguilingly over his half-glasses and I couldn't help but notice how the sun caught the blue in his eyes. "Ah, but it is such lovely, deeply considered bullshit. And my publisher cries for it." He took a sip, pulled his overcoat more tightly around him, and then thought about his words. "Not that that matters either."

Now awake and eager to begin the day's work, I went over to the sink and rinsed out my cup. But I couldn't resist one shot at Michael; he made it too easy. "Hey, Michael?"

He'd begun to settle back into his meditations. "Hmm?"

"Have a nice day!"

The day promised to be a beauty, and even though I had to button up my overcoat all the way, I could tell that spring was chasing the winter cold away. Although I was in such a rush to get at the Chandler journal that I wanted to run to the annex, I forced myself to walk calmly. I'd decided not to drive for a number of reasons: for one thing, Bessy was sounding increasingly rough, and she needed the break. For another, I thought that the walk home would help clear my head at the end of the day, and I also didn't want to sweat through my good clothes or turn an ankle by hurrying too much on shoes not made for hurrying. There's some unwritten rule in library or archival research that says the researcher dresses nicely, professionally. This is in spite of the fact that there's not going to be any real audience to see you, that working with old books can get pretty grubby—what with decaying dyed leather and brittle yellow pages that are turning to dust—and that it would just be more comfortable to wear jeans and a sweatshirt instead of a skirt and heels. I don't make these rules, I just go along with them when it . . . suits me.

My walk also gave me a moment to enjoy the scenery and to make my plans for the day. I was afraid that at least a part of the morning would be taken up with introductions to the staff and to the library protocols. With any luck, I'd be able to look at the journal before lunchtime. I resolved to be patient until then, even though I was dying to see it; the only reason I'd found myself able to leave so late was that I knew the library wasn't open on the weekend. I had been told over the phone that it contained more than cursory entries; this was a relief, as so many early journals were nothing but glorified weather reports rather than what we think of as true diaries.

I'd have to wait and see for myself what I could make of the private thoughts of Margaret Chandler. I knew that a skilled historian could tease facts out of the most innocuous of references and that because I tended to be more aware of mentions of the material aspects of life—archaeologists tend to focus on things they can measure and quantify—I'd lose a lot of information if I didn't pay attention to nuance.

When the library came into view, I did pick up my pace a little bit—I just couldn't help it. Archaeologists spend considerably more time doing research and labwork than working in the field, but opening up a volume like the Chandler journal is as much fun for an archaeologist as putting that first shovel to ground. An even better analogy is to mining gold: Even though you might end up with nothing at all, there's such a thrill in the exploration that you're willing to pan out a dozen times because it only makes it that much better when you hit that one good vein of data that you can mine for all it's worth.

I was at the library annex by 8:55 and found that Mr. Constantino was involved in the perusal of the sports section of the paper. He didn't even say good morning, just wordlessly looked up at the clock, sighed, and carefully folded his newspaper and put it aside reluctantly. Constantino crooked his finger at me, and, ignoring my raised eyebrow, led me down the hall, where I had my photo taken for my badge. Then he lectured me about security for fully ten minutes by the clock. It was then I brought up my complaint about Gary Conner, which was received with boredom and the assurance that I was mistaking harassment for efficiency. Knowing I wouldn't win that argument, I saved my breath—for the moment. Every moment messing around with Constantino was another moment's delay in meeting Madam Chandler.

After I finally extricated myself from Constantino's sterile office, I fled to the library, where I immediately felt more at home. I was greeted by the warm, brown smell of old leather and paper, well-worn carpeting, and wood polish. There were a number of carrelled desks about, and a couple of flat tables on which to spread work. Reference works lined two walls, and a small office was on the third. The last wall had windows that looked out into the dense stand of trees that sprawled out in front of the annex, and I paused there to admire yet another splendid prospect.

"Nice, isn't it?" I was startled by a man's voice behind me. "I'm Henry Saunders, the head librarian. You must be Emma."

The man I faced was a few inches taller than I, and a few pounds lighter, but not weedy, with thinning blond hair and glasses. He was dressed, as are most of the men of my academic tribe, in chinos, a blue oxford shirt, and a tweed jacket. Unlike most of my colleagues, however, the jacket was nicely made out of good wool, and his tie was subtle, interesting, and not spotted with grease stains. Henry Saunders's glasses weren't the usual default gold wire rims, either, but a carefully chosen pair of French frames in a brown tortoiseshell that showed off some pretty compelling cheekbones. This was the sort of guy my Maternal Parent would have picked for me: WASPy, refined, and respectful. But unlike most of the boys my mother liked, Henry had a nicely formed chin with the merest hint of a dimple and gray eyes that were anything but vacant.

"Yes, I am, how do you do?" I said, taken unawares. We shook hands. "The, ah, views . . . around here are very nice."

He had tremendously sexy hands, broad and dry, strong and careful, and he colored ever so slightly at my last thoughtless remark. Okay, not stupid, a little shy—I stopped myself abruptly. What's with cataloguing the men lately, Em?

I tried to remember what else I knew about Henry; virtually nothing. When I was working on my Shrewsbury application, I checked out a few books that I knew had been written as a result of other fellowships. Each of the acknowledgments contained profuse thanks to Henry Saunders for all of his help, but I didn't know anything about his professional background. So far, I knew only that he was good at his job.

Pleasantly businesslike, he began to walk backward, to show me around the facilities. "Let me show you around my kingdom—"

Always alert to Shakespearean possibilities, I seized on this one. "Aha, then that must make you Prince Hal!"

"Actually, my proper title is His Serene Majesty, the Emperor of Bibliopolis," he answered with a grin, "but you can call me Harry. All personal belongings—books, coats, bags—go into the lockers over there—"

Just then, Michael Glasscock swanned past us, dressed now, but still wearing his overcoat. "Morning, Harry. I got the Armstrong catalogue from Faith and Jack's seen it. I'm done with it. You guys bid on anything at the sale?"

"There was an auction of important Americana," Harry informed me. "Well, we tried for a couple of leaflets but the competition was way too tough."

"Pretty pricey stuff, and me without a spare half a mil," Michael agreed. "What should I do with it?"

"Just put it on Sasha's desk, thanks. Oh, and Michael? You really shouldn't take any of the periodicals back to the residence with you without signing them out. I really have to insist."

"Sorry Harry. I forgot." With no real apology in his voice, Michael pulled up a chair and promptly settled in for a nap.

I blinked and looked at Harry, who seemed perturbed. "Michael seems to forget a lot of our policies when it suits him. I asked him repeatedly to leave his coat in the locker, but he keeps 'forgetting.' I'm sure that he really does understand about security, but . . . well. He doesn't seem to worry about it too much. We finally reached an agreement; he can keep it in the reference room, but not in the manuscript room. It was just . . . easier that way."

Harry then dropped the subject. He quickly ran through

the standardized speech about using pencil or a computer only, how the catalogs worked, and how to fill out a call slip for the bound volumes and manuscripts.

"You can help yourself to whatever reference books are out here," he said, gesturing to the shelves, "but no one besides Sasha and me is allowed in the stacks, I'm afraid. We do ask that you limit yourself to one item at a time with the rare books," he said firmly.

There it was: the first hint of the librarian strain, a manifest urge to control the books. "No problem." There was only one book I wanted to get my hands on, and I was only just managing to listen to his spiel politely.

"This collection is important on a number of levels, and we all have to cooperate to preserve it for the future. Quite apart from the monetary value, which, I think is on the order of tens of millions—"

"How on earth do you insure a library like this?" I asked, agog.

"We can't," Harry said simply. "We can't replace a lot of the things here, for starters, and for another thing, we'd never be able to get the security to the point where an insurance company would willingly take a risk on us."

I stared at him, dumbfounded.

"Of course, if we loan something to another institution— a library or a museum, say—we insure the object for transport, but we make the other institution pay for it." Harry resumed his spiel. "In any case, the intellectual and historical significance is utterly priceless, being one of a kind. So you understand why we need to take such care. Unfortunately, it's not only a matter of conservation and protection issues but outright theft. There's a rising market for rare books, manuscripts, and incunabula—"

"Great word," I said, more impressed with Harry every minute. "What's it mean?"

"In the library sense, books that were published before

1501," he explained, "though of course, we only deal with books relating to the colonial period and later. The black market is huge. You may have heard about the thefts from the Van Helst Library in Philadelphia recently."

"I hadn't," I said. "I'm mostly tuned into the problems with the antiquities market, but I guess it shouldn't be a surprise to find it extends to all sorts of rare, old things as well."

Harry nodded. "And it's a problem we take seriously." He paused thoughtfully, then suddenly changed the subject. "In terms of conservation, most of the volumes here are in good shape, but we'll let you know if you need to wear gloves, to keep the damage from body oils and cosmetics down to a minimum. Actually, if you could refrain from using hand creams or perfumes, that would be a big help. There are a few very rare volumes that we will have to get out of the vault, and if you need one of those, you will have to use it in my office or Sasha's, for security reasons." He glanced over at me, and I thought I recognized tentative approval. "But you've done this sort of thing before, of course."

"Oh, yes." I was relieved that Harry saw that I was a member of this club.

"It's nice not to have to explain why we can't let you go romping through the stacks. Too many of our Fellows think that they should be allowed. But we have some terribly valuable things, and it's just not possible." He paused and looked around. "What am I forgetting?" He ran down the regulations about photocopying, the hours the library was open, and the rest of the infrastructural details. "Let's go up to the manuscript section and I'll show you where you'll be working."

I followed him upstairs, thinking about how most people view librarians; they are usually caricatured as stern old creatures out of touch with the rest of the world and with a need for control so great that it drives them to suck the life out of the fun of using a library. The worst librarians act like dragons sitting on a golden hoard, resenting you for threatening to disturb their carefully ordered world. With the best librarians, the sort I so often had a chance to encounter professionally—well, the concern with control was still there, but it was mitigated by their understanding that the care of the books was important but, that theoretically speaking, the books were worthless unless they were used. The good ones try to find out how to facilitate your work while still caring for their charges.

Upstairs was a room of the same size as those below, but differently partitioned. The reading area was similar, but in addition to the small office in the back, I could see a small laboratory to one side. It wasn't anything fancy, just a fume hood and a sink and a couple of work surfaces. A collection of brown chemical bottles sat on a shelf, along with cases of distilled water. I knew that distilled water was often used to clean paper during its conservation. Harry noticed my interest.

"We are lucky enough to have what we need to do some conservation and repairs to the books right here. We are equipped to do most anything short of rebinding, but at the moment, there's no one who is skilled enough to do more than the basics."

"Is that you, Harry?" said a muffled woman's voice. "I'm still worried about the Whitehead—"

"Ah, here's Sasha Russo, our manuscript librarian." Harry was looking over my shoulder and smiling broadly. "Sash, come say hello to Emma Fielding."

Sasha was stooping by a trolley full of books and had been sorting them when she called him. At the mention of her name, she stood up to introduce herself. And stood up, and up, and up. No wonder Harry was smiling; Sasha's legs ended on her about where my ears start on me.

It just wasn't fair. Oh, sure, she was wearing a pair of glasses with thick black frames, a lavender twin set and tweedy brown skirt, and had her hair up in a tight bun. But the sweater looked like it was covering a partial relief map of the Rockies, the hem of the skirt struggled to stay demurely at the tops of her knees, and the glasses looked like a fashion photographer had just decided that smart was chic and stuck them on the pouting face of his latest supermodel creation. And that hair; gold with coppery glints that reminded men why Jason sought the golden fleece, and that was the sole object of every woman who ever tangled with a home bleach kit. Sasha Russo was a manuscript librarian trapped in the body of a Viking goddess.

I'd taken particular care with my appearance that morning and had flattered myself that I looked not only professional and presentable but a little sexy, in a kinky, Edwardian sort of way. Suddenly I felt short, squat, brown, and dull, a toad standing next to a tulip. I consoled myself with the thought that she was probably a bubble-headed miracle of plastic surgery and Aqua Net, with minor talents for alphabetizing and walking away.

"Hi, I'm Sasha Russo," she said, offering me a hand that was strong and delicate at the same time. "I'm so pleased to meet you, I've been telling Harry that it's long past time that someone with real credentials came to work with the Chandler diary. Margaret Chandler's historically been given such short shrift, and so when I read your proposal, I was convinced that you'd be the one to finally do her justice. Welcome."

I never knew how much of a toad I could feel like until I heard her kind words. "Uh, thanks," I croaked.

"Has Harry told you about our surprise yet?" Sasha could barely contain herself, she was so excited, but of course her voice and Harry's never broke a whisper.

"Surprise?" I looked puzzled at Harry, then Sasha.

"I thought I'd leave that to you, Sash," Harry answered.

She beamed at both of us. "When we learned that you

were interested in the Chandler journal, we checked the rest of the holdings to see if there was anything else you would find useful. And what do you think we found?"

Harry interrupted. "*You* found, Sasha. Don't give me any of the credit."

"Nonsense. It's a joint effort, Harry. Always."

I caught a fond glance as it was exchanged between them; as far as they were concerned, they were all alone at that moment. Okay, there was definitely something going on here. "You're killing me with the suspense."

"Letters." The manuscript librarian was practically exploding with delight. "We found part of Madam Chandler's correspondence to a cousin in London. They were collected just recently, in England, and it's clear they're hers!"

I could barely believe what she was saying. "You've got them *here*? Now? For *me*?"

"We do indeed! There is a *tiny* bit of work to be done on them," she backpedaled, in the face of her obligation to the manuscripts. "They should have been put into acid-free folders and catalogued immediately after they came to Shrewsbury. But they weren't and so I need to deal with some mildew before it gets out of hand, but there's little harm done. A bit of foxing, some small tears. Speaking of work," she turned to Harry, "I still can't find the Whitehead manuscript."

"I've found it, I'll get it for you," Harry replied.

"Great!" Sasha was clearly relieved.

Harry explained to me. "Unfortunately, we're still sorting out things since my immediate predecessor. He was a bit careless in terms of tracking his acquisitions and deaccessioning. He came in at a time—years ago—when the library was still being treated too casually as a private collection, at a time when the family still thought it was a bit of a lark to have a good library, but not a responsibility." He frowned.

"It can be a real problem, to have someone come to study documents that were sold five years ago, but we're getting things in order—"

"He left things in a muddle," Sasha agreed vehemently. "It seems to get worse the more we work on it, and I'm beginning to wonder if he didn't liberate a few things on his way out."

"Sasha—"

"I know, but I can't see any reason in not asking—"

Finally I couldn't stand it any longer, and I broke in as gracefully as I could. "If I could just get set up someplace—?"

The two librarians looked at me and burst out laughing. They managed to convey their mirth almost noiselessly.

"Of course, you want to get started!" Sasha said.

"I'll see you later, Emma." Harry left.

Sasha led me to a carrel. "Why don't you settle in here, and I'll get you Madam Chandler." A loud, metallic, grating noise from outside overrode her words. "Oh, drat, we're still at the mercy of the workmen out there," she informed me. "Repairing the grout or something, in the walls."

"Mortar?"

"That's it, it's a mess and a racket and there's been problems with the fire alarms with all their digging around. Poor Harry's been dragged out of bed several times this month when the alarm's gone off in the middle of the night—but you don't need to be worried about all that." She put the annoyance aside and got back to business. "Now there may be a few other folks in and about. We have scholars who visit for a day and a couple of interns to help with the cataloguing and such. And usually Dr. Faith Morgan is up here too, but she's in Boston for a few days. She's been studying some rare examples of Antebellum fiction, doing wonderful stuff on the nature of expressed emotion. With such an interesting topic, you'd think she'd be a little more . . . a little less . . .

you know, more of a people person. I mean, she and Harry get on famously, there's no denying that—"

Something in Sasha's voice changed and her face went red. I was certain that there was at least a little possessive jealousy at play here.

"—and I know the interns are fascinated, she strikes them all as rather mysterious, but she doesn't make much effort with the rest of us. When she does, it's almost like she's trying to push buttons, trying to manipulate you." Suddenly, Sasha realized that she was speaking out of turn again, and a moment hung awkwardly between us so that when her phone rang, she was eager to excuse herself. "I'll bring the journal when I get done. I'll be real quick, I promise."

Her description of Dr. Morgan's project rang a bell with me, but I couldn't remember why. I was too distracted by the length of time that it took Sasha to come back out with the diary—she was taking forever! Eventually she emerged with my book and a slip of paper. "Sorry about that, my phone. It was the director, Evert Whitlow. He likes to have the new Fellows for lunch the first day, but he won't be able to see you until Wednesday."

"Okay, thanks." I paused, not quite certain how to bring up the question I had on my mind. "Dr. Morgan's work sounds familiar to me. Where does she teach?"

"Out in California somewhere, I think." She flushed with embarrassment. "I'm sorry, I shouldn't have . . . before . . . you know, some people are just easier to get . . . and she . . . just . . ." Sasha paused, still holding the diary and apparently reconsidering what she was going to say. Finally, she put the Chandler volume down in front of me. "Well, here's the journal. Good luck. I'll be in my office if you need anything."

All other thoughts fled as I was left alone with my treasure. I moved the journal so that it was perfectly square on the desk before me and examined it as an object for a moment. What would it tell me about its former owner? Already it was more than I expected: So many diaries were simply sheets of paper sewn together with a little cardboard cover pasted on the end pages, simple recordings of the quotidian facts of a life, sometimes only a list of visitors or chores. This one already struck me as different. It was about eight inches long and six wide, with a faded blue leather cover, leafy vines outlining its edge, tooled in gold leaf that still shone. Although the corners of the book were dog-eared and browned with age, the cover and endpapers were clean of mildew and other decay. The only problem was that the pages were a little loose within the binding: there was no way that I could photocopy the journal without damaging it further, if in fact Shrewsbury allowed photocopying of bound volumes. That didn't matter so much, as I would have to transcribe it into my notebook computer anyway.

Taking a deep breath, as if I were about to plunge from the high board, I opened to the first page.

It took my eyes a moment to adjust to the eighteenth-century handwriting, but the first of my several fears was allayed: Madam Chandler wrote with a beautifully clear hand. It would be a pleasure to read this elegant script, and I knew that my work would go so much faster than if I had to contend with poor penmanship. I read the superscript at the top of the page, the once-black ink faded to blurred brown, but still legible:

> *Margaret Amalie Chase Chandler, her IIId Booke,*
> *Begun this Year of Grace 1723*
> *Stone Harbour, Massachusetts*
> *Since it is possible that thou mayst*
> *depart from Life this very Moment,*
> *regulate every Act and Thought accordingly.*

A flood of ideas cascaded through my head even before I finished reading that heading. Her middle name suggested the possibility that Margaret might be part French; the date, I remembered, correlated with the first year of her husband's tenure as justice in the courts in Stone Harbor and Boston; and she herself must have been in her early twenties at the time. Even as I was digesting this morsel, gooseflesh ran down my spine and arms as I realized that this was the *third* volume of her journal—was it possible that the others still existed? A whole series? Hold on a second, Emma, don't go looking for more, when you haven't even read one page of this one!

But the epigram dragged me back to the miracle of this book. I had no idea who had written the quote, but it sounded classical to me. The thing that kept my heart racing was that it was the sort of thing you'd see in a man's journal—it was extremely rare for women to know the classics, even in translation. She was very well read indeed, if she was familiar with the Greek and Latin writers. Margaret Chase's family was rich, but not aristocratic—I had learned from her husband Matthew's documents that her father was a merchant. And it wasn't yet fashionable in Europe for even wellborn women to be so educated. And the tone of the epigram was so strongly religious, that told me a lot about her as well. This was going to be a trip. I could tell it would be an adventure to learn about this woman's life.

I closed my eyes and said a little prayer to Saint Helena, the patron saint of archaeologists, before I looked at the first entry:

> *May 29/This morning took into service Nora, a little blacke Wenche . . .*

That slowed me down a second. The name Nora suggested Irish, while black . . . of course. It was taking me a minute to acclimate to the idiom of the time. In the seventeenth and eighteenth centuries, black or white generally referred to hair rather than skin color. And her spelling, rather than being condemned for its irregularity, would have been praised for its creativity. I continued to read:

> ... *a little blacke Wench cursed with as terrible a Mouthe as I have ever had the Misfortune to heer. Tis little Surprize to discover that she is Irish, and as rabblesome as any who hie beyond the Pale, so I fear Correction will come only at great length of Time and much exercise of Discipline. Insofr as Matthew bade me take her up I will do so, but I would too his sense of Mercy and Justice extended as far as his poore Wife! V. gd—I will keep her, but I will also watch the Plate. V. hot still, set Katie to whip'g the Sleeves of the green Linnen; Jenny to Jellie makg. Tomorrow to visit Rev. Blnchd who has been much troubled with his Wind—I will carry my parsley Tonic to him as he says it is the only Thing that brings ease.*

I could barely keep from shrieking with glee! I had hoped that the journal would not be just a chronicle of the weather and the Sunday sermon's text, but this sort of detail was an unbelievable wealth of information. Servant troubles, household tasks, opinions—and oh, what opinions!—feelings, gassy preachers and their cure! Oooh, what a book this was! What a book mine would be!

Slow down, Emma! I chided myself. This is only the first paragraph; what will you do if the rest isn't as detailed as this? I flipped carefully through the pages, and every entry seemed to be at least a paragraph long. Although most people tended to use the words *diary* and *journal* interchangeably these days, this was a true journal, filled not only with facts but the thoughts of the writer. In other words, the mother lode.

I needed to formulate a plan. Do I read the whole thing

first, get a feel for what's in store? Or take each entry apart as I get to it, analyze it without being influenced by what I knew was to come? This was like finding Tut's tomb as far as I was concerned, a window on another world, and I wanted to make sure that I would get every bit out of it that I could. Perhaps it *would* be wiser to transcribe it as I went . . . I set the book down carefully to consider.

My decision took less than a heartbeat. I would *definitely* read it through first. Although I would take notes as ideas came to me, I needed to begin my engagement with Margaret Chandler, learn who she was, react to her as a person, before I began to dissect and analyze her world. Wonderful woman, tell me how you lived! Surrender all your secrets! Prejudices, prayers, the cost of cloth, neighborly disputes, dinner menus—!

A small cough from Sasha alerted me that my enthusiasm had animated me: unwittingly, I had left my seat and was doing a little victory dance in front of the desk.

Ah, but it can't be the first time she's seen such behavior, not in a place like this! I nodded an unfelt apology, resumed my seat, and got down to the engrossing task of reading someone else's diary.

The only reason I stopped two hours later was because I was in desperate need of a biology break. I found that Sasha also was in the ladies' room.

"Any luck with the missing manuscripts?" I asked, as I finished drying my hands.

"No, but Harry's on it," she said. "He'll get it sorted out, I'm sure, I'm just jumpy right now, about everything, it seems. There's so much going on—what with the way that Mr. Whitlow is reorganizing the structure of the library this year— adding more administrators all the time—and keeping up with the collections management, and all. I can't afford to even think about losing this job; you know how it goes: last hired, first fired. And it always seems that there's money for administrators, but never any for librarians. It's tough."

"Especially with the economy the way it is," I agreed.

"Tell me about it." Sasha dug out an orange stick and cleaned under her nails, quickly and efficiently. "And what with the alarm systems and all, well, you can see why I'd be worried about the state of the collections, especially the things we can't locate—"

And perhaps that is the reason the security staff is acting like a bunch of angry apes, I thought.

"—but we'll sort it out. Harry and me." Sasha smiled without explaining anything more, gave me a little wave, and went back to work.

Although I would have bet heavily against it, I was hungrier than I imagined possible when dinnertime came later on that evening. I would have stayed in the library all night if Sasha hadn't come by to chase me out at the five o'clock closing time, and it was only then that I realized I hadn't bothered to eat lunch. The Chandler journal was so engrossing that the hours flew by, but my questions also mounted. As with the first entry in the journal, others that came after it were detailed, and they also sometimes contained a series of numbers. In some cases, the numbers appeared in the middle of the text. I finally decided that the numbers did not represent dates or verses from the Bible—none of the numbers went higher than the mid-twenties—but were possibly part of some sort of code, perhaps alphabetical. I made a few half-hearted attempts to play around with the numbers, but got nowhere with them. So I simply resolved to keep my eyes open for more clues and continued to read.

*   *   *

Although I enjoy eating, I am by all accounts, and especially Brian's, a miserable cook, preferring to dump my dinner out of one or more cans rather than going to a lot of trouble to create something really tasty. So it was with some surprise that I found, while making my dinner, that I was in fact the gourmet of the house. I figured beans and rice would at least get some vegetables and low-fat carbos into me and wouldn't take more than a few minutes away from work. My housemates, however, had even more efficient solutions to the evening meal than me. Although I saw him eat an orange during the early news, Jack's dinner consisted solely of three or four trips to his Cutty cabinet throughout the early evening. Each time he nearly filled his lowball glass. He had dessert in the form of an individual serving of banana pudding in a plastic container after trip number three and *Wheel of Fortune*.

Michael, on the other hand, took a more traditional route and dumped a frozen burrito into the microwave. He was still wearing his overcoat, which I'd noticed he'd never bothered to remove during his day's tenure at the library, and which seemed to remain with him as a form of security blanket. Bored with watching his burrito spin surreally around on the carousel, Michael hopped up onto the counter to watch me mince some garlic with the wide-eyed curiosity and excitement that children have for fireworks or parades.

"Hey, Julia Child. I think there's some spices or something over there," he said, jerking his head to a cabinet near the sink. "I saw some little cans or jars."

After I determined that the little jars were full of roach powder and sink cleanser, I got some cumin and chili powder from my little store of groceries I'd brought with me, at Brian's suggestion, and dumped it into the cooking beans.

"So where's, ah, Faith, tonight?" I asked. I wanted to ask Michael, with his seeming inclination to share more of his thoughts and opinions than anyone really wanted, about whatever it was that Sasha was alluding to this morning. It occurred to me that Sasha had made a lot of allusions to things I was curious about. But my gambit to get Michael to speak up worked even better than I thought.

"Ice Queen's still off freezing someone's soul in Boston. She'll be away for a couple more nights, then she's all ours again. Just don't leave the bathroom a mess when you're in there before her, or you'll wish your parents had never met."

I frowned and dumped my cooked rice into a bowl and then scraped the beans out on top of that. "Oh?"

Michael was the epitome of archness. "How discreet you are, Dr. Fielding. Why don't you just come out and ask?"

"Okay." I took my bowl over to the kitchen table and began to eat. Around bites I said, "So. Why do you call her the Ice Queen? How do you freeze a soul? Is it just that she's crabby in the morning, or that she's a highly functioning but dangerous psychotic? What makes you think I couldn't take her with one hand tied behind my back? Why would you think that anyone appreciates seeing a messy bathroom in a communal living situation? And how come—"

Even though it was abundantly clear that I was kidding, Michael sternly held up one hand: Elvis wasn't coming on-stage until the audience was properly hushed, Maestro wasn't about to begin the symphony until all attention was focused on him. "It's just my pet name for Faith. I suppose she's no worse than your common or garden variety touch-me-not, sanguivorous neurotic that the ivory tower seems to incubate by the thousands, but on the minus side, she's got more armor than a cockroach hiding in a safe deposit box, a tongue like sulfuric acid, and the same benevolent tolerance for ordinary humanity as a pissed-off Gila monster. Unless you have something that she wants, and then, watch out. She changes like a chameleon."

I swallowed.

Michael finished off his assessment of Faith. "Apart from

that, she's sort of cute. Hasn't published much lately, though."

The microwave bell *dinged*, and Michael hopped down and scooped out the burrito onto a paper towel. He went off to watch the news with Jack before I could ask him any more.

After dinner I was on my way to my room when the phone rang. I picked up the extension in the second-floor sitting area.

"Hello?"

"May I speak with Emma Fielding please?" An oily, faintly familiar voice oozed over the line.

"Speaking."

"Professor Fielding. This is Ron Belcher," the caller announced, pleased with himself.

"Dean Belcher, what a surprise." I was very careful not to say what a pleasure it was; his manner had the same effect on me as biting into sandy butter.

It should have been nothing at all. I don't recall much of the specific conversation, only that he was calling to let me know that the last of my letters of support had been received and that I would still be responsible for the classes that my colleagues and graduate students were covering during my brief leave. Again, these were reminders that no one working for tenure needed to be given, especially not someone as type-A as I am.

It was the last two things he said, after twenty minutes of listening to himself talk, that put me into shock.

The first was that he'd been having a look at my tenure portfolio, and—confidentially speaking, of course—he was almost convinced that it might just be enough. Almost.

The other thing was his mentioning that he'd been good friends with the Shrewsbury Foundation's director, Evert Whitlow, when they'd been at prep school together. He asked me to give Ev his best regards.

I didn't even get a chance to ask what he'd meant about

my portfolio before he hung up. I think I'd remembered to tell him, in the slender openings he'd left for my part of the conversation, that I was having lunch with Mr. Whitlow later in the week. I think that I'd been able to form complete sentences, even while I was on autopilot, the bulk of my brain trying to come to grips with the fact that he'd called me up to cast doubts on my tenure hopes. I hung up automatically, hoping that I'd made inoffensive and polite noises in all the right places. But at some point during the conversation, my eyes had closed so tightly that I was seeing stars and my fists were clenched so hard that the nails bit into the meat of my palms.

He'd called me up to play with me. The dean was twitching the bait, reminding me that my continued presence at Caldwell College in Maine was on the line, just as I'd gotten away from those worries for the moment to submerge myself in my own work, real research for a change. Until now I'd thought of him as a balding, second-rate Dickensian villain, a pain that came with the territory. But I knew from my experiences with him over the past several years, that his call wasn't just insensitivity, wasn't just social maladroitness, he was genuinely screwing with my head, now that he was in a real position to do so.

Congratulations, Dean Belcher. You've just been promoted to sadist, first class.

I looked down and realized that I'd wrapped the phone cord around my hands and was pulling so hard that I'd managed to straighten some of the curls out. I unwound the cord from my hands carefully, noticing how I'd managed to cut off the circulation in them without even thinking about it: The ends of my fingers were red and cold and there was a deep, white groove where the cord had bitten into my flesh. My hands were trembling, and I tasted bile at the back of my throat, the way I do when I've been hit too many times at my Krav Maga class and I'm ready to tear the lungs out of my instructor Nolan's chest if he'd only let me get close enough to do it. I knew from experience that it was a bad place to be, and I felt powerless to do anything about it.

I let go of the last of the cord and turned around to go to my room. I nearly ran into Jack, who suddenly appeared on the stairs, just about eye-level with my fists. He stumbled backward and would have fallen, had I not steadied him by grabbing his shirt.

"Oh, my God! What is this?" Jack said. "I thought it would be quiet out here." He had been wearing his headphones and must have been scared to death to see me appear suddenly.

I flushed at being caught acting so. "I'm sorry, Jack! I . . . don't know what came over me. Yes, I do, it was my dean. I apologize."

"Hmmph." An opportunity presented itself and a sly look crossed his face. "Well, no harm done. Perhaps you would care to join me in a drop of something to calm the nerves?"

I was about to decline, but I felt so guilty about having scared him that I agreed. "Thank you. That's very kind."

As Jack went off chattering and humming to himself, Michael slouched up the stairs, still dressed in his overcoat. I was beginning to believe that he'd been born in a tiny London Fog.

"Care to join us, Michael?" Jack had returned and was very excited to have company in what was clearly his favorite pastime. He'd brought out a bottle of cheap cherry brandy.

Michael eyed the bottle askance. "Thanks, I won't. But I will watch you and Emma enjoy it." A blank expression crossed his face. "I'd have thought you could make it up the stairs without tossing back another shot."

"Oh, Michael!" All atwitter with the unexpected attention, Jack explained the reason for the impromptu party in the sitting room.

I took a sip and instantly my teeth ached to crawl back into my jawbone. My stomach rebelled, and I noticed Michael was leaning back, half-glasses perched pretentiously on his nose, watching me with vast amusement.

"Deans are a malignant force of nature." He shrugged. "Can't be helped. It only gets worse, in our little slice of purgatory."

"Pshaw, you dreadful thing, that's no help!" Jack swatted at Michael, who rolled his eyes. He took another sip, his round little eyes bright with the liquor, and took his glasses off to clean them as he spoke. "Oh, my dear, you must take heart! You see, both Michael and I have been through precisely the same thing, and now look at us. Just fine."

And if the sickening brandy wasn't cause enough, I almost lost my dinner when Jack licked the lenses of his glasses, then dried them off with his sweaty shirttail.

Michael made a rude, wet noise in the back of his throat. "Yes, Emma. Do look carefully at us." He heaved himself off the wall. "That's enough frolicking for one evening. Night all."

I threw back the rest of the thimbleful of liquor so that it wouldn't linger on the palate and said "Thanks, good night" to Jack. But it was with that revolting taste, the churning in my stomach compliments of Dean Belcher, and the thought that I could look forward to grow up to be just like my housemates—seen and unseen—that I eventually fell into an uneasy sleep.

Chapter 3

MADAM CHANDLER KEPT ME FASCINATED FOR THE next day and a half. The journal was just about one hundred pages, covering just a few months. Although I had hoped for a full year, the content of the journal made it perfect for my needs. I wanted to be able to speak about everyday life on the site I'd been excavating, and I wanted to try to say something about the life of women, especially since all the other documents spoke of the public life of Justice Chandler. Margaret recorded much of her activities in running her household, possibly set down to provide an example for the children she had hoped would fill her future.

Two things troubled me as I worked, however. I began to wonder about the location of the other volumes of her journal, if indeed they still existed. More immediately, I worried about the meanings of the unfathomable numbers I found on so many of the pages, since it was clear they held some deeper significance.

As I read the normal text, I knew that something was causing the clouds to gather over her existence. She was concerned with the rapidly declining health of her friend, the Reverend Blanchard, and her sour relations with her neighbors. It was in these passages that the numeric sequences seemed to dominate, and I began to believe that her true feelings might be hidden in a code. Other journalists, like Pepys, William Byrd, and Leonardo, used codes or shorthand to confuse the casual reader and to protect their ideas, thoughts, and sins, so that it was possible that Madam Chandler was doing the same. But as compelling as those numbers were, my first task was to read and transcribe as much of the diary as I could, to take it with me when I finally left Shrewsbury. I'd have to leave cracking that code for later, if it could be done at all.

Even without those questions, I had plenty to occupy me. When you are studying the life of someone you will only meet through documents, it doesn't matter that you have no way of knowing for certain, but you begin to develop instincts about and even feelings for your subject. I began to develop a picture of Margaret Chandler's character. She was certainly strong-willed, so much so that if she'd publicly vocalized the tart opinions that she revealed in her diary, she would certainly have been pilloried for a shrew. She thought well of the way she looked, and by the number of references to cloth and sewing, I gather that she kept at least one maid busy dressing her in keeping with her wealth and station. Margaret knew how to run a household and had obviously been well trained in the domestic and social side of her life: There were many accounts of dinners and parties that apparently facilitated her husband's legal and political work. She was truly pious in a way that I found touching; having no belief myself, I am sometimes envious of faith in others.

And at the end of most of the entries, even the briefest ones, she mentioned what she was reading. Sometimes it was the papers from London. These, it was quite clear, she had shipped over by her family, several weeks' worth of issues arriving at a time, as was evident from the entry, "Tommy obliges with the *Trumpet* and sends word that he will send me others, if he thinks them not too political to be of interest to me." With other books, however, it was clear she was ordering them from booksellers in London and in Boston, or borrowing them from her husband, Matthew Chandler: "Mr. Chandler has recommended Dryden's translation of Ovid to me after I have done with the Plutarch."

It was still just a hunch, but I got the impression that she might have been hiding her voracious appetite for reading from everyone except the man to whom she was referring as "Mr. Chandler, my dearest friend," with increasing frequency. This was compelling for a couple of reasons. Even though referring to one's husband as "Mr." might strike the modern reader as unduly formal, it wasn't unusual right through the nineteenth century. But the use of the expression "my dearest friend" was sentimental and emotional to an almost extravagant degree. Based on what I knew of the times, Margaret was probably shrewd to conceal the extent of her interest in books; wit in a woman was compared to an unsheathed sword, dangerous to herself and everyone around her. And the fact that her husband helped her in this subterfuge indicated that trust and affection, if not true love, was growing on both sides of the marriage.

I knew that I was beginning to like Margaret when I started becoming frustrated with her contempt for the Irish, her class-bound views, and her dislike of life in the rough frontier of early eighteenth-century Massachusetts. I tried to remind myself that they were common views for someone in her position, but cheered for Madam when she recognized some good quality in Nora, the Irish maid she had been so unwilling to take on, or when she observed how the odd manners of her New England neighbors worked well within their own society.

Margaret became a little more real, a little more human to

me in spite of her tremendous personal presence in writing, when I recognized that some of the spatters on a page full of the mysterious code were caused by teardrops. I wondered what the rest of the diary would eventually reveal.

So I was able to keep my professional worries behind me until about eleven fifty on Wednesday, when Sasha reminded me about my lunch with Director Whitlow. I bit back a curse; I had planned on just a quick bite eaten in the staff lunchroom, so as not to take any more precious time away from my work on the journal. Making nice-nice with the officialdom just wasn't as appealing as the life that was unfolding before me.

As I hurried down the hall, I reasoned that talking about one's work, especially with someone who was knowledgeable about such things, was almost as much fun as actually conducting said work. Whitlow, even if he was friends with Dean Belcher, must have some sympathetic qualities if he was willing to take a position as the director of such an institution as Shrewsbury. And although I knew that Belcher wouldn't have lifted a finger to get me the fellowship, it probably wouldn't hurt to have his "good friend" get interested in my project. It was an opportunity I should make the most of.

I was surprised to see how imposing a figure the director was. Evert Whitlow looked more like a businessman than the head of a historical repository, and he worked hard to maintain that image. He wore a crisp charcoal wool suit with a conservative power tie, kept his thinning sandy-reddish hair cut close and carefully, and had a ruddy complexion that suggested an Irish heritage, a lot of weekend golf, and martinis before dinner and port after. He shook my hand firmly.

"I hope you don't mind a working lunch," he said as he showed me to a chair. "I don't like to give up too much time to the nonessentials, not when there's so much work to get done in a day."

"Not a bit," I responded. Even though he was saying exactly what I'd been thinking just moments before, I resented the impression that I was being categorized as a "nonessential."

"I'll just have some sandwiches sent up and we can get started. There's a nice gourmet deli in Monroe with a truck that stops by every day with their classic sandwiches ready-made." He picked up the phone. "It's a real lifesaver for me, timewise. What do you like?"

"Anything's fine."

He told an unseen assistant to order some roast beef and chicken salad. "What else? Chips? I don't know—" He paused to look over at me. I shrugged and he answered, "Well, maybe some fruit salad. And a couple of waters."

He settled himself into his chair and tidied some papers out of the way. "So. I understand you are looking at—" he glanced surreptitiously at a notepad—"the Chandler diary?"

"That's right. Are you familiar with it?"

Whitlow shook his head. "No, not at all."

Trying to be gracious and get him off the hook, I said, "Well, I'm not surprised. It's exciting for me, but compared with some of the treasures you've got here, it is pretty small potatoes."

"I'm not really all that familiar with the bigger potatoes," Whitlow said, shrugging. "It's not essential to my job; I leave that side of things to Harry Saunders and Sasha Russo. They keep me informed with an executive summary. "

I must have looked surprised that he wasn't any more interested in the collection, and he laughed politely at my expression. Fortunately, he received a call, and by the time his assistant came in with a couple of cardboard cartons with our food, I was able to compose myself. Whitlow looked at the labels on the sandwiches and said, "If you don't mind, I'll take the roast beef. My wife would kill me if she knew—cholesterol through the roof, you know—but as long as she doesn't see . . ." He shrugged again, then promptly tore into his forbidden sandwich with gusto.

I bit into my sandwich and was surprised by how good it was. Then I sighed and realized I hadn't been for anything like a proper run since I'd been here and would have to make up for that shortly. If the amount of homemade mayonnaise was any indication, the director wouldn't have been off the hook with his wife if he had chosen the chicken salad either.

After a couple of bites, the director resumed our discussion. "I was hired, just a couple of years ago, now, to get the foundation known, to improve the bottom line, to expand the possibilities of the place. I haven't got time, and frankly, I haven't got the interest, to get too involved in the collections.

"As you know, the foundation started out as a Shrewsbury family hobby, collecting Americana to share. The family would compete with each other, spending the timbering fortune their grandfather had made in Monroe, to see who could bring home the most important, the most antique, or the most curious documents of American history. It developed into some pretty serious collecting and connoisseurship; the sons hired a librarian to keep track of the family passion after a while, but he was a bit of an antique himself, and it took years before things were catalogued properly. When the old man died at the beginning of this century, the family began to invite upper-echelon scholars—you know, the more respectable sort from among their social set—to look at the stuff, and word began to spread. Other researchers began to ask to use parts of the collection, and the foundation was established to make the most of the collection. It was a coup for the Shrewsbury family, who wanted to come off like the big-time philanthropists. In its early days, the foundation had been sort of cozy, unofficial, and unstructured, and that's fine, but these days, there are certain realities that need to be addressed that can be handled without compromising that intimate atmosphere too much, we hope. It's a new world out there, and even such venerable institutions as the foundation can't afford to get too hidebound about traditional approaches that just don't work today."

Whitlow finished half his sandwich and picked up his cup of fruit salad, frowning slightly. He was obviously wishing he'd ordered the chips instead. I munched on my sandwich, thinking about what I'd heard from others of their time working at Shrewsbury. The principal charm of the place was that in addition to the really important early editions of Americana, the Shrewsburys had also gathered the odd, the comic, or the rare. The materials that had appealed to the whimsy of the collectors proved to be so valuable later on because the collection was more eclectic, perhaps in some ways, a more complete record of early America, than a more educated or disciplined approach to acquisition might have provided.

"It would be a shame to sacrifice that atmosphere of . . . intellectual adventure for a few thousand bucks—" I began.

Whitlow protested, in an "I'm an eminently reasonable guy" way: "But nothing's going to be denigrated by trying to upgrade the library, make it into a world-class institution. We need to expand in different directions." He shrugged. "I know it's not a popular perspective, but I have high hopes that my approach will work. The Shrewsbury family left a very generous endowment, which showed tremendous foresight, but even though it was well invested, it doesn't measure up to what our goals are today—"

I silently wondered what would make an already superb collection "world class." It sounded like a vague bit of business-speak, to me. "How are you going to raise the money?" I asked.

Whitlow didn't even blink. "There will of course be an appeal to our more forward-minded donors, but there will also be a reorganization of the staff and some selective, prioritized deaccessioning."

My jaw dropped. "You mean you're going to sell some of the holdings?"

Whitlow put up his hand to forestall my reaction. "Cut away some of the deadwood, streamline the collections, focus on the first editions, the best-known writers, the most important material."

I paused thinking that, depending on his definition of the best material, Madam Chandler's journal might be culled, sold off who knows where. I thought about how it was often that the documents that seemed the least important told us the most; how things like receipts, family photographs, and keepsakes stuffed into boxes best revealed what life was like for ordinary folk. Even a woman like Margaret, who was part of the elite, would have been invisible if it hadn't been for her diary.

Mr. Whitlow frowned again but spoke pleasantly enough. "Look, I can see by your face that you come down on the 'conservative side—'"

I jumped in. "I would say 'preservationist.' "

"Okay, fine. But you don't keep every little scrap of everything you come across in your daily existence do you?"

"I'm not a repository. Shrewsbury is."

"Point taken." Mr. Whitlow leaned back in his chair. "But then you have to agree that every collection needs a periodical reexamination, to decide where not only the strengths are, but where the weaknesses are too. Our goal is to improve the collections. How can you be against that?"

"I'm not against improving the collections," I said. I put aside the fruit cup I had been enjoying so much just a minute ago; my stomach felt a little upset. "I just think it is not a simple thing to deaccession materials from one of the best collections in the world. I'm just against recklessly applying what might be a sound idea in business to something as . . . organic as a library or a museum collection, without it suffering for it."

Evert Whitlow nodded and tented his fingers thoughtfully. I got the sense that this was just a theoretical argument to him, whereas it felt so much more like religion to me. "You know, I heard that there was a superb basilica where Pope Julius wanted to place the Sistine Chapel. If people like you had your way, we wouldn't have the Sistine Chapel today."

"Well, when you think about it, the Sistine Chapel isn't that great, architecturally speaking," I responded. "Where the real interest is, why everyone waits in line to see it, is the Michelangelo frescoes. If you take away the name, just for the sake of argument, what they're interested in is . . . the surface treatment. A Michelangelo, yes, but otherwise a surface treatment on a fairly ugly building. We have other, better Michelangelos; who's to say what masterpieces we lost with the basilica?"

The director slapped his leg, enjoying the debate. "You're calling the ceiling of the Sistine Chapel a more surface treatment? Dr. Fielding, you're something else!"

"I am exaggerating a little," I admitted. "My point is that newer is not always better, and that issues of preservation— whether they are for architecture, archaeology, or libraries—are never straightforward, as business truisms sometimes seem to be."

"Well, we're not treating this issue as an uncomplicated one," he tried to reassure me. "And the staff—the library staff, that is—is doing its best to keep us alerted to all the potential problems. Don't worry, trust me. They're on your side, so nothing drastic is going to happen."

"Well, let me know if I can lend you any of my expertise. I'd be delighted to advise you, in whatever capacity an interested professional could." I couldn't really face continuing this conversation any further with the knots in my stomach, so I changed the topic. "I understand that you know Ron Belcher." As soon as I said it, I realized my tummy would have preferred a discussion of the weather.

But rather than the instant recognition I'd expected based on the Dean's remarks, Whitlow's face was blank. He shook his head vaguely, not placing the name.

"He said he went to prep school with you," I added. "Now he's one of the deans at Caldwell College. Where I teach."

Recognition finally filled Whitlow's face. "Good lord— Ron Belcher? That little guy back in—? Well, it's been some time. Yessir, that's going back more years than I care to admit to. How is Ron?"

"Very well, thanks." There wasn't a whole lot I could add to that, but Whitlow didn't seem to be too interested anyway, his polite inquiry a mere formality, if he in fact truly remembered Belcher in the first place.

"Well, it's nice to hear from old friends," he said simply, and that was that. So much for the much vaunted friendship that Belcher claimed. The schmuck.

The director rose from his chair and wiped his mouth: The meeting was over. "I'm glad we had this chance to chat. I'll let you get back to your work, and look forward to hearing your presentation on your work later in the month."

"Oh, right." I remembered that one of the obligations of accepting the fellowship was to give a talk on the research conducted there. "Well then, thanks very much for lunch."

Whitlow shook hands again, cordially, and then we were both able to get back to the essentials of our respective jobs, worlds and philosophies apart.

But after lunch, a switch seemed to have been shut off, and I couldn't get back into the effortless work patterns I had enjoyed for the past couple of days. I couldn't concentrate properly and couldn't figure out why, other than recognizing that I felt out of the mainstream, isolated and somehow bereft. Maybe my eyes were tired, perhaps the euphoria of starting a new project had worn off a little, but even Madam

Chandler seemed to have lost her vitality in the face of a sweltering summer in Massachusetts. Her handwriting was more cramped than it had been, and more than ever, it was more frequently punctuated with the long strings of numbers. Whatever was troubling her—the entries were terse and made references to situations that I didn't yet fully understand—seemed to have infected me as well. I finally left early and decided that I would go for a run, but when I got up to my room, I was so dispirited, I flopped down on the bed for a nap.

When I awoke in what must have been hours later, it was dark and freezing; March had been reclaimed by a wintry low. Outside my lofty window, the deciduous trees were still barren, and I knew without seeing that the bare ground was brown and raw, carefully raked but badly scarred by the winter. The bluish-black shadows seemed made to order for the haughty isolation of the place.

Oh, come on, Emma, I chided myself, one more minute and you'll be finding yourself in Mr. Squeer's academy, or turning into one of Jane Eyre's unfortunate schoolmates. You've been lonely and depressed before, it will go away in the morning. Call home, see what Brian's doing. It's not like you're trapped on the moors or anything, so stop feeling sorry for yourself.

I realized then that I *was* feeling sorry for myself, wondering of what value all my work was if somewhere down the road, polite, efficient types like Whitlow would clear it all away for what was judged to be more important. Was it worth my trying to resurrect Madam Chandler's life if the remnants of it might be scattered to who knew where, simply because she was not well known or because she'd not written a famous book? And what point was archaeology anyway? It didn't solve any of the world's problems. Wasn't it rather self-involved of me to make up these little questions and answer them for myself and a tiny little audience?

Old, familiar questions reemerged to haunt me, the same ones that arose when I was a teenager working in the field, deciding if I would follow in my irascible grandfather Oscar's footsteps and become an archaeologist.

When I'd raised these philosophical quandaries with Oscar, at first he'd just grunted. "I'd be a shitty dentist. The world doesn't need any more shitty dentists, but it sure as hell could use a few more really first-rate archaeologists." When he saw that his answer wasn't helping me, he'd put down his trowel, stopped working, and spoke very seriously. It was, and remained, one of the most important moments of my life.

"Human beings are funny," he'd said. "Oftentimes they treat the past like an eccentric old relative, something to drag out for special occasions and ignore until the next time they need an example of why things are better now than they were in the bad old days—or vice versa. We modern Americans are the worst like that. But humans need to see where they've come from. They use the past to make sense of how they live, they need the past to tell them how to move ahead, to give them positive and negative examples. It makes them feel a part of things too. And maybe, with any luck, if we use these big brains we're so proud of, we'll figure out how to make fewer of the mistakes we seem to always be making if we pay as much attention to the past as we do to the future."

He looked thoughtful for a moment and then picked up a measuring tape. "Now, stop fidgeting and straighten out that wall before you dig any deeper."

That memory made me smile. Shaking myself free of my funk, I turned on a light, flipped on my portable radio, and turned up the heat in my room. As I looked around the room, my glance landed on the picture of Brian that usually sat on my bookcase at work and was now on the bureau here. It wasn't the best picture I ever took. It's from a birthday party and it's not horrible; I mean, you can tell he's a guy, that he's got cowlicks that resist any sort of tampering. It's not great as a formal portrait, that's all. But the reason I take it with me whenever I leave home is that I'd caught him in mid-laugh, and it reflects a true image of his soul: I love him for his humor, his curiosity, persistence, and optimism, and somehow that all showed up on the print.

The photo was one more thing to cheer me; I wasn't going to cave in to my doubts.

I also reminded myself of why I had finally decided that my work was important. History tends to be about grand events or trends that are dissociated from the common person. Historical archaeology is about everyday things, it's finding out about people who didn't always have a voice or fair representation by those who kept the public records, it's about filling in the blanks. By teaching what archaeology teaches about the past, I was letting my audiences know how people like them made the great things possible. On the good days, I felt like I was a preacher, teaching empowerment, hope, and ownership. On the bad days, like today, I felt like an empty vessel. It was so much a matter of faith, and sometimes faith has to be jump-started by self-discipline. Resolutely, I picked up the last unopened box and began to unpack it.

When I opened it, I was surprised to see two packages, one very small and the other about a foot long wrapped in tissue paper and nestled between my *Chicago Manual of Style* and Grandpa Oscar's much-worn Riverside edition of the complete works of Shakespeare. A brief susurrus and I found that the smaller box contained a small silver bracelet with dense square links, a style that was popular during the Art Deco period. I will reveal under no circumstances what the card that accompanied the gift said; suffice it to say that I was troubled with no further worries about petty tyrants like Belcher and Constantino, or the well-intentioned predations of bureaucrats like Whitlow in the face of the accompanying note. I went into the hall to call Brian, but as he wasn't in, I left no other message on the machine apart from telling him I found his surprise. I didn't want to melt the answering machine.

When I tore the wrapping from the other, larger package, I found a box marked on the outside in chaste letters: "THE MACALLAN, Aged 18 Years." The note that accompanied it was in our friend Kam's handwriting. Kam was Brian's friend and boss, and he'd married Marty, my old college roommate, more than a year ago. They were expecting their first child shortly. The note read

> *Marty and I were concerned about you being in the wilderness without medical supplies—this ought to serve admirably. In addition to being a first-rate sterilising agent and anaesthetic, you'll find it's also effective as a social facilitator. Congratulations on your fellowship again,*

> *Kam*

I noticed that "facilitator" had not been his first choice of words. If dear Kam weren't trying to come off as an older brother instead of a flirt, he would have left "lubricant."

Beneath that was one of Marty's hastily scribbled notes, familiar from our college days together:

> *Dearie, if this child doesn't make her appearance soon, I'm going in there after her with an eviction notice. In the meantime, one of us has to have a good time, so have a sup and think of me and my bottle of fizzy water. À bientôt.*

> *M.*

So, Marty still wasn't telling us what the name of the baby would be. I couldn't wait to see what kind of a mother she'd make, or what the baby would be like, as far as that went. As a matter of fact, I recalled with a frown, it seemed as though all of my friends were considering these issues. I'd just had an e-mail from my friend Jane in England, who told me in her matter-of-fact way that her work on the abbey was moving along splendidly, and by the way, she was due with twins in the early fall: Trust her to fit in one last field season beforehand. A longer e-mail from her husband, Greg, filled in some of the blanks: Jane seemed untroubled by morning sickness and showed no sign of any nesting instinct and was quite her old self, though she was smiling more often now. Before I could embrace the thought that Jane might have mellowed a bit, he followed that news with, "The students and I still feel the lash and are very interested to see what changes the 'bliss' will eventually bring. I suspect the babies will not be as susceptible to Jane's efficiency as the rest of us."

There must be something in the water, I thought, and then caught myself. No, it's not the water. It's how old we all are, it's the time when people decide these things. Well, I certainly haven't time for that, I thought, but then again brought myself up short. If Jane Compton, workaholic extraordinaire and, once upon a time, girl rocketing up the academic ladder could imagine—nay, was actually having—children, then it was entirely possible that I should put this topic on my list of things to consider before I got too much older.

That thought was more than enough for the moment; I slammed the lid on that particular piece of Tupperware and shoved it to the back of the refrigerator of my mind to deal with later. Armed with my two talismans, my whiskey and bracelet, I went down to reestablish my place in Shrewsbury and the rest of the world.

No one was about—a notice on the little bulletin board in the front foyer suggested that the others were probably attending a lecture at Amherst. Fine, I decided, I would just commandeer the house library for myself.

That room was every fantasy a serious reader could have imagined. The walls were covered with built-in bookcases that reached the twelve-foot ceiling; a bank of French windows was opposite the sliding doors I had come through. The plaster design on the ceiling was nearly as complex as the pattern on the oriental rugs that broke the room into discrete areas. An enormous stone fireplace dominated the center of another wall, with matching bookcases on either side. In one corner was an escritoire filled with Shrewsbury stationery, while the other furniture consisted of two plump leather couches and a couple of wingback chairs, closest to the fireplace.

Now, I pondered, if I were a crystal sherry set, where would I be kept? Familiarity with P. G. Wodehouse rather than an in-depth acquaintance with life in grand houses led me in the right direction—the cupboard to the right held a dozen short glasses, several long-banished ashtrays, and a box of matches.

The wood box was not at all dusty and the kindling was free from cobwebs: Someone intended this to be a working fireplace. Emboldened by the bottle and the thought of a fire to add a little emotional warmth to the room, and armed with the matches and the posted instructions, I opened the flue, checked for a draft, and stacked up a reasonably cozy pile of papers, kindling, and logs. It caught almost immediately. I took a glass and my bottle and dragged one of the chairs closer to the hearth.

As I tucked my feet under me and wrestled with the stopper, I tried to conjure up some image of a private club and was startled to realize that all my companions would have been men. Places like the Bellona, Diogenes, and Drones, although fictional, were strictly male preserves, as were the real-life Mohocks, White's, and Button's.

Well, damn, I thought disgustedly. I suppose if you can only afford prunes and stewed beef, there's really no point in having a quiet place to enjoy sherry you haven't got. In that case, I decided, lifting my glass, I will inaugurate the first, occasional meeting of the . . . what should it be called? Something to do with pioneering women, libraries, research . . . Hypatia popped into my mind, but I quickly rejected her name as too bad an omen. She had been a scholar at the library of ancient Alexandria, and met her demise when an angry crowd murdered her, believing that it was inappropriate for women to do such men's work.

I shuddered and quickly ran down a list of other possible honorees: Bradstreet, Behn, Elizabeth, Franklin, Hathshepsut, Mead, Montagu, Roosevelt . . . I realized that I didn't want anything too specific to one woman and immediately came up with the answer: The Bluestocking Club.

The whiskey was sterling. I let the next sip linger a bit more, savoring the sharp peaty bite, and allowed my eyes to unfocus on the fire as it hungrily devoured the dry wood. Lovely. I didn't bother worrying about wretches with too much power and not enough to do, I didn't worry about existential puzzles, I didn't even bother trying to unravel more of the mysterious Madam C's life. I snuggled into my sweater and tucked my feet up underneath me, nearly drowsing as I listened to the crackle and hissing of the fire, letting the smoke of the single-malt mingle with the smell of burning wood. After admiring the dull glow of my bracelet in the flickering light, I was feeling so mellow and content when the door opened a crack, that I didn't even mind the intrusion. I decided that whoever it was would be welcome; the Bluestocking way was to be generous with guests. I would even show Jack what real booze was. Whoever knocked would be voted in with all the privileges, moved and seconded and passed by unanimous vote of one.

It took me a moment to realize that although it was neither Jack nor Michael, I recognized the face that peered from the narrow opening between the sliding doors. "Sasha? What are you—?"

But although there was a superficial resemblance to the manuscript librarian—blonde hair, same approximate height and build—this woman had none of Sasha's vibrancy. Instead, angles and planes seemed to dominate the stranger's profile, as if she was built to deflect unwanted attention. Over a dark turtleneck, she wore a sleek, narrowly cut jumper that I could see was made of a fine wool, but none of its warmth seemed to be conveyed to her features; her skin was as pale and cool as marble.

Then a name from the past surfaced and snapped into place alongside my vague recognition of the work being conducted by the fourth Shrewsbury Fellow.

"Good God, Faith Burnes!" I said with more enthusiasm than I might have without the soothing effect of the fire and the whiskey. "I haven't seen you since . . . well, since Coolidge I guess! What are you doing here? How are you?"

The other woman started visibly at my robust greeting and looked around her, as if out of habit. "I'm not Faith Burnes anymore. I go by my maiden name, Morgan." Then the penny dropped for her too, and her face relaxed into a cautious half smile. "Emma . . . Fielding, right?" she said slowly, working memory from the mire. "It has been a while, hasn't it, since graduate school?" Then, almost reluctantly, "I thought I recognized your name on the memo. It's been a long time."

"It's me, all right," I said. "Look, come in, come in, have a seat, Dr. B—er, Doctor!" I gestured grandly. "Pull up a pew."

"I didn't want to disturb you," she said, backing away quickly. "I just thought I'd left my notebook in here . . ."

There was no notebook, and we both knew it. "Nonsense, disturb! Look, really, let me get you a glass, this stuff is brilliant." Perhaps a little too much "r" in brilliant, Emma? Better slow down, you're overtired and the whiskey's got a kick.

With a little effort, I extricated myself from my nest and

toddled over to the cabinet and fetched another glass. "Honestly, won't you join me? I've had the whole place to myself all night, I've been telling myself ghost stories and I need a bit of human companionship. You'd be doing me a favor. What have you been up to?"

Faith seemed to think about it for a moment, then, as if compelled by something other than her own will, slid the doors together behind her and glided over to the other chair. She picked up the bottle and looked at it thoughtfully, then turned her gaze at me. Her pause was overburdened with contemplation of a decision that had nothing to do with a drink, I thought. "Why not? For old times' sake."

I got the impression that she was talking about old times that had nothing to do with our brief, shared time in graduate school. Even though I'd been in the anthropology department and Faith had been in the English department, we'd ended up together in several classes on early American culture. I poured a measure and Faith drank. As an afterthought, she said, "Thank you."

"Not at all. *Slàinte!*" I toasted, and settled back into my chair. "So tell me about your name. I'm a little out of the Coolidge loop, I guess."

"No, no," she said, "it's not you. I am Faith Morgan now. I took my maiden name back after the divorce. I needed to be someone else after that."

I frowned; that was such an odd way of putting it. But at least now I remembered why Sasha's description of her work sounded so familiar despite the different name.

"I left Paul over two years ago," she explained. "You met him back in Michigan, I think. He was a year ahead of me, two ahead of you. He was in the English department too. I brought him to a couple of functions." She took another sip. "We'd been married a long time. Far too long."

I nodded, only dimly remembering her husband—ex-husband, I corrected myself. Fiancé, when I knew him. My impression of him was not an appealing one; a cold fish, calculating, appraising, demanding. Oh, dear. Now that I thought of it, I also recalled thinking how perfect a match he was for long, blonde Faith. Two icicles flavored with disdain. But I hadn't known her well and only interacted with her under the most constrained of circumstances. She seemed different to me now.

"I'm sorry," I said immediately, taking another big sip from my drink to cover my discomfort. I had friends and bracelets, after all.

"So am I," she replied briefly. She demolished a good inch of liquor. "Tell me, where are you now?"

So I plunged in with a brief outline of the last twelve years, more than willing to help build the bridge she'd started. Oddly, Faith seemed genuinely interested in what I'd done, and this surprised me. I found myself responding to her more warmly than I expected, not with the inflated lists of achievement generally reserved for trumping unlikable colleagues at conference brawls, but a plain history. She nodded throughout my description, then she too filled in a brief resume: several teaching stints, sporadic work on the book she came here to finish, finally settling in to a good job and new life in California after the divorce.

It took more than fifteen years and a thousand miles from where we first met before we could sustain something like a real conversation, give and take of even this limited sort. Not a giddy reminiscence filled with "and what abouts" and "do you remembers"—our earlier relationship had extended no further than cool formality at very best—but a civil exchange. We each had another couple of fingers and I calmed down: My fear that my premature bonhomie would trap me with the Ice Queen gave way to a recognition that we both had moved away from the guerrilla warfare of graduate school. That's all it is, I thought. People can change. The satisfaction of having repaired something mangled by youth has a comfortable heft and a subtle, almond taste.

The warmth of the drink eventually drew back to reveal my underlying weariness, and, swaying a little, I rose to bank the fire and say good night. Then I realized that Faith had asked me for another glass. Unwilling to jeopardize our fragile bond—we were going to be housemates for the next weeks, after all—I poured her another shot, and an eighth inch for myself, and resumed my former position. But was it the dying light of the fire, or was her face more flushed than I remembered? There was something behind her green eyes that troubled me. Her fingers kept twitching at the fabric of her jumper as though they had a life of their own, until she caught herself doing it, and carefully tucked her legs underneath her, replacing the skirt so that it covered her tights to the tops of her shoes.

She noticed that I was watching her, though, and with a hostile glare, she unnecessarily smoothed the side of her perfect chignon. In that instant, I was transported back to Coolidge and my first encounter with Faith, who had evaluated me in this same unsparing fashion. A shadow crossed her face, or maybe the firelight shifted with a falling log.

Whatever I had lacked then, I apparently now possessed, for she said, "You know, I never liked you. No one could possibly be that . . . enthusiastic, that eager, and be for real, I thought. I thought, I assumed, you must be rather calculating. But you seem the same, only quieter now."

She seemed to be waiting for some sort of reply. I shrugged, but I knew what she meant. "Life has a tempering effect," I offered. Strange; I expected to feel more hurt at her admission, but the blisters failed to rise, and I realized that Faith was simply being honest. Her opinion didn't mean anything to me. It suddenly occurred to me that ice is compact and brittle and being aloof is an excellent means of protection.

"Still, I wonder what you would have done. You know, I believe I trust you." Without waiting for a response to that rather startling pronouncement, Faith launched into a narrative I would have given anything not to hear.

"I never believed it could happen to me. Even when I was living it, I didn't understand that I was a battered woman. I mean, everyone *knows* that it's only poor, uneducated women who get beat up, right, Emma?"

Faith's sarcasm, a recrimination—against who knew what—slammed into me like a blow. I wasn't certain I knew what she was talking about, all of a sudden, and yet had a sickening feeling I knew exactly what she was saying.

Faith got out of her chair and filled her glass nearly halfway with whiskey. She stared at a drop that had splashed out of the glass and onto the table, and then ran her finger through it, before she turned away from me and drank deeply. "I'm still learning to deal with the fact that I was too afraid to leave." Faith turned on me. "You told me you married that guy you were seeing in Coolidge. What would you do if he hauled off and slapped you across the face with every ounce of strength in his body?"

Chapter 4

I OPENED MY MOUTH AND CLOSED IT. THE SHOCK OF the question and what it implied was as brutal as the act she described. Faith waited briefly for some quick, easy answer she knew I didn't dare make, before she pounced.

"Right. Can't even get your brain around the idea. Neither could I the first time it happened." She sat down in the chair across from me and stared at the fire. Shadows danced across her profile, which was composed in spite of the harrowing tale she was telling.

"I couldn't leave the house for two days. Paul's handprint was a brand on my face." She raised the glass to her mouth, but then didn't drink. She set the glass down. "The first time. The first time should have been the signal to pack a bag, call the cops, and run like hell, right? Only it's not that easy. I loved him. I knew he loved me. It could never happen again, it was just that we were both so worn out, had such a bad day.

"I say afraid, but maybe I should say vain. It still stings when I think just how classic my case was. Classic." She shrugged. "Ordinary? Me? Of course, by the time I accepted

what was really happening, I was too afraid to leave. But
don't delude yourself, Emma. It can happen to anyone."

I thought about protesting, I wanted to protest, but I knew
that, in a way, she was right: It could happen to anyone.
Without thinking, I reached for her, but Faith went rigid at
the gesture. I wrapped my arms around myself instead.

"The trick is," Faith was saying, "the trick is not to think
about it, ever. Of course you can't, but you try to make this
perfect little shell around you, try to keep everything out.
Drinking's good. Valium's better. But something always gets
through, ruins your concentration, and you screw up. Then it
happens." She picked up the glass and took another swallow
of the whiskey, savoring its bite, considering what she'd
said. For a moment, I thought she was shaping the story as
she told me, but then I recognized that for wishful thinking.
Knock it off and listen, Emma, I rebuked myself.

"It doesn't matter to someone like Paul that mistakes
happen. Mistakes happen every day. And every action begets
an equal and opposite reaction. But . . . it took me a long
time to realize no one ever does anything to deserve . . .
what he did to me. For so long."

I felt ill. Growing colder and more sober by the second, I
couldn't imagine getting up and doing something as homely
as adding another log to the lagging fire. Worse still, the way
that Faith recounted her story left no room for me to offer
comfort, sympathy—even my anger for her seemed insuffi-
cient, like it would be an insult to offer it. I wanted to stop
this outpouring, this *mechanical* relation. I wanted to be a
million miles away, with all of this just a faceless statistic
and in a small, hidden part of myself, I knew I resented her
for personalizing this atrocity.

. The fact that I was spellbound only added to my horror.

Faith held up her glass to carefully observe the last half
inch of amber liquid. Something about her expression was

chilling, as though she was relishing holding us both in thrall with her story. She went on, calmly, deliberately. I had been telling myself ghost stories, and now she served me up a true tale of horror.

"The problem was, that in between times, things seemed really good, just like when we first met. There was always some excuse I could find to explain the last time. My fault or his, it *couldn't* happen again. So things went on, what felt like normal life, until the next disappointment at work, the next too-big credit-card bill, the next . . . there was always a next. And Paul was always very careful to take me to a different hospital, always had a perfectly believable story. Who'd have doubted him? He was gorgeous, well respected—hell, people felt sorry for him, saddled with a wife who drank and popped pills and got herself into the *worst* accidents. He's one hell of a good actor; he believed himself. I believed him. I helped: I developed a talent for lying. I became clever with makeup. I learned about first aid."

I realized that she had been silent a moment and I, needing to fill up that awful silence, asked the only question possible under the circumstances.

"How did you ever manage to leave?"

Faith uttered a short, humorless laugh. "I was in the hospital, but this time it wasn't because of Paul. I couldn't stand the wait anymore. I decided to kill myself.

"Once I thought of that, I knew everything was going to be okay. I felt very calm; the tension simply left me, for the first time in years. There was this delicious sense of anticipation, like I was getting ready for a big date. I bought an expensive bottle of vodka, took a long, hot bath, and dressed in a silk nightie. A Billie Holiday record played as I set out the Valium and the vodka in a nice arrangement."

I bit my lip, trying to resist imagining someone who so welcomed death.

Faith watched me for a moment, then continued. "When I woke up in the hospital, they told me how lucky I was that I threw up all the pills I'd swallowed. Lucky. Can you believe it? Then Paul came to visit. He charmed the devil out of everyone there; only this time I didn't believe his soft words. You see, he'd found my note. I saw the look in his eyes, something I'd only ever seen the edge of before, and I knew, sure I was still breathing, that when I went home *he* would kill me. And no one would ever know about it.

"I decided that was *one* decision he wasn't going to make for me," she said. Inside I cheered, feeling giant relief at this welcome, recognizable emotion.

"So I told the nurse." She said softly: "And then it was like going through withdrawal."

The effect of three rapidly swallowed drinks was starting to catch up with Faith and her words became slurred and more insistent. I tried to say something, anything, but this had never been anything like a discussion.

"I won't bore you with the details. Just let's say that the legal system doesn't do battered women any favors. Despite what you might think, domestic violence is not taken seriously. The day I was most afraid was the day that Paul went to prison. That's when the really hard work began. Hard work on me, reshaping how I thought. But I did it."

Faith got up and jabbed at the coals with the poker, startling hot life out of the embers. Turning, she must have seen me as I felt; horrorstruck, curled up and pressing myself into the back of my chair. She took pity on me, maybe, or maybe she was just getting tired. She shook her head, wobbling a little as she sat again.

"Emma, the good news is I got out." She waved her hand drunkenly in front of her face and her words were slurred. "Don't worry about me. It will take five years. I'm still processing the anger." She drained the rest of the liquor from her glass. "Only now, I'm not angry with me. There's a big long line of folks who deserve it more. And you know, not all of them hit me.

"Some just didn't speak up. Some, after I'd left and they found out, asked in the politest way possible what I'd done to deserve it. There's a negative aura that surrounds a woman when people know she's filed a restraining order— *she* must be dangerous. *She's* the one who's unstable. *She* must be to blame.

"And it was because of that idea that it took me forever, once I spoke up, to realize that *it wasn't me*. Four little syllables, a whole universe away. But I got there." She got up and brushed off her skirt with an exaggerated, almost flippant, gesture and stumbled a little as she walked to the door. "And now I'm here."

"Faith," I started lamely, sincerely, "if there's anything I can do for you, please, let me know. I will do it."

She looked at me and smiled. It was an unhappy smile and not at all reasssuring.

"I know you will, Emma. I know you will." And with that, Faith left me crouched in my chair, all alone in the cold, dark library.

Chapter 5

I DON'T KNOW HOW LONG IT WAS BEFORE I CREPT UP to bed. But the next morning, I awoke with a sore head and sour stomach, both of which were only partially attributable to my excessive drinking the night before. I washed and hurried downstairs to grab several cups of coffee and a banana, then went off to the library, determined to get some profitable work done and a little internal sense of quiet before I decided how Faith fit into my life again. She was nowhere to be seen, and I was guiltily grateful for the chance to collect myself before we saw each other again. How do you relate to someone who has known you only slightly, kept you at arm's length, and then, later, reveals stunning intimacies to you? If nothing else, I needed to blot some of the emotion from last night's revelation.

Most days with research, you know you're doing the best part of your work. The rush you get as you chase down clues only builds as you move toward a better understanding of your subject, as you find references to people or events, understand the use of an obsolete word, or make a connection to a historical event that actually had an impact on the folks

you study. Research is in many ways a marvelous withdrawal from the world, a private challenge and pursuit, what
the uninitiated think is the sum total of life as an academic.
It is solitary and exciting, trying to read the letters amid
blotched ink and bad writing, trying to put those pieces together—what is that letter missing on the torn edge of the
page, where did I see a reference to sewing before, is the
maid who spoiled the candles the same one who scorched
the pudding? I prayed that research would take me away this
morning and set my troubled mind and emotions at rest.

But today was one of those days where research is a
plague and a Herculean struggle, and makes me pine for the
honest, straightforward labor of fieldwork. Virtually every
cross-reference I tried to track down was a nonstarter, each
book I needed seemed to be checked out on interlibrary loan
to somewhere in Witwatersrand. The photocopier was broken, and I got into an unnecessary argument with Sasha
when she erroneously claimed I had used pen and smudged
one of the art books I looked at trying to find a portrait of
Madam Chandler. It was only after I accidentally slammed
my finger in my locker that I realized that I could best profit
the world through seclusion, fasting, and prayer: I decided to
forget work and go for a run.

As soon as I put on my running shoes, I felt better. I left
the house and hit the road before any of the others got home.

Something was finally going right; my brand-new CD
player had fresh batteries, and there's just something about
the beat of rock music that makes my legs work like they're
supposed to. Of course I don't really listen to Red Hot Chili
Peppers myself; I listen almost exclusively to classical music. This was on one of the CDs I filched from my sister
Bucky.

The air was warming up, and although I still needed a
sweatshirt under my windbreaker, the thaw was close
enough to springlike weather to wear shorts. I tore around

the hill, heading toward the annex, not worrying about my pace just yet—I love to run flat out at the start, get away from it all. My head cleared as I made the crest and began to regulate my pace once clear of the downslope. A long, relatively flat patch; I got past the doggy, draggy, warm-up point, to where joints made of wet leather suddenly feel Teflon-coated and now all I had to do was let my legs take over, and I could enjoy the view. The air was still cold, but not with the bitterness of winter, and the sun, as it periodically fought clear of the clouds, let it be known that spring really was winning out. More and more green shoots had struggled through the duff, and the first brave daffodils dared to show off a bit of bright yellow to celebrate the true rebirth of the year.

The birds were also starting to come back, and I was pleased to be sharing my little bit of the planet with other beings, especially since they were nonhuman. A squirrel chased another across the road in front of me, and the two careened around the thick trunk of an oak, crazed or ecstatic with chemical instinct. After a while, with a little physical distance, I felt less muddled, less thwarted, and could consider the return to civilization and humans after all. I would miss the trees when I left here, I thought, already anticipating my month of study over. So many and so huge, they also reminded me, with a sharp pang, of the closed-in feel of home. Once the inside of the Funny Farm was completely finished, I fantasized, Brian and I would hire a landscaper to put in some oaks, cedars, mast-pines. I'd pay for it with the multimillions from my best-seller-in-the-works, I thought, and then throw in a terrace, complete with peacocks and a sweeping vista. Then I recalled what my editor said a really hot academic work would bring, and decided, that if there was enough left over from taking Brian for a decent meal, I would buy some more tulip bulbs.

I also decided that perhaps the day wasn't a total waste,

as I'd crossed a good many things off my list, and the better part of science, I lectured myself easily as I chugged along, was eliminating the obvious. Sasha would obviously find that I hadn't been responsible for that smudge, as I take better care of my books than I do of myself.

And Faith's courage, her guts in leaving Paul, now impressed me more than the sadness and anger of her story. It even took away some of the resentment at how she ambushed me with it. My admiration for her grew the more I thought about it and that let me know that I dared to face her again. She had been drinking an awful lot, and maybe she'd not intended to share any of it with me, but I would just be there for her, and if she were pleased to continue our renewed relationship, then we'd see where that took us. I wouldn't take it personally if she regretted telling me her story—it was pretty clear she needed to talk to someone.

Whoops! My right foot landed and rolled on a twig, and I momentarily lost my balance, only avoiding a fall with a couple of quick, awkward catch-up steps. Time to turn around, I thought, no sense in pushing it too far, just when I'm starting to feel good. I made it to within sight of the annex in good time. I'd go back past the house and then see how I felt about tackling the hill down to the guardhouse and back.

I started back the way I came, along the little stream that delineated part of the extreme western boundary of the property, and followed the road a way. The light improved now, a big gap in the clouds combined with the last full light of the day. The bare trees, made darker by the recent wet weather, stood out starkly against the gray sky. The blackness of the stream similarly acted as a foil for the new green leaves of the daffies, and a single shaft of light hit the water just right, suddenly placing me in a backdrop as wistful and romantic as a pre-Raphaelite painting. A bit of Oscar's sonnet came back to me: "Bare ruin'd choirs, where late the sweet birds sang." It wasn't Oscar's, of course, but I always associated my grandfather with Shakespeare. It didn't matter—the view was privately magical.

I pushed a little harder, to see what reserves I had, how fast I *could* go if I wanted, when something caught my attention. When you've spent more than twenty-five years picking out grubby artifacts from rocks and dirt in the bottom of a screen, you get used to all sorts of distinguishing clues, no matter how small: I *notice* when something stands out of its context. A sharp edge or corner, not usually seen in nature, or a glimpse of bright color where you might expect to see only dull soil and broken roots; it's what I do.

It was a flash of white that distracted me from my concentration. A patch of snow, I thought. But the recent rains had cleared nearly all of the remaining snow away out here. I sighed and jogged back, slowly now, just to satisfy my curiosity. A plastic grocery bag, I wondered, or possibly a weird reflection of the stream in this Burne-Jones sunlight?

I got closer to the place, and slowed down to a walk, stunned by what I thought I saw. And when I realized that I wasn't mistaken, I skidded down the leaves on the muddy slope from the road to the edge of the brook.

I found Faith Morgan lying facedown. Her head and torso rested in the stream, her hair spread out and tangled around her on the water. Dead leaves surrounded her body, but they more resembled a nest than rubbish to be cleared away. I rolled her over carefully, hoping that she had only just fallen, but that was more of a fervent wish than a real possibility.

For a split second, I thought I could wake her up; she would catch cold without her coat. She needed to run to keep warm, like me. But even before I pushed back some of the hair from her still face, I knew she was dead and I mustn't disturb her further. I tried to slow my heavy breathing, the only intrusive thing in this place. Although I remotely understood that I must leave her in the water, I couldn't resist moving some more of the wet hair from her eyes.

Something besides life had left her, and I sat a moment, trying to figure out what the change was. Her lips were bluish, but it did not detract from the look of peace—that was it. The bitter, haunted look had left her, possibly for the first time in our slender acquaintance.

The light shifted again, and the golden beams were blocked behind another bank of clouds. The wind was picking up again. I sat with Faith a little longer to keep her company in the lonely afternoon, until I realized that I was getting cold too, and that someone should be told. I told her I would return quickly, brushed the leaf duff from my shorts, and scrambled back up the shallow bank to the road.

It felt silly to be running again, I felt childish, suddenly, in my sneakers and windbreaker, goose-pimply legs churning fast again, with no thought as to managing my pace. I knew I wouldn't do Faith any good with speed, but I needed to feel the blood moving through my body again, and she at least deserved the respect of urgency.

I pounded down the road toward the house, noticing how the clatter of bare branches overhead is a very lonely sound.

Chapter 6

A S I GASPED MY WAY UP THE FRONT STAIRS, I FUM-
bled for my key in the pocket of my windbreaker. I was
hyperventilating now, and between that and the sweat pour-
ing into my eyes, I could barely fit the key into the lock. It
clicked open; I stumbled into the foyer and heard someone
coming down the main staircase, the clink of ice on glass
audible. I skidded across the tile to the phone, but regardless
of my haste, Jack started in as soon as he realized he had an
audience.

"Well look what the cat dragged in!" he announced from
the stairs. "And dragged over hill and dale by the looks of
you!"

"Jack, just—don't! Faith's dead!" I dialed 911 and told
them we needed an ambulance and police at Shrewsbury, and
said I would meet them at the spot. Then I rang the security
desk at the annex. Jack never stopped blathering the whole
time, the old fool. He should have known he'd get more from
listening to my calls than he would by pestering me.

"Dead? Faith?" he was stammering. "How can she be
dead? Are you sure?" Jack took another big draught of his

drink, then set it down, then picked it up again, leaving a big wet ring on the hall table.

I hated him for his frail, human incredulity, and for making me think more about this than necessary. "That's why I get these scholarships, Jack," I snapped as I hung up. "I notice when someone's lying on the side of the road."

"On the side of the road? Was she hit by a car? Perhaps she's only unconscious," Jack offered eagerly.

"I don't think so. I think she's been dead for hours, maybe since last night, maybe this morning. It looked like the leaves had blown around her for a while," I said, pausing to retie one of my sneakers. "I'm heading back there. If anyone calls back, tell them about a half mile from the house, on the road by the stream. Not as far as the gazebo, but within sight of it."

"Not dead this morning," he mumbled, picking up his drink and emptying with one last gulp. "That can't be, it just can't. I—"

But I shut the door on him and his unhelpful fretting and hurried back to Faith. I walked quickly, but sped up when I saw a security vehicle already there. Someone was moving down the bank, crashing through the branches and leaves like an elephant through that fragile place.

"Hey!" I gasped as I ran, but I was still too far off to be heard. "Wait a minute!" I picked up speed, but my legs were trembling now with the exertion and nerves, and I knew I was heading for a big muscle crash.

"Hey!" I shouted again, my chest heaving violently as I reached the top of the bank. A guard was rolling Faith over. "Get away from her! For God's sake, don't touch anything!" I couldn't believe that he was just pawing Faith like that. No one could be that stupid, that insensitive. At least I'd had the hope that she might still be alive.

I couldn't see clearly, I couldn't be sure, but then I thought I saw "Officer" Gary Conner put something into his pocket.

As I slid down the bank, he released the body, which rolled back into the water with a small, sickening splash.

"What the hell are you doing?" I was revolted by his discourteous treatment of Faith. "What did you just take? Give it to me now!" I stuck out my hand, actually expecting that he would hand over whatever it was. Had he really been going through her pockets?

Gary's face was maddeningly deadpan. "I didn't take anything. You must be seeing things."

"Bullshit!"

"Look, just move back," he said pompously. "We don't need any civilians messing up the crime scene!" He actually grabbed my arm and tried to jerk me away, but I wrenched myself away from him, using more force than he expected.

"Keep your damned hands off me!" I said. "And don't give me that 'civilian' crap! You're nothing but a rentacop! And what makes you think it's a crime scene, anyway?"

For a minute I swear he looked panicked but the unease was quickly replaced with cunning. "You just said so," Gary replied smoothly.

"I don't think so," I answered, rubbing my arm as the blood rushed back painfully into where his fingers had been snapped away. "All I know is that you were messing around with a . . . a *body* and I'm sure as hell going to—"

I was interrupted by the arrival of the EMTs on the scene, and off in the distance, I could hear the insistent warning of other sirens coming from town. Gary Conner took the opportunity to step away and murmur something into his walkie-talkie, and as badly as I wanted to hear what he was saying—and to whom—I was caught up in the barrage of questions that the ambulance driver had for me. He took a look at her and tried to find a pulse, then stepped back and asked me who she was.

Another Shrewsbury security vehicle pulled up, arriving

at the same time as a Monroe patrol car, their lights adding to the general confusion. I was momentarily discouraged about the possibility of anything getting sorted out, of even being heard, when, after a plain car pulled up and the door opened, a sharp female voice cut through the mayhem.

"Okay, folks, a little order, if you please! Tim, Steffie—" here the authoritative voice addressed the EMTs—"If you would sit tight for just a minute. Mr. Constantino, what have we got here?"

"Excuse me, sir!" The authoritative voice called out again, and a woman dressed in plain clothes stepped forward as Gary began to climb back down the slope.

A look of disgust crossed the woman's face as she recognized Gary. "Oh, it's you, Conner. You get back here and keep yourself planted 'til anyone tells you to move."

Reluctantly Gary climbed back up to the road and stood sullenly behind Constantino, who had emerged from the second security car.

The woman spoke briefly with the patrol officers and then addressed us. "Now. Let's start from the beginning. Who found the deceased?" As the EMTs stood aside, I saw the plainclothes officer clearly for the first time. She was a hair shorter than me, with dark, mannishly cut hair. I could tell that she was slender, even under her thick gray jacket, but her heavy belt and jeans looked as though they were molded to her.

I stepped forward, shivering. "Me, I did. She's Faith Morgan."

"And who are you, ma'am?" The detective's gaze flicked over me like a lash, taking everything in. I knew what she saw; I sure as hell didn't look reputable.

I hate being called *ma'am*; I know what it means, but it sounds like it's short for mammary or mammal. "Em . . . Emma Fielding," I said, trying not to chatter too much with the cold and exertion.

"Detective Sergeant Kobrinski, Dr. Fielding is one of our researchers here," Constantino offered in that patronizing tone of his, as if that explained my eccentric appearance. I noticed that he appropriated my title to bolster his authority, but she rejected it just as easily.

"Is that so?" the detective said, eyebrows raised. She looked me over again, apparently not impressed with what she saw. "In that case, I bet Ms. Fielding can answer for herself, can't she, Mr. Constantino?"

Constantino backed off, which surprised me; one of the patrol officers took him aside and began to ask him questions. The detective turned back to me. "Can you tell me precisely what happened?"

I gave her the story, including my observation of Gary moving Faith's body around. I was pleased to see how much that seemed to bother her.

"Now, even you should know enough not to screw around with a situation like this, Gary Conner. Did you take something from the deceased?" Detective Kobrinski asked, though I got the impression that she already knew what the answer would be.

"I was just checking to see if she was really dead," Gary insisted, as if hurt.

"I told you she was dead when I called!" I protested disbelievingly. "I think I can tell when someone is dead!"

"Ms. Fielding, if you don't mind," Detective Kobrinski cut me off, then spoke to Gary with deceptive lightness. "Now, of course you *know* I can't search you, not unless I arrest you for something, right? Is there any reason you know of why I should do such a thing, Conner? Any outstanding parking tickets or anything?"

Conner didn't move at all, but he looked like he could easily strangle the life out of her without thinking twice about it. He murmured, "Fuck you," barely moving his lips, just loud enough to be audible.

"I didn't catch that, Gary," Kobrinski said threateningly. "Did I?"

Constantino stepped in. "Detective, I think it's safe to say that Dr. Fielding here was seeing things." He gestured to me with what was supposed to be sympathy, but it came off as an indictment. "She's clearly upset by this experience."

It wasn't fair: I didn't look the part of a detached witness. I was soaked with congealing sweat and shivering with cold, overexertion, and low blood sugar. My chattering teeth and the "Red Dwarf" sweatshirt I had stolen from Brian were not the best witnesses to my sober observational skills.

"I'm not hysterical!" I said defiantly. "I was alert enough to notice her in the first place and not make a mess of the scene—" here I shot a look at the younger guard that I fancied would have dropped an angry cobra in its tracks—"then make the calls, and get back here to meet you all. Where I saw him take something from Faith!"

Detective Kobrinski eyed me, weighing my words. "Why don't you go over and have a seat with Tim and Steffie over there, for just a minute, while I sort this out?" She crooked a finger at one of the EMTs, who came trotting over. "See if you can't dig up a blanket, or something, for Ms. Fielding here, before we get another corpse on our hands."

I wanted to stamp my foot and protest, but one look from the detective assured me that I would lose this battle. I convinced myself that the only way I would get ahead here would be to cooperate and appear as rational as I knew I was, but it rankled that this was just what she wanted anyway. The EMT named Tim gave me a cup of water from a cooler and one of those shiny silver sheets. It looked flimsy, but it was warmer than I expected, and I thought I looked even goofier than before, like a potato wrapped in tinfoil.

I tried not to think about Faith lying down there in the water with us wrangling up here. Part of me was shocked that she had been alive and talking to me just last night, part wasn't at all surprised that she was gone, and a corner of my mind held onto that alien, tranquil look I'd seen on her face. I couldn't sort things out, and yet, the nasty idea darted through all my confusion that Faith had been setting me up. Had already set me up.

Someone, Steffie, I guess, poked me in the shoulder gently, and I turned to face a chocolate cupcake head-on. "You look like you could use a little glucose right about now," she said, offering the snack to me.

"Thanks," I said, "but I'm not feeling real hungry."

"You're not going to do anyone any good if you drop before you can answer her questions, are you?" Steffie said reasonably, jerking her head toward the detective.

"I'll try." I decided I'd take the damn thing just to make her happy. It was one of those packaged chocolate cupcakes, without an ounce of real anything in them anywhere, and a shelf life of . . . no, make that a *half life* of fifty years, easy. Just the sort of thing Brian's been trying to wean me off forever, claiming that he had pictures of what such a thing did to the internal organs of lab animals. I had actually gotten to the point where I believed I didn't like them anymore.

The thing was gone, and I was licking the crumbs from my fingers before I knew what happened. "Thanks," I said. "I guess I really did need that."

"Hey, I think I've got some Fritos in the glove, if you want . . ." she offered.

"No, no thanks," I said, embarrassed by my sudden gluttony. "I feel much better now." I looked over to the little scene by the bank and pulled my rustly silver blanket closer around me, drawing my knees up onto the inside of the door of the ambulance.

Detective Kobrinski had led Gary Conner over to one side, far enough away to be out of everyone's hearing—I could see Constantino straining to hear what was going on, while the other cops made sure he did nothing more than try

to eavesdrop. In a vivid pantomime, I saw her go on perfectly calmly while Gary grew increasingly more agitated.
He never moved from the spot he stood on, but the shifting
of his weight, the flood of color to his face, and the hunching
in his shoulders all indicated that he was seething. He didn't
hand anything over to the detective.

Finally, she turned and left him standing behind her,
when I saw him say something very briefly. She stopped,
slowly turned, and even more slowly walked back to face
Gary again. She didn't say anything that I could see for the
longest time, just stared at him with those dark laser eyes of
hers. Finally she responded just as briefly to him and returned to her car where she spoke for some time on the radio. Gary walked back over to where Constantino was
standing, but I noticed he never turned his back on Detective
Kobrinski as he passed her.

I never thought I'd envy Constantino for anything, but I
knew that he'd find out what they'd said to each other long
before I did.

The Detective Sergeant moved carefully down the hill to
take a look at Faith. She squatted carefully and then reached
down towards Faith's skirt. She hesitated and pulled her
hand back, and I realized she'd just successfully resisted the
urge to twitch Faith's skirt modestly down over the bare skin
of her exposed legs. Suddenly within the melee of emotion,
I was overwhelmed with gratitude: Someone was finally
paying respectful attention to Faith. Kobrinski got up and
surveyed the surroundings briefly. She nodded to herself and
returned to speak to the other officers, then went to her car,
where she spent some time on her radio. I moved closer to
the main knot of activity, the better to observe what was
transpiring.

One of the cops went to the trunk of his cruiser and without a word, began to fasten a bright line of yellow flagging

around a tree on the top of the slope about ten yards above where Faith lay. The other spoke into his radio.

"How long is this area going to be cordoned off?" Mr. Constantino demanded. "There's a fund-raiser next week and I've got the landscapers coming. Mr. Whitlow wants it all—"

Detective Kobrinski arrived just in time to hear that last; she looked at him with something close to humor and said, "Mr. Constantino, straight to hell with your landscapers. I'm blocking off this half of the road to traffic for just as long as it takes me to get done investigating."

"You can't be serious," Constantino protested. "We certainly can't have—"

"I'm sorry that this woman's death is going to ruffle the quality of life here at Shrewsbury for a while," the detective broke in coldly, "but that's the way it's going to be. I promise I won't take any longer than necessary. But I can't speak for the State Police detectives or the medical examiner's people." She grinned wickedly. "Honest." She walked along the top of the slope, conferred with the patrol officers, and gave orders, apparently unaware or unconcerned that Constantino looked like he was longing to shove her down the side of the gully.

"Look, it seems pretty clear to me that you're making a federal case of an accident—"

"No, not a federal case, not yet," Kobrinski called. "Not unless you know of something that would indicate that this is a felony." She moved a little closer to Mr. Constantino, as if to include him in on a little secret, but she didn't lower her voice. "You know, as much as I love the fact that my being here is crawling right up your ass, I'm not going to need to take any more advantage of it than necessary. But rest assured, Mr. Constantino: I am enjoying this." Detective Kobrinski smiled and I saw little pointy teeth bared.

Constantino looked as though he were going to burst a blood vessel. Truth be told, I was amazed at the way Kobrinski was standing up to this supercilious windbag. But of course, she was trained to do just that. I relished her enjoyment of the situation—you go, girl!

She turned back to me, and I smiled to express my approval and our sisterly solidarity. The detective, however, wasn't interested.

"Let's start from the beginning. I want you to tell me precisely what you saw," she said, without a trace of recognition that we shared anything—even our distrust of Constantino—in common. "I want to know everything you did and thought from the moment you noticed Ms. Morgan down there. Don't leave anything out."

For the next half hour I repeated my every step, my every breath, what I touched, what I thought about thinking. She went back over every point to clarify and expand on every detail. By the time that I finished, I was convinced that she must know everything I did. I was starting to feel slightly ill, from the stress and muscle cramps, when she asked one last, surprising question.

"Okay, ma'am, what do you think happened?"

I answered before I had time to think about it—some of my best thoughts come without invitation. "I . . . I think someone drowned her." My own words startled me.

"You think she was murdered." Detective Kobrinski arched one eyebrow.

I continued, explaining my opinions to myself as much as to her. "She has no coat on, and it was freezing last night. No way would anyone choose to go outside without a coat. Even if she just wanted a breath of air—what would she be doing nearly a half mile away from the house unless she had a damned good reason?"

"Hmm." Kobrinski was no more encouraging than that. "What else?"

"And she didn't have any tights on," I said. "Faith was wearing them with that dress yesterday. And," I said, relieved to finally identify what had been bothering me, "her shoes are really clean. There's no dirt on the heels or bottoms of them, at least, not enough to indicate to me that she walked down the hill by herself. Not with the mud." I showed her my own caked sneaker.

"Why do you say last night?"

"Faith, she would have never worn the same dress two days in a row, and like I said, she was wearing that one last night."

"What time did you last see her? What were you doing?"

"I'm not sure, maybe midnight." Here I paused out of an instinct to preserve the secrets that came out during our talk. I shook myself—nothing could hurt Faith anymore, and now the truth was important. I took a deep breath and said it. "We talked about her leaving an abusive marriage, starting over in her work."

"Did you know her ex-husband?"

There was something about the way she said that, like she knew something but was too polite to let me know she knew it. "No, not at all. I met Paul a handful of times a long time ago. I'm afraid I wasn't as charmed or impressed by him as other folks were. I barely knew Faith, really. We were just in some of the same graduate classes together."

Detective Kobrinski nodded and asked equably, "Did you get along well?"

"Not particularly well, but you have to understand," I hurriedly added, aware that this wasn't coming out the way I wanted, "our personalities clashed and we were just happier avoiding each other. She was . . . I don't know . . . controlling, you know, or she could be a little haughty. We actually had a fairly pleasant chat last night, before she told me . . . about leaving Paul."

"Hmmm," was all she said again. "So you met up with an

old . . . what—competitor? rival?—for the first time in years last night—"

"Hey, I didn't say—"

"Oh, what, you were friends then?"

"Hang on there," I said, finally determined to set her straight. "We weren't enemies, we just didn't care for each other. I'm just trying to be honest and you're twisting my words around—"

Detective Kobrinski brushed my concerns aside. "Okay. What happened after you two finished talking?"

"I went to bed, I was very tired—"

"Oh?"

There was that damned provoking skepticism again. Was she determined to believe nothing I said?

I tried again. "Well, she kept me up late, and I'd had a few drinks—"

"Drinks." A whole ocean of implication soaked the word, but I let her imply away. She wasn't going to get my goat; I just nodded.

"And then you went to bed. Can anyone verify that? Were you alone?"

"Yes, I was bloody alone!" I said, abandoning my good intentions. "Look, you are making a lot of unfair assumptions here—"

Kobrinski looked at me with maddening calm. "You're telling me a bunch of facts, I'm just trying to see how they might fit the truth."

"I'm telling you the truth!" I nearly laughed in frustration.

That seemed to prick her more than anything I'd said so far, but her anger was a hot, quiet burn. "Do you understand why I'm asking you these questions? This looks like it's a murder investigation! I'm going to find out what happened here. Are you aware that the murderer is usually the first one on the scene?"

It was almost as though she was taking this personally,

and the fact that she was showing genuine emotion drove away the thousand smart-aleck retorts that sprang to my mind. "Yes, I did know that," I answered. "This isn't the first time I've been asked about a murder." I gave her Sheriff Dave Stannard's name and number at the Fordham County Sheriff's Office, the place we'd first met several years ago, when he was investigating the death of a friend of mine, in which I'd been implicated. "He'll tell you. I'm really just trying to tell you what I know."

Just like that, the utterly professional facade slipped back into place. She noted down the number and said, "Thank you, Ms. Fielding. I think I've got everything I need for now. Just don't make any plans to leave Shrewsbury for a while, okay?"

Chapter 7

"ARE YOU GOING TO BE SAFE?" BRIAN SOUNDED AS though he wanted to climb through the phone line late that evening. "I thought that place was supposed to have tons of security! I think I want you to come home now."

I didn't tell him I couldn't, even if I wanted to. "I'm fine. There are cops all over the place, and besides, we don't know that it wasn't an accident—"

"You just said you don't think it was!" he protested.

"Well, what do I know about anything?"

A pregnant pause hung between us for a minute.

"Brian, trust me. I'm all right. You know how cautious I am."

I was not reassured by the length of time it took him to answer. "Lock your door at night, sweetie," he sighed. "Don't do anything exciting."

"Exciting" was a compromise word by which Brian meant "stupid," "rash," or "dangerous" for the situations I might have described as "expedient" or "necessary." He and I both knew what he meant.

"Relax, I'm just here to get some research done. Other folks are looking into the matter, don't worry."

"Uh-huh."

"Really," I said. "Everything's cool."

Brian didn't say anything, and I felt the need to convince him of my coolness.

"It's just a little weird around here. That's all. The cops were asking questions in the library. People whispering to each other, after. And they were looking at me, like they think I caused all this trouble just by finding Faith."

"They're just scared, Em," he said quietly. "Something bad happened near them and they're just trying to make sense of it."

"But when do we get a normal life?" I asked suddenly. "Work, the house, then something like this? All this drama, all the time, is a little much. It's starting to wear on me, you know?"

"Hey, it's okay, sweetie! It sounds like you've got some other stuff going on in your head too. Want to talk about it?"

I wasn't sure I really wanted to, but it seemed like a good idea. "I was just thinking. For years, we've been struggling, for our degrees, our jobs. Getting a house, and now working to make it habitable. Us against the rest of the world, and that's fine, but it's been . . . years. And for a while now, all I seem to hear about is how people are starting to think . . . you know. About themselves. About life, not just work. Marty and Kam. Hell, even Jane is going to take some time off, and you know what she's like."

There was a long pause at the other end. "Emma . . . are you telling me you want to have kids?"

My jaw fell open. Was that what I was saying? The thought was so large, so important, I needed time to give it more careful thought. "I don't think so. I mean, I don't want to have that conversation right this minute. But we haven't discussed that in a while, and well, shit, if we're going to talk about it, we should do it soon." I licked my lips and tried to take up the thread of my present worries. "Like I said, it seems that all we do these days is for something else, it's always work, and I think maybe I need to make some time for some other things too. I just get so tired, you know?"

"I know."

"I mean, I know it's important to do what we're doing. The last push on the tenure grind was this year. We need to work on the house, and it's too easy to lose momentum. But I just . . . need to do something with you that isn't about everything else. For a while."

"I can get behind that. What if—?"

"And as for this thing with Faith? Well, it was weird to see her again. It was okay, at first, and then it went horrible. It just seems like that's on top of me too, and I don't like it."

"Okay, first thing? That has nothing to do with you," Brian said firmly, once I paused to take breath. "Absolutely nothing. It's just bad luck, it's . . ."

He paused and I was surprised by how anxious I was to hear his reasoning.

". . . It's just a matter of distance. Everyone has lots of weirdness happen near them in the course of their lives, but most of the time, it happens to someone they know, you know, someone who knows someone who knew someone— friends of friends. You've just been unlucky, a couple of times, because . . . you're at the center of a karmic vortex," he said confidently. "Not your fault."

"Hmmm," I said, willing to be convinced. "Is that some kind of Chinese philosophy?"

"I think I got it off *Buffy the Vampire Slayer*," he said. "Or does it sound more an old Bowie lyric? I can't remember."

"What a rip-off!" I laughed. "Here I thought I'd married into a five-thousand-year-old tradition of wisdom and I get—"

"The all-American boy. Trust me babe, I'm the best thing that could have happened to you. You're laughing, you sound better. Do you want me to come out there?"

"I do feel better," I admitted. "Just come Saturday, like we planned. I'll pick out a nice restaurant, so bring a clean shirt and some shoes. Real shoes, I mean, not sneaks."

We dawdled over good-byes and I didn't even realize I'd been so depressed until I hung up feeling better. Brian fixes me when I don't even know I'm broken.

The next day, Friday, stumbled by in a disorienting blend of the ordinary and the surreal. While things at the library were shaken up by the ongoing investigations—there were police cars by the road in the morning, when I went up to the library—there was a tacit understanding that work and life should continue. And oddly, the inhabitants of Shrewsbury were confused and uneasy, but nobody really seemed to be mourning Faith. It was more like they were trying to cover up the bad opinions they held of her in life.

It was a little unnerving for me to see the alterations that death had wrought on Faith's memory as it was collectively held by the staff. Day readers, interns, and administrators who ordinarily blended in with the background were suddenly jarred into visibility, as they shamefacedly transformed Faith into a kind of heroine by using words like *tragic* and *remote*. Before her death, Jack and Sasha had hinted and fumbled, trying not to use obvious adjectives; Michael had spoken outright about the difficulty that one could expect in living and working with her. Now Jack spoke seldom, just scurried about and kept his head down and Sasha went through the motions of her job with pursed lips and brusque motions. Harry was purely morose. Michael seemed much the same as usual, which is not to say normal.

And as if reflecting the emotional chaos around me, Madam Chandler was continuing to provide a few puzzles of her own. The text was starting to change and more and more of the encoded passages were appearing, sometimes in the middle of a paragraph, sometimes for a page or so near the end of an entry. I was trying to transcribe the words faithfully, but it was clear that something was not right in Margaret's life, so I recorded my own feelings along with her words to keep track of those all-important first impressions. I grew less and less comfortable even as she herself seemed to become wary:

Jul 16—(Truth stumbles in the Market-place and Honesty is kept out.)

There is an Increase of Concern over Rev. Blanch'd's sudden passing. Matthew has been pressed beyond all Fairnesse to quiet Dame Rumor, and Rev'd Affleck e'en went so fr as to preach a Sermon that signified his support of my Parte. His Text, Isaiah LIX, was much spoke upon, but more for its Ambiguity than its Direct'n and Succor to the Congrega'n (24 11 8 9 5 10 2 5 19 5 2 22 2 10 10 5 16 10 9). The Weather is evilly oppressive, but has bro't forth the most remarkable Blooms, poss. the only thinge of Merit in this superstitous Wildernesse is its heath'nish Hues and monstr's Flowers. The Herbs and Foxglove thrive, as does the Nicotiana virginiana *and the wild, thorny Roses. This leads me to consider the Goodnesse of the Creator—perhaps He offers Comfort thus, though I cannot but think that His choice of Messengr mocks me (24 5 5 16 1 12 3 16 7 8 2 1 8 3 1 6 11 17 19 2 3 20 11 5 17 5)*

Today I notice in Nora a Vertue unlooked for . . .

The whole passage confused me; if she was so concerned about the Reverend's death, then why the hidden text and the long description of her garden? And what was it that the heretofore sullen Nora had done to earn that grudging encomium? I made a note to try and locate some biographical data on Reverend Blanchard: Obviously her parsley tonic hadn't had its hoped-for effect. And that remark about rumors savored of careful circumspection.

The hairs suddenly stood up on the back of my neck, as the feeling of being watched made me look up. I was surprised to see Harry Saunders standing over my carrel, looking at me sympathetically. There'd been no sound of his footfall on the carpeted floor.

"Oh, gosh, I'm sorry," Harry apologized. "I was trying to be discreet. So many chatty Cathies around here today—" he looked around disapprovingly at a little group who was buzzing off to one side, watching us. "Maybe I should have been a little more noisy."

"It's okay, I'm just a little preoccupied," I said, sliding an acid-free bookmark into my place.

"And no wonder," he said. "I was just going to offer you my office, if you like, just to have some quiet today."

I knew that by "quiet" he meant privacy. "Thanks, Harry, I'll be fine. Everyone's being polite; they can't help but be curious."

"Of course, please, just let me know. Is there anything . . . ?"

"Nope, I'm just working through the Chandler manuscript, right now, but I may want to have a look at the town histories for Stone Harbor. Something was definitely happening at the time Margaret Chandler was writing her diary. Have you read it?"

"No," he said brusquely and turned away.

The blunt, almost curt negative startled me. "Are you okay, Harry?"

He turned back suddenly and blurted out, "If you want to

talk about finding Faith, please don't . . . keep it bottled up inside. I'm . . . I'm a good listener." Harry needlessly adjusted the knot of his tie to cover his embarrassment.

At first, I was so angry, I could feel my stomach contract as if preparing to take a punch. I felt betrayed: It seemed that this was just a ploy for Harry to hear firsthand the morbid details of my discovery of Faith. But I saw something in his eyes that was beyond nosiness, something that looked a little more like grief endured. Faith had been here for several weeks before she died—what if Harry'd fallen for her? From a distance, Faith was an easy person to have a crush on, regal looks and brains too. Had I been wrong about him and Sasha?

"I'm sure it was very quick," I said, shrugging. I didn't know any such thing, but it couldn't hurt, I reasoned. "I just hope the cops can tell us what happened soon."

Harry said nothing, but nodded sadly and then withdrew without another word. I guess we all have our ways of coping.

A piercing wail unexpectedly tore through the room and I jumped up, not knowing what to expect. "Shit!"

"Fire alarm!" Sasha called calmly, as she locked the glass-fronted offices. "Everybody out through the front!"

I followed the small group out through the front doors and stood under one of the great pines in front of the building while Harry, Sasha, and a security guard went through their procedures, counting heads and double-checking that everyone was out. Everybody was huddling together without their coats: The weather had turned gray and raw since the almost-spring of yesterday. It suited the general mood of the place, or maybe just my own.

Sasha came over to where I was standing, freezing. "You really should have left that, you know," she said sternly.

I looked down and realized I'd carried Madam Chandler's diary out with me. "Sorry, I didn't think."

"It's okay, next time, just leave the books inside." Her remonstration delivered, Sasha smiled kindly. "Completely understandable reaction. I had to train myself out of it when I first arrived. It's hard to leave these behind sometimes."

We watched as the fire truck pulled up outside, and the marshal conferred with Harry. They both went back inside.

"Probably just the darned construction work again," Sasha explained. "It's been tripping the alarm lately, day and night, even when it's disarmed. We just have to live with it until the repairs are done."

She smiled bravely, but her voice began to quaver. "There's just been too much going wrong here lately, and so sad too. Faith, Dr. Morgan—" She broke off and dabbed at her eyes with a handkerchief and then blew her nose, finally, as if determined not to completely break down.

I patted her arm, feeling like a louse for not sharing her tears. "I know. It makes you feel vulnerable."

An unmarked police car pulled up too, and a grim-looking Detective Sergeant Kobrinski got out. She looked around questioningly and then spoke with Mr. Constantino. On my way to the library that morning, I'd seen her and a couple of officers combing through the damp leaves along the bank of the stream. They had planted little colored flags that stood out in contrast to the dark earth exposed where the leaves had been raked away.

"She doesn't have it easy either," Sasha sniffed, watching the detective sergeant read something off a clipboard to an increasingly unhappy Constantino.

"No?"

"We both grew up in Monroe. Pam Kobrinski and I went to high school about the same time." She shrugged. "It's tough to be in charge where everyone's watched you grow up the hard way."

Before she could elaborate, we were interrupted when the woman herself approached. "Sasha, how're you doin'?"

"Okay, Pam." The librarian corrected herself awkwardly: "Detective Sergeant."

Detective Kobrinski didn't seem to notice Sasha's hesitation. "Can I have a word, Ms. Fielding?"

She led me apart from the group. "I just thought I'd let you know, since you knew the deceased. Faith Morgan died by drowning."

"Was it an accident?"

"We're still looking into that," Kobrinski answered briefly.

"Well, thanks for telling me," I said. "Let me know, will you, if I can help you out in any way."

Detective Kobrinski's mouth twitched, and I was reminded of a fox's nose and whiskers flicking, testing the wind. "Oh, don't you worry about hearing from me."

A general murmur rose from the small group of staff, and people began moving back into the library.

"Sasha says the alarm's been going off a lot because of the construction," I explained.

"That's a damned waste." She frowned. "I know, it's the insurance companies, probably, or something, but other folks who really need the fire department won't be able to get them." The detective sergeant looked as though she'd just had an idea. "Have you—?" But just as quickly, she reconsidered whatever it was she was going to ask me and turned to leave. "Never mind. I'll be in touch."

I decided to spend the rest of the afternoon catching up on my departmental paperwork, composing e-mails to the colleagues and students covering my classes, and losing myself in that other world. When I got back to the house, I found I was the first one home from the fray, but I hadn't even grabbed a soda when Jack stumbled in.

He didn't bother to conceal the fact that he was loaded, and went directly to his cupboard, where he emptied the scant remainder of one bottle of scotch into his glass, drained off that inch, and then opened another bottle immediately. He was wearing his headphones, and I could hear another synthetic jazz tape playing, but slowly, the sound distorted by the failing batteries.

What am I doing here? I thought miserably as I watched him. These people are one nervous tic away from the loony bin. Not even the Funny Farm. Brian's right, I need the real world, not more obscure factoids and isolation in the midst of these freaks.

Only after Jack had refilled his glass halfway to the top and added one lonely ice cube did he seem to slow down, noticing my presence there with him and pulling off the headphones. "Faith's death. One feels *surrounded* by malignancy. Terribly upsetting."

"Yes it is," I said.

"But of course, you were the one to find her," he acknowledged. As if that fact were reason enough, he took another gulp. "Horrible."

Despite his drinking, there was only just the *hint* of a slur on "course."

Jack looked at me apprehensively, then breathed, "Do you think she was *murdered*?"

It took me a long time to say it. "Yes. I don't know who or why, but she wasn't out there by herself that night," I said.

"That night, Wednesday night! But that's the thing that confuses me," he exclaimed, scrubbing the back of his neck as if that would clear his thoughts. "I could have *sworn* that I saw her yesterday morning!"

"What?" I almost dropped my soda.

"You see, I can't be certain." Jack looked anguished. "I just can't be certain."

"What time did you see her?" I asked. "Was it before breakfast?"

"Oh, not *morning*-morning," he explained. "It was still dark out, about three-thirty, I think it was. I don't sleep well, you see."

I said nothing, thinking about the disruptive effects of alcohol on sleep.

"I'd been tossing and turning, and I thought a wee dram might ease things a bit, you see. Calm me. I happened to look out the window, and I could have *sworn* I saw her walking down the road, toward the gazebo. But I just don't *know*."

"Well, when you were down here in the kitchen, did you hear the door—?"

"Kitchen?" he asked, puzzled. The ice popped in his drink, reminding him it was time to take another large sip.

"Yes, yes, kitchen," I said impatiently. "If you could see her, she must have just left—"

"Oh, no," Jack said. "I wasn't in the *kitchen*."

"I thought you said you got a drink?"

"Well, I keep my small bottle of brandy in my desk, you see," he admitted unwillingly. "You remember, from the other night? And like I said, I have trouble falling asleep sometimes."

"I see." I recalled the sickeningly sweet stuff he'd shared with me.

"I just *happened* to glance out the window, as I said, and I saw her heading down the road. I recognized her by her dress, you see."

"Jack," I asked softly. "Were you wearing your glasses?"

He looked uncomfortable, a thin glaze of perspiration creeping across his balding head. "No, of course not. I was just . . . getting my drink, you see. Didn't need them. But I did remember that dress of hers, all . . . whatever you call it. Billowy, full."

I thought about the narrow cut of Faith's jumper, and I knew now for certain that Jack had seen no such thing. "Didn't you think it was odd that she should be out so late, with no coat on?"

Jack was silent for a moment. "I remember thinking that she seemed to be in a hurry. I thought she was going to the library."

"Jack! The library closes at five o'clock! What on earth would she be doing going there at that hour? Wait, are you sure it was really three-thirty? Did you read the clock wrong?"

"I don't know, I don't know," he said wretchedly. "I just don't remember much, maybe I'll remember better later, after the shock has worn off some. Perhaps another small sip—"

"Damn it, Jack! You don't need another drink! You need to tell Detective Kobrinski all about this!"

"I will, I know I have to tell her," he snapped, suddenly angry. He slammed down his glass. "Just as soon as I figure out what it was, I'll tell her. I'm no shirker, *I* know what *I* have to do. So just leave me alone, Emma, leave me be!"

Under other circumstances his hopping about might have been funny, but now I was alarmed, convinced he was going to have a heart attack. Jack was nearly purple and sweating like a racehorse.

"Jack, I didn't mean to—"

"You have no *idea* what it's like," he continued, unmindful of my interruption. "No idea at all, and you just start in on *me*, do this, do that!"

"I'm sorry, I just—"

"*You* don't know anything," he insisted angrily. "Just go away. Leave me alone! Why can't you all just leave me alone!"

Jack stomped out of the kitchen, bringing his glass with him. Stunned by his outburst, I stared after him a minute be-

fore I started pulling out the ingredients for dinner and began cooking.

"Smells good," someone whispered into my ear.

I jumped about six feet in the air. Michael had come into
the kitchen without making a sound.

"Holy snappers! Michael, don't *do* that!" I exclaimed
when I came down out of orbit. "What is it with people
around here, always sneaking around?" First Harry, now
Michael.

"It's a library, Emma," Michael said, leaning against the
doorway. He looked like he'd do it again the next minute, if
he would get the same reaction from me: he was the very
picture of a little boy teasing. "Skulking is the first thing
everyone learns."

I frowned at him and turned my attention back to my fry-
ing onions.

"I keep forgetting, people are a little edgy around here
since yesterday." He unbuttoned the omnipresent overcoat
and then massaged his hand as if it were sore.

"You seem to exclude yourself from the rest of us, the
way you say that."

Michael shrugged and pulled out a packet of cigarettes,
then, catching himself, swore quietly and put it back into his
pocket.

"I didn't really know Faith all that well." He shrugged
again, shook his dark hair out of his eyes. "She died. It happens."

"You know, that sounds a little callous." I cracked some
eggs violently into the pan with the onions, then picked out
the eggshell. I deliberately turned my back on Michael to
stick some bread in the toaster but he didn't say anything until I had turned around again. I noticed he was rubbing his
wrist again.

"What's wrong with your hand?"

"Nothing. Look, it's a shame Faith's dead. If she was

murdered, then that should be looked into. But I'm not going to cry crocodile tears over it. What am I supposed to do?"

I sighed as I dumped my scrambled eggs onto a plate. "I don't know. Maybe it's other people you should be thinking about now, not how *you* felt—or did not feel—about Faith. The library is full of scared, shocked people who might not see it from your angle." Some of the egg had stuck to one side of the pan, and I scraped at it irritably, got the toast, then took my plate into the dining room and began to eat.

Surprisingly, Michael followed me. He twitched aside one of the curtains to sit on the windowsill, despite the fact that there were five perfectly good chairs free at the table. "Do you always go around thinking about what other people think?"

I put down my fork and looked at him sarcastically. "Well, Michael, that's sort of the definition of what anthropologists do."

"But you're an archaeologist."

"Right. I generally think about what dead people thought." Then I heard what I had just said and suddenly, I didn't want to finish my dinner. The eggs sat on the plate looking cold and greasy.

"Sounds like a lot of work to me. And depressing too."

"Then I guess that's why you don't bother," I said shortly and then got up to throw away the remains of my dinner. I hadn't even made it to the door when Michael stopped me.

"I don't see *you* crying into your tea towel, Emma. Could it be that beneath that carefully groomed exterior, you're just as 'callous' as I am?"

"Look, you," I snapped. "My relationship with Faith was minimal and complicated and just plain weird right up to the minute we said good night. I'm still sorting things out for myself, so just cut me a little slack, okay?"

Michael nodded. "And yet, I wonder what you would have said if that's what *I'd* told *you*." He stood up, then without warning, brushed past me. "I need a cigarette. Don't wait up worrying about the parlous state of *my* soul, Auntie."

He left me stunned. As I washed my dishes slowly, I wondered: Just what had his relationship with Faith been?

Chapter 8

FROM THE SOUNDS I HEARD EARLY SATURDAY MORN-
ing, as far as Jack was concerned, I wasn't off the hook
yet. My plan to sleep in late *and* avoid my cranky housemates wasn't working. I heard Jack coughing and hawking
his usual morning symphony on his way to the bathroom,
and I noticed that he added a few extra slams and dropped
items just for my benefit. He obviously remembered my inclination to sleep in and was making the most of the chance
to act out. At one point I could have sworn he threw the bathroom scale out of spite, but I couldn't be certain. A phone
rang, and I buried my head under a pillow; everyone seemed
to be conspiring against my getting a little extra sleep.

I finally decided that there was no point in trying to wait
until we all cooled off, as no one was cooling, especially me.
I felt crabby and decided that I hated everyone: The only
thing keeping me in this nut bin was Margaret Chandler. Besides, I had an evil caffeine-deprivation headache that I
could only wish on Republican politicians.

The news channel blared from the parlor and then went
dead, followed by a slammed door as I descended the big

staircase. Good, I thought, that was Jack. I watched the coffee drip with maddening slowness into the pot, and was glad that Jack had left the house: I wasn't ready to be the peacemaker. We were all in this together, and you didn't catch me pitching any tantrums.

Brian said that he'd show up for his visit around noon or one. That meant three hours until I had a little relief from the tumult here. I figured a trip down to the library would keep me from dwelling on the situation. Even if the stacks were officially closed on weekends, I could still get to my carrel to sort out my notes and look at the reference works that were available to us. Good: A plan and a monster mug of joe were positive steps toward staying sane.

And speaking of sane—"Honey! You cooked for me!"

I was mildly shocked to see Michael, fully dressed, subdued smart-casual, overcoat, and all, practically waltzing into the kitchen.

"Michael?"

"Gooood morning, Auntie!" He pirouetted over to the counter and helped himself to a cup of coffee.

This was not the enigmatic, secretive man I remembered from the evening before. "Pardon me for saying so, Michael, but you seem . . . happy . . . about something."

"Oh I am, Emma, I am." He set his cup down and, hopping backwards, tried to hoist himself up to sit on the counter. His right arm buckled, and with a little groan, he missed the counter, smacking his butt hard on the floor.

Although he winced when he rubbed his wrist, even that didn't seem to faze him. Michael reached up for his coffee and continued as if he'd achieved precisely what he'd intended. "The gods punish me for attempting to be spry: I offer them the fit meat of hubris, and every time, they eat it up. But still I resist, I try." He thought about that and then frowned briefly. "Unfortunately, that's the clinical definition of hubris and one doesn't really beat the gods at their own game. But no matter."

"Look, Michael, I've been thinking about what you said last night—" I began.

His dopey adolescent grin returned. "Last night? Last night? What happened last night?"

"Well, we both used the word *callous*, and I think—"

I stopped when Michael continued to look confused. For a minute, I thought he was trying to embarrass me into recounting the entire situation, but then his face cleared. "Oh. That? You actually listened to what I said? And then you *thought* about it? To borrow a phrase from Jack, dearie gracious me. Ah, no matter. I'm pretty certain there should be no lasting harmful effects." He vaulted up onto his feet, actually no mean trick as he was still entangled in the loose tails of his coat. "Down, boy, down!" he said, slapping the overcoat away. "My editor said that those tests that the FDA performed on my last book were inconclusive at best."

"As long as there are no hard feelings—" I offered.

Michael abruptly coughed violently, spraying a mouthful of coffee all over the sink. Startled, I tried to pat him on the back, but he waved me off while he tried to draw a clear breath, coughing all the while. And standing so close by, I was forced to notice that he was wearing an unabashedly musky cologne; I was suddenly and forcefully reminded of all the documentaries I'd seen where they described how male animals marked their territory and attracted mates by smell. Jack's Brut seemed like a meek afterthought, by comparison.

"Ach, Nicole Miller ties are not enhanced by staining— good thing I had my overcoat, eh?"

I shook my head sadly.

"You speak of hard feelings," he continued, "not knowing I'm about to meet the vituperative Wife Number Three. She rang up this morning, trying to get more alimony out of me, when she knows there can't possibly be a farthing left in the coffers. Numbers One and Two—"

My jaw dropped. "You've been married three times?" He couldn't have been too far off forty-five, at most.

"Four, actually." Michael looked annoyed. "I was about to say, Numbers One and Two are currently plotting with Number Four. I think Number Three is acting on her own this time—the other Weird Sisters would never consider anything so banal as mere finance. The four of them are constantly scheming, fighting, dispersing, regrouping. And yet, always to my disadvantage."

He went on thoughtfully, index finger raised as if trying to articulate a bit of life wisdom. "Never marry anyone who teaches at the same college you do, Emma, you wouldn't believe how it can work against you."

Michael raised a second finger to tick off the next of his tenets. "And if you do marry someone who teaches where you do, make sure you don't do it more than three times— I'm pretty sure now that four's beyond the safe limit." He sipped. "Anyway, Number Three is meeting me in Boston today to wrangle."

"Oh. I'm sorry." I remembered that I had been meaning to ask him about the quote in Madam Chandler's diary, but other events had distracted me. "Well, maybe after you get back, you'd be willing to look at a quote for me. I think it's a Classical philosopher, but I don't know for certain. That might cheer you up—"

Michael was impatient and forgiving all at once. "Dear child, there'll be no need of cheering." He explained: "When Number Three says she wants to discuss money, she really means that she wants to work herself into *such* a violent froth of animosity that the only relief for the little piranha is to rend our mutual clothing and attempt to subdue me through coitus. I'm happy to say that I give in every time."

I was still trying to wrap my head around this when Michael took his leave, still looking uncharacteristically jaunty.

"Ta-ta, Auntie. Send the SWAT teams to the Parker House if I'm not back by Sunday night." He rubbed his hands together greedily. "With any luck, there'll be a hostage situation!"

I watched as Michael started up his rattletrap Mazda and roared off with one of Edith Piaf's melancholy songs blaring through the rolled-up windows. He had to be the most outlandish, most mercurial person I'd ever met; jaded and charismatic, incisive, rude, brilliant, and at times, just plain weird.

And if I was being perfectly honest, damned attractive. I'd found myself carefully resisting his odd charm a little more vehemently than I liked. I frowned. Michael was exactly the kind of guy who would have gotten me into trouble in high school, whispering rude and witty things so that I laughed and got busted while he wore an angelic look on his face. I didn't want to find him amusing. I didn't want to think him attractive.

I also noticed that I never did get around to asking him about his relationship with Faith.

After a brisk walk to the library, I decided I'd spend my time tracking down some data on Reverend Blanchard, but what I found in my carrel was enough to detour me from that mission. A handwritten note on top of my stack of reference books was waiting for me.

Emma,

You are certainly not *forgiven for being such a bully. I am not the dunce that everyone seems to think I am*

*and I would consider it a tiny kindness if you might
keep that in mind.*

JACK

P.S. I'm sure you'll be extremely *pleased to know
that I did think of something else, and will be dis-
cussing it with the detective shortly.*

Whew! Jack certainly has his priorities straight, tick me
off first, then let me know that he did actually come up with
something about Faith's movements early Thursday. I
looked around but he was nowhere to be found, and I
couldn't tell when he'd written the note.

I worked for a while after that, but Jack's comment about
the authorities got me wondering about a number of things,
and I realized with a start that I actually knew someone who
might be able to answer my questions. I dug out my cell
phone and getting a tolerably good signal in the lobby,
punched a number that I never suspected I remembered and
hardly believed I would ever use again.

"Fordham County Sheriff's Office. How can I direct your
call?" a crisp voice with a mild Maine accent answered.

"I was wondering if I could leave a message for Sheriff
Stannard to call me when he gets in on Monday."

"Ma'am, he's in the office today, would you like me to
put you through?"

"Thanks, yes."

A momentary pause was followed by Muzak. Sheriff
Dave Stannard had stood by me when others had pressured
him to arrest me as a suspect in a murder; he'd also been
willing to listen to my opinion when he was out of his depths
in looking at clues, where they overlapped with my professional expertise.

Part of me realized that I'd given Dave Stannard's name

and number to Detective Kobrinski for exactly the same reason that I was calling him and not Detective Bader, even though Bader lived and worked in Massachusetts. I didn't have much of a personal relationship with Detective Bader; I kept in touch with Dave through occasional e-mails and cards that had followed me doing a talk about archaeology at his girls' schools, but he was in Maine and I was now living in Massachusetts. Brian had a much higher probability of running into Detective Bader than he would of finding out I'd been asking questions of Sheriff Stannard.

Almost as though the thought of him summoned him, the man himself answered. "Dave Stannard."

"Sheriff, this is Emma Fielding. The archaeologist. You remember, I—"

"It's been a while, Professor Fielding, but I doubt I could forget you." His voice was as warm and comfortable as buttered toast with tea. "What can I do for you?"

"I just had a few questions, but if you're busy right now . . ."

"Naw, there's nothing going on." The sheriff chuckled pleasantly. "I'm just in today because so many folks called in with the flu. Good thing I'm not partial to college basketball, or I'd be out sick too. What can I do for you?"

I knew better than to be fooled by that down-East, good ol' boy patter. Dave Stannard was indeed down East and the Yankee equivalent of a good ol' boy, but there was nothing but shrewd thoughtfulness behind it all. Recalling that, I was suddenly a little shy about telling him the reason I called.

"I'm sort of . . . helping out with . . . another investigation."

There was a pause before he spoke. "I guess by investigation you don't mean some fraternity pranks over at Caldwell College," he said briefly.

"No, I'm not in Caldwell right now, I'm in western Massachusetts, near Monroe."

Another barely detectable pause before he said, "Okay, what have you got?"

I told him about finding Faith and about my confrontation with Detective Sergeant Kobrinski. "But what I was really wondering about was . . . well, how Faith died. I know it sounds stupid, but I don't know what happens when someone drowns. Could you answer some questions for me?"

There was such a long silence that I almost imagined I could hear the waves crashing on the wintry beach just five miles away from the Sheriff's Department. "You know, Professor, I'm not sure I'm real comfortable second-guessing a fellow officer—"

"Oh, no, I'm not trying to get involved," I hurriedly reassured him. "I was just the first one to find Faith. And . . . I sort of . . . knew her from a while ago."

Another moment passed while Stannard digested that little morsel.

"Look, I really am just trying to do a little research," I pleaded. "Faith's death, accidental or not, has been bothering me, and I thought if I understood a little about what actually happens when a person drowns, physically, I mean, I might be able to sort of . . . calm down. Focus on my own work again. Honest. Can you help me out? What about . . . the person I met in your office a couple of years ago?"

There was a long pause. "You mean Dr. Moretti?"

"Yes, I think that's right."

He took so long to answer me that for a moment I wondered if he was going to.

"Hello?"

"I'm still here," Stannard replied. "I'm just thinking. She's got a really odd way about her sometimes. I wonder if you wouldn't be better off just looking in the encyclopedia or online or something."

Suddenly, my stomach went queasy as I recalled my first encounter with the ME. I realized that although I had intentionally blotted her manner from my memory, she was exactly who I needed to talk to. "You think she'd be willing to answer a couple of questions?"

He gave a short laugh. "Oh, yes. You won't have any trouble getting her to tell you all you want to know. The trick is to get her to . . . well, to be honest, getting her to stop." Dave Stannard sounded a little reluctant.

"Look, at this point, I'll take anything," I reassured him. "Can you give me her number? And is there any chance she'd be in on a Saturday too?"

"I'm almost positive; she's dangerously in love with her work." He gave me Dr. Moretti's number.

I scribbled it down. "Okay, thanks, Sheriff. I really appreciate this. And don't worry. I just need to know these things so I can make sense of them for myself. I won't be a nuisance to the detective. I've got my own work to do."

"I'm sure you'll try," Stannard said. "You know, Emma, I kind of got the impression that you're one of those folks who can't help themselves when they get an idea in their heads. Now, I'm not going to tell you what to do, and you already said that you're going to let the police do their work. But look after yourself. Take care."

"Oh. Yeah, sure, Dave. Thanks for your help."

"Talk to you real soon." The sheriff hung up.

I looked up at the clock and figured I had enough time for one more quick call before I went back to the house. Then I dialed the number that Dave Stannard had given me hesitantly.

"Morgue," came the impatient answer. It was a woman's voice, a 1940s-cinema soprano loaded with creosote and cigarette smoke.

Even though I recognized it immediately, I stumbled

mentally, remembering the gnomelike woman. "I'm trying to reach Dr. Theresa Moretti."

"Well, don't strain yourself too hard, chickie-pie, you got her."

I cringed at her creaky joviality. "Sheriff Stannard gave me your number, thought you could answer a question for me—" I started.

"Well, isn't that nice of him! Boy-o thinks I got nothing better to do than be the Shell Answer Man!"

"It won't take long," I promised. I'd dealt with plenty of cranky folks; I could handle her, I thought.

"Who is this, by the way? Momma told little Terry never talk to strangers. Speak up, I got a couple of friends here that aren't getting any sweeter waiting on me! Oh, hang on a second—"

I heard the phone's mouthpiece muffled ineffectually, and the voice carried on like a rusty coffin hinge haranguing someone who was apparently in the room with her.

"No, no, no, Ernie! For the love of . . . Nooo!"

There was a very long pause on the other end of the line.

"Oh, for Pete's sake . . . Well, *pick* it up. G'wan, it won't bite! I know it's got dirt on it, but I won't tell if you won't . . . Just wash it off, little dust ain't gonna bother him any, now . . . Weigh it before you put it back in!"

Eeeeyew! I thought to myself. As the hapless Ernie received more abuse, I remembered that Theresa Moretti had reminded me of a diminutive version of the Wicked Witch of the West, voice, attitude, and all. Make that the Wicked Witch of the Down East, and you'd have it just about right.

"—What? Half a kilo? Jeez Louise, I guess we know what got *him*, huh? No, *you* figure it out—what are they teaching in schools these days? No, I *can't*! I've got some chippie on the phone thinks I'm a public servant or something . . ."

Chippie indeed! I thought. "Hello!"

That brought her back to my world. "What?"

"My name is Emma Fielding, and right now I'm out near Monroe, Massachusetts. I believe we met when a friend of mine was murdered several years ago, Pauline Westlake."

"Out by the Point?" the voice demanded, now giving me full attention.

"Yes, that's right—"

"The crushed skull? Then that other, the convallotoxin poisoning? You the archaeologist?"

I was torn between relief, having found a connection at last with this odd creature, and irritation that my dear Pauline should be reduced to the description of her demise. "That's me. I was wondering—"

"I remember. I thought you did 'em both, and pretty bold work, far as I could tell from what I could tell. Bodies just seemed to start piling up when you wandered into town—"

Maybe Dave Stannard was right, I thought crazily to myself. Surely the encyclopedia would have been a better idea.

"—but his nibs says not, not that *he* ever caught anyone else."

I felt obliged to come to the sheriff's defense, not that he really needed any help from me. "The sheriff solved the case; it was just that the real killer, well one of them, escaped—"

Dr. Moretti snorted, obviously not convinced. "Oh, yeah, yeah, yeah, the straight party line. Well, so long as you weren't actually busted. What do you want to know?"

I paused, amazed that she should wave her suspicions around like that and yet still offer to answer my questions. But my desire to defend myself lost to my curiosity and my fascination with this ghoul. I said, "I've got a question about drowning."

"Drowning, huh? We do some of that around here, occasionally."

We must have had a bad connection: I distinctly heard lip

smacking. "Well, what generally happens to a person who's drowned?"

The medical examiner giggled. "Well, *generally*, they die."

I shuddered. "I mean, what changes does the body go through? Is it easy to drown someone?"

"Depends," she said, warming to the subject. "Have you got atelectasis following aspiration or do you suspect laryngospasm?" Relish of her work and a clear love of the professional jargon dripped from every word. "Atelectasis" was pronounced like it was a beloved name.

I blinked. "I beg your pardon?"

Dr. Moretti sighed; obviously I had joined Ernie among the ranks of the hopeless. "Have you got lots of fluid in the lungs—and it doesn't have to be water—so that the cells stiffen and the lungs can't expand? Or was there just a little fluid, enough to constrict and close the airway?"

I hated admitting my ignorance. "Um, I don't know."

Rather than pouncing on my lack of knowledge, the medical examiner seemed convinced she'd made a point. "That's the problem with drowning"—I heard a slap on a counter, emphasizing her argument—"Even when you got some idea, you still don't know! You can never prove drowning, you can only rule out everything else, and it's damned tricky stuff."

The ME sounded like she was describing an admirable adversary as she continued. "And do you know for sure, fr'instance, that it *was* murder? Drowning's a real unusual means of killing or suicide. Hell, you get close to four hundred bathtub drownings every year, and I'd be willing to bet that most of the accidental drownings involve alcohol. Asking for it, just begging! Have a drink, slide down into a nice, hot tub, and never come up again! Why not just lie down in front of a Mack truck with no brakes? At least that way, you'd have your clothes on when they found you!"

Obviously, the ME had very strict ideas about how one should die.

I thought guiltily about the whiskey Faith and I'd drunk, but before I could reply, Dr. Moretti was off again after more interesting prey.

"*Now*, let's say it *was* murder," she said, sounding gleeful and pleased, like she just spied the dessert cart. "You gotta consider, what size was the victim, what size the perp? Was the deceased conscious, or even alive, when he hit the water?" She ran down the list of questions, cooing like other people do when they see a basket of kittens.

"I suppose you could look for defensive wounds," I mused out loud. "Bruises or scratches, right?"

"Ooo-eee, bright girl! Yes, yes, yes . . . but!" Dr. Moretti exclaimed, lobbing the ball right back to me, caught up in the spirit of the game as she saw it. "But! The body can get real banged up, scraping along the bed of the water body during unconsciousness. You can even get weeds or gravel lodged in the mouth this way, if it happened in the great outdoors! It looks like a struggle when it's just dumb luck!"

Heavens preserve me from Dr. Moretti's brand of luck.

"Here's the trick, though, Miss Smartypants. Look for material in the *lungs*! Water alone won't tell you much, but if you find plant remains or gravel or other such trash in the lungs, *then* you can make a good case for murder."

She sounded like she'd like to make a good case for murder and keep it as a pet. "Well, I won't actually be looking myself—"

Dr. Moretti didn't hear me, however, still caught up in her explication. "Still, it's very iffy—even if you got none of those markers, you still might just have a killer who's real quick and real strong. And stone-cold brutal. Man, when a person drowns, if they're conscious, they struggle, hard, right to the end! It's a desperate fight that takes a long, *long* time to lose. Minutes! You'd have to be one *mean* sonovabitch to hold someone under like that!" That fact awed her whereas all the others had just been interesting tidbits.

I mulled this over. "That helps me, I guess. I was just curious, and the police and coroner out here haven't released any details yet—"

"Where are you? Monroe—that's Redfield County? Well, I can't say's I blame you for being impatient," Dr. Moretti said scornfully. "I know 'Tigger' Bambury and he's even a bigger stiff than most of his patients. Oh, he knows his stuff, just no real *feel* for the subject, let's say—"

All of a sudden, I had far too vivid an idea of what "a feel for the subject" might involve.

"—That it? I've got to go. Genius Ernie here is getting in deep and doesn't know his gluteus maximus from his proximal radius—just put that Stryker down, Marcus Welby, Mother's coming!—You can call again."

"Thank—"

But the medical examiner had already hung up. I got the impression that not many people were welcome to call back, and I wasn't certain that I could handle another exposure to that side of investigations. Dr. Moretti might know her stuff, but her lack of respect for the dead always made me cringe, particularly after I'd been trained for years to treat the human remains I might find with due dignity. No one should like her job that much.

I thought about what she'd told me as I walked back to the house to meet Brian. Once again I passed the place in the stream where I found Faith Morgan and I remembered what I'd seen that day. I hadn't seen any sign of a struggle at all; I'd thought the leaves looked like a nest around her body.

The stream was awfully shallow there, less than a foot deep, and Dr. Moretti's words about alcohol and accidents came back to me with a surge of guilt: Maybe I'd been responsible in some way for Faith's drowning . . .

C'mon, Em, stop it! Common sense spoke up, unexpectedly on my side for a change. You didn't force her to drink anything, you didn't tell her to go out roaming in the middle of the night without a coat or even stockings, and besides, what about her clean shoes? There was no way that she fell down that hill without getting mud all over them. You told the detective that you thought she was murdered and that's still what you believe in your heart of hearts, so stop looking for even more trouble for yourself.

Even though I hadn't got more than a lick of work done and, frankly, had got more questions than reassuring answers from my phone calls, I did feel a lot better than I had since Faith had died. My improving mood was bolstered when, just over the last hill, I saw Brian's blue pickup crunching over the gravel to the parking lot behind the house. I waved even though there was no chance that he could have seen me. I picked up the pace a little, but enjoyed watching him get out, stretch, and walk around, without him knowing that he was being watched. Oh, goody—by the looks of him and the truck, he'd been working on taping and mudding the drywall in what was going to be our dining room at the Funny Farm.

I approached but was still too far away to call when I saw a pantomime beginning. A Shrewsbury security vehicle pulled up with a bounce and a squeal of brakes. Mr. Constantino, obviously reenacting some B-grade cop show, emerged and slammed his door angrily, shouting. Brian wiped his hand on the seat of his jeans, obviously going to offer it, but something Constantino said made him rather curl his fingers into a fist and stuff it into his pocket. He started jiggling the change in his pocket, a sure sign of agitation as long as I'd known him.

Brian pulled his fist back out again, still clenched hard, when Constantino jabbed him in the chest. I started to run toward them.

Chapter 9

DESPITE THE RACKET MY FLAT LEATHER SHOES slapping the pavement made, neither Brian nor Constantino noticed me until I was practically on top of them. Brian's jaw was rigid, and I could see his teeth working under the skin of his cheek. His eyes flashed over to me, without registering much recognition. All his attention was reserved for Constantino.

I had no idea what was going on, but fear dictated that I interrupt, defuse whatever was happening. "Hey, sweetie! You made good time! Any trouble finding the place?" I swear dogs could have heard me for miles around, my voice was so high.

"This guy's your husband?" Constantino asked. He already knew the answer, I could tell.

"Of course he is! What the hell's going on? Brian?"

"Nothing's going on. I'm just checking, doing my job." Constantino smirked, and suddenly, I knew precisely what was happening.

"Good to see you, Em," Brian said. He finally turned to

me, sliding his hand casually over my hip. I knew what he was asking, and I moved in closer to him.

Thinking "Do it!" as loud as I could, I dropped my briefcase onto the gravel and wrapped my arms around him.

Brian generally limits public displays of affection to hand holding or quick brush of lips. There was nothing quick or brushing about this kiss, and I forgot that anyone might be watching. Somewhere beyond the true limits of awareness, I heard the sound of a car door slamming and vaguely realized that Constantino had pulled away.

By this time, the anger had drained out of Brian's embrace and had been replaced by something a little more agreeable, though no less intense. I didn't care; anyone kisses me with that degree of emotion, I pay attention.

A moment or two later, he sighed, then whispered in my ear, "I'm sorry." We straightened up.

"It's not you, it's not your fault. We've just been lucky, for the most part, that's all." I rested my head against his.

"I shouldn't drag you into it like that. It was childish."

"There's no dragging, there's just no way to win with someone like Constantino." I couldn't tell him not to be stupid, it was *our* problem, because that was only part of it. "And besides, what were you supposed to do, punch his lights out?"

He held up a forefinger and thumb of one hand, separated by a scant inch, showing me just how close he'd come to doing just that. "I hate getting yanked around like that. I hate that an idiot like him can push my buttons like that."

"What'd he say?"

Brian sighed, and looked down the road at the retreating security vehicle. The breeze ruffled his hair. "C'mon, let's go inside. It's too cold to stand around out here."

We lugged his stuff up to my room, and I dug out a towel for him to shower. But instead Brian began to methodically straighten the things on my bureau, kick my laundry into one big heap in the middle of the carpet, take the books off the bed and stack them into neat piles on the desk.

I watched him sort things out for a few minutes before I tried again. "So what happened?"

"Ahhhh, nothing. It was stupid." Brian shook his head as he closed the armoire door. "He saw the truck, he saw me wearing work clothes. He saw I'm not white. I guess he thought I was here to do some repairs or something—"

"There've been workers up at the library."

"Then 'Possum-head there—"

"Constantino."

"—got shirty because he thought I was trying to park where I wasn't supposed to, or at least that's what he was saying. I protested, so naturally he thought I was trying to pull something and he started the dick waving." He smiled wryly. "Guy's got a short fuse.

"Anyway, he began crowding me. I was getting mad but just told him I was here to see you. Constantino relaxed, said there must be some mistake. I relaxed, figured he was going to apologize, but he just said he should have known, the contractor was a friend of his and he wouldn't hire anyone who wasn't American."

"Jesus."

"The man's an idiot." Brian shrugged, too elaborately. "You could tell that last little shot was just a reflex, nothing, really. He wasn't even thinking about it, it was . . . a reflex." He gathered up his towel and his boombox and kissed the top of my head, then made as if to hit the shower.

"We've heard worse," I agreed carefully.

"But you know," he said, turning around suddenly. "I get so damn tired, sometimes. There are whole weeks, sometimes, when I'm not reminded by someone that my great-grandparents landed on the wrong coast, got off the wrong ships, but then boom! It comes out of nowhere. It gets real old, having to be so *aware* of who I am." He shut the door behind him.

Down the hall, I heard the bathroom door shut, the shower start. I heard the loud bouncy reggae dancehall music start and just as abruptly stop, followed by a pause. The ensuing music was soberer, a melancholy dub. I picked up the cassette case Brian had left on the bed and saw it was Bob Marley and the Wailers, *Babylon by Bus*. Cold experience told me that there was nothing more I could do, so I resolved to keep my mouth shut and let Brian find his own way out of his funk.

Whatever private exorcism he had performed had apparently worked, for he didn't look nearly as weary when he emerged. There was, however, something else on his mind.

"Did you make reservations at this place you told me about?" he asked, ruefully flicking at the tie that was sticking out of his duffel bag. "I don't really feel like getting dressed up."

"No, we don't have to, if you don't want. I just thought you might like French for a change. Something fancy, a treat."

Brian brightened. "French, huh? Well, that's what I had in mind! And if we go to the place I'm thinking of, I won't have to wear the noose, neither."

He sent the hated necktie flying across the room, and it landed suggestively on the headboard. Then raising one eyebrow in his best John Belushi–Bluto Blutarsky fashion, Brian whipped off his bath towel like a magician and dove under the messy covers of my bed. "You know, we've got a little time to kill until the restaurant opens."

Smothering a grin, I said, "Great. So, how about some cards?" But I was already unbuttoning my blouse and kicking off my shoes.

Brian said, "Sure. Got any twos?"

"Nope. You go fish."

After, as we got dressed, I was still a little worried about Brian's alternative restaurant. He'd told me that jeans were fine. "Where'd you find out about this place? It's near here?"

"A little drive. Roddy told me about it. You'll love it."

"Ummm." I thought about the little archaeological assemblage Roddy-down-the-lab had left in the pickup that he'd sold to us. Under the seat was the latest Victoria's Secret catalog, two Jolt Cola cans, half a moldy microwave burrito, a nearly full can of chewing tobacco, and a dog-eared copy of a Klingon-English dictionary. The truck runs fine and he gave us a fair price, but somehow I couldn't see the *Guide Michelin* calling Roddy for pointers on where to eat. "And it's French, you say?" I asked, not entirely convinced.

"Kinda French! Come on, the sooner we leave, the sooner we get there!"

We drove west into the hill country. "I'd hate to be out here in the winter," Brian remarked, after the third time he'd only just made a curve at the last second. "That's a hell of a drop, and with this wind—"

"I'm glad we took the truck," I remarked as calmly as I could. "I don't think Bessy can take much more of this." I tried not to be obvious about digging my fingers into the upholstery.

"How's she running? Any problems on the way out?"

"Not too bad. Struggling a little up the hills, but nothing major. There's a noise though, that's starting to worry me."

"We'll get it checked out when you get home."

Eventually we pulled up outside a long, low wooden building that bore no sign other than a few neon beer advertisements. It was the sort of place that made you look instinctively for a row of choppers out in front, but I saw mostly mid-size imports.

"Are you sure this is it?" I asked nervously. The place looked like it was going to collapse any moment, perhaps under the stress of the pounding rhythms of the band inside.

Brian rubbed his hands together in anticipation. "Absolutely."

The place was surprisingly crowded, even for a Saturday night, but we lucked out and got a booth not too far from the dance floor. A fiddler swooped into a complicated, climbing solo, and the mob on the dance floor went wild when she hit the peak and the rest of the band joined in. Brian whooped, startling me. I looked around and saw people having a good time, just more raucously than I was used to.

Frowning, I picked up my menu. It was half barbecue and half Cajun recipes. So much for "kinda French"; I was having no luck at all translating the names of the dishes and had to rely on the descriptions. "She's pretty good," I offered, nodding at the fiddle player.

"Pretty good?" Amazement crossed Brian's face. "Katie Boudreau's a certified genius! Queen of the Cajun fiddle! And take my word for it, Le Fevre Acadien is the next Beausoleil!"

"Oh. Does Beausoleil play Cajun music too?" I asked.

Amazement changed to pity. "Look, I know I have my work cut out for me, and that's fine, I love you dearly, but at times, you're just *so* unhip . . ."

"I am not! I'm just . . . differently hip." I turned to the waiter who came for our order. "I'll have the chicken caesar salad and a glass of the house white—"

"Oh no, no, no!"

The waiter and I both paused to look at Brian, who had a horrified look on his face. "You don't really want a chicken caesar salad, do you? Not here?"

"It's on the menu," I said defensively.

"Take a walk on the wild side," he pleaded. "Just give it a shot, this once."

"Fine, whatever." I threw my hands up. "It's your party, just nothing too spicy, okay?"

He brightened. "Then how's about . . . two large orders of ribs, an extra side of sauce, two plates of rice and beans, and a bunch of deep-fried okra. A Blackened Voodoo Lager for me, and a margarita for my differently-hip wife—or do you want a Turbo Dog?"

Turbo Dog? I didn't dare ask. "It's completely up to you, I renounce all responsibility," I said. "I'm going to find the bathroom. Don't start your cholesterol-induced heart attack 'til I get back."

It wasn't as easy as that, however. The dance floor was packed, but the waitstaff were moving so quickly around the tables that I didn't see any other way over to the door marked "Les Filles," so I just dove in and slinked around the dancers as best I could.

Just when I thought I'd made it clear of the two-steppers, I got jostled. I stuck out a hand to keep from falling but a woman in tight jeans and a bright red silk shirt caught it and saved me, turning it into a dance step. She twirled me around, gaily shouting, "*Et toi!*"

I managed to follow her a pace or so without stumbling. "Thanks," I shouted over the din. The sultry warmth of all those moving bodies was enervating, seductive.

"'S'all right, *chere!*" Our eyes met and then the smile fled her face, fading with her fake Louisiana accent. "Oh."

It was Detective Kobrinski. She stopped dancing.

"Yo, Pam!" A compact blond man, muscles clearly delineated under his T-shirt, grabbed her hand and swung her around. "*I'm* over *here!*"

I made it to a relatively empty space near the bathroom and looked back at Pam Kobrinski and her date, moving swiftly and surely around other less skilled couples. One more turn and she met my gaze briefly, then deliberately turned away and focused on keeping up with her partner.

The food was on the table by the time I navigated my way back, and Brian had already accumulated a small pile of neatly cleaned bones on his plate. I looked at my plate and saw a length of ribs that looked like it had come off something from a natural history museum.

"Bar-*baric*," I said. My husband had a smear of barbecue sauce on the corner of his mouth and it was all over his hands. He looked as though he'd been in a bad fight.

"Oh, man, it's great! Dig in!" He threw back a couple of nuggets of batter-dipped okra and shoveled in a spoonful of rice after that.

I eyed the spread dubiously. "You just pick them up? No forks? Hey, look at the ends of the ribs! You can see that they were sawn! You know, by looking at the way the bones were cut, you can tell a lot about the ethnic tradition the chef is following, or what was available to him locally. Now if they were snapped off the ribcage, or cut with a knife, you'd see a much more jagged edge—"

Again came that pitying look, mixed with exasperation. "Em. God almighty. Grab one. Start gnawing."

I started in, tentatively at first, but rapidly becoming obsessed about scraping more of the tender meat off the bones. The smoky tang, the crunch of the cooked fat, and the morsels of sweet pork, were more than enough to convince me. "Whoa, Bri—"

"See what I mean?" he asked, tossing another cleaned gray-white bone on the heap. "It pays to chuck the Emily Post every now and then."

"Easy for you to say." I sucked the meat off another rib. "You don't do anything, you eat everything in sight, you never gain an ounce. I, on the other hand . . ."

"Yeah, yeah, yeah." He eyed my plate and the ribs that I hadn't got to yet. "So, are you going to finish those?"

"Take a hike!" I pulled my plate protectively closer.

"Spoken like a convert!" He signaled the waiter for another round of drinks.

But even after some truly dedicated eating on my part, Brian had to help me clean up the last two. "You got another Wet-Nap?" I held my sticky fingers up.

A voice came from over my shoulder. "I've heard some interesting things about you, Ms. Fielding, but nothing to suggest the way you can put away the barbecue."

I looked up to see Pam Kobrinski, still flushed from dancing, standing over our table. Her date loitered impatiently by the door with their coats, checking his watch in an obvious way. I wiped my hands off on my jeans as best I could, trying to decide if I was supposed to invite her to join us.

"Look, I don't usually do business when I'm off, and I generally come way out here because I'm not likely to run into anyone I know." She smiled wryly. "But since we're both here, could you meet me Monday morning? For breakfast, maybe? We should talk."

I groaned. "I'm never going to eat again!"

Kobrinski looked at Brian, who shrugged. "Neophyte," he explained. "She doesn't know she'll be craving another pile in an hour."

The detective sergeant took out a card and wrote on the back of it. "Not at the station. Meet me at Nancy's Breakfast Nook. It's right on Main Street in Monroe, about seven?"

I groaned again, but she turned to leave, saying, "Have a nice weekend," before I could suggest a later time, even lunch.

"You know her?" Brian asked, watching her don her coat.

"She's the cop investigating Faith's death." Saying it out loud cast a shadow over a fairly promising evening. "Damn."

But apparently, Brian didn't notice. "She doesn't dance like a cop," he said admiringly.

That woke me up out of my funk. "Hey! What are you doing, watching other women dance?"

"Just looking at the scenery, porkchop. Unless, of course, you wanted to—"

"I'm just waiting for you to ask!"

"Ah, here we go," he said, leading me out onto the floor, where the band was playing a slow waltz instrumental. "Now, isn't this nicer than *La Vache Qui Pede*, or wherever it is you wanted to go? I couldn't step all over your toes there, could I?"

But if there was anyone stepping on toes, it was me. My mind just wasn't on my feet, it was on my chance meeting with Detective Kobrinski. "Yeah. You know, I've been worrying over whether Faith was murdered and never stopped to think of a motive."

Brian pulled me even closer and murmured into my ear, "Oooh, my darlin', zat's why I love you sooo; you feed ozair women drinks and bar-bay-que, take zem danzeeng, and what do they sink of? Ze sex! Le monkey lust hot! And zat's it! But you, you speak to me in ze dulcet tones of murdair, ze mayhem." He led me into a slow twirl, returning back to our close embrace, rubbing his cheek against mine. "Ahh, what man could ask for more?"

I kissed him, snuggled into his shoulder. "Sorry. Kind of jarred me, running into the investigating officer and all."

Brian looked me in the eye. "And you noticed she was having fun, didn't you? She wasn't working. Well, not working *much*," he hastily amended.

We glided back, even dared a small dip. "I'll make a deal with you," he said. "I'll talk all you want tomorrow about Faith, work, the house, whatever, just let's have fun now, okay? Just you and me, nothing else. After all, I won't get to see you next weekend, remember? United Pharmaceuticals is recruiting at Stanford, and I pulled the short straw."

"Oh, shoot, I didn't remember." I shook my head. "You're right, anyhow. It's hard to shut it off, sometimes."

"That's why I'm working so hard to distract you," Brian said. "And if you'll remember all the way back to this afternoon, you'll recall that it's better when you help."

"Gotcha."

By the end of the third song, we'd managed to whittle my unsure movements into a respectable two-step and decided to quit while we were ahead. As we left the music behind us indoors, the comparative quiet of the pickup was a shock and the ride home uneventful.

"Man, they don't skimp on their drinks," I said, as we pulled into the Shrewsbury parking lot. No hassles getting in this time.

"You all right?"

"Oh, fine. Just feeling a little loose, that's all."

"Should make you easier to catch, then." Brian opened my door for me.

"Ha! I'll show you who's easy to catch!" I said. I dove out of the truck, not too unsteadily, and flew past him, bypassing the kitchen door and running three quarters of the way around the house to the front door. I looked over my shoulder—no Brian. That'll teach him, I thought smugly, as I climbed the front stairs.

"Boo!" He stepped out of the shadows, startling me.

I shrieked gratifyingly and somehow through the ensuing game of slap and tickle managed to unlock the door and get us in. Brian faked right, then went left. I dodged him and ran into the parlor, waiting for him to get closer again. He caught up with me, both of us giggling, and we'd just about fallen over the back of the couch when the overhead light snapped on.

Brian yelped in surprise and jumped back; I fell clumsily to the floor with a squawk. I squinted against the light trying to see who was there, trying to slow my racing heart. "God almighty!"

A heavy sigh identified the other person more eloquently than any introduction could have done. "Evening, Auntie. Please don't let me interrupt."

"Uhhhh, Michael! I thought we . . ." Brian gave me a hand up and I tried to collect my wits. "I thought you were in Boston."

"Obviously. But my weekend didn't go exactly as I'd planned," Michael said. He looked woebegone and considering his intentions this morning, distinctly undersexed. He went over to a chair, flopped into it, and closed his eyes. After a moment he said, "Just carry on as if I weren't here. The rest of the universe seems to."

Brian rolled his eyes at that response, and I dug a finger in his ribs. "This is my husband, Brian Chang. Brian, Michael Glasscock."

I have to give my husband credit: Brian didn't blink as I made the introductions or as Michael took his hand without ever actually opening his eyes.

"We didn't mean to disturb you," I said.

"Frankly, I'm fairly certain I couldn't get any more disturbed if I stuck a rabid weasel down my trousers, but it is nice to be thought of. Good meeting you, Brian. And Emma, if you would be so kind—"

"Of course, Michael," I said, snapping off the light.

We snuck up the stairs in the dark. "Does he always just *sit* like that?" Brian whispered. "Weird! And what was wrong with his hand? He had a big bandage on his wrist."

"It was bothering him this morning. Yesterday too. *I* didn't notice the bandage though, that's new. *I* was too busy being mortified."

"What do you have to be mortified about?" Brian said. "We were doing what normal people do on a Saturday night!"

"Normal's not exactly the word I'd use to describe most of the folks at Shrewsbury, sweetie." I let us into my room and shut the door on the outside world for the night.

The next morning, nice and late, I was sitting, watching Brian pack up to head home.

"You were really chasing rabbits last night," he said.

"Sorry?" I shook off my inattention.

"What were you dreaming about? You were tossing around so much you practically knocked me out of bed. It's not like you."

I frowned. "I don't remember. I haven't been sleeping well. Maybe it was the spicy food."

"Maybe." He zipped up his bag. "Toss me some of that letterhead, would you?"

I reached over to the desk. "Sure. What do you want it for?"

"Address." He sighed heavily. "I figured I should write a letter about our naughty boy, Constantino, to the board of directors. Best to get right on it, unless you think it would make things difficult for you politically? I can wait 'til after you're done."

"No, do it up. What can they do? I'm already here."

Brian shrugged. "Probably won't do any good, but you can't fix anything by not speaking up, right?"

I rubbed his arm. "It's a good plan."

He dug out his keys, which had a little note stuck on the ring. "God, I'm getting old. I've brought a couple of messages for you. Bucky called to get your number. She'll call. She wants her tapes and CDs back."

"She's my sister, I don't have to give them back. Union rules. Anything else?"

"Nolan called, but to tell me about a reschedule." Brian paused, then said, "But he told me you're developing a real edge."

That was high praise, and Nolan was stingy with it; he probably also knew that Brian would tell me. Which was nice, but it also meant he'd want more from me during our next session. I couldn't tell when that would be, however; it was difficult to schedule my Krav Maga during the school year, and almost impossible during the field season. I'd managed to keep with it with an individual lesson every couple of weeks or so.

"Some edge," I snorted. "It just means I can occasionally hit him back, now. He should be paying me for being his personal punching bag." Maybe this was just Nolan's way of getting me to pick up the pace a little; maybe he sensed I was thinking of dropping our sessions altogether.

"Well, keep at it. You get all these sexy muscles when you've been training."

That's the way we always talked about my sessions with Nolan, carefully avoiding the reason I'd started taking them in the first place. After my run-in with a homicidal maniac years ago, I had decided against buying a gun, the thought of which gave me the willies anyway, but opted for self-defense lessons in the form of Krav Maga. Brian and I made a point of not taking classes together, because when we sparred with each other, it was too easy to take it personally and get upset.

"How're you doing, these days?" I said.

"Well, it's been a while since I've done anything like exercise—"

I personally believe that Brian's long-distant days of surfing and skateboarding did not count as exercise, not the same way running does, but didn't tell him so. Those activities seemed too much like fun to be good for you.

"—but I'm hanging in there. I've got a new bruise for my collection." He pulled up his sleeve and showed me a corker on the back side of his arm, just above the elbow. "It was my fault, I didn't move fast enough."

I leaned over and kissed the bruise. "Poor baby. I'll try and land one on Nolan for you. He's such a meanie, picking on you like that."

"Oh, it wasn't Nolan, it was one of the ladies in the class," he said cheerfully. "I don't know why you think he's so mean, though. He's always perfectly nice to us. Well, not nice, nice. You know, professional."

"Maybe he's got it in for me."

Brian snorted. "Maybe he knows that pushing you is the best way to get you to learn anything."

"Mmm, maybe." I didn't want to think about Nolan, now. I sat back. "You know something? This is nice. We haven't done this for a while."

He thought a minute, then nodded. "You mean, talk about something that wasn't work, wasn't the house, wasn't a deadline? Wasn't a problem?"

"Yep." I wasn't quite sure how to continue. "I really miss that."

"Nothing wrong with that," he said slowly, sensing something was up.

"But I don't want you to think that I don't like my job or my house—"

"Or me?"

"Right. Or you. It's not that. And I like the fact that we can work together as a team, that's really cool. Just, sometimes, I . . . I've been thinking about grad school, and how we didn't have to worry about a house, and we didn't have to worry about cleaning, because the place was too small, and work was a given, but at least we were young enough not to notice how tired we should have been. We managed to squeeze some fun in then, seemed like all the time. Now . . . it just seems like we're not a romantic couple so much as a strike force."

Brian thought about that, and then nodded. "Last night was our first date in a while."

"Yeah. It was fun." I glanced at him. "You had fun, right?"

"Yes, tons. And dinner and dancing after was good too."

I punched him in the shoulder, remembering to avoid his bruise. "I just want to know that you still want to have fun with me."

He looked very serious. "I don't want you to ever think I don't want to have fun with you. Only you. We should do something about this."

I laughed, even though I could feel the heaviness sink back into my shoulders: This felt just exactly like what I was talking about. "Great. I'll make a list, you go online to see what can be done about it."

Now it was Brian's turn to poke me. "No, not like work, not like the house. We can do something right now. Should we institute a date night?"

"We should do that anyway, but I need more than that." I took a deep breath, a little surprised by what I was going to propose. "I want to call a moratorium on the house stuff. We've let it consume us."

Brian blinked. "I thought you wanted to keep at it until it was all done."

I returned his confused gaze. "I thought *you* wanted to keep at it until it was all done."

"Aha."

"Aha, indeed."

"Good, then there's one possible solution," Brian announced. "We give it a rest until we've had a chance for a little extra R and R."

I nodded. "I figure, we're weather-tight and the toilet works. We've nearly got all the big stuff out of the way—fixing the floors and getting the insulation in—so most everything left on the list is cosmetic. Except for the barn."

"Except for the barn, but we can pull that down anytime. So after the dining room's done . . ."

"We put the tools away and think about how to enjoy what we've got for a while."

"Cool. I like it."

"I feel better."

"See?" Brian said. "Old dogs can learn new tricks."

I nodded. "They can even learn to do no tricks at all."

We tramped downstairs. Michael was now lying on the parlor floor, fully clothed and coated, and we had no way of determining whether he'd been there all night or had simply gotten up early for some extra brooding.

"Nice meeting you, Michael," Brian called after he'd kissed me at the door. We looked at each other and shrugged: What was the protocol for saying good-bye to someone flaked out in a public space?

Just as I was beginning to worry that Michael wasn't just moping or asleep, a hand rose from the floor and flapped once, twice, in farewell.

Sunday dragged on and on interminably after Brian left, and then Monday started badly, then just got worse as it went on. And apparently I wasn't the only one feeling it. Not the best of early-morning risers, I'd slept through my alarm, making me already late for my breakfast meeting with Detective Kobrinski. I tore down the main drive in the Civic and I saw Harry and Sasha just pulling in—extraordinarily early for work by anyone's standards. I thought about honking, but reconsidered when I saw that there was a heated argument going on behind the other windshield. Then while Harry was waiting at the guardhouse for the barrier to rise, Sasha got out, slammed the car door and began to hike up the slope by herself, a long, lonely, and chilly walk to work. They didn't even notice me as I left by the opposite side of the same gate.

The drive would have been nice at any other—read: later—time of day. The sky was bright blue, without even fair-weather clouds, and it was almost possible to smell young plants struggling to break through the ground's surface. Large, predatory birds soared on the thermals, and in the distance, I could see a factory clocktower, reminding us all that time was wasting. After twenty minutes of being buffeted by high winds along the hilly roads, I pulled into Monroe.

Main Street was pure downtown U.S.A., late nineteenth- and twentieth-century buildings converted to shop fronts in the 1940s, and not much changed since then. The wide street was just waking up and had few cars parked along it. When I got out, the wind was howling through the valley and the bitter cold made my eyes water. It wasn't done being winter here just yet, not by a long stretch. I paused and out of habit checked my cell phone. Plenty of signal here. I found Nancy's Breakfast Nook right in the middle of town, obviously a cornerstone of the community since its construction.

I began to perk up a little when I saw the interior: a counter of worn linoleum and chrome banked with stools, a menu on the sandwich board over a grill that hadn't been changed in twenty years, and a few bright booths—complete with coat hooks and cracked vinyl seats—near the windows. To my infinite delight, at one end of the counter was a plastic pie keeper with three pies in it. By the looks of things the breakfast would be decent, I thought, though why Kobrinski had to pick the middle of the night for a chat was beyond me.

By the time I arrived it was 7:05 and the detective was already pushing back an empty breakfast plate.

I slid into the booth in the far back corner and wondered who it would be this morning; the provoking, impersonal authoritarian or the fleet-footed queen of the bayou. The person I found was neither: Detective Kobrinski looked like a woman on the horns of a dilemma.

But when I caught her eye, the official mask slid easily into place over her consternation, so quickly and so smoothly that it spoke of years of practice. "Good morning," she said pleasantly.

"It's morning all right," I acknowledged. A waitress came over with coffee carafe in hand, bless her, and poured a cup without being asked. After taking my order, she took another, closer, look at me and left the carafe on the table.

"Thanks for stopping by," Kobrinski said. "Enjoy the band Saturday night?"

"Definitely, they're the next Beausoleil," I said, easily appropriating Brian's knowledge. "You looked like you were having fun."

Mention of my having observed her outside her professional capacity *almost* disturbed that impervious facade; I thought I detected just a hint of annoyance.

"We-ell, you know." She smiled lazily, so quick a recovery that anyone not seated across from her wouldn't have seen it. "Everyone's a Cajun when the band starts playing."

Or maybe the detective wasn't quite as practiced at concealing her feelings as she wanted to be, for she waited until I actually sipped my coffee before launching her surprise attack.

"So, let's start from the beginning. I gather this isn't your *first* murder investigation."

Chapter 10

FAITH *WAS* MURDERED THEN. THE THOUGHT POPPED into my head even before I had the opportunity to register my surprise over the abrupt change in the conversation, her use of the word, or the fact that she'd obviously heard more about my past involvement in a couple of homicide investigations. Placing my mug down with excessive care, I said, "No, I guess not. You spoke to Dave Stannard?"

She brushed her bangs aside with elaborate nonchalance. "He spoke to me. He called Saturday, wanted to vouch for your character. He said I should pay attention to what you had to say. Said you look at things differently." I noticed a slight compression to her lips. "I don't like being gone around."

"There was no going around," I returned. The coffee snaked a path to my cerebral cortex, lighting the ways to comprehension and insight and cheekiness, apparently. "*I* don't like being left in the dark. Look, I only asked about drowning, I didn't talk about this case specifically. I was upset, anyone in my position would have asked some questions."

She snorted. "I'm not certain they would. But Sheriff

Stannard was very careful to mention that you didn't talk any specifics about this case," she admitted. "Several times."

Detective Kobrinski wasn't convinced, and I realized just then that she thought I was challenging her authority. I thought about being a woman cop—a detective, no less—in a rural place like Monroe, or anywhere else, for that matter, and knew I was going to have to be very careful here.

"This is just my way of coping, trying to fit the pieces together," I said. "I find myself in the middle of something like this—again—and I feel lost, out of control. Asking questions helps me sort it all out."

Her eyes narrowed. "Maybe we can do something about that. An exchange." Kobrinski reached into her jacket pocket, pulled out a small, foil-wrapped package, took two and offered it to me. "Tums?"

"No thanks."

She carefully unrolled the package and popped a tablet into her mouth. All around us were the sounds of cutlery on plates, food preparation, and early morning conversation between people who'd known each other for years. My breakfast came while I waited for her to continue, and out of habit, I lifted the thick ceramic plate up carefully to look for the maker's mark underneath. I wasn't surprised to see the familiar impression of a buffalo so common to diner ware.

"What, not up to your usual standards?" The detective's sarcasm reminded me to behave like a normal person.

"Just a bad habit," I said, putting the plate down. "Archaeologists like marked pottery. You mentioned an exchange?"

She sighed. "Back it up a minute. You've got something I'll never have, and that's access to Shrewsbury."

"What do you mean, you don't have access? You're a cop!"

Kobrinski looked at me as if I were dim, and maybe I was. "You may or may not know that there's some friction between Shrewsbury and the Monroe community. Always has been and it's gotten worse since the new director, Whitlow, took over, trying to make it into a 'business.' The town-and-gown thing is a real pain, and as soon as I show up, no matter what for, people start thinking 'protect the library.' It makes my job difficult. And it makes me mad. The fat cats around here get away with too damn much and I don't like it."

"You sound like you have a grudge."

"I don't like being railroaded," she replied tartly. "There's always that little extra bit of leeway that Shrewsbury gets, and it's not going to happen this time."

I smelled a battle being drawn along class lines, and possibly it was a personal one for Detective Kobrinski. It was no surprise, really. Monroe struck me as a working-class town and I got the distinct impression from my discussion with Whitlow that the Shrewsbury family had treated the place as their own personal preserve. That could either make for very strong loyalties or for long-lived resentments, depending on how those relations were handled.

The detective's face soured, and I looked behind me. Constantino had walked in and ordered coffee to go. He surveyed the place like he owned it, but stopped when he noticed us staring at him from our corner booth. He took the coffee, threw his money down on the counter, and left.

She turned back to me. "I smell a lot of rats at Shrewsbury, and the biggest one just walked out the door."

"What do you mean?"

"I'm getting pressured to lay off the investigation, go with the obvious suspect—"

"Wait a minute!" My head was spinning. "What obvious suspect?"

"Paul Burnes."

"Faith's ex?" I hadn't gotten as far as thinking about suspects. "I suppose that makes sense, if it's murder—"

"It is."

Too many things were happening at once, and my head was spinning with this sudden onslaught of revelations. "But wait a minute, he's . . . he's in jail!"

"*Was* is the operative term. He was released nearly a year ago."

If my jaw dropped any lower, it would have landed in my pancakes. "But he almost killed her!"

Detective Kobrinski shrugged. "The story I've been getting through official channels is a little different from the one you told me. I'm still trying to figure out what was going on between the two of them. They're both crazy, if you ask me—"

This wasn't making any sense. "Yeah, but he . . . she told me—"

The detective shook her head. "Like I said, I think the situation was a little more complicated than the side you got from Faith Morgan. She doesn't seem to have been an easy person to pin down. Apart from Harry Saunders, people in the library didn't seem to like her very much, and I got the impression that he was being kind—"

"But that has nothing to do with Faith being trustworthy!" I protested.

"You said yourself that you thought she was 'controlling.' Sasha Russo actually used the word *manipulative*. I think she was feeding you her side of the story, maybe a little jazzed up."

I refused to believe this. No one would—could—make up such things. Could she? But I frowned when I remembered how I felt after Faith's confessional monologue, that she had been setting me up as an audience, playing me. It just didn't feel right, given her story. But then, I didn't know Faith all that well, did I?

Detective Kobrinski seemed unaware of my internal conflicts. "—but we are trying to locate Burnes now. He hasn't shown up to his job for a week. No one can find him."

I put my fork down. "Oh, my God."

"It gets better or worse, depending on your point of view," she continued. "The forensics people lifted a blurred partial of his from a hair comb she was wearing on the night of her death. It could be an old one, though. It's hard to tell."

"You think it was Paul?" A small, guilty part of me willed it to be so.

"It's a good possibility, considering their history," she conceded wearily.

Their history. I frowned and bit a corner off my toast, thinking. "So why do you need me? If you've got Paul Burnes, why this little party?"

"There's very little evidence to go on, and until we locate Mr. Burnes, I'm not going to sit and twiddle my thumbs, especially since it's Constantino who's asking me to do just that."

She flicked another Tums into her mouth and crunched it violently, staring at the wall to one side of me. "I need what you can see, what you know about the workings inside Shrewsbury. I need it and I don't like it, but I'm asking you anyway, because I'm damned if I'm going to let this case get away from me."

Kobrinski sighed, carefully refolded the silver paper over her antacids, and buttoned them into her pocket again. "I don't like asking for help, especially from someone from inside the gates—" She flushed a little and looked up at me quickly. "I didn't mean it like that—"

It didn't bother me much; at least I knew where she stood. "Yes, you did."

I watched a brief skirmish of emotions battle for possession of her face. Defensiveness eventually won out. It was then I noticed just how the dark smudges under her eyes emphasized the paleness of her skin; she hadn't had much sleep lately.

"Okay. I did, but I'm just saying that while I ordinarily wouldn't trust you, I've been told by another cop that you're reliable." She turned her empty plate over and tapped it meaningfully. "That you look at things differently. So I'm taking a chance and I'm admitting that. The least you can do is help me out." The detective sergeant gave me a little "so there" nod.

I nodded slowly myself. "Okay, fine, now it's my turn to be honest. I told Sheriff Stannard that I would stay out of police business, and that also happens to be my personal preference." I hurried along. "But if you need help and I can give it, well, I will. Because . . . because I . . . owe Faith at least that much. And it will help sort things out."

Kobrinski relaxed ever so slightly and nodded agreement. "It will sort things out."

"But why do you need me, when you've got Jack?"

"Jack?" She closed her eyes to flip through the mental Rolodex. "Right, John Miner. I haven't seen him since . . . the interviews last Thursday. What about him?"

"I'm not sure," I said, thoroughly confused—so much was happening that didn't make sense to me. "Friday I, ah, I upset him, he stormed out. But he left a message for me at the library Saturday saying that he was going to talk to you. You say he hasn't tried to reach you?"

She frowned. "When was the last time you saw him?"

"Saturday morning—I heard him in the bathroom. He was still angry at me." I tried unsuccessfully to smother the irony in my voice. "He knows I hate early mornings."

"Heard or saw?"

"Heard. I didn't run into him at all."

She looked sharply at me, the way she had when she'd first arrived to take over the investigation. "What about this morning?"

"Are you joking? I left too early. People in the house, the Fellows, tend to take off for the weekend—he'll probably stop by today."

"When did he leave the note?"

"Early Saturday morning, I guess. Before I got to the library, at any rate."

Kobrinski made a note on her pad. "I've got to talk to the state police, but I'll stop by later, make an opportunity for him to tell me this afternoon. Maybe if you're free then, you could answer a few questions." She closed her notebook and stuck her pencil through the wire rings.

"Whatever you like," I said nonchalantly. "Perhaps you'll have a few more leads to share as well. To help me sort things out."

"Could be," she nodded thoughtfully, and slipped on her coat.

"We're both of us being very careful, aren't we?" I asked.

"Nothing wrong with being careful, as long as you say just what's on your mind."

I got the impression that Detective Kobrinski wasn't saying everything that was on her mind, and rather relished our tense, somewhat combative relationship. Ever seen a cat smile? It happens occasionally, but there are a lot of teeth and you wonder what they're thinking about.

"Nancy, I'll see you later," she called to the woman behind the counter. She nodded to me as she left. "Ms. Fielding."

"Hey! Watch out there!"

Michael's angry exclamation woke me out of my ponderings an hour later. I was still mulling over my conversation with Detective Kobrinski and I'd walked right into him and his armload of books that were now scattered on the reference room floor. It was the first time I'd actually seen him doing any work since I'd arrived at the library. The titles I saw didn't indicate he was buckling down now, however: William Byrd's *Diary* and Lawrence Stone's *The Family, Sex, and Marriage* were both known, at least by undergraduates, for their racy passages. I picked up one of the others: *The History of the Nude*. Didn't seem to be much of a connection with the Transcendentalists, as far as I could tell; the mere thought of Bronson Alcott naked seemed a good reason for a night light.

"Sorry, Michael. My head was elsewhere." I stooped to help him retrieve the rest of his volumes. "Say, you wouldn't have time for that quote of mine, would you?"

"Probably won't take any time. Lay it on me."

I screwed up my face, trying to get the wording right. " 'Since it is possible that thou mayst depart from life this very moment—' "

"Yeah, yeah, 'regulate every act and thought accordingly,' " Michael finished for me. "Marcus Aurelius, *Meditations*. The sort of thing your eighteenth-century intellectual would have lapped up: resignation, order in the universe, all the appeal of the classics and no conflict with Enlightenment Christianity."

I looked at him, amazed. "Really? You recognize it just like that?"

Michael ignored my disbelief, more pressing matters clearly at hand. "You haven't seen Jack around, have you? I've been doing nothing but taking his phone messages since last night."

"No, sorry, I haven't. Has he picked up the messages?"

Michael shrugged. "How should I know? I stick them under his door." He stood up, and I handed him the last book. "He's probably just sleeping it off someplace—"

"Michael!"

"Well, what do you think?" He glanced over the top of his reading glasses. "He's certainly gone to ground."

I checked another polite, *pro forma* protest. "I suppose so. It's sad he should waste so much time and energy on theatrics."

"It will catch up with him," Michael said darkly. "Don't

forget, Emma, it's not the trial that's the bitch. It's the judgment that really sucks. See you back at the ranch."

"Nuttier than squirrel burps," I muttered as Michael strode out of the room.

"I'm sorry, Emma?" Harry emerged from his glassed-in office.

"Michael's just a mass of contradictions. I can't figure him out."

Harry smiled. "You're not the only one. You ever read his last book?"

"No. Why?"

"Take a look at it sometime. It's won every prize in history and the history of philosophy you can imagine. Rumors were that he came within a hair's breadth of a MacArthur 'genius' award after it came out. Don't confuse how he acts with how he thinks. Michael doesn't act like the rest of us, but it seems not to do his scholarship any harm. Quite the opposite; there's nothing at all childish about it. I was impressed by it, but a friend of mine was terrified by it. Said there was a coldness to the logic he was using that scared her. She said it exhibited an almost alien detachment from the human race."

"That's quite an evaluation," I said idly. I needed to be thinking about my day's work on Madam Chandler's diary, not the quirks of my colleagues as assessed by friends.

"That's her job, she's in the field and she was reviewing the book for the *Times Literary Supplement*," Harry answered.

I looked up, surprised.

Harry continued, polishing his glasses carefully. "Danielle was so unsettled, she asked not to do the work on it. The guy who finally did the review loved it, though. Still. Personalities differ in person and print, don't they?"

They certainly do, I thought.

Harry continued. "Anything I can get for you?"

"Just the diary, thanks. Let's see what surprises Madam

Margaret has for me today, though frankly, after the morning I've had, I don't know how much more I can take!"

"Sorry, Dr. Fielding, time!"

I was so engrossed I could barely remember where I was.
Sasha had bustled in to collect Margaret's web of intrigue
from me at the end of the day. I glanced up at the clock and
was startled to see that it was four forty-five.

"Oh, you can't!" I pleaded. "I'm right in the middle of the
trial!"

"Trial? Who was on trial? You make it sound like you're
reading a romantic thriller!"

"Madam Chandler! And get this, she was accused of
murdering the Reverend Blanchard! I flipped through the
Stone Harbor town history this morning and found a brief
reference to it. It turns out that the dates of the most heavily
encoded entries correspond with the dates of the trial! *Her*
trial! All I know so far was that she was eventually acquitted,
but before that, some townspeople were even hinting that
there was witchcraft involved!"

Sasha gasped in astonishment. "But wasn't her husband . . . ?"

I nodded. "One of the presiding judges. He apparently
had such a reputation for honesty that the people refused to
allow him to step down when he asked. He was afraid of not
being impartial enough. They'd only been married a few
months."

"How horrible," she said. "But it's exciting too! I'll have
her letters ready for you by the end of the week—maybe
they will help. Thing is, I didn't see anything in them about
a trial," she added apologetically.

"Well, at this point, anything would be a help. Jeez, I
know so little of what was going on with her! Besides the
work I've already done at home—which didn't mention any

of this—I've only got this poky town history to work with."
I gestured to a frayed reference book next to the diary. "It's
one of those town bicentennial things, from about 1850, and
it's heavily biased—you know, Stone Harbor firsts and hoary
ancestor worship. What's more important is this other diary,
from about a century later. The writer records an anecdote
that her grandmother told her about the trial. It seems the
records of the trial were suppressed, though. Is there any
way I can get hold of the court records to check?"

"Massachusetts Docket for the Exeter County Court District, 1700 to 1750," Sasha said promptly. "We've been trying to acquire one for years, but the supplemental copies,
like the one you need, are very hard to come by. Harry's
been driven to distraction trying to find a copy of the original edition, but we can get one through interlibrary loan for
you. If I call right now, it'll be here tomorrow."

"Great, thanks. I'm just surprised you haven't got it,
you've got everything else."

She laughed. "Harry treats it like a personal affront; last
time one was available, we didn't have the funds for it. And
since we got the Whitlow endowment—"

"Ah," I said. "As in Director Whitlow?" Suddenly, a lot of
things were making sense.

"That's right. His brother." Sasha looked around as
though the mere mention of the name would bring the man
himself. "Since we got that money, there's not been one to
be seen: If you ever want to see fireworks, just mention it—
Harry becomes a bear at the very mention of it. You just
keep plugging away with the diary and the letters, and the
court records will be here before you know it."

I began to back up my work for the day and shut down my
computer. "It's difficult, to keep calm and work methodically, even though I already know the outcome. I had no idea
about the trial," I said. "There are only hints in this book,
and until I crack the code, there's no way of knowing what

Margaret was going through. I can tell her handwriting is changing, the quotidian descriptions are shorter and shorter, as though she had only the strength to conceal her feelings so far, and no further. She was in big trouble, I think."

Sasha frowned, and I imagined that a similar frown sent all the warriors of Greece loading into their ships for Troy. "But why write a *diary* in code?"

"They weren't necessarily private, the way we think of them today," I explained. "They could have been records of historical events, they might have been more an on-going soul-search. Some parents kept them to show their children how to live a virtuous life, some kept them to record a history of the family. And Justice Chandler would have been well within his rights to demand to see his wife's journal."

Sasha shuddered. "I've always heard that he had a reputation for being cold and heartless. That his was a stony sort of justice."

I shook my head. "I get that too, Sasha, but from the town history, not the diary. Margaret doesn't write much about him, but when she does, it's as though she's learning about a respectable stranger. She's in awe at first, then later you start to see moments of fondness occasionally, and then some very sentimental language—Margaret was clearly falling in love with her husband. But when the trial starts, all references to Matthew disappear. Into the code, I guess."

"Imagine sharing a bed with the man who might hang you!" she breathed, then crooked her finger. "I hate to do this, but it's past time for closing."

"You're such a stickler," I teased. I regretfully handed her the book.

Sasha took the book and sighed mournfully. "You're not the only one who thinks so." She seemed to get caught up in a fog of melancholy.

I prompted her. "Sasha?"

"Oh." She sighed again, coming back to the present. "Harry and I had a disagreement this morning—"

I remembered their argument ending with Sasha slamming the car door down by the gate.

"—and well, you know we've been having trouble over the records from the last librarian—things sold and not recorded in the accessions. Well, I say call up the former librarian and ask him what his system was so we can find the missing books and papers. Check the accounts against what he says. Makes sense, right?"

I nodded.

Sasha threw her hands into the air. "Harry won't bother; he says that it will all get sorted out with a little more time. I can't blame him for being reticent, really. The former librarian was friends with Mr. Whitlow and no one wants to bother *his* friends. Jobs like this are scarce as hen's teeth, and there are rumors of cutbacks, you know?"

I did know, I thought; Director Whitlow had told me so himself.

"I know I want to keep my head down; and I'm in no financial state to try and buck the system. But it's such a little question." Sasha shook herself. "You know, I believe you're trying to distract me so you can have more time with Madam Chandler, but it won't work! Shoo, Dr. Fielding, you can come back tomorrow morning!"

When I got back to the house, Kobrinksi's unmarked car was parked out front, and Detective Kobrinski was just about to ring the bell.

"Good timing," she said. "You can let me in, and we'll start solving mysteries. Is Jack Miner in yet?"

"I don't know," I said. "We can have a look."

Jack wasn't watching television in the parlor, so we went

to knock on his door. As we climbed the stairs, I decided it
was time for me to get some answers.

"Did Faith drown?"

"Yes." The detective paused, one hand on the railing.
"But not in the Shrewsbury stream."

I stopped in mid-step. "So she was moved there after?
Was there any evidence by the stream?"

"Hard to say. There was a lot of disturbance from everyone traipsing down the bank—"

I bridled, but kept my mouth shut.

"—and you said that Gary Conner moved the deceased,
that didn't help either." A thought struck Detective Kobrinski. "Could you see for sure that he removed anything from
the crime scene?"

"I couldn't tell for sure, but it looked like it. He was being
pretty rough with the . . . with Faith."

She thought it over. "Her handkerchief was inside her
pocket, but it was muddy, like someone had pulled it out and
then stuffed it back in. And I think there's something missing from her room. And I'm not really certain why her body
was moved to the stream."

"Maybe the murderer was trying to hide it?"

"Didn't do a very good job, did they?" the detective said
with a flash of black humor. "You found her less than eight-
een hours after she died. That's a guess, by the way, based
on degree of rigor mortis; we can't be any more accurate because of the cold temperature of the air and water. But why
not dump her in the woods in back of the library? No one
ever goes there. Why not remove her from the premises altogether?"

"Not enough time?" I suggested.

Detective Sergeant Kobrinski furrowed her dark brow.
"Could be. The way I figure it, either the perp was trying to
dump the body in the stream to wash away any trace evi-

dence—very efficient, by the way—or he or she was trying to make it look like Ms. Morgan drowned there in the stream. That's a possibility. But why not throw her whole body in?"

I thought over my newly acquired, grotesque insight into death by drowning. "Did you find anything in her lungs?"

"I'm not at liberty to say at the moment," she said abruptly as we reached the top of the stairs. "Which is Jack's room?"

I led the way, but there was no answer to our repeated knocking. The detective looked frustrated, but I pointed out that it was still early yet and maybe Jack had gone into town to meet her.

"I'll call and check," she said. "But just so's not to waste the trip, let's take a look in Ms. Morgan's room. You knew her the best of anyone—"

"I knew absolutely nothing at all about her," I answered resentfully.

The detective frowned again, but took a key and opened Faith's room across the hall. "It's been processed, so you don't need to worry about disturbing anything. I'm looking for something in particular; let's see if you notice what I did."

Smothering my annoyance with the policewoman's games, I looked around the room, not furnished too much differently from mine. Clothes, tailored to an extreme degree, still expensively perfumed, hung in the closet, with shoes lined up as if for military review beneath them. Books organized by subject were in ranks on the bookcase, all of the bindings exactly one inch from the edge of the shelf, just like the ones Faith had kept on the top of a Victorian drop-front desk. The papers on the work were all lined up at right angles to the edges of the desk.

Unlike my room, however, there were no comforting

piles of papers and books and scraps of notes left hither and yon for discovery and inspiration. No heaps of clothing on the floor and all of Faith's underthings were carefully folded and put away according to type. She had been a person with a high degree of interest in order. A fine layer of dust had settled over everything, only noticeable because of the uniformity of the blanket, presumably only accumulated since last Wednesday night. My room had little patches cleared away where I needed a clean surface, leaving everything unevenly coated.

Something prompted me, and I moved over to the old desk and opened the drop front.

"There's nothing in there," Kobrinski said, leaning against the closet door. "Just some Shrewsbury stationery. All of her work was sorted into the files and on her desk."

Looking at the books, I recognized only the Foucault among the secondary sources, and aside from battered annotated copies of the works of Cooper, Rowson, and Irving, there was no modern or recreational fiction to be found anywhere. There was a gap quite noticeably left on one side.

"That's where her diaries were," the detective supplied when she saw me pause. "We've taken them to the lab and have been going through them. Absolutely religious about keeping them, every day. They end about two months ago."

"What are they about?"

"Everything. I wish she had written one during her stay here," Kobrinski grumbled. "That would clear up a lot for us, the way she wrote. I get the impression that the person who wrote them was a different one than the person all of you knew. It's . . ." She shook her head. "cold—"

I thought that assessment was spot on, myself.

"—but you'll have to look at them and tell me." She traced a pattern going through the carpet with a toe.

"So why did she stop?" I asked. I closed the desk.

She shrugged. "Most of it was about her recovery, after her suicide attempt. You wouldn't think that someone would be quite as . . . analytical . . . about themselves. Almost like it was about someone else. I don't know. Maybe she figured she'd done all the work she could and was moving on."

I arched a disbelieving eyebrow and Kobrinski shrugged again. "The last entry is on the last page of the last notebook," she said. "Sort of makes me think that there should be another one."

I nodded. "Yeah, just look at this room. You'd think she'd keep on with something as disciplined as a diary, especially since she brought the others with her. Did you look for another volume?"

The detective nodded and reached for a Tums. "All the usual places, between the mattress and boxspring, *in* the mattress and boxspring, in the grate, all over. I tried to think like her, I tried to think paranoid, I tried to think scared—perhaps she was already afraid for her life before she was murdered. But we found nothing. I wondered if it wasn't taken from her the night she was murdered."

"Well, we'll never find that out until we get the murderer, or at least know who it is," I said. Who would want her dead? I asked myself. I didn't know enough yet.

"There's only so many places in this room a book like that could be, and be hidden," Kobrinski muttered. "It must have been taken from her."

A thought, an incredibly distressing one, hit me between the eyes. "Oh, my God. The library!"

She looked doubtful. "Hide the diary in the library? Wouldn't that be dangerous?"

"It would blend right in," I said. "What better place to hide a needle than in a haystack?"

We both slumped; she knew as well as I did that going through all those shelves could easily take days and that we'd be cross-eyed at the end of it. "All right, we'll go have a look around the reference room," Pam Kobrinski conceded reluctantly. "You have to admit though, it takes balls to hide something in plain sight."

I had been staring right at the Victorian desk when the detective said that, and a second brainwave, stronger and truer than the first, hit. "What did you say?"

The detective misunderstood me. "Okay, *guts*, it takes a lot of *guts* to hide something in plain sight. That better? This political correctness thing is a real pain in the—"

"No, no not—" I shook my head; she'd misunderstood me. "Just hang on a minute. The diary's not in the library. I know where it is." I crossed the room.

The detective folded her arms across her chest, clearly annoyed by my changeability. "Well?"

"It's just when you said, 'hiding in plain sight,' you reminded me of something I heard in a class a long time ago," I murmured, almost to myself, as I gazed at the old desk. "A class about decorative arts. In particular, the lecture on nineteenth-century furniture."

"Huh? There's nothing in the desk, I already looked," she said impatiently. "I even looked under the drawers, behind the damn thing. It's not there. We don't even know if another diary *exists*."

"Yes we do, and I know where it is. Faith wouldn't let her diary get too far away from her, particularly not if it had something important in it." I pulled down the drop front again and tried pushing one ornate panel at the back of the desk. Nothing happened. "You see, the Victorians loved tricks, secrets, hidden meanings." I tried poking a beautifully carved section of vine. Nothing there. " 'Springes to catch woodcocks.' "

"You think there's a secret panel," the detective sergeant said, doubtful.

"I know there is." I opened the door to a little cubbyhole in the center of the desk and pressed the back, but to no avail. "At one point, I had a pretty good idea of where the secret compartment was located in most of these old desks. That was a long time ago, though. I could have sworn it would be at the back of that cubby. That's what's speaking to me." I peered at some ornate tracery, trying to distinguish a crack or a hinge. "Come on, where are you?"

Stepping back, I tried to look for the obvious that wasn't obvious. I kept coming back to that little door. And then I smiled triumphantly, reached forward, and pulled at the decorative wooden pilaster on the right side of the door. It slid out easily, the linear decoration concealing the fact that the column was just the front of a tall, narrow drawer. It was empty, but as the detective stepped forward eagerly, I pulled out the left column and inside was a small, modern exercise book with the date January 15, 2003 written on the front of it.

"Faith took that class too," I said.

I handed the detective the diary feeling distinctly smug; she hadn't been able to find it. But to my amazement, she only put the diary in a plastic evidence bag.

"Hey, aren't you even going to take a look at it?" How would you feel if you handed someone a light blue box from Tiffany's and they just chucked it into a closet?

"It's got to go through the lab first," she said. "Then we'll both—"

She was interrupted when we heard someone pounding up the stairs and a crash out in the hall. We started out of the room to investigate, when Michael stumbled into the doorway.

"I . . . I found him. I found Jack," he gasped. He was sweating, pale, and breathing heavily, obviously distressed.

"Where?" we asked simultaneously.

But I almost knew the answer even as he said it. A prickle

ran down my spine and the hairs stood up on the back of my neck.

Michael looked like he was ready to faint. "In the gazebo. I think he's dead."

Chapter 11

THERE WAS JACK, LYING SLUMPED AGAINST THE latticework railing of the gazebo, just as Michael had described. The three of us drove over in Detective Kobrinski's car after she called for the EMTs and crime scene squad. We paused a moment after we arrived, all for different reasons, I suppose. I faltered at the stairs because I was waiting for the joke to be exposed, waiting for Jack to jump up and shout "Gotcha!" and for him to congratulate Michael on a well-executed gag, even though I knew that would never happen, no matter how much I wished it would. I saw Detective Kobrinski hesitate to glance quickly over the weathered wooden floor before she walked on it, presumably for any clues as to the cause of Jack's death, because it seemed to me that anyone could tell just from looking that he *was* dead. Michael, for his part, never even climbed the stairs leading up to the gazebo. He just waited at the foot, looking in any direction but ours, his hands thrust deep into the pockets of his overcoat. It looked like he was trying to keep his face blank, but I noticed the strain of queasiness across his features.

When I finally walked around the gazebo, I could see that Jack was wearing his usual dark blue janitor pants and his gray duffel coat, which was unbuttoned, exposing a frayed pale blue dress shirt and a couple of sweaters. His headphones on his head, the tape player almost falling out of his coat pocket, just the way I'd always seen it when he was alive, and Jack looked for all the world like he'd just decided to hang out in the gazebo and listen to his tapes. In one hand, he still clutched an empty whiskey bottle, and based on the faint smell coming from the body, not much of it had been emptied by spilling or evaporation. Jack had been on a world-class bender.

I looked at his face even before I could decide whether I really wanted to. It was now trapped in a permanent grimace, the sort of face he had made before when I spoke of exercise or archaeology. One difference was that there was a distinct bluish tinge to his exposed skin and particularly to his lips that I couldn't attribute to the dying light of the afternoon. The other was that a thick rope of dark vomit had crusted down his chin from the corner of his mouth. I looked away hurriedly.

"Looks like he froze to death, or maybe he choked," Detective Kobrinski said, echoing my own thoughts as she squatted down beside him. She was looking intently, but still didn't touch anything.

I had a quick flashback to last Thursday, when she was looking at Faith just the same way. That thought reminded me of just how much was happening around me, and I quickly shoved it aside. "I don't think he could have been out here since Friday or Saturday, though, could he?"

Kobrinski looked at me and frowned in a "Who the hell invited you?" fashion, before she answered, more politely than I expected. "You would have seen him before, wouldn't you, when you came by here since then, right? Hey," she called to Michael, who was shuffling through the pebbles around the base of the gazebo, "when was the last time you saw Mr. Miner here alive?"

"Friday, I guess," he said slowly, as he traced a pattern with his toe. "No, wait, maybe it was Saturday?"

"But Saturday was the day you went into Boston early," I pointed out. "I heard him in the bathroom. Did you see him before you left?"

"Maybe it was Friday," Michael corrected himself hurriedly. "I didn't see him all weekend after that."

"Well, do you if know if he was gone the whole time?" I persisted. "I couldn't tell if he was just avoiding me because of our little to-do."

"I said"—he scuffed out his pebble lines impatiently—"I haven't seen him all weekend."

"Do you have any idea where he might have gone?" Even though I could tell I was irritating him, I just couldn't stop asking the questions that popped unbidden into my head. "Hey, wait a second! I didn't hear him slamming around in the bathroom this morning! Did you?"

Michael finally looked up at me. "What kind of ghoul are you?" He stared in revulsion. "I mean, how can you ask if I heard Jack taking a piss this morning, when he's lying there like . . . like . . . fuck it! Like a piece of meat!"

"Hey Michael, come on! There's no need to be like that," I said. "I'm just trying—"

But Michael just scowled, batted a hand dismissively at me, and stalked off across the field, following the stream road back toward the house. His overcoat flapped around his heels like a faithful dog.

I stared after him and called, "Hey, wait a minute!"

"Umm, Emma—"

"Where's he going?" I asked, turning to Pam Kobrinski, who was watching the exchange. "We need to figure out—"

"Say, here's an idea," the detective offered lightly. "How

about you ask me your questions, and I'll deal with everyone else?"

"What do you mean?" Her mild criticism on top of Michael's stung more than I expected. "I was just—"

"I know you were just." Kobrinski sat back on her heels. "I think things will work out better if you focus on observing and I'll do the interrogating."

"I wasn't interrogating," I insisted. "I was just asking Michael some questions."

"Still." She paused to hook her bangs out of her eyes with a pinkie. "We'll start at the beginning. Let's have a look at Mr. Miner here and try to decide just how he died."

The discussion was closed. She'd let me off very gently, but it didn't help much.

I took a deep breath. "Well, he could have been drinking and then passed out and froze to death, right?"

"Yeah." She nodded. "Seems to be lots of alcohol flowing around this place. There was a high, but not legally intoxicating, amount of alcohol present in Ms. Morgan's blood."

"Jack was worse than most, though," I pointed out. "He'd been drinking steadily and more heavily ever since I found Faith, and he was pretty much in the bag every night before that, according to Michael. As far as I could tell, it was a regular ritual."

"So this isn't inconsistent with previous behavior."

"But the fact that he's outdoors," I said. "That is."

Detective Kobrinski grunted. "And we need to know how long he was here."

"Won't the autopsy help with that?" I couldn't help shivering, not only because the sun was going down and the wind was picking up, but also because I thought of the glee with which a certain medical examiner would have tackled the problem.

"Maybe. Might even tell us if it was alcohol poisoning

and not the cold, if he drank enough. But again, as with Ms. Morgan, it's going to be difficult to determine the time of death with the cold weather the way it is, altering rigor." Detective Kobrinski gently prodded Jack's arm. "You didn't notice him this morning or this afternoon, right?"

"Right. You know, I can't imagine what would have brought Jack out here. He hated the cold, he hated the idea of exercise, and his car's back at the residence."

Kobrinski looked up. "Interesting."

The dying light reflected off Jack's Walkman in a peculiar fashion, giving me another idea. "What about the batteries? He used the rechargeable sort, there was always a set charging in the kitchen. That might help with time of death."

"Maybe. Hang on a second." The detective took the pencil out of her little spiral-bound notebook. "He used these all the time?"

"Between that and the scotch, it was like Jack was trying to block out as much of the world as possible," I said. Suddenly I couldn't look at the face of the sad little man and focused on the Walkman.

"The radio?" She moved the portable stereo a little with the pencil, to better look at it.

"No. It was almost always tapes. Fake jazz, that sort of thing. Always cranked way up. Why?"

"The tapes would use up the batteries faster."

"Oh. Of course." The odd light attracted my attention again and this time I knew why. "Could I borrow that a second?"

She handed me the pencil and I reached over and pressed the eject button with the pencil eraser.

We could both see it then. Jack was wearing his headphones, but there was no tape in the cassette player.

"Still, it doesn't mean it was murder . . ." the detective mused.

"Huh? Who would want to murder Jack?" I stammered, not thinking.

Pam Kobrinski sighed and looked about a million years old. "Who'd want to murder anyone? You'd be surprised at what would prompt someone to kill someone else. It doesn't take much, I'm sorry to say. But you gave me a motive yourself this morning."

"Me?" My mind raced back to our breakfast meeting and screened the possibilities, until one hit me right between the eyes. "Oh, my God. The note."

"Right. The note that Jack left for you in the library. Where, as far as I can tell, almost anyone could have seen it. It said that Jack knew something and was going to tell." She stood up and stretched casually, but looked tense.

"But . . . but . . . the note. The note was on my desk. What if . . . what if . . . ?" My words trailed off even as my imagination, as overfed as it had been in the last week, took off like a greyhound, haring after the worst possible conclusion.

"What if whoever saw the note, *if* someone saw the note, thinks Jack also spoke to you?" The detective had trouble concealing her unease. "I'm afraid we can't rule out that possibility."

Everyone was remarkably tolerant of me, not asking me to move off the bottom step where I had sunk down until they actually had to. They finally removed Jack's body, hauling it off in the bag on the gurney forty minutes later. At the news that he might have been murdered and that now it might be a good idea for *me* to be worried too, I'd sort of collapsed in on myself, head on my knees, arms wrapped over my head, willing everything to just go away. Flashbulbs flared, notes were taken, the surrounding ground searched, little puffs of breath hanging in the air around Pam Kobrinski and a State

Police officer and the ambulance EMTs who showed up promptly. But I was oblivious to it all. While it was still possible that Jack hadn't been murdered, that he'd just forgotten a tape in his drunken stupor and succumbed to the cold, I didn't think so. It was too big a coincidence after Faith's death. Something horrible was going on at Shrewsbury, and I was no longer just on the edge of it all; it was moving closer and closer, threatening to envelop me.

"I think we're done here, for tonight," Kobrinski said. She was rubbing her hands together trying to warm up. "C'mon, I'll give you a lift back. I'm going back to the house to have a look at his room now."

The thought of being cooped up in the car even for the half a minute it would take to get back to the house was utterly abhorrent to me. I shook my head. "No thanks, I need to stretch a bit, warm up. I'll walk back, see you in a minute."

"You sure?" she asked impatiently; she didn't really have time to mess with me. "It's getting pretty cold out here."

"Yeah." I didn't tell her I wasn't certain I could even face being back in the house, closed up alone with my thoughts. "I'll see you in a bit."

"Okay." She looked doubtful. "I'll need the note, if you've still got it."

"I think it's in my wool jacket. I'll check."

The detective peered at me. "You sure you're all right?"

"I'm fine."

"Don't dawdle. It's going to be a long night for us all."

I nodded and watched her pull down the road, headlights on even though there was still a little light left in the deepening dusk. And as soon as her car pulled around the bend, out of sight, I knew I should have accepted the ride.

I was overwhelmed with the most extraordinary sensation

of isolation. I felt exposed, on the edge of the woods at the foot of the mountains in the middle of nowhere, with nothing for miles around but me and spiraling catastrophe. I could see the glow of ambient light from Monroe blinking on against the pinkish blue and black of the gloaming, and it only increased the profound pall of loneliness. The dark obliterated any trace of the emerging spring, and all I could see were the ghostly branches that rocked in the cold wind. A single star appeared, winking palely, watching with a distant chilly light.

I want to go home, I thought miserably. I want Brian. I want to hide under the blankets until this all goes away. Thoughts of familiar things and the security of them sent a pang of longing through me. Even Quasi, the feline Prince of Darkness, would be a welcome sight.

But it was the thought of the cat's disinterested malevolence that actually changed my mind and bucked me up. I got up from the gazebo steps to think it through. If I was being completely honest, it was impossible for me to leave now. I simply couldn't desert Madam Chandler. It was though I had a physical craving to find out what happened during the trial to save her from being hanged. There was no way I could abandon the diary, not with the letters about to be released from conservation, not with the transcript of the trial about to arrive at any moment. I'd be throwing away half of my evidence by leaving the diary *itself* unstudied. Who knew what information would be revealed in the fabric of the diary itself? Perhaps by a closer examination of the pages and binding, something would be revealed to me. I needed all of the diary's clues to crack the code. I started to walk.

Brian might categorize this decision—and I realized in that instant, it was a decision to stay—as "exciting," or worse. I wasn't too sure how bright it was myself. I just knew that I was as close as anyone had been to finding out the truth about her journal and the trial. Call it instinct or call it conceit, I needed to stick it out for Margaret.

There was another thing, too. I couldn't do anything about what had happened to Faith or Jack, but I could sure as hell try and help find out what had gotten them both killed. Kobrinski was right: I had access.

I hadn't changed a thing except myself, but it was surprising what a difference that made. I was still only dealing with speculation, there was no real reason yet to think that Jack had been murdered. And if he hadn't been, then I had nothing to worry about, really. And we'd find out what happened to Faith, I was willing to bet, now that we had her diary.

As I came around the bend to the final stretch of the road leading to the front of the house, I realized that someone—not Detective Kobrinski—was leaning in to the front seat of her car. It took a moment before I realized that this wasn't right.

"Hey," I whispered, suddenly self-conscious, then again, much louder, as I realized that something was very wrong. The figure straightened as I began to hurry forward. "Hey! Stop! What are you doing?"

The figure didn't bother to turn to me but began to sprint across the open ground, heading for the library and the woods at the back of the estate.

It was like a spring that had been wound too tight finally let go, and I took off after the figure. I hadn't been for a proper, long run in what felt like weeks, but so far from feeling out of shape, I was nearly ecstatic—I could finally *do* something.

Channeling every ounce of frustration, fear, worry, and anger into forward motion, I tore across the back field and had made it to the top of the grassy slope before I even knew I'd started up the steep hill. Adrenaline and endorphins flooded my system, and I now understood why you should never run on painkillers. It felt too good. You ran too fast. I ignored prudence and let the sensation of speed consume me, wipe my mind clear of every thought but the chase.

But even at this speed, the figure eluded me. I could make out a bulky form I presumed to be male, though the clothing could have easily concealed a woman. Whoever it was was in good shape and had come prepared to leave quickly; with the light from the house I saw the white soles of running shoes showing up against the dark of the evening.

The figure left the road and entered the lightly wooded area on the way to the library, and we both had to slow somewhat. There were no clearly marked paths, and the increasing dark forced us to dart more carefully through the underbrush and low branches. I was at a disadvantage here, not knowing the terrain as well as did the other runner, but I never lost sight of my quarry.

I was able to keep up but not close the gap between us and was beginning to wonder what I would do if I *did* catch up when suddenly a dark blur streaked past me. I was running as fast as I ever had in my life, but Detective Kobrinski was moving like Diana on the hunt and in complete control of her every movement. I had just a moment to watch her go with awestruck fascination before a charley horse abruptly immobilized the muscle in my right thigh and sent me tripping across a thick root.

With a cry, I stumbled and fell to the ground, and it seemed like I skidded for the entire length of a football field, but in reality it was only a yard or so. Somewhere past all the pain, I heard the tinny ring of clanking metal and looked up to see whoever I had been chasing clambering up a section of chainlink fence that formed the rear boundary of Shrewsbury.

"Freeze! Police!" the detective shouted. She was nearly at

the fence herself by the time the figure had made it over the chainlink, hesitating briefly to untangle his foot from the bent wires at the top.

She didn't stop but seemed to fly up the front of the fence herself. If she touched the links with hand or foot, I couldn't see it.

Kobrinski too got tangled at the top, her bulky jacket slowing her down. She landed at the bottom on the other side and shouted her order again, but the figure had by this time made it around the bend, presumably to a waiting car, and roared off without turning on the headlights.

"Damn, damn, damn!" she roared, kicking the fence angrily. "Ahh, damn it all to hell!"

She climbed back over the fence, but this time I could hear the effort she took in scaling it. She paused, straddling the top, taking care to remove something from the top link without touching it too much herself. By the time she reached me, I was up and limping around in small circles, using every curse that Grandpa Oscar had taught me and a few that would have made him blush. I was trying to get my thigh to loosen up. If it had been wrapped around a walnut instead of my femur, the nut would have cracked in a second.

"Are you okay?" she asked. "What's wrong?"

"Cramped up," I half gasped, half groaned, massaging my leg. "God, it hurts!"

"Dehydration, probably, and oxygen deprivation in the muscle. Keep moving, keep rubbing it, and make sure to drink a lot of water when we get back," she advised. "Let me give you a hand." Sweat beaded on her forehead and I could feel the heat the two of us were both radiating in the chilly air.

"Huh—how in the world did . . . did you do that?" I was just starting to get my wind back. "You were in the h . . . house when I took off!"

She nodded, catching her breath now that the moment of pursuit was past. "I heard you shout and booked it."

"Booked it! That was nearly supersonic!"

"I wouldn't have made it this far if I didn't have you to follow. You kept up pretty good there. Not bad at all."

"Pretty good?" I sputtered. "Not bad? I ran my heart out! I'll never run that fast again, never in a month of Sundays! I nearly cripple myself and you—!"

Kobrinski was laughing, silently, showing all those little pointed, catty teeth. *She'd* regained her wind in no time, while I was still huffing and puffing. "You'll be fine."

"Huh," I said. Bite me, I thought. Since when did she have a medical degree?

"Would it help to know I had a four-year track scholarship to UMass Amherst?"

"Yes," I said, slightly mollified.

"Of course, that was a long time—years—ago. I've slowed down considerably since then."

"Go to hell." I paused to rub my throbbing thigh.

Again came the silent laugh. "All I can say is, it's gonna suck to be you tomorrow."

We limped along slowly, and by the time we reached the back field, I was hobbling along by myself. I would be feeling the effects of the night's escapade for a while.

"What did you find on the top of the fence?" I asked when I could finally divert some of my concentration to other matters.

"Our friend left a small piece of electrical tape," she answered.

"Electrical tape? I thought he caught his foot up there. Was he trying to hide the running shoe design?"

"Maybe just to help camouflage them; so many are white or reflective these days and stand out in the dark. Ever heard the one about the kid who was ripping off VCRs and went to a whole lot of trouble to dress like a ninja? Problem was he was wearing those running shoes that blink red lights when you run in them. And he didn't have a clue how the arresting officer was able to follow him."

I thought about it. "Not much in the way of footprints going to be left on the pine needles and stuff, but there may be something in the dirt on the other side of the fence—"

She wasn't convinced. "Maybe. And there may be tire tracks and there may be prints in the house."

I nodded. "So did you find anything in Jack's room?"

"Jack's room?" I could hear the confusion in her voice. Kobrinski shook her head. "I was going to Jack's room but ended up in yours. I hate to say this, but it looks like it's been tossed pretty good. I think whoever we were chasing was in your room. Must have gone down the back stairs as I came up the front."

"Oh God, what happened? My computer, my notes—!" The full implications of this were only just starting to settle in on me when suddenly I heard the detective sergeant swear hotly and run the last few steps over to her unmarked sedan parked in front of the house.

I was about to ask what was going on when I saw the broken window glass scattered around the driver's side door, illuminated brilliantly by the lights from inside the house. I hobbled up as she tore open the door, looked inside briefly, then just as quickly slammed the door shut again. She turned, as if to explain to me, then turned back just as quickly, slamming the roof with her hand in a white hot rage.

The violence of her actions scared me, and I could only shrug and shake my head dumbly, waiting for the explanation, when she did turn to me.

"I'd locked Ms. Morgan's diary in the car, but it's not there now. It's been stolen."

Chapter 12

"**N**OOO! LET ME GO!" I COULDN'T UNDERSTAND why I couldn't move.

"Owww! My eye! Damn it!"

"She's still out there!" Someone was holding me back. I fought to get loose. "In the water!"

"God's bollocks!"

"I have to get out there!"

"Emma, wake up! There's no one in the frigging water, damn it! You're asleep!"

"The water! Meg!" There came a jolting realization that I wasn't where I thought I was, and all the images that had been so real, so urgent, just a moment before, completely evaporated. I found myself in the hallway outside my bedroom trying desperately to hang onto the vanishing remnants of the dream, thoroughly confused, just a second too late to get the vital clue that I sensed waited for me.

Michael was gripping my right shoulder with one hand, pinning me hard against the wall outside my room with his forearm. He cupped his left eye with the other hand. It was the shock of his proximity and the sudden realization that he was naked from the waist up that really woke me up.

"You okay now?" Michael finally asked, not willing to move away until he was sure of me.

I swallowed and nodded, not trusting myself to speak. He smelled of clean sweat, warm sleep, and, unexpectedly, baby shampoo. He looked tired and scared, worried for me. It was nothing like his daytime mask of terminal ennui. I was still shaken from my nightmare, my heart racing like twenty. Certainly he must be able to feel it pounding, pressing so close. I became acutely aware of the fact that I had been trying to shove him away from me and that my hands were still on his bare, flat stomach. I could feel chest hairs curling under my fingertips that normally would have been concealed by a shirt and the omnipresent overcoat.

He hesitated, but as soon as he stepped back, releasing me, I fell forward, only keeping my balance by grabbing his arm. Again I realized that he was stronger than his usually careless posture would have suggested: I'd been struggling very hard.

As soon as I'd steadied myself, I pulled my hand away as though I'd touched a furnace, embarrassing us both. I realized I couldn't just dive back into my room and hide, but neither could I speak yet.

"Where's the light? God, my eye hurts! My poor glasses, I hope they're all right. That's some mean right you have." After a moment, he found the hall light, then looked around. His glasses were on the floor a few feet away from us, and he picked them up, then he quickly scuttled into his room.

"What happened?" I asked, swallowing again.

"I thought you could tell me," Michael called. He returned a second later, his overcoat tied closely about him. He paused, looking at his glasses. "Good, they're not broken."

He didn't put them back on immediately, but smoothed out his tousled hair, collecting himself. "I was reading, nearly asleep, when I heard yelling, screaming, not to put too fine a point on it. I figured the house was on fire. I ran out just in time to find you going berserk about someone being in the water. I tried to keep you from running down the stairs and you landed a smart one on me."

"Oh God, I'm sorry—"

He walked over and checked himself out in the hall mirror. I was horrified to see a bruise already rising around his eye.

"Oh, pree-eetty. This is going to look real nice." He made a fierce face at the mirror, probing the contusion carefully. "Between this and the hand, I'm starting to look like Frankenstein's monster." He held his hands out in front of him and tried out a stiff-legged walk.

"How'd you hurt your hand?" I asked, too quickly.

Michael desisted with his monster imitation and waved my question aside. "I don't remember. Whacked it on the lockers, I think. One of the doors is broken, it sticks. What were you dreaming about? Faith? Who's Meg?"

"Faith?" I could barely remember what had been driving me before. "Yes, it was Faith. No, wait, I don't think so. It was where I found her, in the stream, but not really, and not her, if you know what I mean. Meg's . . . a friend of mine. A student. A long time ago, I was afraid she'd drowned." I shivered, remembering that stormy night out at Penitence Point; at the moment, that memory was the thing I could make the most sense of. "At the time, I was afraid I was going to drown too."

"Hmmm. Go get a bathrobe, or something, you're starting to shiver," he said, not looking over from the mirror.

I hobbled into my room and threw on my robe, an absurd silk trifle that had been a gift from Marty. I brought it only because it fit into my suitcase. I found myself wishing it was a thick, shapeless piece of terrycloth, and was profoundly grateful that it was still March. If it had been June, well, I wouldn't have been wearing my long johns to bed. I took a moment to gather myself in hand, sitting down on the bed and resting my head on my knees, waiting for my heart to slow down.

I don't sleepwalk. I don't generally have dreams that drive me to it. And I almost never have experienced the sort of physical shock I had just encountered with Michael. I just don't get that wound up about strangers, even good-looking ones. I'm not the sort to get wound up—

Emma, I told myself, the word you're groping for, if you'll pardon the expression, is *aroused*.

Whatever you want to call it, that's not me, I insisted. I just . . . don't. What the hell is going on here?

Once I settled myself, I took a deep breath and went back out into the hallway to make my apologies.

"I really am absurdly sorry." I was more than a little freaked out by what I'd done and how I was feeling. "Maybe we could get you some frozen peas or ice or something for your eye?"

Michael put his glasses on, adjusting them carefully, seeing how they looked with his shiner before he put them away in his room. He was Michael the enigmatic again. "Emma," he said disapprovingly. "You know how I feel about vegetables of any sort. I doubt there's anything so politically incorrect as a raw steak in the house? No? Well, come on downstairs anyway, Lady MacBeth. I don't think I could possibly get to sleep again after all that drama."

I limped after him, my leg still sore, and checked the big clock at the foot of the stairs. Three thirty. We'd only got to bed around one, after Detective Kobrinski and the state police crime squad had sealed Jack's room and we'd had a look around my own devastated room. Nothing appeared to be missing there, and nothing was really damaged, as far as

I could tell. Papers were strewn about the room, the covers were torn off the bed, and the mattress was on the floor. All my clothes that had been in the armoire were in a heap on the floor, and all of the drawers had been taken from the bureau and emptied, then they were thrown on top of their contents. But my computer was on the desk where I'd left it, and I found the note from Jack still crumpled in the pocket of the jacket I'd worn Saturday morning. Nothing had been destroyed.

For all the lack of damage, I still felt creeped out; someone had handled my stuff, been near to what was important to me. Ours is a culture that values privacy and has a sharply defined notion of personal space, so much so that fights can break out over an unintentional bump on the sidewalk. The sanctity of my de facto home had been violated and even though the little interior door lock had been absurdly easy to break through, it represented a shattered social code of respect for privacy and safety. I had to resist the urge to wash all the clothes that had been thrown about, even though they hadn't even been on the floor long enough to get wrinkled, simply because some unknown person had handled them.

The detective sergeant had taken my statement and went off to take Michael's, leaving me to clean up the mess as best I could. I hadn't seen Michael since he left the gazebo—not until my nightmare dragged us both from our respective beds.

After a quick look in the freezer, I tossed Michael a package. "Here, put that on your eye."

He looked at the plastic bag askance. "I suppose Tater Bites don't really count as veg, do they? Jack won't want them now anyway." He clamped it to his eye, and stretched out across two chairs on the far side of the table. I could just see the tops of his bare feet, his hands as he gestured, and the bag as it sat on his head.

A very bad parody of what was presumably an Austrian

accent issued from behind the table. "Soo, vat vere you dreamink. Tell me, vat haunts you zo?"

"It was just a bad dream, that's all. I don't remember anything else."

"You are then very often tearink around der house screamink blau murder?" Michael got bored with Freud and switched back to his normal voice. "You know sleepwalking is pretty unusual in adults? Do it often?"

"No. No, absolutely not. Almost never."

"Almost never?"

"Cocoa?" I offered, hopping up from my seat.

"Oh God." A vast sigh came from behind the kitchen table. "When a man takes a poke in the eye, from a *woman*, who's *asleep*, he wants something a little more butch than cocoa to soothe his ego."

I almost told him about my Krav Maga lessons, as if that might be balm for his ego. Then I reconsidered; I didn't particularly want anyone to know about whatever slight resources I might have at my disposal. Just in case. Nolan would be very proud, though: I'd finally figured out how to stop overthinking my moves and land a good punch. All I had to do was be asleep.

Instead, I pulled the Macallan out of a cupboard, then hesitated.

"What's wrong?" Michael propped himself up on one elbow, still clutching the cold bag to his eye.

"This is what Faith and I were drinking the night she was killed." I looked at the label, daring it to make some sense of what was happening at Shrewsbury.

"So what, are you afraid it's cursed?"

That was precisely what I was thinking. "No, 'course not." I annoyed myself by reacting to Michael's sarcasm. "Anything older than twelve years is proof against curses."

"You're making puns? Now?" He paused. "Maybe you

think it's poisoned," he suggested in an odd, cold voice. "Maybe you even spiked it yourself."

"Don't be stupid." I poured two shots and banged them on the table irritably, worried about what he might be, even as he bluntly accused me of murder.

Now Michael heaved himself up on his elbow, eye level with the drinks. He hesitated, then made a big production of scrutinizing the glasses, switching them around, and around again, looking up at me to see what I thought of his antics.

"Stop being dramatic."

He still waited to take his first sip until I drank first and only then raised his glass. "Chin chin. Here's to the dramatic: It may keep you from being dead."

I sighed heavily. "Faith wasn't poisoned, Michael. We don't know how Jack died. And I had nothing to do with either of these deaths."

"Never hurts to be careful, does it? We're down fifty percent in one week, you know. I think even the British officers in the Crimean would have reconsidered in light of those numbers." He paused and took another sip. "We don't know each other, we band of happy scholars. We don't know who's lurking around here."

"The important thing is we don't know *why*." And as long as we were on the subject . . . I took a deep breath, then blurted out, "Did you trash my room?"

He rolled his eyes and set his glass on the table, sinking out of sight to recline across the chairs again. "No, I did not trash your room. Did you?"

"Did I what?"

"Toss your own room. I wondered about that." A bandaged hand snuck up and reclaimed the whiskey.

"No! Why would I do that? What, you mean like a diversion or something?"

I saw the bag of Tater Bites wobble unsteadily, just visible above the surface of the table, as Michael shook his head. "I have no way of knowing that I'm not living across the hall from a murderer. Your door wasn't even busted. It *does* make for a nice diversion. Ought to give any thinking person pause, yeah?"

I shook my head. "For all of Mr. Constantino's much-vaunted concern with security, any dodo with a credit card could get by these indoor locks. A good swift kick is what did the trick, according to Detective Kobrinski. You'll just have to take my word for it. It wasn't me."

"I don't think either of us ever got by on faith, have we, Emma?" Michael shook his head again and clucked. "And I don't think that we can afford to start now. Just think about it. Faith herself . . . ah. You know, we started off with the four of us, and quite frankly, none of this excitement started until you came along—"

The same thing that Dr. Moretti had said. "Oh, for heaven's—"

"—and now there's just us twain. *Ten Little Indians* was hardly less subtle. So I'm all for excessive care—dramatics if you like—until we know what is going on. I like you, Emma, but I don't think I should trust you; you know too much about door locks and credit cards. You spend too much time, by your own admission, in the heads of dead people. Contrariwise, you'd probably be smart not to trust me."

I thought about that for a minute, realizing that he was right and not liking it. "Did you see or hear anybody go into my room?"

"Nope. I was sitting in the parlor, by myself. Having a think. I wasn't paying attention."

And sitting in the dark was perfectly useless as an alibi, I thought, especially when the parlor was so close to the front of the house, where the detective's car had been parked while she was upstairs. That back staircase made it very easy to miss each other, it was designed to do just that, to shield the Shrewsburys from the sight of their scurrying servants. "You never did tell me what your relationship with Faith was."

"No, I didn't."

"Well?" I still couldn't see Michael's face, hidden behind the table and the makeshift ice pack.

It was a long time before he answered. "Suffice it to say, we knew each other only slightly and had nothing in common but a bleak outlook on life. We just expressed it differently."

"You seemed a lot more upset by Jack's death than hers. Big difference between this afternoon, yesterday, I should say, and last week."

"I didn't find her," he said quietly. "I didn't know Faith the way I knew Jack. Jack and I had . . . history."

I pushed on recklessly. "What kind of history?"

"We just knew each other, conferences and such. The random contacts of our mutual field, poor bastard. You can't tell me you don't know how small the academic world is—you meet someone by chance, and they seem to pop back into your life for real shortly after that." Michael was clearly getting impatient. "But what do you care? What are you, the emotional hall monitor?"

"No. And for the record, I'm not a ghoul either," I said. "It's just something I do. An extension of my work. It only seems fair, that's all; someone ought to care, want to get at the truth. But whatever the reason I feel compelled to . . . peer and poke, at least I feel like I'm doing something useful. And that helps."

Michael sat up and tossed the soggy, limp plastic bag in the sink. "I suppose that's better than some avenging angel complex, but it doesn't comfort me much."

I slammed my glass down. "Then why don't you leave?"

"Gots to pay the bills, sweetheart. There's the eternal

and various spousals to support and last time I checked, food and books cost money. Here, they'll feed me and let me at the books for a whole six weeks. It's the closest thing to patronage this side of the Renaissance, and it's keeping me out of the cold and wet until my next stop in New Haven."

I took a sip of my whiskey. "Sabbatical year?"

He laughed hollowly. "I'm supposed to be regenerating, reinvigorating myself, but it's really just a peripatetic prison sentence with half pay. I've got three more lined up between now and August, and then it's back to the salt mines and the full pittance."

"Oh?"

"Just got done at Philadelphia, next New Haven, then Berkeley."

"Oh." Something about Philadelphia rang a bell, but I couldn't remember why it seemed significant.

"So I haven't really got a choice," Michael explained loftily. He was definitely one of those jerks who got off on complaining about being broke and an academic, like it ennobled him somehow. "What's your excuse? Why don't you leave?"

"I can't. I'm . . . I'm helping Detective Kobrinski."

A wet, rude noise came from the other side of the table. "Yeah, right. I'll try again. Why not leave?"

"I . . . I can't." I shrugged helplessly. "The diary, Margaret—"

He gave a short humorless laugh and swung himself up from his reclined position. "I see. Well, it looks like we're both stuck here, whatever the result. It would be nice if we're both alive at the end of it all."

"Michael, cut the attitude, would you?" I put my glass in the sink, trying not to let him get my goat, but it had already been got.

"It might be attitude, but it's mine and it's honest." He got up, took the soggy bag from the sink, and slammed it into the wastebasket. The violence of his gesture startled me.

"I think things are going to get a whole lot worse before they get better," he said, "and frankly, I'm going to be keeping my head down. I suggest you do the same. 'Night, 'night, Auntie. Don't let the bedbugs bite."

"Holy shit!" Late the next morning in the library I read the paragraph a third time to make certain I hadn't made a mistake. I hadn't. "Holy—"

"What is it?" Sasha came over to my carrel. "Are you okay, Emma?"

"I'm fine, but Madam Chandler sure isn't!" I gestured to the diary. "Sasha, you have to read this! When I came in this morning, I found that the rest of the diary was in code from where I left off. I didn't even bother trying to transcribe it all, just skipped to the next bit of English. This is the last entry and it's a lulu!"

Sasha leaned over and read out loud while I paced back and forth behind her, practically reciting along with her, the words had so seared themselves into my memory:

August 3rd. It is over. For the first Time in my Life I hve succomed to a Woman's, nay, a Mortal's Weaknesse, and believe yt my God and Creator has abandonned me finally. Perhaps it is more of a Comfort to believe that then to accept that this may be His Plan, which is too much for me to beare; no One should be made to suffer so. I write these last Lines plainly, I have no Reason further to conceal my Despair, and perhaps it is no coincidence they fill the last Space in this little Booke that has been the best Keeper of my Confidence, my secret Soule. I have proclaimed my Innocence in the Matter of Reverend Blanchard's Death publickly, I will do so once again here: I am innocent but I have not the Means to demonstrate it. *I have finished my Will and I hope that it will be taken into consideration after I am gone. And perversely, while I have written that I am so empty of Faith that I must sound like an empty clay Jar, hollo' and fragile, I still cling to the Notion that even if God has quit me, perhaps Matthew has not . . . Enough, I cannot afford Hope, it is too costly a Garment for my present Estate. I must compose myselfe for tomorrow. Adieu, Matthew, you have been a loving Friend as well as my Huzband and you have done your Dutie, I cannot hold you responsible for being what you are any more than you could save me from what I am. We will meet again in the seat of the Almighty and at least I am able to rejoice in that sweet Knowledge. Adieu, adieu, yr loving Margaret.*

She looked up in shock. "But we know that she lived until much later than this date, 1723. We *know* she didn't die the next day!"

"Right, but we don't know how she escaped being hanged!" I said excitedly. "It's like missing the climax of a serial, where you've left off with the heroine hanging off a cliff, and the next time you see it, she's fine, but you don't know how she got out of that impossible situation." I got up and paced three steps. "Damn! How soon will those letters be done?"

"They're being dried now, I can have them for you tomorrow. But the trial transcript in the records should be here today." She checked her watch. "Any minute, in fact, if the librarian at Amherst sent the book out last night. I'll go check the mailroom for you."

"Thanks! I don't think I can stand not knowing a minute longer."

"What you really need is to crack that code," Sasha pointed out. "Have you tried that yet?"

"I've been too afraid to try," I admitted. "I haven't the faintest idea of where to start. I'm no cryptographer."

"Well, Margaret Chandler probably wasn't a cryptographer on top of everything else," Sasha said reasonably. "It can't have been too hard, just enough to keep the maid from peeking, I suppose."

I looked at her in amazement. "You're absolutely right, Sasha. And if I can't figure it out, I'll find someone who can."

"This is so exciting!" Sasha exclaimed. "This is *just* what it's all about! There's never any money, there's never enough resources, but every once in a while, this service, this slaving away really pays off!" Her eyes were shining with a thrill I hadn't seen in her before.

I cocked my head. "Service?"

"You know, Emma, I'm sure you do." Sasha poked me in the arm playfully. "It's like religious orders, isn't it? It must be the same for you? Oh, I sound like a nut!"

I shook my head. "No, you're right, you just use a different word. I think of it as vocation, but it really is the same thing."

She continued. "There are days when you wonder, why do these wretched, old tatters of paper run my life? It's just leftover scraps from vanished lives, right? And they seem to control your every waking thought, all of your movements, even how you breathe, sometimes, with the fragile stuff. Your whole life. But then something comes along, a clue or sometimes even the solution to a puzzle, and it sets you on fire!"

I looked at Sasha, never realizing that kind of passion was hidden inside her. It's just a fluke, a flaw, maybe a wish of this society that trains us to believe that the pretty people must also be shallow. "The next thing we have to do is try to locate other volumes of the diary, if they exist. What's the first step?" Then I caught myself. "I'm sorry, I'm acting like you're just here to help me."

But I needn't have worried. Sasha turned a blinding smile on me. "Oh, don't be silly. That's exactly why I'm here. And this is one of the good days! Aside from poor Dr. Miner, that is—but, you know, he just wasn't doing too well, was he? His drinking and all. It was bound to catch up with him, wasn't it?"

As per Detective Kobrinski's request, Jack's death was being treated as an accident. I still thought Sasha was taking it remarkably casually.

She continued, nearly prattling. "And these things always happen in threes, don't they?"

I must have shown a little surprise, because she backtracked hastily. "I'm sorry, that's really more with movie stars, isn't it? Famous people seem to die in batches of three. I guess it's taking a while to hit me, that's all. Look, I'll run to check whether the mail's come in, then we can start checking out other possible repositories for the other volumes, if they've survived. You have a look at that code!" She did a little bob, dancing, trying to restrain her excitement. "So exciting!" she practically squealed and left me alone in the room.

I looked at the diary again, although I had looked at it a thousand times already, trying to find some clue as to the code. I looked at the first line of the code that was present and tried a simple substitution, 1 for A, et cetera. When that didn't work, I reversed the alphabet instead, but that made an even worse mess than before.

Then I thought about trying the old method of working backward from the small words, *the*, *it*, or *to*, that might give enough of the letters to the big words to start sorting them out by the context and arrangement of the letters. No luck there either; the spacing between numbers was just too even.

And with that, I'd exhausted my entire repertoire of code-cracking knowledge. I'd have to call Brian; he was the one obsessed with crosswords and puzzles of that ilk. Hell, he made a living trying to convert the code of natural drugs into synthetic ones, he was bound to have an idea.

"We're in luck!" Sasha returned with a large Federal Express box in her hands. "Oops, we'll want the biographical dictionary as well, won't we? I'm sorry." She laughed. "I'm not really co-opting your project, I'm so excited I just can't help myself!"

With an ease that I would have thought impossible, she took the Fed Ex box in one hand, and reached over her head to single-handedly grab the dictionary off the shelf. Both items were about the same size, nearly a foot square and four inches across the spine.

I watched the tendons stand out in Sasha's wrist and fingers as she carried the books over to me. "Whoa, look at you! Those must weigh a ton!"

Sasha looked up, surprised, then realized what I was talking about. "Oh, these. You get used to it, things go faster if you don't have to use two hands on every single book—but we always use two hands on the rare stuff, of course! You should have seen me the first week, though—I was a mess. But now I can reach nearly an octave on the piano and I can whip my little brother arm-wrestling whenever I go home to visit." She swung both massive tomes down in front of me with easy grace.

I picked up the Fed Ex box; it weighed five pounds, easy.

"All it takes is practice," she insisted. "By the way, when are you planning to do your talk?"

I stopped breaking into the box long enough to look at her. "Talk?"

"You know. All of the Fellows are supposed to do a presentation while they're here. Nothing big, but we invite the members of the Library and staff to come hear. I have to print up the notices and I thought, some time the beginning of next week?"

I'd completely forgotten about this obligation and didn't spare any thought to it now. I just wanted to find the record of Margaret Chandler's trial. "Fine, whenever you like."

"You got a title in mind?"

I didn't, but I came up with one quickly to get back to the transcript. "Yeah. How about, 'At the Intersection of Emotional Reality and Historical Fact: The Chandler Family, Public Records, and Private Lives?' "

When Sasha made an ill-concealed face of alarm, I hastily amended, "No, that's a bit much, isn't it? Not bad for a conference paper, though. How about we chop it after the colon and add archaeology: 'Historical Archaeology and the Chandler Family: Public Records and Private Lives.' "

She looked vastly relieved by that suggestion, but a voice came from behind me. "Still sounds a bit of a drag, Emma. Don't you know the rule? You gotta have sex or death in the title to be a real draw."

Sasha giggled and straightened her skirt.

I just rolled my eyes and turned to him. "Morning, Michael. My, where'd you ever get that fine-looking mouse?"

I should have known it wouldn't have fazed him. "Got it wrestling with my conscience, Auntie. Tell her, Sasha, you never go wrong looking for sex or death in anything."

"He's right, Dr. Fielding—"

Suddenly I was Dr. Fielding again, and not Emma as I had been all morning. Michael Glasscock hadn't been married four times already for no reason.

"—we got one of our biggest audiences ever for Dr. Glasscock's presentation."

"Okay, now I have to ask. What was the title of *your* paper, Mikey?"

Michael couldn't have looked more pleased with himself.
" 'The Erotic Tension Beneath Transcendentalist Philosophy: Work, Sex, and Thought in Utopian Communities.' It
was nothing, really. Dumbed it down a bit, but kept all the
juice."

I snorted. "Nothing, indeed! How'd you pull that one
off?"

"Simple." He smirked. "I took a lesson from my Lit Crit
colleagues and veered slightly from the history of philosophy to the venerable topic of who slept with whom in the
American Transcendentalist movement. Never fails. Of
course, afterwards I felt like a two-dollar whore who makes
change, but that's life in the Ivory Cat House, isn't it,
Emma? A long, downward spiral of cheapening compromise
in the name of survival."

Sasha giggled again, but there didn't seem to be anything
humorous in either Michael's face or words, though his tone
was careless as usual. I thought about Harry's words, "an
alien detachment," and found them appropriate.

"I think I'll stick with my title," I said. "Usually 'archaeology' is enough to get people interested."

Michael slunk over to a carrel, flopped into a chair, and
for all intents and purposes, promptly went to sleep. I
opened the book hurriedly, a copy of the original handwritten text, and flipped to the date of the trial, and read it with
growing disappointment. All there was, was a brief entry
saying that the records were sealed, written out in a cramped
clerk's hand. I tried not to look as heartbroken as I felt as I
explained what I'd found to Sasha.

She took it more philosophically than I and headed back
to her desk. "That's the way of it, isn't it? Some days you hit
the mother lode, most days you pan out. Not your fault,
right? There's a copy of Blackstone's *Commentaries* on the
top shelf of the reference section, over by the door, if you
think that will help." She jerked her head toward a big

wooden bookcase just opposite the door and went to the back to sort through the rest of the mail. "Though it was published a little later than this trial, it may help explain some of the terms," she called.

I sighed and dragged one of the antique wooden stepladders over to the shelf she indicated and climbed up to the top. Out of the corner of my eye, I could just make out a quick movement as I stretched to get the large black volume. I was so engrossed in trying to balance on top of the steps and flipping to the entry for "murder" that I didn't realize someone had grabbed my shirt and yanked sharply backward until it was too late. I had already started to fall off the steps.

Chapter 13

"EMMA!" IT TOOK ME A SECOND TO RECOGNIZE Sasha's voice.

I opened my eyes and found myself on the floor of the library. Sasha and Michael were staring at me, a halo of books and overhead lights behind them both.

"Oh, man. I fell, I guess. Knocked me silly."

"You must have overbalanced," Sasha said. "Oh, don't!" she cried, reaching out for me as I tried to sit up. "Your head!"

"I'm fine," I said, but it wasn't until she said that that I noticed a sharp pain right at the back of my skull. I touched it gingerly and felt a lump. Looking at my hand, I was relieved to see no blood, and I pulled myself up the rest of the way, leaning against a carrel.

"You okay?" Michael was strangely unsure of what to do with himself and kept twisting the tail of his overcoat. "You want some ice or something?"

"Uh, yeah. Thanks."

"There's an ice pack in the guard's office," Sasha suggested. Michael all but ran out of the room.

I tentatively felt for the bump again.

"I heard you yell and found you on the floor," Sasha said. "I couldn't figure out what you were doing." She flinched, watching me explore my scalp. "Take it slow now."

Michael returned shortly with the ice pack. "Sorry, they didn't have any Tater Bites." His nervousness was almost palpable.

I took the pack and applied it, wincing as the cold hit the hot lump. Then I noticed the copy of Blackwell's *Commentaries* on the floor next to me, the heavy cover splayed open and the pages folded underneath the weight of the book. Its violent sprawl brought the memory back with a rush.

"I didn't fall. I was pulled." Amazement crossed their faces. "Somebody pulled me backwards!" I looked at both of them. "And *neither* of you saw anything?"

"Emma, you couldn't have been pulled," Sasha protested. "There was no one here but us. Are you *sure* that's what happened? Maybe you got caught on something or missed a step. Your head hit the carrel there."

"No, I definitely felt . . . I saw a movement behind me, out of the corner of my eye, and then felt myself being pulled backwards. I'm sure about that. Michael?"

He shook his head slowly, looking to Sasha for confirmation. "I was almost asleep—I've had a couple of late nights in a row. I didn't see or hear anything until Sasha shouted. She was already beside you by the time I woke up enough to figure out what was going on." He backed away and leaned against the bookshelves, watching us, troubled.

I scanned both their faces but couldn't see anything but confusion and concern. It didn't reassure me in the least: I knew what I knew. What bothered me was that I was actually starting to suspect both of them.

"Would you like a glass of—?"

Sasha's offer was interrupted by the blare of the alarm and the piercing wail went straight through my already fragile head. "Oh, damn it all! I thought they finally found the problem with that thing! Let's go everyone." She began to go through the evacuation procedure and went to check on the rest of the floor.

Surprised by the sudden noise, Michael said something much less innocuous than "damn," then gave me a hand up. "It's definitely a bad time to be a Shrewsbury Fellow. This time two days ago, there were three of us alive. Now even the two of us are looking a lot worse than we did last night."

I winced as he yanked me up, but was made more uncomfortable by the reminder of my violence toward him the night before. "Michael, I'm sorry about—"

"Pish," he said airily, "I've always wanted to start a rumor. I've originated three different stories about how I got hurt, and I'm dying to follow the paths of each one."

"I honestly don't go around popping people in the eye—" I insisted he listen to my apology. "I'm sure it's just the stress—" I again debated whether to tell him about my sessions with Nolan; maybe it would assuage his ego. Maybe it would warn him against thinking I was an easy target. Just in case.

"At least I know why I got hurt and that it was an accident," he broke in impatiently, and suddenly my window of opportunity had slammed shut. "Unlike some around here."

We moved outside, standing under the pines with the rest of the staff. There wasn't even the usual joking about missing the math test, the alarm problem wasn't funny anymore. Nothing was funny at all.

Michael made the most of the opportunity and lit up a cigarette immediately. "Ahhhh. God, that's good." He took a long drag, his eyes glazed over with pleasure, then blinked, coming back to the real world: the respite was temporary. "So that was a hell of a racket you made this morning. Got a couple Sumo wrestlers in your room?"

When I didn't answer he said, "I moved my desk in front

of my door, too. It's probably a good idea under the circumstances."

"The lock is broken, and I just didn't want to disturb you again. In case I decided to take another midnight walk."

"Ah. Very considerate," Michael said tonelessly.

I could tell his attention was not on our conversation. He was watching Sasha intently.

"You know," he continued, "the first thing I saw when I woke up was Sasha leaning over you." He lit a second cigarette from the first, then pinched out the old cigarette just above the glowing ember with a quick thumb and forefinger, flicking the butt away. "Just saying it sounds crazy, like an implication, but it's the truth. In fact, I'm starting to scare myself, thinking about what's been going on around here. But Sasha?" He shuffled uncertainly as he watched her across the road.

"I don't know what to think," I said, and it was the truth. "Sasha doesn't really radiate the sense of being that cold-blooded, if you know what I mean. She'd have to be awful bold to try something like that in front of you, or me, for that matter. And why would she do it at all?"

I didn't realize how long I'd paused in thought. Michael said, "Well, I didn't do it. I believe you when you say you were pulled, but Sasha was the only person I saw near you. After the fact, admittedly." He was still watching Sasha as she spoke with one of the interns.

I couldn't stand to think too closely about what he was suggesting, even though I knew I ought to. I flipped the ice pack, putting the cooler side on my lump. "All I know is that if this bump gets any larger, I'm going to have to give it a name."

"You know, I think you ought to be more worried than you are!" he said in exasperation. "If there's a connection between Faith's death and Jack's, then you could be next. You were the last one to see Faith *and* Jack and according to

our lovely detective, he left you a note saying he knew something. If I were you, I'd consider getting out of here, pronto,
diary or not."

Before I could think of an answer, Michael's expression
suddenly dulled as Harry joined us. "Harry, you've got to
help me out here."

Although he was still dressed with impeccable care,
Harry had dark lines under his eyes and a careworn look on
his face. "How's that, Michael?" he asked obligingly. But his
quick smile vanished when he saw my ice pack. "Emma,
what's wrong?"

"She fell," Michael said brusquely. "I've been having no
luck locating the papers I need. Could you give Sasha a hand
looking for them?"

His patience obviously strained, lips compressed, Harry
said, "I'll look into it right away, Michael."

Michael watched everyone filing back, then turned to me.
"Think about what I said," he said emphatically, then walked
back toward the library.

Harry stared, puzzled, after him.

"What was that? Michael seems somewhat . . . preoccupied."

"He thinks I should leave." I flipped the ice pack again,
but realized that all the cold had gone out of it. "He thinks
it's dangerous here."

"We'd be happy to let you come back, finish up another
time," he started, reluctantly. "You know, that might even be
best, everything is very disorganized at present and heaven
knows, there's a lot going on around here just now."

"Thanks Harry," I said absently, watching Michael out
front through the window. He jumped up and pulled at an
oak branch, shaking melted ice onto a couple of young interns, who giggled playfully. "I think I need to work on
Madam Chandler's code, though, and I need the original
copy of the journal for that, I think. I can't just leave it. It's

not just the story, it's not just the work that is going to help me when I go back to work on the site, it's as though if I stick with it long enough, it's going to help me make a connection that's going to give me some fundamental understanding of how I work. How I think . . ." I shrugged.

Harry stared at me quizzically, and I knew I'd lost him.

"Well, that's just what I tell people," I joked. "It's really just because this way I get to read diaries and no one will call me nosy."

"It's a powerful fascination that these little bits of paper, leather, and thread hold for us," Harry said. "Literally captivating."

The man was such a diplomat, I thought. "It really is. Sasha called it service"—at the mention of her name, I saw Harry's face light up—"I call it a vocation. Funny how we all look at it in those terms."

"It's a sickness, isn't it?" Harry asked, laughing. "Sasha and I, well, we're lucky to be able to work with the things we do. But you won't believe the lengths to which some people will go. People have been murdered over rare books, overgenerous donors have committed suicide after realizing they couldn't bear separation from their collections. Some collectors, faced with starvation, were recorded as spending their last penny on a rare book instead of food. There's no end to the stories of extreme bibliomania."

"Come on," I said, disbelieving.

"I'm serious. A former monk in nineteenth-century Spain was thwarted in his attempt to acquire a rare book; shortly thereafter, his successful competitor was found dead in his burnt-out book shop. This happened a few times, and when the ex-monk was finally arrested for the murders, he was more distraught that a book he had stolen was not unique than the fact that he was going to be executed."

"You're joking, right?" I asked. "That's, like, an extraordinary example, right?"

"Oh no. Far from it. What about Petrarch? He devoted his life to rescuing the lost classics and wrote letters to the authors whose works he'd recovered, even though they'd been dead for hundreds of years," Harry said. "And the librarian of Cosimo III—no one knows his name—eschewed a private apartment, choosing rather to sleep in a hammock slung between bookcases in the great library over which he presided in the seventeenth century. He lived 'on titles and indexes, and whose very pillow was a folio,' and died looking like a beggar in spite of his high status, but left his own thirty thousand books to the people of Florence."

"No one's that nutty," I muttered. "I love books just as much as the next person, but—"

"Of course," Harry said. "*We* manage to keep our loves in check. But the market for rare and antique books is thriving. Did you get a look at the catalog for the Armstrong collection?"

My mind flew back to my first day, and the conversation between Michael and Harry. "No. Never got the chance."

"Everyone knew the bidding would be hot, but no one expected that the sale would bring in the millions it did. One copy of Champlain's *Voyages* went for close to $400,000."

I let out a low whistle. "I wouldn't mind owning that one myself."

Harry laughed. "Well, I can't get the book for you, but we've got a copy of that catalog around here somewhere. I'll get Sasha to track it down for you. And if you think that's something, the black market is even more busy these days. You read about it constantly and it gets worse and worse. Just last month, two valuable nineteenth-century manuscripts were stolen from the rare book room at Van Helst Library. You should ask Michael, he was down there in Philly at the time. I bet he'd know more of the story."

"Michael's seen a lot of excitement lately." A split second later I thought more closely about what I had just said.

"I suppose we all have," Harry said tactfully. "Lately. Just Michael's bad luck that he's been in the wrong places at the wrong times."

Suddenly a deafening rumble started.

"You'll have to excuse me," Harry shouted over the din, and I followed him over to where the workers were finishing one section of the foundation repointing and starting to open another with a ditch witch, one of those small machines used to excavate narrow ditches. All around were scattered the tools of their trade, including trowels, crowbars, and a dirty wheelbarrow filled with water for the cement. Over the noise, I heard the end of a hollered-out, extremely bawdy joke, and immediately thought of the gravediggers from Hamlet.

I saw one of the men in work clothes say something as they noticed us. The other one stood up and brushed off his hands, and put on a cap marked "Martini Brothers, Contractors," preparatory to doing business. With a signal from him, the other man turned off the machine and the sudden silence overwhelmed us.

He started with his hands in the air in a gesture of forestallment before we could say a word. "Look, before you start again, Mr. Saunders," came a voice that would have been well at home in the Bronx. "I keep telling you, it's not us. It's your electrician or your alarm service. *We* are not tripping your alarm." Apparently this was Frankie Martini himself, if the embroidery on his shirt pocket was any indication.

"Isn't it at least *possible* that your work is disrupting things?" Harry asked, obviously frustrated. "None of this started until you started."

"Just our bad luck," muttered Martini brother number two. His shirt was embroidered JOEY M.

"It does not have anything to do with us," said Frankie firmly. He turned to me and explained courteously. "See, when you've been using one of these things as long as I have, you can feel everything. Rocks, roots. You know what you're hitting. And something like the PVC pipe that those new alarm systems go through, it vibrates different. We'd never in a million years cut through one of those."

I peered over into the narrow trench to have a look at the soil out of habit, looking for artifacts that might have been churned up. Frankie Martini nudged Joey Martini.

"Looks like you got a girlfriend over there, brother. Takin' an interest in your work."

I caught myself—not everyone feels compelled to investigate every hole in the ground they encounter. This was just another old habit, like analyzing the assemblages in my neighbors' recycling bins. "No, sorry. I'm just looking to see if there's anything interesting in there; I'm an archaeologist."

"Oh, yeah?" The Martini Brothers exchanged the patented half nod, curled lip, and raised eyebrows that denote discovery of the unusual.

"Archaeologist, huh?" Joey said. "I bet you could tell me where to find some good arrowheads around here? I like to dig them up with my kid."

"Well, you know," I started wearily, "you're really not supposed to do that . . ."

Joey Martini looked offended. "Why not? My kid loves them, got a whole roomful of them. We go looking every weekend in the summer. I'm a good father," he added irrelevantly.

I thought about trying to explain about context and preservation laws and realized that this guy wasn't going to stop no matter what I said. "Sure you are, but you'll put me out of a job."

"Oh, I get it. Better not tell you what I found last week, then?" Nudges and guffaws followed. "Not for nothin'. *That* was a beauty."

Harry stared at us impatiently, then turned to Frankie. "Perhaps you could just take it a little easier, guys?"

"Oh, sure, whatever you say, Mr. Saunders. I'm just saying. But for you, we'll be extra careful." The reply wasn't convincing; Frankie Martini went back to adding more water from a bucket into the cement bin. He reached over and hit a switch, the racket from the ditch digger conveniently obliterating whatever caustic comment brother Joey might have made under his breath.

We walked away and Harry just shook his head.

"You know, they're right, Harry," I said when we were well out of earshot.

He looked at me.

"It's got to be either the electrical or the alarm system itself. It shouldn't be so sensitive, certainly if they're not actually cutting through it."

All at once, the weight of his work was apparent on his face: Harry looked frazzled, overworked, and underpaid. "I'm not being an ogre, Emma, I just want those guys to be careful, that's all. It's an expensive system and we're trying to expand it. And I can't afford these problems right now, not with everything Whitlow is dumping on us. None of us can. His new plans—"

"I know, Harry, but I've done some work with alarms before and what they're doing shouldn't bother it."

He stopped strolling. "What do you know about alarms?"

"Oh, not so much about the theory behind them," I said, "but I've done some contract work with alarm companies, watching out that the installation doesn't disturb any important archaeological sites, that sort of thing. Those systems are smart. They don't go off for no reason. And those guys who do the actual excavation, they really get a feel for what's in the ground. They may not be able to keep their pants buckled up around their waists or their shirts tucked in, but I've known some who can tell when they're hitting waterlogged wood or even a piece of bone with a backhoe. If they work with archaeologists long enough on these projects, they get to be real artists."

Harry looked at me thoughtfully. "Well, that's helpful. I'm not really the one in charge of this, Constantino is, of course, but I'll ask him to check with the alarm company again, see if they should try testing something else."

"Yeah, it's probably a good idea," I agreed. "It may not be what you think." I made a move to reenter the library but Harry stopped me, led us away from the door again.

"Emma, I need to tell you something." He looked very troubled.

"What's that, Harry? Oh, not something about the letters!" I told him about my situation with the abrupt ending of the diary.

"No, it's not about them, but it is about a letter. Mr. Whitlow received a letter today and he's very troubled about it." He paused significantly, waiting for me to catch on.

I shook my head. "And?"

"It was a letter from your husband, complaining about a problem with Mr. Constantino. It was disturbing to think that such a thing could . . ." he trailed off delicately.

It all came back to me now. Brian had written the letter and overnighted it. When he decided to act, he acted fast. "Good, it should be disturbing! Constantino's behavior was offensive, and it shouldn't be tolerated."

"I agree," he said quickly, "but that's not what he's concerned about. He views you as a troublemaker now, after your other complaints."

"*What* other complaints?" I didn't think of myself as being high maintenance. In fact, I rather prided myself on being a trouper, when you got right down to it.

"About Gary Conner, for starters, and your behavior over Dr. Morgan's death. They see you as a problem. Not that I agree, and I've been arguing on your behalf. But I just wanted to let you know, you've put a cat among the pigeons."

"Yeah, well, if they think I'm a problem now, wait until they, what I look like when I'm trying to be a pain," I said, but then I turned serious. "Honestly, though, everything that Brian wrote or I said was true."

Harry shrugged helplessly. "They see it as you being overly sensitive to necessary security procedures. Perhaps it's not such a bad idea to leave things—just for now, I mean—and let things cool down a bit."

"Look, if they're disturbed by the truth, then there's never going to be a good time for me here," I said, scratching the back of my neck; I touched the bump by accident and flinched. I sighed; none of this was Harry's fault. "Shall I have a talk with them, do you think that would help?"

"No, I shouldn't," he replied. "Let's not fan the flames. Director Whitlow isn't favorably disposed to explanation, so it's probably better not to bring it up at all. I just wanted to let you know." He adjusted his tie imperceptibly, looking tired. "I've got to get back and try to find those manuscripts."

I watched him walk back inside.

Maybe I was the only one who believed me, but I knew that I hadn't just fallen off the stepladder. I had been pulled, and hard—it was no accident. Maybe I was wrong imagining that everything going on was connected with Faith's death—I still didn't know what *that* was connected to. But Harry's comments raised another disturbing idea: Was it possible that Constantino had pulled me off the stool, either in retribution or to scare me off?

My gaze traveled over to where the two workmen were repairing the foundation. They didn't seem put out by my distressing morning, I thought ruefully, then immediately re-membered the line from Hamlet, "the hand of little employ-ment hath the daintier sense." They were just doing their work, they didn't need to embroil themselves in the mess at Shrewsbury. But by that logic, I did, I thought. And I realized that it was time for more than just sticking it out and offering my observations to Detective Kobrinski; I had to start look-ing around in earnest. She was right, she just didn't have the access necessary to make any sense of what might be going on here. I was at the heart of things and I thought, as she was so fond of saying, "Let's start at the beginning."

It wasn't such an outrageous idea, once I'd actually thought it. But it did mean that I'd have to start thinking obliquely, because I wasn't getting anywhere, just going over and over how Faith and Jack had died. I had to find out why. It was time for a bit of discreet prying.

But discretion wasn't necessary. The means of observation presented themselves almost immediately on my return to the library a moment later. Sasha looked as distressed as she had after the news of Faith's death, and Harry's face was drawn with concern. The door to the library was open and neither of them was lowering his voice, so I went quickly past the door, instead of through it, stayed in the hallway, and studiedly tied and retied both my shoes on the far side of the door. Looking through the doorway, I could follow their conversation.

"I haven't seen them since Dr. Glasscock had them out two weeks ago," she cried. "I know I put them back and now they're nowhere to be found!"

"Are you certain they went back to the correct spot? No one's had them since?" It was immediately clear that Harry had asked those questions many times before. Although he was pacing agitatedly back and forth, he seemed to be going down a well-rehearsed list.

"Harry! I *know* how to do my job!" Sasha nearly shouted through her tears. "They're missing! Along with all the others!"

"Sasha! Ssssh! Not so loud!" For the first time, Harry sounded worried. "This is a problem that we can solve. We just need to stay calm!"

"You keep saying that and things aren't getting solved! More things are missing, and now it's not just because they've been mislaid by Mr. Talbot! This happened since then! Is it possible that Michael took them, and just forgot? He's done it before. He could have—"

Harry pulled Sasha into an embrace. "Sssh, it's okay, we will find out what's happening, Sasha. I promise."

She mumbled something into his jacket that I didn't hear, then seemed to compose herself. "I'm sorry, it's just that so much is going wrong lately, Harry. I don't know what's happening anymore. What's happening here, what's happening with us? Lately you've been so—"

"Sshh, shhh." He stroked her head comfortingly a moment, then set her firmly away from him. "Go get some air, collect yourself. I'll start sorting this out right now." He looked at her with concern. "Okay? We can fix this. This is not a problem."

She nodded and went into her office for her coat. I took the opportunity to slip back past the library to return the soggy ice pack to the guard's office. No one was in, but I could hear a muffled but heated phone conversation being conducted in Mr. Constantino's office. I threw the ice pack into the freezer of the little refrigerator then dodged out as quickly as I could. Virtue and righteousness might be on my side, but that didn't mean that I wanted to run into Constantino this minute. I'd had enough grief for today. Actually, for a long time to come.

Glancing out the window, I saw Sasha pacing to and fro outside the library, her collar turned up and her arms wrapped around her for warmth. I decided that there was no time like the present to start asking a few innocuous questions about library procedure.

Just as I exited the library, a man rushed from behind the building and grabbed Sasha by the shoulders, jerking her around. She screamed shrilly as I ran toward them. As I neared, I realized that Sasha's assailant was now staring at *me*. We froze, locked in a moment of mutual recognition. I stopped and the man threw Sasha aside. He ran down the main road toward the front gate.

Just as he rounded the bend, I saw with relief that Pam Kobrinski's car was pulling up the hill toward us. Glancing at Sasha to make sure that she wasn't hurt, I waved my arms frantically. Detective Kobrinski pulled up, her window rolling down as she pulled to a stop.

"He attacked Sasha!" I shouted. "Brown leather jacket and a pair of jeans—you can still catch him!"

Without a word she roared past us, around the circular drive and back down the way she came, her siren wailing.

I looked down and saw Sasha was still sitting where she'd landed, hyperventilating and shivering.

"Sasha?" I helped her up and she started crying again, clinging to my arm.

"It happened so fast," she gasped. "I couldn't see his face, I don't know what he looked like, why did he—?"

I heard the mumbled blare of a P.A. system and knew that the detective had seen the fleeing man.

"Shhh, it's okay," I soothed. "I saw him. He won't get away now. I know who it was."

The librarian looked at me with amazement, wiped the tears from her face with the back of her hand, and hiccoughed. "You know who it was?"

"It was Paul Burnes, Faith's ex-husband," I said grimly. "I think we'll get some answers now."

Chapter 14

IF I'D HAVE KNOWN WHAT WAS GOING TO HAPPEN AT the police station later, I never would have taken Pam Kobrinski up on her offer. She told me that I could help evaluate Paul's state of mind, I could help tell her if I caught him in any obvious lies. And I thought that by going, it might help quiet my mind, sort out my fear and confusion about Faith and Jack's deaths. And, I admit it, there's always the excitement, that hungry little demon of pride that comes with having information that others don't and being able to reveal it. That was part of it.

We were both wrong. Worse. I was a fool for believing that I knew anything at all, and she was mistaken in telling me that I'd be quite safe behind that two-way mirror, in that building full of cops.

It was just a God-awful mess.

I drove down with Sasha—still shaky over Paul's attack—who was going to give her statement. Once we got there, Detective Kobrinski led me to a small observation room and warned me to keep quiet and to keep the lights out or I'd be visible behind the two-way mirror. The interview room wasn't really what I'd expected. I had suspected that there would be no other windows, and there was a video camera mounted on the wall opposite me, the images it recorded played in tandem on the monitor in the room with me, creating a weird sense of unreality, seeing the scene before me in two sizes. But other than that, it was just a room that was painted white, with a cheap, cafeteria-style table off to one side and a few plastic chairs near it. Hell, with that big, institutional black-rimmed clock on the wall, I could have been in my high-school guidance office, if you scattered a few college brochures around. I guess I'd been expecting something out of the Inquisition. Hoping even, truth be told.

Pam Kobrinski entered the room, and then another officer, whom she'd introduced as Officer Campbell, marched in with their prisoner. With that big beetled brow, nutcracker jaw, and shoulders a yard across, Campbell looked like a refugee from the Neander Valley, but Pam told me he was a pussycat.

Paul Burnes looked like a calf facing the mallet.

"You may as well sit down," Kobrinski said. "We've got a lot to discuss, Mr. Burnes."

It wasn't until Campbell actually placed a large hand on Paul's shoulder that he sat down, unresisting. The few times I'd met Paul back in Michigan, I hadn't liked him for his deliberate distance, a carefully cultivated, almost clinical detachment that he never let drop under any circumstance. That distance now took the form of an inward retreat. His blue eyes were devoid of emotion or even recognition, I could see that his clothing was unkempt. His hair, in a long, bristly crewcut, showed more gray in the brown than I remembered, and his face was now deeply lined. His strong features still gave him the qualities necessary for handsomeness, but something in his personality had always detracted from his looks, as far as I was concerned. Clean-shaven years ago, he now had a beard that needed a trim.

"You know you've been playing pretty rough with the ladies?" Officer Campbell asked.

Paul ignored him, sunk in his own thoughts.

"And the ad agency you've been working for is wondering where you've been," Kobrinski said thoughtfully. "You must have gotten pretty excited about something to just up and leave them all hanging like that."

So Paul wasn't teaching anymore, I thought.

There was a long pause, and then Paul mumbled something.

"You'll have to speak up, Mr. Burnes," the detective said impatiently.

"I said I had to see her."

"You had to see who?"

"My wife. Faith."

"I think you mean ex-wife, don't you?" Detective Kobrinski asked. She already knew the answer. "Faith Morgan? I don't get the impression that she had any interest in seeing you. No sir, not after what you did to her."

"I had to see her," he repeated dully.

Officer Campbell shifted his weight behind Paul, and leaned down so that his face was nearly level with Paul's. "Okay, now why don't you tell us something we don't already know. Like why you killed your ex-wife."

The effect that his statement had on Paul was like flicking a switch, the torpidity was replaced with alertness: He believed they were trying to trick him. "Killed her? What the hell are you talking about! I thought this was about trespassing or something and running into that . . . other woman?"

Campbell threw his hands up in the air. Detective Kobrinski got up.

"I find that a little hard to believe, considering your past relationship with her. I haven't gotten your file from Michigan yet, but I think we can safely say that the two of you had your ups and downs."

"Ups and downs?" The restored Paul actually smirked. "Don't make me laugh. She drove me insane. But that was our business, and no one else's."

"Oh, that's where you're wrong, buddy," the detective said. "Everybody has their problems, but not everyone tries to solve them with violence. I got a real low opinion of wife-beaters, bud. Real low." Kobrinski turned away in disgust, but Campbell was watching Burnes intently.

"Oh please. Come now." It was like magic. The confident old Paul was back, superior sarcasm and all. Suddenly I knew there was something going on here and that Detective Sergeant Kobrinski wasn't picking up on it. I caught myself just before I rapped on the glass to get Kobrinski's attention: I didn't want to reveal my presence behind the mirror. All I could do was watch and remember so that I could tell her later.

"I can read, Mr. Burnes. And even if you stole the last diary your wife kept, we know about the rest of—"

"The diary?" Paul snorted derisively. "That tissue of lies? You know, there's a very good reason my wife studies Early American fiction. She's got a real talent for creating it herself."

Pam wasn't buying any of it. "I think we have plenty of other evidence to corroborate—"

"For example?" He might have been in a seminar, setting a trap for an overconfident student.

"We have other witnesses who can describe what you did to Faith."

"Witnesses? Who?" Paul gave a short, incredulous laugh. "People she's been feeding a line to from the moment she said hello? Like I said, what was going on with us was strictly our business, no matter what she told outsiders."

I thought about the evening Faith and I had spent in the library together and how . . . *greasy* it had made me feel.

"Whatever you say, but we've got the forensic evidence—"

Paul looked at her disbelievingly. "Forensic. Wait a minute, you're, you're *serious*. Faith's dead? This isn't just . . . ? Oh, God, what have you done?" Paul seemed to be talking to himself because he certainly didn't seem really connected with what was going on in that little room.

"Spare me," Kobrinski said, bored. "It's a little late for this."

"Spare *you*?" Paul scrubbed his face with his hands, rubbing his chin as if that would help him make sense of what he was hearing. "What the hell do you know about it? I love Faith, and she loves me. And you're telling me she's *dead*."

This was getting too weird for me. I had never seen Paul in so unguarded a moment as this, and the way that he spoke about Faith in the present tense made my skin crawl.

Detective Kobrinski said, "When we get your complete record I think we'll find—"

"What record?" he insisted, then paused. "Now that's interesting. What *do* you think you're going to find?" The old Paul again, the Paul that I knew, raised his head again and stared arrogantly at the detective. I shifted uncomfortably even though I was safely unseen behind the mirror: I wouldn't have changed places with her for a million bucks.

"You know what we'll find, don't you?" she answered, inviting him to fill in the blanks.

"Let me guess. I savagely beat her until she tried to kill herself." Paul said the words in a sing-songy chant, like he was running down a very old, oft-recited list. "Or was it that I was impotent and took it out on her? Or was it the one where she couldn't conceive and my taunting her drove her to self mutilation? Or was it—"

I realized suddenly that he knew what Pam was doing and was toying with her. Again came the instinct to warn her, but I couldn't, not without revealing my presence. I just had to watch and remember.

The Detective Sergeant was shaking her head, uninterested in Paul's theatrics. "When I get those records, they'll show that you've a long history of violence toward your ex-wife—"

"The records. Right, maybe. But what if they show this?" Paul stood up suddenly and pulled his shirt out of his jeans. "Did you read about *this* in her diaries? I'd be very interested to see that particular text myself."

A six-inch scar ran jaggedly from just left of his navel across to his side. The ugly wound was closed and the stitches were out, but it was bright pink still. It hadn't been that long since he received it. I wondered at this; it had been a couple of years since they'd split, according to Faith.

Campbell shoved Paul back into his seat, but that didn't stop him from talking. "She used a pair of scissors. The doctor said that if I hadn't moved in time, I wouldn't have made it. That's when she split. I came here to see her, but—No." Paul closed his eyes and relaxed all his muscles, then shrugged off the other officer's restraining arm. He opened his eyes again, totally stony-faced but for the calculation in his eyes. "Fuck you. I want a lawyer."

"It's your right, Mr. Burnes," Kobrinski said, moving a step toward him. "And I think given your situation, it's also a very good idea." The detective glanced at her wristwatch. "Officer Campbell, will you join me outside for a moment?"

She and Campbell left the room. I could see through the open door that she was heading to join me when she was accosted by another officer. She shut the door carefully behind her.

Paul was left alone with only me to watch him, though of course he didn't know that. Quite changed from the broken creature he appeared to be when they first escorted him into the room, now that they'd left, he looked animated now, alert, and edgy. Twisting a heavy gold ring that he wore on his right hand, Paul seemed to be gauging his predicament, and I could almost see him as he mentally traced the different pathways, calculating what would happen, as if he were playing chess in his head. I'm no good at chess; any luck I've had on the board has come from knowing my opponents rather than anticipating every possible move. Paul was a master.

He began to pace back and forth in the small room, measuring off the length of the floor repeatedly and methodically. Paul was deep in thought and what his face showed wasn't panic. It wasn't fear, bravado, or anything that I would have imagined someone faced with this situation might experience. He was trying to puzzle something out, and the ramifications of that conundrum had an effect far beyond the confines of that little room. There was something else going on here, and he was the only one who knew it. Besides me.

Watching Paul, I had the sensation I was observing a dangerous animal from behind the slenderest of blinds. The sensation was heightened when he suddenly stopped and turned toward the mirror that shielded me. I held my breath. He began to approach. Not me, I reassured myself. He can't possibly see me while the light's off on my side. It's his reflection.

It was all I could do to keep from running away. At the same time, I was fascinated, dying to know what Paul would do. The tension that built up on both sides of the mirror was electric. Every hair on the back of my neck was standing up.

He seemed to be drawn by something he saw in the

mirror, and he approached it almost reverentially. He locked eyes with his own reflection, but given that he was standing in front of me, it was as though he was actually staring into mine. I didn't dare move. Paul leaned over and gently touched his forehead to the glass, slowly rocking from one side to another, still maintaining eye contact with his reflection.

He reached over finally and gently brushed the glass with the back of his fingers, as if he were caressing the cheek of someone he saw there. Beyond the mirror. He rested his palm against the glass as I stared right into his unseeing eyes.

"Oh, baby," he whispered. "Where have you taken us now?"

I shivered as my own private horror movie played, forcing me to watch things I found grotesque and inexplicable. Reality as I knew it was distorted, turning inside out and parading itself before, daring me to pick out the truth. I was trapped in a web of voyeuristic intimacy. This was too private to bear and too hypnotic to flee.

The spell was broken abruptly when the door opened behind Paul and he hastily composed himself as Officer Campbell entered the room.

Then I turned and ran out of the observation room, Alice escaping from Looking Glass Land, where everything was recognizable but too sinister to be familiar. I almost ran smack into Detective Kobrinski, who was coming to fetch me.

She shook her head. "Something else, huh?"

"Ladies' room. Where?" I managed to gasp out.

"Down the hall, second door on the left," she answered, stepping back out of my way.

* * *

The door opened as I was reaching for the coarse brown paper towels on the sink. Detective Kobrinski came in and shut the door, leaning back against it quietly while I dried my hands and face. After a moment, she said, "You sick?"

"No." I looked into my bag, to avoid looking in yet another mirror, and found a comb I didn't even know I had. I combed out my hair by feel, even if it didn't really need it.

Pam looked quietly triumphant, convinced she had the right guy. I was no longer so sure, in spite of the weird confidence Paul had unknowingly just shared with me.

"Quite a case, huh? That guy is about as cold as they come."

"Sounds like the Paul I knew," I said, putting my comb away. I turned to her. "But after you left . . ." I told the detective what I'd seen. "It was downright eerie," I concluded.

She took it in and nodded once or twice. "You know, I wouldn't trust that guy as far as I could spit him," she said thoughtfully. "Guys like that honestly don't realize that they're doing anything wrong, and that gives their words the ring of truth. As far as they believe, they didn't do anything and can't understand what all the trouble is about."

"This was eerie," I repeated. I didn't yet have the words to explain what convinced me that she was on the wrong track.

"I wonder," the detective mused. "Everyone knows that those mirrors are two-way. It was probably just a little performance for whoever was back there. You told me what he was like. And I'll be able to review it on the videotape, too."

I shivered. "I don't know. I know I might have said I remembered that he had been calculating, but I don't think anyone is that good a liar. Something was going on there, something that we don't entirely understand yet."

Kobrinski waved my doubts aside. "In any case, it will all be cleared up when I speak to the folks in Michigan. Look, Ms. Russo will be done with her statement in a minute, and the two of you can get back to Shrewsbury." She put her hand on my arm and looked genuinely touched for the first time, not evasive, not sarcastic. "Emma. You've done really well with this. It's been a big help. Thank you."

I wasn't convinced I'd done anything at all, so I just nodded and sat down where she told me to wait. I was aching from my fall, and I wanted to get out of there. I wanted to stop thinking about what I saw, but that wasn't going to happen. A subdued scuffling in the hallway caught my attention and when I saw it was Paul, I found myself automatically shrinking back, trying to press myself into the wall. He walked by unresisting, led by Officer Campbell, but he started to balk when he recognized me for the second time that day.

"You!" he called, as if searching to place me. "I remember you! You tell me! Is Faith really dead? I'll believe *you*."

It was no compliment that Paul should believe me. The implication of course was that I was too stupid or unimaginative to lie.

I really didn't want to answer him, but Officer Campbell stopped, obviously wanting to watch Paul's reaction.

"Faith's dead." Then the absolute burning need in Paul's eyes drove me to say more than I meant to. "I found her."

He looked stunned, the way he did when I first saw him in the interview room, until Campbell said, "C'mon, you," and yanked his arm brusquely. When he looked back at me, Paul's eyes were dull and dead again.

Sasha emerged hesitantly as soon as Paul was gone. "I wasn't coming out while *he* was here." She was still pale, her eyes red and puffy. "Are you okay? You look kind of green. Is your head bothering you?"

I sighed. "It's been a rough day, Sasha. How about you?"

She shrugged and smiled wanly. "I'm okay. It all happened so fast. That's all."

When we reached my parked car, I paused to fish out my keys.

Sasha blurted out, "I didn't press charges."

That surprised me. "Oh?"

She fiddled with her hair, trying repeatedly to get one short strand to stay behind her ear. "I mean, I don't think it was really *assault* or anything—"

I was unable to quash an impatient impulse to explain the niceties of the law as I had learned it first hand. "Yes, it *was*—"

"—and besides, they've got bigger things than me to worry about with him. I just came along to tell the detective sergeant my side of what happened. What I knew."

We got into the car. I wanted to know, too. "Did Paul say anything to you? Anything at all?"

Sasha paused before she said, "It was creepy. When he grabbed me he said, 'You promised.' That's all. Then he got a good look at me and seemed really surprised. Then he saw you and ran."

"Yeah, he recognized me, but I don't think he remembered who I was right away." After a couple of tries, I got old Bessy to turn over and catch. I pulled out of the parking lot, and headed us back toward Shrewsbury. "What did he mean, 'you promised'?" I said almost to myself.

The librarian shrugged. "How should I know? I never saw him before. That's all he said."

"He was after Faith, I bet," I said. "Must have been. I mean, your collar was up, you and she have a similar build, close to the same hair color . . ."

We drove along in silence until I noticed that Sasha was weeping again. "Hey! Hey, what is it, Sasha?" I pulled over onto the side of the road, just shy of the Shrewsbury gates.

The sound of the tires was muffled by the fallen pine needles on the gravel.

Sasha covered her face with her hand and leaned against the window, unable to stop. I cast about for a Kleenex, but the last of my stock of fast-food napkins had been used to wipe off the windows days ago. I settled for patting her arm, and she startled me by grabbing onto my hand and holding on desperately. She pulled out a handkerchief of her own and wiped her face but couldn't seem to stop crying. It took about five minutes before she calmed down, then let my hand go. I was glad, not only because I hoped she would tell me what had been troubling her, but also because I had been leaning against the shift, and my leg was going to sleep.

Her first words chilled me. "It wasn't supposed to be like this." It was almost like an echo of the beginning of Faith's story.

I waited what seemed like an eternity before she took a deep breath and continued. I couldn't seem to get one myself, half of me dying to hear, half of me wishing that she'd reconsider and clam up.

"Everything was supposed to be so much better, you know, once I got this job, moved up here. But now it seems like everything just gets more and more confused and stressful, and—" She sighed. "I don't know. Even on top of everything else that's going on. The libraries going through a really big shake-up. There will probably be cuts."

"What's been stressful, Sasha?" I knew I had to tread carefully here: I thought that "everything else" probably meant the deaths, but I didn't know for sure. The part of me that wanted to hear won out, but I don't think it was entirely a matter of moral fortitude or compassion. Call it professional curiosity, the lure of an impromptu interview that insinuates you into the middle of something. You could also call it a part of my avocational interests.

She leaned back against the black vinyl headrest and closed her eyes to collect herself. "The books, the manuscripts we can't find. I'm just so afraid I'll be blamed for it, since I was the most recent hire. Harry thinks that it was the former head librarian, Mr. Talbot, but even he seems unsure about that lately, and of course, he's got even more to lose than I do, so I can't blame him for being cautious about it. I mean, Director Whitlow and Mr. Talbot were—are—great friends, and if there are jobs on the line, no one wants to stick out too much. But I don't think they were deaccessioned, I don't think they were misplaced. I think . . . I think someone's, right now, stealing them."

I sat, amazed. "Who?"

"I don't know," she answered wearily. "Someone with access, someone who knows how our security system works. Someone who knows how much these things are worth." Sasha suddenly giggled, then opened her eyes. "Of course, we spend an *awful* lot of money on brochures telling everyone just how rare and valuable our collections are, then we invite total strangers to come in and see things for themselves." There was an uncharacteristically bitter note in her voice.

"Come on," I protested. I knew she was right to some extent, but she touched a nerve in me. "You do security checks, you keep track of everything that gets examined. Unless you want to keep the materials locked up and never allow them to see the light of day, there's always going to be some risk. Otherwise, you should just call yourself a storage facility and not a research library."

This was the eternal conflict between scholars and the people who had the works they needed to study. What good was it to preserve these things if no one got any use from them? What good would they be if they were lost or destroyed?

"You're right, you're right," she answered, less sad now and more angry. "I'm just tired, I'm scared—people have been dying around here! That's not supposed to *happen*, and it *keeps* happening! Can we go?" she asked impatiently. "I've got to get back. I've got work to do."

"We're going." I started the car up again, and pulled onto the road. A brief skid on the sandy verge was the only betrayal of my annoyance with her moodiness. My head ached. I'd been assaulted, disbelieved, then had that followed by an episode straight out of a bad dream, and no one seemed to care. Sasha didn't even recognize that I'd actually come to her rescue.

The icing on the cake came when I drew up to the guardhouse at the entrance, and one of the older guards told me that Mr. Constantino wanted to see me right away.

"Any idea why?" I asked.

"I couldn't tell you," he said. His nervous tone suggested he could and wasn't going to.

"I'll stop by presently," I said. "I've got a few things to take care of." What I really needed was a little time alone to pull myself together. I turned to Sasha as we neared the library annex. "I'm going to drop you off here, okay? I'll be back in a bit."

"Great. Fine." She shut the passenger side door with such force that it shook my poor little car. "See you later."

"Not if I see you first," I mumbled under my breath. "Thanks for the ride, Emma. Thanks for listening, Emma, you're so sympathetic. You were right there, when I couldn't even turn to my boyfriend. Oh, no problem, Sash, happy to do it." I didn't bother watching her walk away, I didn't care if she was okay. Well, I did, really; I was just willing to take the dose of guilt later on for being angry with her now. I don't know why I should have felt guilty, I hadn't done anything to justify it. But that never seemed to matter.

* * *

Once I got to my room, I wondered what to do. I knew I should get back to the library to wait on the letters or work on transcribing more of the encoded parts of Madam Chandler's diary, but I didn't want to. Not yet. I continued to change into a pair of clean jeans and one of Brian's flannel shirts, for no better reason than I wanted to shed my skin, put the scene at the police station behind me, and maybe in doing so, take a little comfort in the order of the universe.

Calling Brian, I was chagrined to find that he was not in his office, and I took it out on his voice mail. "Hi, it's me. Paul Burnes, Faith's ex, was just arrested. So you can relax. Stop worrying about me. I'm fine. Everything's fine. Call me tonight. I love you. Bye."

A glance at the clock in the hall told me that even if I didn't want to get any more work done, I was going to have to move it if I was going to rescue my computer and notes from the library before the reading room closed for the evening. Everything was still in a panic, even though there was a chance now that the mystery was solved, I thought.

But it wasn't all solved, I remembered with a frown as I drove down to the library annex. I still needed to find out whether Jack's death was an accident. And now Sasha admitted that books were going missing as well.

As I locked up Bessy, I suddenly realized there was an undue amount of noise and bustle that I couldn't attribute to the ongoing repair work—the Martini brothers usually knocked off around three. I got close enough to see a couple of police cruisers, radios squawking, and the sirens now off, but lights were still whirling, parked in front of the library.

Then I watched as Pam Kobrinski was leading Michael Glasscock out the front doors.

Drawing closer, I realized that she wasn't leading him,

but that he was talking and she was taking notes. I had just reached them when the real center of excitement emerged beside us. Two very burly officers, who might have been clones of Officer Campbell, were having a hard time holding onto their prisoner, who was screaming at the top of his lungs and thrashing violently against them.

"—bullshit! Fucking bullshit! It's a fucking setup! I didn't—"

I didn't immediately recognize Gary Conner in his civilian clothes, but he stopped dead in his tracks when he saw me. That lasted only a split second before he hurled himself toward me, and if the two policemen hadn't kept their grip, he would have made it. The fact that he was handcuffed didn't seem to make any difference at all, and he nearly dragged them along with him.

"This is your goddamned fault!"

I stepped back involuntarily against the force of his accusation.

The cops dragged him along toward one of the cruisers, and Gary managed to get his feet up against the side of the car, preventing them from stuffing him into the back seat. They struggled a while longer, and he twisted around just long enough to spit venomously at me.

"You watch yourself, cunt!" he screamed. "I'll be back for you!"

Stunned, I stared at the spit as it soaked into the pine needles by my feet, trying to make sense of all this. I was glad for the number of cops that was there, and wished for a few dozen more.

The door to the cruiser was finally slammed shut. Gary, now incarcerated in the back, had swung around on the seat and began kicking a rear window with both feet. After a few warnings, the two cops got in the front of the car and started the engine.

I could still hear the dull thumps as Gary hurled himself

at the windows and doors. It must hurt, I thought. It must hurt him to do that. Good. And still, he persisted. What the hell had happened? What did he think was my fault?

Pam Kobrinski was saying something, but I didn't comprehend a word of it, as I watched the police car start slowly back toward town.

Chapter 15

"**Y**OU KNOW," PAM KOBRINSKI WAS SAYING, "I think we just Mirandized our last loose end."

"Hang on a second," I said. "What the hell just happened?"

"Gary Conner quit," she answered with satisfaction. "And when he went to clean out his locker, Dr. Glasscock here noticed something Gary shouldn't have had."

Michael was drooping against the doorway, eyes closed, big black overcoat almost hanging off his shoulders in a hugely Byronic display of world weariness. "I was walking past the security office. He had a stack of books in his locker. Books from the library."

"So you put him in a headlock and called the cops, there, Batman?" I asked, skeptical. The image of Michael hanging by his ankles for his preprandial nap seemed to make more sense than the thought of him tangling with Gary physically.

"I could have, if I wanted to," he said with an adolescent shrug, eyes still closed. "Instead, prudence being the better part et cetera, et cetera., I slunk away and squealed on him to *les flics*. I'm no fool."

"So, wait, I'm confused." I turned to Pam. "*Gary* didn't kill . . . ?"

Pam shook her head violently. "No, no. There are two separate situations here—"

"Situations." Michael covered his face with one hand, shook his head, and blew a wet raspberry by way of editorial comment. "I love your use of the language. I must check my dictionary to find out when *situation* became a synonym for *murder*."

Kobrinski smiled patiently at the unkempt man; she could afford to be indulgent now. "Let's start at the beginning. I believe Paul Burnes was responsible for drowning his ex-wife. A crime of passion. Then Dr. Miner, because Burnes was afraid Miner had seen him. According to our medical examiner, Dr. Bambury, Jack Miner died of alcohol poisoning all right, but it was probably a substantial amount of iso-proponol—like rubbing alcohol—in his booze. There were lesions, eruptions, all over his trachea. I suspect that Paul Burnes saw Miner spying on him as he carried his ex-wife's body to the stream that morning and decided that no one else should know about it."

"Where *was* Faith killed?" I asked. "I know she didn't die in the stream where she was found."

"We found traces of cement mortar in her lungs," came the grim reply. "She was probably killed over by—"

"The library," I interrupted automatically. Kobrinski stared at me, agape, and Michael really seemed to wake up and take notice for the first time. "There's been a big tub of water out there for the repairs, the whole time I've been here."

"Right," Pam said slowly. "I think that she agreed to meet Paul by the fence behind the library—it's hidden by all these trees and it's close to the road, as you well know from our lit-tle race the other day. But I'll bet Paul Burnes was waiting for her on the wrong side of the fence and drowned her there."

I thought about what Dr. Theresa Moretti had told me about the sort of strength and the emotional coldness that it took to hold someone under water until they stopped breathing forever. After Paul's performance behind the two-way mirror, I was convinced he could have done it. He could have seduced the Sphinx, he could have outwitted Loki. And Jack would have taken a drink from Guyana Jim Jones; Paul certainly would have had no problem talking him into a little outdoor party for two and poisoning the bottle.

The Detective Sergeant continued. "But both of these deaths are different situ . . . er . . . circumstances from the theft of the books, which I understand has been going on for some time. I think we can safely say that Gary Conner was responsible for that."

That news surprised me. "I didn't know that the library had reported the thefts," I said slowly.

"They didn't," the detective replied tartly. "So how did *you* know about them?"

"Sasha confided in me this afternoon. On the way home from the station."

Pam scrutinized me a moment longer, until she apparently decided that I was telling the truth. "Oka-aay," she said reluctantly. "Well, when I was called this afternoon, I asked Mr. Saunders about the books we found in the locker, and he admitted that he was about to call me. Apparently, the staff had been trying to determine whether the materials that were missing were actually gone or simply misplaced because of the change in . . . ah . . . accessioning policies. That's whether they keep or sell or buy books," she explained.

"I know what accessioning means," I snapped. "So you're saying *Gary* stole the *books*?" I shook my head vehemently. "That doesn't work for me, not at all. No way."

"Henry Saunders identified the books as being some of the missing ones and has also furnished me with a list of the ones we haven't recovered yet." She smiled confidently. "But I suspect that we'll uncover the rest in Gary Conner's apartment.

"The theft from the library, and don't forget, the vandalism of your room, Emma," Pam Kobrinski continued, "seems to fit in with Conner's being the disgruntled employee—"

"He wasn't disgruntled last I heard," I interrupted. "And I would say my room was searched rather than vandalized. There's a big difference, I think. What happened with Conner?"

"He quit after your complaints. Said something about a letter, that he didn't have to take it . . ."

"That much does make sense, Emma," Michael pointed out. "Rather coincides with your accident this morning."

I turned on him—what did *he* know about it? "It doesn't make *any* sense. This doesn't jibe with whoever tossed my room. That letter from Brian had nothing to do with Gary, and nothing to do with *me*. *That* was all about Constantino." I described Brian's encounter with the head of security.

"The letter aside," she answered, "you'd already had a couple of nasty encounters with Gary, and that makes this make sense. Whoever we were chasing was pretty familiar with the grounds here, whoever stole the books was able to get past the security system." Kobrinski flipped the cover over her notebook and buttoned it away with a sigh. Contented with the outcome as she seemed to be, she still took out a Tums and started to chew, crunching away like she was grinding Conner's bones between her teeth. "Well, that's it for me. I'm heading back to town. I'll probably be in touch with you tomorrow, depending on what we get tonight. Gonna be another long one."

* * *

We watched in silence as she started up the cruiser and headed down the road. "She'll be back," Michael said, as the headlights of the police car snapped on.

I raised one eyebrow and he shook his head, eyes open with disbelief that I should doubt him.

"She *craves* me. Couldn't take her eyes *off* me. You saw it, I practically had to restrain her from climbing up my leg."

"Get ahold of yourself, Michael." I couldn't help laughing at his sincerity, though. It was hard to resist his charming self-involvement.

"I won't need to, if our valiant maid in blue returns as soon as I think she will," he said smugly.

"For your information, she's got a boyfriend the size of a refrigerator," I told him. "He could snap you like a twig."

"He'd have to catch me first. And I'm thin but wiry."

"Try spineless but obnoxious."

Michael shook his head, dismissing my barb. "I'm heading back to the house. You coming, or are you just going to stand there and malign me?"

"Just let me get my stuff." I ran in, decided to ignore Mr. Constantino's request for an audience, and returned within the minute.

"She really has got it all wrong," Michael said more seriously, once we were in my car and starting down the road. "I hope she figures it out in time."

"Why do you think that?" I thought so too, but I wasn't going to say anything to him, yet. Not until I had my thoughts sorted out enough to go straight to Pam Kobrinski with them.

"The books in Gary's locker didn't work for me. For one thing, I didn't see any of the missing manuscripts that I'd needed—"

"They could be long gone by now—" I offered, but Michael just ignored me and plowed on.

"—and there was an encyclopedia in there. Volume GLO–HOP, to be exact. Tucked in all snug and cozy with a first edition of Cotton Mather's *Magnalia Christi Americana* and a copy of a 'Treatise Concerning Religious Affections' by Jonathan Edwards."

Michael mentioned all this so pointedly and was so unbearably smug about it that I just had to let him know I knew what he was saying. "Right. I can see Gary walking by and grabbing a random book, just a little 'screw you' on his way out. But I doubt that he'd be bothered with two works of important Early American religious writers. I mean, how would he know about them? Though he might have been working with someone who was telling him what to steal, I suppose." I thought about it, chewing my lip.

Michael shook his head. "I don't think so. That would mean he knew his way around the library well enough to find the volumes that were locked up—"

"What about the problems with the alarm? That would explain it."

Michael looked pained. "I can't believe you think it was Gary, too. You're killing me, Emma."

"I don't think it was Gary, and neither do you," I retorted. "I'm just playing devil's advocate."

"Well?" he challenged.

"It's all focused around the library," I explained. "I don't think that Faith's death has to do with her freaky relationship with Paul; not that I feel I can trust what she said anymore, after what I saw today. . . . I just don't know what to think about that. But I do think she saw something she shouldn't have. She was killed near the library. And then the murderer killed Jack, because he saw the note he left me. In the library."

"Why do you say *library*? I mean, *he*?" Michael asked. He kept his face carefully blank, but there was an intense gruffness to his voice that caught my attention. "It could be a woman."

"Could be *she*," I agreed slowly. "I'm just using the impersonal pronoun. Unless you prefer *shim* or *he/she*?"

"I do not. I just think . . ." He trailed off, and for once seemed to be gripped with real uncertainty, and genuine distress.

"Michael, what is it?" I waited for him to speak up.

"I don't like to say it before I know for sure, but neither do I want to find myself with an icepick between my shoulders because of prudence." He looked up and grinned crookedly. "Veronica, Ayeesha, Marian, yes, but never Prudence." Michael sobered again and sighed. "This sort of thing seems to be following me around. You may have heard about the theft from Van Helst Library in Philadelphia about a month, six weeks ago?"

My breath caught and I nodded dumbly, recalling what Harry had told me just this morning.

"Well, I was there at the time it happened, though I don't think the detective knew that, or she wouldn't have scampered off so happily." He shook off his distraction. "It was the same thing, a couple of rare manuscripts, Early Americana, priceless. Or at least they had so many zeroes to the left of the decimal point as to make no difference."

I nodded again, my heart pounding as he confirmed what *I* already knew about his proximity to that theft. "Go on."

"I was there," he said slowly, scratching his chin, "but someone else was there too. Someone who is also here. Now. At the library."

That made me forget to inhale. So much for what I thought I knew.

Michael polished his glasses thoughtfully, taking a long time to do it. "Like I said. I don't like to say anything. It's all so circumstantial."

"Michael! Will you just tell me!"

Finally he put his glasses back in his pocket and looked straight at me. "Sasha. Sasha was there, working at Philly when I was there."

"How can that be?" I said, amazed. "She's been here for at least a year."

He nodded. "And how do you know that?"

"I know it because . . ." Now it was my turn to hesitate. "I just had the impression that she was new, but not that new. I guess it was because I thought she and Henry had some history, if you know what I mean." I parked, and we got out of the car.

Michael began to fumble through his pockets for the keys to the kitchen door as we climbed the steps to the house. "I do know what you mean," he resumed, "but I can only tell you that I know what I know. I saw Sasha Russo working at the rare book room in Van Helst Library when I was there, when those manuscripts were stolen. And now she's here. In time for me to find her standing over your prostrate body, in time for more manuscripts and books to go missing, in time for far too many things!"

Even with the door open, neither of us went into the house yet. The cool breeze picked up suddenly, the gust dramatically whipping Michael's overcoat.

"Are you sure it was Sasha you saw there?" I finally said.

Michael brushed past me into the hallway with a look of pure pity. "My dear Dr. Fielding. I collect women. I am entranced by them in every instance, even when they are dancing a collective fandango on my all-too-susceptible heart. I yearn for them, I worship them, I admire what extremes they are capable of making me feel. How could *I* forget someone who looks like *Sasha*?"

I remembered the humbling effect that standing next to the Viking Goddess for the first time had on me, in spite of my insusceptibility. "All right, all right, if you say so."

"I do. Here, let's settle this right now. The Philadelphia library is open until six. I'll call." He dropped his briefcase with a thump and started to dial.

I took off my coat. Michael didn't bother, of course; bedtime wasn't for hours yet. "You can remember the number? Just like that?"

He tapped the side of his head meaningfully. "All right here. Everything, always." He listened briefly, then turned mischievous, suddenly thrusting the receiver into my hand. "Here! You're the one who's so curious!"

I tried to shove the phone away, but I could already hear someone answering on the other end. Michael danced away, just out of reach with his hands held high over his head. He sat down on the back of the couch in the parlor, arms crossed over his chest and grinning, to watch me squirm.

"Good afternoon, Van Helst Rare Book," I heard a disembodied voice say.

"Is this Van Helst?" I said, stalling, scrambling for a ruse. Michael cocked his head to one side, frowning slightly: I was disappointing him so far. Hell, I was disappointing myself.

"Yes, the rare book room. Can I help you?"

"Yes, thank you. My name is," I took a deep breath, "Margaret, ah, Mallowan"—I could see Michael shaking his head, mouthing my new name, his brow furrowed—"and I am calling for Dr. Michael Glasscock." I turned away momentarily, gloating, while Michael jumped up from the back of the couch, shaking his head, silently pleading, "No, stop!"

"Ah, yes, he was here just a short time ago. I remember him quite well." The female voice—gruff, dragonlike, and not at all collectible—chilled noticeably and suggested to me that there had been moments of tension between her and Michael at the time of his visit.

I added just a hint of knowing amusement to my voice. "Oh, well, he's not the sort you forget in a hurry. In any case, I am cawling"—a generic bit of New York City drifted into my accent—"because Dr. Glasscawk wanted to make certain that he had the cor-rect names for your staff in his acknowledgments and asked me to as-cer-tain whether my list was accurate?"

In the parlor Michael nodded, giving grudging approval to my gambit.

"Just a moment, I'll check who was on call that month." I heard the tapping of computer keys as, presumably, schedules were brought up. "Here we are. Let me read them to you . . ."

She ran down a list and I echoed it, making assenting noises after checking off an imaginary list. I noticed that Michael had brought out his notebook and was writing down the names as I said them aloud; he'd forgotten them himself.

"Oh, de-ah," I said. "I have one more name, I can't quite make it out—"

"His handwriting made one grateful for computers," the librarian grumbled. "I could barely make out his call slips."

"Oh, his penmanship is just dread-ful," I agreed. Michael, who had by now sidled up to me to hear the conversation, stuck out his tongue. "This one looks like Sarah, Ruskin, Russian, something like that?"

"Of course. Sasha Russo. She had been with us for quite some time, then left for a new position. She came back for two weeks on her vacation to assist us with a grant project she'd been listed on before she'd left. I'm not surprised he had *her* name," the librarian muttered.

"That must be it. Thank you so much for all your help. Good night." I hung up and looked around for approbation.

Michael nodded. "Okay, okay, but . . . Margaret Mallomar?"

"Margaret Mallowan," I corrected. "I was going to use Margaret Chandler, but I figured there was a chance that someone working in a library might have heard of her—"

"Oh, good call," he said sarcastically, nodding even more vigorously. "That would have given us away, especially after Demi Moore popularized the character in her last film."

I ignored his caustic remark. "Well, just in case, I used Mallowan, after Max Mallowan, the archaeologist. He also happened to be Agatha Christie's husband," I added. I decided to push on. "Michael, so you were down there too, the same time as Sasha, the same time as the thefts—"

"Yes, I was. No, I didn't do it," he interrupted in a bored voice. "Don't you think it'd be stupid to pull the same stunt at two different places? Please, enough. I'm tired. I want to eat."

In that second, I realized just how skillful Michael was at manipulating situations through force of his character. People made excuses for him because of his genius. I made excuses for him because of his brains, and because he made me laugh. Harry's words came back to me, reminding me that the activities of my erstwhile colleague might not be able to stand much scrutiny . . .

The phone rang. I answered brusquely. "Hello?"

A man's voice asked, "May I speak with Emma Fielding, please?"

My husband sounded so shy and cute and sweet that I would have kissed him to pieces had he been there in front of me. "Brian, it's me."

"You sure didn't sound like you. Look, I checked my machine; I've got a few minutes before the cab comes for the airport. What's wrong? I thought everything was okay."

Right. I'd forgotten all about Brian's impending recruiting trip. "It is, but everything's gotten pretty exciting around here." I quickly told him what had happened in the past twelve hours.

"Oh God, Emma, I can't tell you how relieved that makes me feel," he said after. It sounded like he just took his first deep breath for a long time. "I almost decided to cancel the trip, I was so worried."

I didn't bother to tell him about my private belief that this wasn't as neatly tied up as the detective might have wished. Not when I needed to give Michael Glasscock a little more consideration as a suspect. Not when Brian's cab was coming soon.

"Tell me about home, I need to hear about home." Brian obligingly ran down what had been going on at the Funny Farm and I listened to the details hungrily.

"And Marty? The baby?"

"She's huge and really more than ready to whelp. It should be any minute now."

"And is Kam still going to look in on Quasi?"

"Yep, he said that if the baby came, he'd get Roddy to do it. Otherwise, he said he'd pop a couple of Benadryl and bring the twelve-gauge along. In exchange for a little wine shopping I'm to do for him while I'm out there."

I chuckled softly. Kam was always so infuriatingly composed—in person and dress—that one of my favorite memories was the sight of him, runny-nosed and teary-eyed, when we discovered that he was violently allergic to our cat. Well, Brian's cat, really. Ever since Brian brought him home as a feral kitten, when he promptly revealed himself to be a cross between Satan, a Maine coon cat, and who knew what else, Quasimodo's been a one-man cat. Adoring eyes only for Brian, evil-assed attitude for anyone else. I was tolerated—barely—for my opposable thumb and my ability to use the can opener.

The realization that Brian had been speaking brought me back to the present conversation. "—and so now you can focus on your work, which is why you're there anyway."

"Oh yeah, I remember," I said ruefully, and sighed. "Something about a diary? God, that code's driving me nuts. What do *you* know about codes, sugar?"

"What kind of codes? Genetic, Morse, area, zip, bar?" The buoyancy in Brian's spirits was audible in his enthusiastic chatter. "Did you know that there used to be a journal called *Bar Code Weekly*? I haven't looked at supermarket scanners the same since—"

"I'm talking encryption," I said. "If I'm going to get anything useful from Madam Chandler's diary, I've got to crack it. I've tried everything I can think of, which wasn't much, but I figure the code can't be too difficult."

"Yeah, just enough to keep you scratching your head! You're right though, it doesn't have to be complicated to be effective."

"Madam Margaret's got groups of numbers, nothing higher than twenty-six."

"So it's alphabetically based," Brian said confidently. "Okay. You've tried a Julius Caesar code? Just slide each letter, say, four letters forward each time, so A is D, B is E, et cetera?"

"Yep, a couple of times. I couldn't make any sense out of it—there's no order."

"In that case, my best guess is that it's a code based on a book or a poem or something. You know, you take a passage with a lot of different letters in it and number the letters according to their appearance in the passage. How about those?"

"I could try that," I said slowly. "She read an awful lot, though. I'd have trouble pinning down what was the most important book in her life."

"I thought you were always telling me that the Bible would have been the one book that most people knew. Y'know, in the olden days."

For Brian, a native Californian and born hard scientist geek, the olden days were those prior to 1960. "It was and I'll try that first, but I honestly don't think it's going to be Genesis chapter one, verse one, you know what I mean? I think she was a little more sophisticated than that. But it is a starting place."

"Oops! Cab's here, gotta go. You'll do it, sweetie, just start at the begin—"

He hadn't even finished the word, but Brian's unconscious use of Kobrinski's mantric phrase hit me like a speeding freight train. I knew what the key to Madam Chandler's code was.

"Start at the beginning! Holy snappers!" I looked around frantically for my briefcase. There! By the chair!

"What?" I heard his voice over the phone, but now it seemed as though it was coming from a very great distance. "What's wrong? Emma?"

"Nothing, but you've got to hush, I can't—" The phone cord wasn't long enough for me to reach my briefcase, even though I strained every inch of muscle. "I think I know what the code is—hang on!"

"I can't!" Brian insisted. "Look, you're okay, right?"

"Yeah, but I just need two minutes to check whether I'm right—"

"Look," he interrupted. "When you sound like that, you're right. Don't worry, just go do it, okay? The cab's here," Brian said. "I'll call you if it's not too late when I get into Stanford, okay? I love you."

I felt torn in half, rotten for ditching Brian, desperate to check my new theory. "I love you too, I really do—!" But even as I was saying it, I was scrambling over to hang up the phone. It took me a couple of tries to get the receiver back on the cradle, because it kept bouncing off, with all the force I used.

I pounced on my bag like a hungry lion on a slow gazelle. I tore the buckles open, and ripped through the thicket of le-

gal pads, folders, and filing cards until I found my research
notebook and my computer. Flipping the screen up and
switching the machine on, I then rifled through the notebook
until I found the first page where I'd copied out the first epigram that opened Madam Chandler's third diary for Michael
to look at:

*Since it is possible that thou mayst depart from life this
very moment, regulate every act and thought accordingly . . .*

During the eon that it took my computer to boot up, I sat
there on the floor and started numbering the letters in con-
secutive order as they appeared in the quotation: 1 for S, 2
for I, and so on.

```
S i n c e  i t  i s  p o s s  i  b  l  e
1 2 3 4 5  6 7  8       9 10

t h a t t h o u  m a y s t
 1112        13 14   15

d e p a r t  f r o m  l i f e t h i s
16      17 18

v e r y  m o m e n t,  r e g u l a t e
19                    20

e v e r y a c t a n d t h o u g h t
a c c o r d i n g l y
```

Okay, "it." I is repeated, so T is 6, skip to P, that's 7, O—
"Oh, man! It's going to work!"
Finally my word processor program came up, and I
opened the file that contained my transcription of the diary,

so far. Excitement flooded me, and I kept overshooting where the first series of code numbers started.

Finally, a brief entry with code appeared and I struggled to calm myself to compare the series of code numbers with the key I had just worked out: 12, 14, 8, 1, 6, 6, 5, 17, 17, 2, 9, 10, 5, 16, 12, 15, 9, 17, 5 . . . Then I wrote down the letters that corresponded to each number.

"A, M, O—" Amo? That didn't make any sense unless— Please God, no! Don't let her be writing in encoded *Latin*, my tired heart just won't take it! Amo was "I love," and that was about the extent of my knowledge of Cicero's language. Never mind, Emma, keep going, keep *going*!

"A, M, O, S, T, T, E, R, R, I—" That double T didn't look like Latin after an S. Keep going, keep going! There's still a chance.

"—B, L, E, D, A, Y, B, R—" I kept scribbling down letters, not even looking at them, just praying that I would get enough to tell me how to start making sense of them. The problem was, there were a couple of letters that weren't contained in the quote, so I knew that I'd have to get them from the context.

And then suddenly, magically, the letters seemed to shift into place, separating themselves into words I could recognize. In English. Once my eye distinguished the first couple of words, breaking up the rest was easier:

"A MOST TERRIBLE DAY BREA22S AND I 22NO24 NOT IF I HAVE THE STRENGTH TO FACE IT . . ."

"A most terrible day breaks and I know not if I have the strength to face it . . ." I whispered to myself. A quiet calm stole over me, and I automatically assigned J, K, Q, W, X, Z—the letters that weren't in the quote—the numbers 21 through 26, thus completing the key.

Sitting on the floor, I stared at the translated sentence in silence. Almost three centuries ago, a woman found herself in a strange new world, isolated from her family, her husband, and her community. Alone in that wilderness and faced with the threat of being hanged, she poured out her heart into a book that was her only companion. I thought of Margaret Chandler trying to exorcise her fear by writing. She'd literally written volumes. I imagined the burden of complete despair she must have borne by the end of this journal, when she was convinced she would be executed and still, in plain, uncoded words, steadfastly maintained her innocence. I thought of the pride she must have had to keep those fears concealed from casual glance, even in the face of public condemnation. The woman carried herself with outward dignity with those thoughts carefully hidden away. Hidden until I had cracked her code and read the secrets in her heart.

"Margaret, now I know," I whispered.

Realizing that I couldn't properly do work on the hallway floor, I gathered up my papers and computer into my bag and bounded up the stairs. I had a long night ahead of me, but at least I knew that I would be in the best of company.

Chapter 16

A DREADFUL POUNDING WOKE ME THE NEXT MORN-
ing, and it took a moment before I could determine
whether it was a real noise or a product of the eerie dreams I
fled. Vague images of a shadowy forest with fluttering letters
pinned to every tree fled irrevocably as the banging persisted
on the door to my room. With an effort, I pried open my eyes
and was brutally assaulted by bright sunlight streaming in
through the windows.

Over the racket at the door, I could hear Michael calling
my name. I froze, trying to gather my wits. Harry had un-
consciously made some pretty damning comments about
Michael's proximity to all of the events here. In spite of
Michael's apparent willingness to share his theories with
me, I had only just started to consider his role when I had
been distracted by Brian's call and my epiphany that led to
breaking Margaret Chandler's code.

Shaking myself awake, I decided I needed to keep my
suspicions hidden until I had better evidence. "Hold your
horses, I'm coming," I called grouchily. The clock told me
that it was after nine o'clock. I'd had only five hours of sleep

and was exhausted, and it took a huge effort to shove myself upright on the bed. As I did so, a cascade of printed pages slid off my chest, where apparently they'd rested all night after I fell asleep reading them. They sailed gracefully along the floor until they were hampered by a pile of dirty clothes. I kicked the whole mess to one side and, with a grunt, managed to shove my desk aside and open the door before it splintered under another burst of hammering.

Michael stood there, panting slightly, looking red-faced and expectant. His hair was curling every which way; his eyes were bloodshot, but that didn't detract from their appeal.

"Well?" I said.

He was practically hopping. "Don't you 'well' me! Where the hell have you been?"

I could tell he was really ticked off, but why, I didn't know. "Well, what do you think, Michael? I'm in sweats, in a locked room, where I retired last night. To sleep in a little. What do you think I was doing?"

"I just came back to make sure you were okay," he answered pettishly. "When no one saw you arrive at the library at your usual time, I wanted to make sure you weren't languishing in a ditch somewhere. Around here lately, being absent could mean being dead. That's something you of all people should have thought of, you know."

And why was he so suddenly interested in my whereabouts? That "should" and the fact that he was right only nettled me further. I've always hated the "you should know better" sort of remonstrance more than any other.

"For a change, I thought I'd work on my *real* work, what brought me here in the first place. Sue me," I said, feeling prickly.

He ran his hand through his hair and I was startled to discover that I wanted to do the same thing. "Snipe all you want, but in spite of Detective Kobrinski's optimism, nothing's been conclusively solved yet. I prefer to know your whereabouts. Purely for safety's sake, if not yours, then mine." With that he turned and headed downstairs, but called coldly over his shoulder, "If you want the luxury of forget-fulness, you might leave here."

Again, he seems to want me out of here, or at least ac-counted for, I thought. I was so beleaguered with confused thoughts of retort, apology, and suspicion that he got away before I could say anything, which was probably all to the good. I didn't have time for him, anyway, not until I had some better proof, because Sasha had promised that the Chandler letters would be ready today. At the thought of be-ing able to learn more about the trial of Madam Chandler, I didn't even bother showering, but tied my hair back into a short pony tail, dressed fit to be seen, grabbed my notebook and jogged to the library.

Sasha was nowhere in sight. Maybe she was still recovering from her ordeal at the station yesterday, maybe she was on break, but there was no way I was waiting for her, so I took a chance and headed upstairs to Harry's office. As soon as I got there and raised my hand to knock, I almost turned around and left—Harry was obviously on the phone, speak-ing in an angry, choking voice. As much as I knew I shouldn't listen, I couldn't help myself. It sounded as though his world was coming to an end.

"—You can't do that! It's a travesty! We've discussed this already, and you swore to me . . . No, that won't work. How can you even consider . . . ? This is outrageous! . . . No, no, I'm coming right down."

I heard the phone slam and had just decided that I wouldn't bother knocking, in fact, I would scurry away as quickly as possible when the door was flung open. Harry was as tidily dressed as ever, pulling on a smart gray overcoat, but the real evidence of his emotion was in his eyes. They were red-rimmed and agony-filled.

That's what a saint looks like, I thought, the instant before he's accepted his martyrdom. I was so stunned by the force of this pain that I was rooted to the spot.

For a moment, I didn't think that Harry would recognize me, or even stop, but to our mutual embarrassment, he did. "Emma. I'm sorry." He cleared his throat; he took off his glasses and carefully began rubbing at them with a clean linen handkerchief and I was reminded of how a cat washes itself to cover embarrassment. "Have you been waiting long to see me?"

I couldn't believe his voice was as normal, as calm as it was. Not with those eyes. "Er, no, Harry. I was just going to knock." Fortunately, my hand was still raised, preparatory to that action.

"What can I do for you?" He sounded insistent, as if he wasn't going to allow his unseemly show of emotion to interfere with his work.

"No, sorry, it can wait. You look like . . ." Hell, I thought to myself. "You look like you're on your way someplace. I'll wait 'til I can find Sasha. I was just going to ask for the Chandler correspondence, that's all."

"Oh, I can get you that." He started off for the conservation room and I followed dumbly behind.

"You don't have to do that, Harry," I protested. Though I was desperate to see the letters, I didn't want to add to whatever was dismaying him so.

Harry sighed as he unlocked the door. "Between you and me, I need a moment to count to ten, if you know what I mean. I just got a call, and well . . . You know. You think you've got something important settled, finally, and then someone comes along and ever so casually upsets the apple cart. Hard not to feel like Sisyphus, some days. But I'll get it straightened out."

I was considering how large a rock it was he was pushing, or whether the tipped cart contained the golden apples from the garden of the Hesperides, to evoke that kind of response. And yet, here he was obliging me on his way to remedy the situation, above and beyond the call of duty.

"How's work on the diary going?" Harry asked briefly as he handed me the folder.

"Harry, I managed to decipher Madam Chandler's code!" Even as I said it, I marveled. I hadn't even said the words out loud since I'd done it. It almost was like I was realizing the implications for the first time myself.

Harry looked shocked, then a delighted smile broke through the clouds in his face. He grabbed my hand and began pumping it enthusiastically. "Congratulations! My God, congratulations! Emma, that's wonderful! This is extraordinary! Tell me, tell me all about it!"

"I *did* it, didn't I?" I sat down suddenly at a table and tried to collect my wits. "Well, it was based on the quote with which she started the diary. It was there all the time. Waiting for me. Or, you know . . . whoever."

"Emma, this is a discovery of the first water! I don't know what to say." Harry was as dazed and happy for me as I could have been for myself. He shook my hand again, encasing it with his left hand as well, grinning with childish excitement. "Thank you, Emma! I have to go now, but you . . . you know, you've just about managed to restore my faith in humankind!" And it was with a great lightness of step that he went off on his delayed errand.

Still dazed by Harry's warm response to my news, I realized that Christmas wasn't over, that there was one more package under the tree with my name on it. I composed myself hastily, found an empty carrel, and opened the folder. On top of a pile of sheets of heavy linen paper, each encased in its own clear plastic conservation envelope, was a typewritten conservator's report, prepared, no doubt, by Sasha, who had been hard at work in the little conservation lab.

I took a look at the report to prepare myself for the goodies that lay beneath. Under the Shrewsbury laboratory's letterhead it read:

Chandler MSS. 2/2/3. Three letters (one incomplete) in fair to good condition, on linen rag, oak-gall and iron ink. Work completed by S. T. Russo (see attached conservation notes). Correspondence between ("Madam") Margaret (Chase) Chandler of Stone Harbor, Massachusetts, and Daphne (Radcliffe) Mainwaring, of London, probably dating 1723.

Biographical Notes: Madam Chandler and Mrs. Mainwaring were cousins through the maternal line. Margaret Chandler was wife to Justice Matthew Chandler (see Alarick Springer, 1933, *Lives of Massachusetts Jurists, 1620–1750*, privately printed; Records of the Quarterly Courts of Massachusetts, Exeter County, Volume II) and has been remarked as a diarist of the colonial period (see Chandler MSS. 1/2/1; Alison Lairde, 1902, *Helpmeets and Housewives of the Old Bay Colony*, Boston). Mrs. Mainwaring was married to John Mainwaring, and after his death, later married Sir Robert Chomondeley (1725); Sinclair Deauville (1732); and Peter, Lord Buckleigh (1740) (see Debrett's *Peerage*).

Keywords: Domestic life, social events, childbirth, 18th century, London, colonial Massachusetts, housewares, clothing.

In careful, faint pencil beneath, Sasha had left a note to herself: "See also Fielding, Emma J., 200–(article? book?)."

Bless the girl, she was already anticipating my own work on the subject! I thought gleefully. I wouldn't disappoint her, not when I had to live up to Madam Chandler's own high

standard. I picked up the first envelope, feeling the plastic
folder buckle a little as I examined the letter inside, hoping
for the answers to all the questions I had about the trial. I
recognized Margaret's clear, elegant hand and was immediately disappointed to find that the first letter was a fragment;
the first two pages were missing:

-3-

*I must finish quickly if this is to find a Place with the
Post bound for Capt'n Sherman's Antelope. As you
will already have read, I cannot stress too greatly Mr.
Chandler's Role in my Salvation. It was his Faith in
me, his entire comprehension of the Truth, and his
Perspicacity that rescued me, and had he not the Fortunate Willingness to give Credence to my Observations, all would have been lost.*

I realized with a sharp pang of disappointment that the
first part of the letter probably had contained a description
of the trial and Margaret's escape from a death sentence. I
read on, hoping to find some other clue.

*His sense of Justice is so utterly even-hand'd that had
it not been impossible, I sho'd have worried about his
strict Preservat'n of the Law. As it was, I was rather
more concern'd w/ the immediate Preservation of my
Selfe, and will keepe as a dear Lesson that Truth is
more than a Summe of Factes. But all's well that ends
so, and we are quite—happily!—returned to a well-
regulated Life. Please take Care in how you mention
this to my Mother, as I have been reluctant to trouble
her with Details until I knew the Outcome for certain,
and have just sent her Worde.*
  We are determined to continue construction on the

*new House, and I cannot fathom why I sho'd be so dis-
appoint'd to leave this one. It is a very anchient and
creakey sort of Place, fantastickal in its Antiquity, but
I have discovered a Fondnesse for it that is nigh on inexplicable. Perhaps the Reason of it lies meerly in that
it was the first place I set to House-keepinge. I wish
you would send me, as soone as is Convenient, a new
Suit of Bedcloths, Vallances (with a Fringe), Bolsters,
Coverlids, and Curtains, embroider'd, a dark Greene
if it can be got, otherwise Blew, but not so light a
Shade as that we saw in Mistress Stephen's new
Chamber. Also, if you can send some Holland diaper
Napkins, it wo'd be a blessing to me, for Mr. Chan-
dler's Guests must expect the best. I have given the
Monie (£50)to Capt'n Sherman for this.*

*Au voir, Daphne, and With all wishes for God's
Blessings from*
Your devoted and grateful Cousin,
Margaret

*Post scriptus: Do you remember our Wager? I may
have News for you soon . . .*

I sat stunned for a moment: there was not a scrap about
the trial. I hurried on to the next, shorter, letter, not in Margaret's hand; the writing was not as well formed, but was
still readily readable. Maybe there would be some reference
there.

September 30, 1723, London,
My chere Margareta,

*I was pleased to perform the office of Nurse to your
pore Mother, who was so distress'd at your news, that*

she fainted away and could not be revived without several glasses of French Brandy, in which I was forced to share, to lead her in a good example. Had I known that your letter to her had been delayed leavin London, I shouldn't have announced (thinkin as I did, that I brot the best of news), "Margaret is saved from Hangin!" Really, you sho'd take grater care in your corespondence. I was obliged to recount the whole tale, instead of retirin, as you know I prefer, to a quiet corner to observe the Company at hand, so that I was quite the focal point of interest and was begged to tell the tale again and again. I am happy to take this trouble for you, but I hope that in future you will not be so thotless. I make this a present of advise (not so very stern a rebuke) to you, from your older, more experienc'd couzin. I was pleazed to hear that Matthew was so much a part of the relief of your distress, for Caroline Denbigh ust to call him "that grate, lumberin mute" (much aginst my protests, for I knew your warm feelings for him), and he has never been much outspoken, at least in polite company, but I knew myself that he had hidden qualities.

I have dispatched the beding and the Napkins for you, and have encluded a few trifels more, though what use they can be to you in that Howlin Wilderness, I cannot imagine. Who is there *to pleaze? Though, of course, you will want to keep as much with the Times as possible, against your Returne (I hope soon?) to England. Also, I've sent patterns of this years silkes, if you wish to be o current in matters of dress as well. If you can send me more of that Barbadoes Rumm, I would be thankfull. It is a soveraine remedie for female weaknesses, which you remember have been a burthen to me as long as I can recall. Not the New Englande rumm, which is harsh and fit only for dosin servants.*

You had very much better send two barrels, for Mr. Jack Mainwaring sometimes likes to make a Rumm punch. I am afraid he will go all to excess, mixin limes and oranges and hot water with it (which increaseth the potentcy), and often advise him to take it in some less excitin form, neate and unmixed, as I do. When I am ill.

I do not remember a wager between us; you know I never take wagers, unless they be verry small and not even then, savin as a jest. You write of news, but I cannot think why you did not tell me in your last letter; tell me plainly what your news is. You must learn to carry yourself as a Woman, and leave off Girls games and foolin and you won't find yourselfe in such troubles.

I keep this short, and not start another sheet, to prevent you payin much postage. I must go visitin now, and then plan our ball for the opening of the Season. I am a slave to my duties, as you know, and if you do not come home soon, you may not see me alive again, I am so troubled with them. But I undertake all, as cheerefully as any woman in the world, and do my Christian work.

Your ever-lovin couzin, Daphne

The last letter was from Margaret, and while I was let down that it did not have any news about the trial, I should have remembered that nothing ever works out the way you expect in historical research. I'd had so much luck so far, it seemed greedy to want more—but it was the only really crucial part of the mystery I didn't yet understand.

22 November 1723, Stone Harbor

My Dear Daphne,

I am disappointed that you do not recall our Wager, for I believe I sh'll be the Winner. A Shame for I sho'd have taken Delighte in choosing the bolt of silk, but no matter: I will not hold you to it as the Object itselfe is too important. My Newes is this: An it pleases God, there will be an Heir to our House in the early spring. The Justice behaved like a Man at my telling him soe, that is to say, cut an Antick Caper and made the Parlour ring with Shouting, then was very meeke and bid me sit, to rest myself, then stand, that I might not crush the Babe, then sit again. He then decided that I must not come to Travaille here but return to England post haste and was in an extasy of Worrie about the Winter Storms for a Crossing and so in a space of two Moments determined I must remain here and you must send a Woman to me, for my time comes in April, I believe and I sho'd not attempt the voyage then. I wish you wo'd too, send me someone, for I know as much as any One about common or domestick Physick, but it wo'd be a Comfort to know that there was Another to help me.

I am sorry to say that since my announcement, my dearest friend Matthew has beene a sore tryall to his Clerks and me, much distrackted unlesse he sits in Sessions, where he is much like himselfe, but away from there he forgets his Hat or rends it in thinking and planning, but I will forgive him the Repairs. He is only anxious for my Sake. I am well enough now, and sho'd continue so. Mother is kind to remind me that my Healthe is rude enough for a Shepherdesse, and I am content to leave my Fate and Soule in the Hands of the Almightie, but sometimes must battle an excess of Melancholie, which is the Babe making me humourous. You must send what is needeful for the little Stranger to come among us and I inclose a Bill against Morgan's for the Expence. It is too bad of you not to

*recall our Wager, for I wo'd have prefered a Rose silke
Satin . . .*

  *Write more if you like, I do not mind that Coste, but
I think you are rather more busy than worried for my
Accompts. I want your Letters more now, than ever,
and remain, dear Cousin,*

  Yr. faithful Loving Cousin,

  Margaret Amalie Chase Chandler

I flipped back and forth through the letters. There was no
way to get around it: I wasn't going to find out about the trial
from anything here at Shrewsbury. As disappointed as I was
about the trial, I had to admit that what I found instead was a
little jewel. Madam Chandler announced the imminent arrival of her first child with a mixture of pride and playful triumph, but I noticed a little nervousness worked in amongst
her remarks about Justice Chandler's reaction and her careless mention of her good health. Besides death by fire,
mostly suffered from working stooped over in an open
hearth with long skirts, childbirth was the leading cause of
death for women in the seventeenth and eighteenth centuries. Faced with that knowledge, I might have been a little
skittish myself. That reminded me that I should call Marty to
see how she was doing.

  I checked my genealogical notes and found that she had
been safely delivered of this child, and had seven more who
survived to adulthood—quite an impressive feat for the
time. Again I was struck by the irony of already knowing all
the answers to the questions Margaret would have had about
her life even as I was trying to piece together the shape of
the quotidian existence she knew so well. For a moment I
wished there was some way that I could reassure her that

everything would turn out well, but then suffered a pang when I realized that Margaret had been dead for more than two hundred years and I would never get to meet her. It was difficult, at times, to remember that this research was a journey that I would make on my own, with no one to greet me at the end and confirm my conclusions. I alone was responsible for breathing life back into Margaret's story.

At the same time, I knew that I was coming to a kind of crossroads in my own life and wished someone might give me a few answers to that story too. I shook myself and returned to my work.

Her cousin Daphne seems to have been a central character in that story—her name showed up often enough in the diary and her own hand revealed much of the truth at which Margaret hinted in her journal. Daphne Mainwaring obviously fancied herself the coming family matriarch and was what P. G. Wodehouse might have described as "acutely alive to the existence of class distinctions." For all her bluster and her posturing, however, I got the impression that she was goodhearted, though, and her remarks about the "trifels" she sent to Margaret and her wish for her return almost balanced her obvious desire to be the center of attention and the bearer of any news. Almost. That line about Margaret's "thotlessness" was a pip. It was possible too that she wrote in jest—for all of her refusals about their wager, I noticed that Margaret still told her what she wanted for a prize; there might well be something more between them than the light tone of her letters suggested. And there must have been something in Daphne to have attracted such a series of husbands. Good grief, I had enough trouble just keeping up with one, never mind four in a row. She certainly didn't have any of the stereotypical widow's troubles in remarrying. I'd have to look into Daphne's life a little further.

It was that thought about historical realities that reminded me that I needed to get to work on my presentation for Monday—just five days away, now, and I would have to work through the coming weekend. I gathered up my computer and notes and carefully replaced the letters in the folder, set them on Sasha's desk, and returned to the house.

Michael was nowhere to be seen: good. It made it that much easier to ignore my growing concerns about him—for the moment. I made a couple of sandwiches, grabbed a carton of orange juice, and headed upstairs to get to work.

I started sketching out an outline for the talk. Sasha had said about fifty minutes, so that meant about twenty pages if I read formally, or about five outlined pages if I were more casual about it. A little bit about my work on the archaeology of the Chandler house, which presumably was their new one, a little about other famous diarists—better throw in a little about Laurel Thatcher Ulrich and her work on Martha Ballard, to get the point across about the importance of scrutinizing even seemingly banal details as well as the relevance of women's lives.

The sound of the ringing phone scared the hell out of me. I thought about ignoring it, but habit got the better of me. It was Pam Kobrinski, and she didn't have good news.

"I have to release Gary Conner," she announced briefly. "I thought you should know."

My heart sank. I hadn't realized until just then how much I had been counting on his being guilty, even though I didn't think much of him as a suspect. "Why?"

"His fingerprints were found only on one of the books in his locker."

"The encyclopedia," I said.

"Right. How did you know that?" Kobrinski asked.

"I couldn't see Gary digging into the Puritan theories of praxis. What about other people's prints?"

"Not any we can identify. Some old ones of Harry Saunders, but that's to be expected."

"No one else's?" I asked, then made myself say what I was thinking. "Were there any of, y'know, Michael Glasscock's?"

"No, why? Ah, because he was the one who happened to observe all this," the detective answered her own question. "No, none of his. The others, the religious ones, had blurs and partials, and none of them looked too fresh. Gary maintains he's innocent, and we couldn't find a damned thing in his apartment to suggest that he's not. He finally admitted that he did take something off the victim's body—"

"What was it?

"Two twenty dollar bills." She shrugged. "I think I believe him, he's real scared now, but there's not a lot I can do to prove that now. Constantino isn't interested in prosecuting on the strength of an encyclopedia—hell, he's taking Gary's side, saying he was just looking something up. I called because . . . because I thought you'd want to know."

The way she said that reminded me of the rage that possessed Gary on his way out of the library. A little shiver ran down my spine, and I decided that I wouldn't want to bump into him on a dark street. "Thanks for the warning."

There was a longish pause. "That's not the only bad news. Legally, I'm also about three seconds away from having to release Paul Burnes. He'll probably go this afternoon."

I gasped and she continued, angrily. "There's not much I can do. At this point, it looks like he was on the plane at the time when his wife was murdered. I've got him until I can get a definite statement from the airline and from our ME, Dr. Bambury, but that's it. Damn it, every time I get close to something in this case, it evaporates into nothing. People were killed, I've got leads—then—nothing!"

I had to agree, thinking about Paul's disturbing behavior in the interrogation room and my own sensation of being Alice in an overturned world. "Everything looks like the oppo-site of what it is. Smoke and mirrors."

"Yeah, I know," she said. "Like the first time in history the guy who beats his wife isn't the best suspect for killing her. And it happens on my watch. Any defense lawyer in the country would eat it up with a spoon, anyone else I bring in for this. I don't know what else to do and I'm running out of options."

She sounded so frustrated that it was more out of a sense of pity than having any real solution that I made the offer. "Why not meet with me tomorrow? We can talk about other options."

I could hear paper ripping on the other end of the line and presently heard the munch of Tums as the detective mulled it over. "What other options? There are no other options."

"I'll try to dredge up some other ideas. Just blue-sky. What can it hurt?"

She sounded resigned and unconvinced. "Why not? I'm not getting anywhere fast at the moment. Make it breakfast early tomorrow?"

I shuddered. "Make it lunch. I had a late night last night. And the night before."

"What are you working on there, anyway?" she asked. "I mean, officially?"

"Journal of an eighteenth-century woman. Actually, she was caught up in a murder too, and when it was all over, she said, 'The truth is more than a sum of facts.'"

"Smart lady," the detective said.

I barely heard her. Suddenly, there was a roaring in my ears, brought on by the force of the idea that I'd just had. If I'd been a Zen student getting whacked in the head by an ir-ritated monk, the impact couldn't have been any more sharp or illuminating. Unfortunately, the notion that just occurred to me was as terrifying as it was sudden and irresistible.

"Why don't you come hear my presentation on Monday?

I'm suddenly struck by a number of parallels between my research and this case that I think you'll find interesting. I'm also betting that there'll be one other person in the audience who'll be impressed by the similarities as well. I'll tell you all about it tomorrow, but for now, I may have a plan to flush out the killer!"

Chapter 17

I RESOLUTELY WENT BACK TO MY ROOM, DETERMINED to continue framing my paper for the presentation on Monday, but despite my resolution it wouldn't happen. Not a damned word. I stared at the screen. I thought about making another sandwich. I considered going for a run. Nothing. My heart just wasn't in my lecture notes now, and my brain was entirely elsewhere.

I realized that I'd been landlocked for too long. As much as I loved the library, I needed to see some landscape a little more lively than that on the estate. Water, if possible, deeper than wading depth. I needed to get out of there altogether, truth be told. I'd already told some friends at a local historical society that I'd be by for a visit at some point, and that trip would expand my horizons for the afternoon, at least. I left a note on the table, the phone rang; it was Sasha asking if I was okay, because I hadn't shown up. I told her my plans and got into the car.

* * *

As I drove farther away from the complex, losing myself on the highway, I felt as though a weight was falling from me; not only had my horizons been limited by the trees and buildings of Shrewsbury, but my spirit had been bound up by the place as well. It was almost as though I hadn't taken a good deep breath in weeks, something that felt too much like distress, as opposed to plain old common or garden variety stress.

And speaking of stress . . . Ol' Bessy made an uncomfortable grinding sound as I shifted gears going up another foothill. It wasn't so bad the next time, but it persisted nonetheless. All of this gearwork was taking its toll on her, and this time I was convinced that there wasn't going to be a nice, cheap quick fix for whatever was making that noise. It sounded terminal. I didn't see any lights go on, and I had checked all the fluids repeatedly since I'd come out here, but I got the impression that if I made it through this trip, I'd be lucky.

It was fortunate that the last unkind hill had brought me within level distance of my destination, the Redfield County Historic District. My friends Nell and Chris were in charge there; having started out years ago as the archaeological component of the visitor center's crew of six, dwindling funds and increasing cutbacks insured that they now covered everything including geology, history, natural history, and, occasionally, archaeological fieldwork. Still, they were happy about it; the schools who perennially dropped off thousands of students from all over the state were happy about it, and they just kept crossing their fingers every time budget time came around.

The visitor center was an ugly, squat concrete building that was meant to look exciting and modern but only managed to look like a bunker, stark and hideously out of place against its wooded location. The last hopeful gasp before the funds dried up in the 1980s, the building was just one story tall, with long banks of windows that afforded good views of the outside.

I pulled into the parking lot, recently repaved to repair the damage from the frost heaves. It was a patchwork quilt of filled-in potholes, the tar stained with salt like the edge of a margarita glass. I found myself noticing, out of habit, which ones overlay others and were therefore later repairs. At one point, I was so busy following one long patch of purplish asphalt that I found myself observing that a break in the surface resembled two fragments of broken pottery that would mend together. I shook my head and thought, I need to get out more often. Really.

The door to the building opened and a heavyset man stepped out, wearing a down vest over a dress shirt and tie, along with a wool cap. As I approached, Chris sipped on a can of soda and leaned against the frame of the closed door, letting the weak March sun warm his teddy-bear face.

I guess he hadn't changed much in the years since we first crossed paths, archaeologists studying a similar time period and working within a couple of hours' drive of each other, but the lines on his round face were a little deeper, and I got the impression that the cap was covering an ever-diminishing amount of wavy brown hair. The times we met were at conferences for the most part, though our e-mails were filled as much with personal updates as bibliographic exchanges. He and Nell were good people, into the work with a good balance of reality and idealism, juggling their growing family with complicated schedules, diminishing state and local budgets, and their mutual passion for colonial reenactment.

I waved and he responded, tentatively, until I walked closer and he recognized me.

"Hey, Emma! You still driving that piece of shit?" Chris and I had been friends since Bessy was a proud and recent acquisition.

"Not for too much longer, if that nasty sound it was making up the last hill was any indication." We shook hands warmly. "How you been, Chris?"

"Overworked and underpaid. Damn glad it's spring, though it always seems to come later and later out here. How about you?"

"Much the same. Also underappreciated."

"I hear you." He sighed and scratched behind his ear, under the cap. "Why, just last week, I managed to trim my budget without taking too big a bite out of the new programs Nell wants to do next year and without having to cut back on the old stuff. What thanks do I get? The finance committee got on my case for not having made the changes in the first place, and I caught a ration from Nell, who also called me a butcher."

"Sounds rough."

He shrugged. "Nah. It's just the same crap every year. It doesn't even bug me anymore. It comes with the seasons, right? I go home and complain to my wife about what kind of a magician I have to be to do the job I have and how whiny my staff is, and Nell comes home and complains to me that even after four years, her ungrateful boss asks her to do more and more with less and less. Then we have a drink and get the kids out of hock, and it's cool."

I furrowed my brow. "Please tell me that by out of hock, you mean you pick them up from school or something."

"Daycare, but Todd's off to big-boy school next year. He's very impressed with himself." Chris took another swig of soda. "God, listen to me. Between the bureaucracy and the kids, my vocabulary has gone into the poo-poo toilet. Save me, tell me what you're up to. Something adult and archaeological, with artifacts and everything."

I briefly filled him in on the Chandler journal and what I'd been doing at Shrewsbury. Although he'd heard about the murders—how could he not?—Chris only stopped me to ask whether I was okay. I didn't elaborate any further on that situation than to reassure him I was fine.

"I just needed a break, you know?" I finished. "Get out of there, get out of myself."

"I hear you," and that was the end of his questions. I breathed a sigh of relief.

"Look, if you want, Nell's in the activity room with a batch of fourth-graders. You can go watch her for a bit if you want, she'll even put you to work, if you don't move fast enough out of her reach. Or if you want, you can go check out a couple of the cellar holes we're going to take a peek at next year. We have two definites—they've got flags—and one possible. We're going to break for a late lunch in about twenty minutes, but they're not far."

I knew right away how I was inclined. "I think I'll take a walk and see if I can't discover any more of your cellar holes. With the way my luck's been running, I'll probably find one by falling into it."

"Don't knock it; it worked for me. That's why I leave the fun to Nell these days, and hide at the desk. I can't believe how much it takes out of me. It wasn't that long ago that we were all indefatigable, was it, Emma?"

He sighed, but looked content enough, I thought. "Not that long at all."

"Okay, I'll see you in a bit. Just follow the trails around back. We trust you enough so you can move off the paths, no matter what the signs say." He wagged a finger at me. "Just don't go taking anything, now, young lady."

"Damn. There goes my funding for next year."

I went around back and paused at the window to watch Nell for a minute. She was a graying ash blonde, slender and looking lost in one of Chris's old sweaters. The waiflike look was misleading, as I knew that she was all whiplike muscle from fieldwork and wrangling her toddlers at home. It took me a moment to figure out what she was doing; the window was shut tight, blocking out the sound in the class-room, and she had a group of kids helping her make a cake. That didn't make a lot of sense until I realized she was teaching them about stratigraphy and how archaeologists look at the layers of soil on a site. The plate was put down first, the earliest "layer." Then one layer of pound cake, a thick smear of frosting, a layer of sprinkles, another layer of cake, more frosting, some chocolate chips, and a final layer of cake, the frosting on top of that, and then gummy bears on the very top.

My stomach rumbled as I watched her, as if by pan-tomime, show that to get to the earliest layers, a careful ar-chaeologist or cake-eater had to work from the top down; I also noticed that she had them jot down how they ate the cake, recording the layers as they carefully exposed them with plastic spoons. I suppose that went a long way to take some of the sting out of hearing about how we learned about dating things, reasoning the layers on top were deposited later in time relative to the ones on the bottom. If she threw in a few of those gold-foil candy coins or some other good-ies, she could have gone on about how we can work with ar-tifacts whose dates we do know.

God bless her, I thought, for having the guts to work with ten-year-olds, though perhaps their parents wouldn't love them having a big chunk of cake at school, or learning to eat their food in layers, which didn't bode well for future meals of lasagna, sandwiches, or s'mores. The kids were probably old enough to understand the concepts she was teaching them, but I personally never felt comfortable talking to any-one under twelve, in the instructional sense. Though if Marty's kid was going to be my godchild, then I'd have to learn. But Nell had the knack of getting across to any age group, which was a talent I just didn't have, nor did I have the patience to work on acquiring it.

Nell caught my eye and held up a finger for me to wait

for her until she'd finished, another minute. Then as the kids were cleaning up, she came over to the window, and raised it up.

"Hey, you! What are you doing out here in the back of beyond?"

"Clearing my head. You're finishing up soon?"

She glanced at the clock. "Another twenty minutes or so? Got time to stick around for a chat?"

I nodded. "I'll catch you on my way out."

"Good deal. See you then."

I followed the trail for about ten minutes. It was well maintained, different paths marked for different destinations, difficulty, and distances, and what's better, it was nothing like the manicured woodlands at Shrewsbury. There was just enough honest mud, frozen, dried, and hardened into boot-shaped ridges, to remind me it was March. Even the air was different, more of a bite, and I could hear the sound of an eagle screaming as it soared overhead. The sky was pale blue and unbroken by clouds; it seemed to go on forever. Out by the highway, it seemed almost to race the stony hills to the horizon; here in the woods, the trees were the columns supporting the sky like the roof of a cathedral.

As I walked along, I kept my eyes open for clues that would lead me to a cellar hole. Openings in the trees, perhaps a sparse stand of younger trees that had grown in the area after the house was abandoned and had collapsed over time. Collections of stones that were not natural, something more than glacial deposits. Stones that were squared off, worked, perhaps even with the telltale tool marks left by the feather and wedge used by some stonemason long ago to dress them. Fruit trees, perhaps the remains of an orchard, or roses, anything that had been introduced and cultivated by humans, or maybe even some clusters of native but opportunistic plants that throve on the edges of habitation sites, where there might be disturbed soil, waste dumps, or animal pens. Just one more example of how so often studying humans comes down to looking at their trash.

The smell of dried leaves and earth was restorative, and settling into my old habits of field walking was a balm. I paused on the trail, squinting off to the left. Sure enough, in amid some fairly old oaks was a small cluster of flat stones, tumbled perhaps, but still in a roughly rectangular shape around an indentation. Taking advantage of Chris's permission for me to go off the trail, I ventured into the woods to get a better look. It took me a moment, but then I found the flagging that my friends had used to mark the area. Satisfied that I hadn't lost my skills, rusty as they presently might be, I continued on the path.

I was just about to turn around, having walked for about twelve minutes, when I heard a gunshot. Hunters, I thought automatically, though the notion didn't cheer me much, being dressed in dark colors and without any fluorescent safety gear. I didn't think it was actually hunting season, but the shot sounded remarkably close by, though I didn't have any idea how sound carried in the hills around here. More than time to get back, I decided.

That's when the second shot came, and this one was undeniably close.

I whirled around crazily, but couldn't see anyone sporting hunter's orange. "Shit! Hey! There are people out—!"

At that point, a third shot rang out, and I heard a heavy thud beside me; I felt a sharp pain in my cheek. I abandoned the ideas that it was hunters, licit or illicit, and I didn't care to find out why anyone should be so careless. I was still hoping that it wasn't deliberate, as I broke into a run. A fourth shot followed, and this time I could tell a tree had been hit, within feet of me.

I tore down the trail toward the visitor center, but realized that the path was probably the least safe option: Whoever was shooting at me would know exactly where I was heading. I certainly didn't want them to be able to find me, and I sure as hell wasn't going to lead them back to the visitor center and all those kids, either. Operating under the assumption that whoever had the gun was behind me, I left the path and hit the woods, heading roughly back the way I'd come. As I entered a small clearing, I heard another sharp crack and dove behind a slight rise in the ground. That hurt as much as the shelter comforted me; leaves covering rocks in a shallow concavity didn't much help to break my fall.

"Emma? Emma!"

I could hear that it was Chris: I didn't want to answer, but I had to warn him. "Chris, don't! Someone's shooting at me!"

"They sure as hell better not be!" he shouted even louder now. "I don't know what the deal is, buddy, but I'm armed and you should get gone now!"

I strained to hear, but couldn't make out anything that sounded like anyone retreating. At the same time, there were no more shots. I waited still, unsure of what to do.

"Emma?" Chris called. "Come on out, toward me. Keep talking so that I know it's you, okay?"

"Uh . . ."

"It'll be okay."

"All right." I had a last look around, and couldn't see anyone, not even Chris. "I'm coming out now. I don't see anyone . . ."

"That's good, just keep coming toward me. Follow the path, if you can find it again."

"Uh, no problem." I tried to think of something to say. "Um, I think I found another foundation hole for you."

"Yeah?" Chris called back, his voice cracking a little. "That's good. Pretty big one?"

"Not too bad." I thought about what I'd used it for. "I would have liked it to be deeper, though."

"Well, come back next summer. It will be pretty deep after we get done excavating it. You think you can find it again?"

By this time I could see Chris. True to his word, he had a shotgun in his hand, but he was sweating bullets, and breathing heavily, a Day-Glo orange vest hanging half off him.

I hurried the rest of the way down the path. "Chris, I didn't want to lead whoever it was toward the center. Toward the kids."

"Nell just put them on the bus; everyone's fine. I doubt they even heard it." Then he saw me up close. "Shit, you're bleeding!" The alarm on his face made him look almost babyish. "Did you get hit?"

"I didn't think so—" But some of those shots had come pretty close, I recalled with a shiver. I reached out to Chris instinctively, and clutched his sleeve in my hand.

"I think I see a piece of bark," he said, going paler, holding my arm tight. "Maybe it's just a splinter. Let's get you back and get you cleaned up. And I'm going to call the cops."

"No! Don't!" A panic almost as great as that in the woods threatened to engulf me.

Confusion filled Chris's face. "Emma? I gotta call the cops, I can't just . . . ."

I shook myself. "No, you're right . . . you have to call them."

"What's wrong?"

"I . . . nothing. I . . . just didn't want any more police."

Chris didn't say anything. We walked the long way around to his office, avoiding the windows of the classroom, just in case. He picked up the phone and looked at me. I nodded, and Chris called the police. He then pulled a first aid box out from a steel cabinet and put on a pair of surgical gloves. He probed gently at my face, and I felt a sharp pain as he hit something. "You got a big-assed splinter in here. I'm going to take it out, okay?"

"Yeah, sure."

He worked carefully, but I could feel the blood flow when the splinter was removed. Chris took his time blotting it up and applying disinfectant. "By the way, I don't advertise that I keep a shotgun out in the truck. I don't like to take any chances, not with the kids around."

"Gotcha."

"Did you see anyone? Do you think it was . . . something to do with the other stuff? At Shrewsbury?"

"I didn't see anyone, but the bullets just came faster when I called out to whoever was there."

"Hmm. Any idea who it might have been?"

"Not really." But the number of suspects had just been increased by two, if Detective Kobrinski had to release Paul Burnes and Gary Connor. I felt a sharp pain as the disinfectant found its way into the wound. "Ouch!"

"Now, you're all right. I'm done," Chris said with the practiced calm of a father. He cleaned up the discarded wrappers and gloves and put the box away. "I don't think you'll need stitches or anything." He paused as he shut the cabinet door.

"Emma. Do me a favor? Talk to your cop about this, okay?"

I nodded. "I'm going to call the investigating officer as soon as I get out of here."

Chris looked at me funny, and I realized that he seemed a little sick.

"What the hell is going on here?" Nell was suddenly in the doorway, her face waxen. "Christopher Marlowe Hensley, you tell me what I just heard outside! And what is that thing doing around your neck?" She tugged at the hunting-orange vest that still hung crazily off Chris.

"Uh. There were shots. I was worried about Emma."

He didn't need to say anything more. Nell saw the shotgun propped up against the cabinet.

"You asshole!" She crossed the office in two steps and shoved her husband in the chest. "Don't you know—?"

"Yes, of course I do. Why do you think I . . . ?"

By this time, Nell was sobbing, hanging onto Chris by his shirt. He was crying too, not making any noise at all. I wished I was a million miles away; this *was* all my fault, I couldn't help but think.

Sirens sounded nearby.

Nell quieted down; Chris pulled out a hanky and handed it to her. She shook her head, pulled out her own, and wiped her eyes and nose. "Trust us to get pregnant, right before a vacation."

"I knew we would, we always do. St. Bart's?"

"Better hope it's a boy. What would we name a girl?"

"Bartina? Guadalupe?" Chris screwed up his eyes, concentrating. "Maybe Gustavia?"

Nell shuddered. "Better hope it's a boy." She turned to me. "We were going to St. Barthelemy in a couple of weeks. We name the kids . . . well, usually we go on vacation, we even think about going on vacation, we get a kid."

I was about to suggest she change travel agents, but I bit my tongue. "Congratulations."

Nell turned suddenly on Chris. "And you, if you know I'm pregnant, don't go running into the woods with a shotgun!"

"This is my fault," I interrupted. "If I hadn't been here . . ."

"Don't be stupid, Emma." Nell cut in. "You don't know who was out there. Big guy should have a little more sense, no matter what."

"I was thinking of you . . ." he began, but he already sounded lame. "I wasn't going to let anyone hurt you."

"Don't be a dope." She kissed him again, suddenly all business.

I wasn't about to bring up the fact that Chris had probably saved my life. I didn't want to believe the shots had anything to do with me, and admitting that he had would bring it home to me.

The three of us went outside and waited for the cops to come. When the squad car arrived, Chris and Nell looked relieved.

"Burke's a friend of mine," Chris explained. "Good guy."

"You guys okay, Chris?" the officer called as he emerged from the vehicle.

"Yeah, Burke, we're okay. This is Emma, she's the one who was out there."

The cop was on the shorter side of average height, but with a barrel chest that seemed to compensate for his lack of inches. "What happened, ma'am?"

I quickly told him my part of the story, and he noted it down. He looked concerned, confirmed Pam Kobrinski's name and number, then asked Chris his side of things.

"And there were no more shots after you called out?"

Chris shook his head. "Nope."

"Okay." The policeman excused himself and spoke into his radio for a few moments. When he returned he announced, "I'm going to check out back. I doubt there's anyone still around though."

We waited inside until he was done, about twenty minutes, then Burke returned and he and Chris spoke away from me and Nell before he departed.

"I want to go pick up the kids," Nell announced suddenly, watching the cruiser depart. "I want to see them right now."

Glancing at the clock, Chris said, "They won't be ready for another—" But then he got a look at his wife's face. "Right. It won't matter if they leave a bit early today. Emma, I think—"

"I've got to get out of here." I hugged them both, and after reassuring them both that I was fine, and being reassured in turn that they were both fine. I headed for the door.

"Drop by the house before you head back home, okay?

Some weekend. A real visit, with lunch and drinks. You can see the kids." Nell was trying hard not to seem relieved that I was going, but wasn't protesting. Neither was Chris. I couldn't blame them in the least.

"Right." And hold the gunfire, I added silently.

When I got back to Shrewsbury, I called Pam Kobrinski, who wasn't at all thrilled with my description of my afternoon, and I had to bite my tongue to keep from telling her that it wasn't like I was doing anything wrong. She informed me that she would indeed be speaking with Chris's friend the cop and warned me that I might be asked for more information. I agreed quickly, but inside, my heart sank. Just thinking about what I'd had to go through in the trial of a murderer who'd gone after my sister not so long ago was enough to make me want to limit my participation as much as possible, but I knew that she was right. It was my responsibility.

I made yet another sandwich, went back to my room, and tried to write, as if it would be easier to work now, but that was a faint hope at best. So, trying to ignore my throbbing cheek, I began to write down the new ideas that *were* flooding my head. I took out a piece of paper and began writing down the names of the people who were in this mess with me, and then I started writing why each one might be a likely candidate for murderer.

Paul Burnes: Obsessed with Faith. Long history of weird, probably mutually abusive relationship—crime of passion? Good motive. If not absolutely confirmed as liar then certainly unreliable. Coincidence, his showing up just after Faith's death? Attacked Sasha—why? Thought she was Faith? Or is something else going on here? Very charismatic—could have poisoned Jack (if Jack saw him). Did he trash my room? Pull me off the stepladder? Problems: Access to the library (especially to see Jack's note for me)? Could he have talked Faith into meeting him before he killed her? Time problem with arrival? Awfully convincing in his denial at the station. He gets released, I get shot at . . .

I loitered over Paul for quite a while before I took a deep breath and began working on the folks at the library. I didn't want to think these things about most of them, but if I was going to do things properly, I wasn't going to let my own biases get in the way. That was just bad science.

Harry Saunders: Has access to everything. Knows the worth and could easiest of anyone remove things without being caught. Dragging his feet over the problem with alarms? Too well dressed for librarian's salary? Waited to tell the cops that the books were being stolen.

I paused there, realizing that I would need two lists—all of the things I'd written for Harry had to do with the theft, and nothing to do with Faith or Jack. I kept writing dutifully:

Everything's been happening at the library. Motive for killing Faith or Jack? Knew them both . . . Problems: Is he strong enough to have held Faith under water? Motive? No clue there. Books another story. Did he get caught by Faith? What was she doing out there? Did they have some sort of affair while she was here? He looked really broken up the day she died. What about Jack? How would Harry have known I was in Redfield?

Sasha Russo: Obviously very upset about something. Connection with Paul??? Didn't press charges against him after attack . . . Stronger than she looks—Fed Ex box. Looks superficially like Faith—significant? Passionately involved

with Harry—motive for killing Faith, she said he was distraught over her death—could be jealous of Faith because of
Harry's interest in her? Certainly seemed to be. Has been in
several places where thefts have occurred, has access to the
library and the grounds. She was in Philadelphia when similar thefts occurred. Seen over me after pulled off stepladder—did she do it? Problems: too good to be true (likes my
work). Motive? She's said she's broke, she also mentioned
that there will be cuts, and if she's the last hired, would she
be first fired? Is she stealing the books and selling them off?

Here I hesitated again. I thought about erasing the line
about liking my work, but left it in anyway. Underlining the
most damning thing, which was that she showed up in two
places where similar thefts had taken place, led me directly
and all too easily to my next suspect.

Michael Glasscock: Obsessed with women—vague about
previous relationship with Faith. Connection between this
and Faith's looking like Sasha or vice versa? Shows up in
both places where thefts occurred and where Sasha has
worked. Also charismatic. Also rude, cynical, brilliant
(knowledge of books, all stolen were his period—reli-
gious/philosophical??), scatological, arrogant, moody = violent??? Remember what Harry said about his book being
cold, inhuman. If he turned his mind to crime, it wouldn't be
a problem for him. Smartass. Sits alone in the dark being
enigmatic. Hand hurt after Faith found—also, didn't spend
night in Boston with Wife #3 as he planned? Seems too suspicious of Sasha? Perked up when I mentioned things happening at library—nerves for himself, or interest in my
observation? Was there when Gary cleaned out his locker—
planted books to implicate him?—there when I was pulled
off stepladder; Jesus, he found Jack, there in the house when
Faith's diary went missing and my room was trashed?????

Motives? Broke from alimony, stolen books either his subject (so he has only access to them or can sell them). Affair
with Faith? Knew Jack professionally before we met here—
competition, some other knowledge? I don't know yet. Murders to cover up thefts? Crime of passion, viz. Faith? Said
they had a complicated past. Problems: Has same access I
do, that is, not to stacks. Has been truthful about everything,
including fact that he doesn't entirely trust me and fact I
shouldn't trust him—Ten Little Indians crack. Bizarre, self-
confessional attitude = distraction from inherent truth? Said
I should consider leaving for safety—mine or his??? Again,
shortly thereafter I am shot at—did he see my note? How
would he have found me out there?

I was startled at how much I had written so quickly, and
that started to make me nervous. How much had I been ignoring, possibly to my own peril? Casting an educated eye
over what I wrote about Michael, I was struck by two things.
I had written more personality traits down about him than
any of the others, and if I had been reading an entry like that
in Madam Chandler's diary, I would have suspected her of
some sort of interest. And I had filled up a goodish space
with far too many damning coincidences. Holy snappers.

After I sat pondering that for a few more minutes, I realized that a part of my visceral attraction to Michael could be
chalked up to my romantic associations with libraries. After
all, I'd met Brian at the library in grad school, and certainly
libraries had afforded some private spaces for necking in my
life before that. But that alone wasn't enough to account for
my reaction to him, and I soon saw that it was the way that
Michael lived—seemingly devoted to his work, taking little
responsibility for students or even his wives, for that matter,
not much caring how he appeared to people—that was appealing to me now. Who wouldn't see the allure of being that
selfish, while juggling a spouse, a house, and a job? It wasn't

so much that I wanted Michael, though he was attractive; it was more that I wanted the luxury of his attitude. I sighed; my life was so nearly ideal, if only I could manage juggling it all a little better.

Chewing my pen's cap, I considered writing down the names of the interns that I'd run into, or the other security guards, but dismissed them. I just didn't know enough about any of them. But there were two others that should definitely be placed on the list:

Mr. Constantino: Jerk. Vain. Arrogant. Bigot. Not nice. Doesn't like women with any kind of power, me or Kobrinski, and probably not Faith, either. Access to everything—dragging his feet over problem with alarms? Enough brains to sell stolen books? Motives: More for thefts than murders, don't know his relations with Faith or Jack? Strong enough to drown Faith, but why? Framed Gary with books? In league with Gary about books? Problems: A menace to polite society, but is he the murdering type?

Gary Conner: Ditto above, with bells on. Has access to everything, books found in his locker. Problems: Motive for murders? Found messing about at Faith's murder scene, then called Constantino first, not cops. Did he have the brains to take the books found in his locker? Problem with encyclopedia vs. Mather or Jonathan Edwards?? Violent, has it out for me. P. K. thought enough of that to warn about his release (and then shots go whizzing past my head—how did he know I was going to be out there?). Did he trash my room? Pull me off the ladder? Knows the grounds. Take the diary? Why? Also, what connection between him and Faith or Jack?

Once again the phone outside began to ring, and this time I went to answer it with relief: I was getting more questions than answers with my little exercise. That of course was all too common an occurrence in archaeology and it was much less pleasant an experience in murder investigations. But by the time I got out into the hall, the phone had stopped ringing. I leaned over the banister to hear Michael on the extension in the front hallway.

"No, she's not in. I'll leave her a note. Yeah, bye." Michael hung up and, I noticed, did not bother to write a note for anyone.

"Hey, was that for me?" I shouted over the railing as I descended the stairs.

"Leaping Vishnu!" My gloomily cloaked colleague staggered a few steps and clutched at his chest. "Goddamn. Through too many years of being chewed on by members of your sex, Emma, my heart is merely a tattered, flapping piece of gristle, a pump not fit for a goldfish bowl. Certainly not made to take that kind of shock!" He paused a moment, thoughtfully. "I think I just wet myself."

I scowled. "Knock it off, Michael. Was that for me?"

He pulled a face at me. "You, you, you, that's all you ever think about. You wouldn't have a spare Depends on you, would you?"

"Michael!"

He seemed distracted still, suddenly pulling out a notepad on which he scribbled a few notes. "Yes, it was for you. Call your husband. Tomorrow. He's going out now. He's changed hotels. What's with the bandage on your face? What happened to you?"

"I cut myself shaving," I said impatiently. "What hotel is he going to?" I was anticipating another showy display of his eidetic memory.

"How should I know?"

I looked at him doubtfully, my skin shivering. "Brian didn't tell you?"

"Yes, he did. I've just forgotten. You scared it out of me."

"So how am I supposed to call him? Were you even going to bother giving me the message?"

"Yes, probably. I'm generally good about that sort of thing. I've got a lot on my mind right now. It won't happen again. Dial star six nine, if you have to. Now if you don't mind . . ." He started to go upstairs.

I stomped my foot; since it was bare, it hurt like hell. I didn't care. "Damn it! Do you have any idea of how bloody inconsiderate that was? What if there's an emergency?"

"You anticipating one, Emma?" he said nastily. "I said it won't happen again."

"Yeah. Well. It better not." I muttered at his retreating back. Michael, I'm trying hard, but you're not doing a damned thing to save yourself.

Tortured thoughts like that didn't help my writing any, the whole rest of the day, and I went to bed in a foul mood, taking the usual precautions. I called Brian's cell phone and left him a message.

By lunchtime on Thursday I was feeling reckless, ordering two grilled cheese sandwiches along with a cup of Nancy's high-test coffee while I told Pam Kobrinski about what I'd found in the diary. Her reaction to my plan for Monday's talk reminded me of one of a cat nearly stepping into a puddle of perfume. Disgust was replaced by horror, which gave way to disbelief on Pam's features.

"That's got to be the stupidest idea I've ever heard," she said.

I didn't really expect that she would be over the moon about my plan, but that rather hurt. "There are obvious parallels between this case and the one in which Madam Chandler was involved," I explained. "There's the diary, the notion that none of the evidence is quite what we think it is, the intelligent, strong-willed woman within a small community. I thought that if I hinted at some of the similarities and then just let the killer's imagination take over . . ." I sniffed. "I thought that it was pretty slick, all things considering."

"Slick doesn't count for much when your ass is on the line!" Kobrinski slammed her coffee mug onto the table. "I don't see how getting the killer riled is going to get us any closer to the truth. I mean, do you think someone is going to jump up and confess? Worse yet, maybe, jump up and take a shot at you? Oh, wait!" She gestured at the bandage on my cheek. "Maybe he already has!" Her eyes and mouth narrowed with disgust. "Jesus Christ on a pony!"

I carefully finished the last bite of my sandwich before I answered her; her sarcasm was best ignored. "Most everything I'll be saying is completely innocent. Everyone knows there is a lot of police attention here right now. The murderer will have to be very careful and not give himself away before he can find out what I really know. I figure, I'll just keep my eyes open for any extra attention and then call you. Right away."

"It's a stupid idea," she muttered stubbornly.

"Have you got a better one?" I shot back.

"No."

"Are you going to be there on Monday?"

"You gonna go through with this whether I am or not?"

"Pretty much."

She sighed and pulled out her Tums. There was only one left, so she went up to the counter to buy another package. I could tell she was stalling.

"You just bought one of these six packs," Nancy said. "You eat them like they're candy, Pam. You gotta take better care of yourself."

"It's my butler, Nance. He was late with my bonbons and pedicure this morning and it throws my whole day off," Pam replied lightly, to the proprietor's laughter. She sat down again with a scowl for me and began peeling the paper off the newly purchased roll. "I don't like it."

"What's the scoop with Paul Burnes?" I said when she plopped back down, to change the subject.

It wasn't a happy change, as far as Kobrinski was concerned. She looked completely haggard. "He was flying somewhere over the Midwest when Faith was killed. He didn't land at Logan until *after* the outside time limit for the time of death. I was able to hold him only until I got a positive make on him from one of the flight attendants." Her last statement sounded like it was being rung from her. "It couldn't have been him."

He, I corrected her grammar mentally, for the sake of something to distract myself. I pushed the crumbs around my plate, gathering them into little piles while I took in her news. I wasn't surprised, but now I had to come to grips with a new disturbing scenario.

"Tissue of lies," the words Paul had used to describe Faith's stories, her diary, rang in my ears over and over again. "He's one hell of a good actor; he believed himself." Faith's words also returned, like the memory of a bad dream. I couldn't tell who was lying and who was being honest. Either I believed Faith's story, and ignored everything that everyone at the library had to say about her and what I knew about her talent for exploiting her audience, or I believed Paul wasn't acting in front of the two-way mirror, and had to admit that I had been used by Faith as an accessory to their grotesque relationship.

A surge of anger engulfed me, and I thought about that night I had spent in front of the fire listening to Faith's story. I felt used, like I was being laughed at for a sucker, even though I had no idea of how much of anything was true. I resented not knowing how big a fool a dead woman thought me, and hated myself for thinking such things of a woman who'd claimed to be battered.

But maybe, I thought, inspiration suddenly spilling over, it wasn't the facts as I experienced them, but the truth of the little world that Paul and Faith embraced as their own that I really needed to understand. Whatever emotional fallout seeped out past the confines of their twisted relationship just *wouldn't* make sense to anyone else. It still sickened me to think of the hurt that these two people inflicted on each other, but there was that backward, Looking-Glass logic that was perhaps remotely comprehensible if it was—well, the way they *were* together. Their own private drama, a mutually destructive symbiosis.

Faith's missing diary became more important than ever, if we were ever going to unsnarl this tangle of hurt and deceit and, more important, find out who else might have been involved with her enough to want to kill her.

"You okay?" Pam said wearily. I could tell she was at the end of her rope. She had nothing else to go on. If she hadn't been so exhausted, she never would have let me see her like this.

Sighing, I reached into my coat pocket and took out my folded list of suspects and suspicions. Carefully smoothing out the creases, I slid it across the table to her without a word. Behind me, I could hear the hiss of the high-power dish sprayer, the clink of heavy dishes; orders were called out and the sizzle of the grill answered them.

She took it with a glance that warned me of betraying her with hope, and scanned it quickly. "You know, you've written more than twice as much for Mr. Glasscock than you have for anyone else here. Pretty incriminating stuff too."

"I know."

A little spark of vitality seemed to ignite her eyes. "Looks like some overlaps between here and events at the Philadelphia library. Maybe I'd better give a call to the Philadelphia police, find out what they know about those stolen items. Maybe call the Parker House, ask some questions."

"Maybe."

Obviously feeling a little more her old self, Pam Kobrinksi said sternly, "Under no circumstances are you to go setting traps in your talk."

I gave her a sour look that informed her precisely what I thought of her order, and got up to leave. "Monday. Two o'clock."

She caught me by the sleeve as I passed her and I had to stop. "Dr. Fielding?"

That was the first time she'd used my professional title since we met. Up until now, she'd been very careful to use the more democratic "Ms." "Yes, Detective Sergeant Kobrinski?"

"Shots in the woods. A list of suspects. The library teeming with corpses. All of a sudden I've got an idea we're getting close to this. Do me a favor, would you?"

"What's that?"

"Watch your back."

Chapter 18

THE GRINDING NOISES COMING FROM UNDER THE hood finally convinced me that they weren't going to go away, so I stopped while I was in Monroe, to get Bessy checked out. The mechanic's initial assessment was grim, both for my pocketbook and in his prognosis for my car's long-term future. He agreed to do what he could, and gave me a lift back to Shrewsbury.

Back at the residence, the next assault I experienced came from the last place I was expecting—my sister Bucky—and that was really more the threat of an invasion. Bucky called to tell me that she'd found "just the cat" for me.

"I'm sure I don't need to tell you that I already have all the cat I need, or that Quasimodo would make short work of any other cat that darkened his doorstep." Our present cat was still not certain *I* would get to stay.

As usual, Bucky disregarded anything that was inconvenient to her. "You overreact to Quasi. He's a pumpkin, really, just with a strong sense of territory and limited people skills. He'll be fine with Minnie."

"Minnie? What, as in Minnie Mouser?"

"Minnie as in Minerva. The shelter brought her into the surgery for me to check out, and that's what they're calling her. She's really bright, so it fits her. I call her Skinny Minnie, though, because she's a tiny little thing, mostly bones at the moment. She's got a real pretty color, and once you meet her, her personality—"

"Bucks, you're talking like I said I'd take this cat. The truth is I couldn't even if I wanted to. I've got too much going on in my life with work right now, my tenure portfolio is being reviewed, the house is still a mess, and, well, there's just too much going on here at the moment for me to even consider adding anything else to the pile."

"You need to get a life."

"Excuse me? I thought I just got done telling you I had too much already!"

"No, you got it wrong—"

"I *beg* your pardon?" There really is nothing like a sister to crawl up your nose. Nothing besides nails down a chalkboard, grit in a salad, or bamboo under one's fingernails.

"You got it wrong when you said 'the truth is.' Those are just facts, Em; the *fact* is you're overworked and otherwise busy. The real *truth* is, you need a life. Don't confuse the two things."

"Jeez, thanks for the lesson in semantics." I was feeling distinctly nettled; it was what I'd been talking to Pam Kobrinski about, what I'd been pondering as I studied Margaret's diary.

Bucky sounded pleased with herself. "Makes all the difference in the world. Yes, you say you have Quasi, but he's not really your cat, is he? Big difference there. Now, when do you get home? Or should I just drop her off, and have Minnie waiting for you when you get back?"

"Bucky, don't! We'll talk about this later."

I think I managed to convince her that she wasn't going

to visit this cat upon me, but when I finally hung up, I realized that what Bucky'd been saying about the difference between truth and fact was exactly right. That seemed to be what unstopped the genie's bottle, and I finally got to work on my paper.

All the rest of the weekend I was caught up in the flurry of writing and rewriting my presentation, and by Monday, my nerves were a jangling mess. Finally, after riding the roller coaster between believing that I was writing pap I would have shot a freshman for spouting and knowing that I was just the best thing to happen to archaeology since cold beer, I made my last edit, had a final read-through, and pronounced it good enough for government work.

Which would have been fine, except that this wasn't just a conference paper, something to provoke comments from colleagues. This time I was trying to provoke a killer's curiosity. I wished for the long-ago days when I thought that a word choice in a paper would make or break my career, not this surreptitious prodding and poking, like an experiment that might blow up in my face.

Monday morning I went downstairs for a gallon of coffee, still in my sweats and silly robe. I was too beat to worry about getting dressed before stimulants.

Michael was there, of course, staring out the window as he always did. He didn't bother turning around either, and today I noticed he had *Le Monde* and *Die Welt* to one side with *The Sun* open now. For apparent language skills, however, he seemed stuck on page three of the London tabloid. "Morning, Auntie. Ready to dazzle us all this afternoon?"

I may have mentioned, I'm a little slow in the morning. I stared at him, wondering how he knew it was me. "How did you—"

"You're the only one left, aren't you?"

He sounded so damned spooky that I missed his next question. "What?"

"I said," Michael repeated slowly, exasperatedly, "what are you going to wear?"

"Ware?" I was thoroughly confused now, thinking that he was talking about ceramics, and fumbled for the coffee pot. I needed to feel that exquisite sensation of my poor, overworked skull being cracked open, reborn to the possibilities of the universe. The coffee had been sitting a while, but I drank it greedily anyway, burnt offerings to the gods of intellect.

"For your talk," Michael explained. "Gonna get dressed up for it, right? But I hope you're not like some of my overeager chums in the English department who feel they have to dress the part of their lecture. I have one colleague who feels obliged to wear a big white shirt and Polo cologne whenever he's doing the Gothics. I personally leave the building when Oscar Wilde comes up in the survey—the sight of him in a velvet coat and a Hermés scarf soaked in Chanel No. 5 gives me the willies. Absolutely no pun intended. It wouldn't be so bad if he were gay, I suppose, maybe then he'd know how to wear the clothes, but he still ends up leaving more first-year girls for me. So what kind of perfume do lady archaeologists wear?"

"Obsession," I answered promptly, saluting him with my mug.

Michael turned around, critically surveying the resurrected wreckage of me from over the rims of his reading glasses. "God, it's like taking the cover off the parrot cage, isn't it? In any case, I'd suggest the dark green silk shirt, that's a nice one with your hair, and you haven't got a pair of black leather trousers, have you?"

"I do *not*."

"Pity. With a string of pearls . . . well, never mind. I'd just lay off the gray wool skirt, that's all. It doesn't exactly make you look dumpy, but—"

"You are the last person I'd take fashion advice from!" I

rinsed out my mug and left it in the strainer. More than time to get out of there. I couldn't bear any further banter with Michael, not when I've just given the police a bunch of good reasons to look into his activities.

"You don't need to look like a model to be an *artiste*, sweetie." He turned back to the engrossing and wholly artificial charms of Miss Page Three.

He can't be the murderer, I thought desperately, I just can't see it. But he's the best candidate so far. I just have to remember to be careful, not let him get past my guard.

I ended up wearing the green shirt anyway, just because it was the last clean one I had.

As I entered the lecture hall down the hall from the library that afternoon, all my anxiety fled. Even noticing Pam Kobrinski over in the corner, I felt completely calm. The sensation was almost like a light buzz, a state of relaxed alertness. An actor friend of mine described the same feeling once. "The lights go down, the intro music goes up, the adrenaline floods, and *poof!* You're in character. You're not worried about hitting your marks because you're Hamlet worrying about regicide, you're Willy Loman worrying about making the next sale."

So nearly twenty years of habit came into play while Harry introduced me to the audience, a good-size crowd of staff and museum members. I smiled benignly—wasn't that nice of him to say those swell things about li'l ol' me?—and, to show my professionalism, gave the audience a somber little nod as I reached the lectern. I shuffled my notes and then let rip with an impish half-grin that said, *Hey folks, hang onto your hats. You're gonna love this*, as I started to read.

My calm lasted long enough to get through my plans for further archaeology on the Chandler homestead, my description of my work on Margaret's journal, and a little background about women's history. It wasn't until I got to the part about how the official record doesn't tell you the whole story that I started getting edgy. I managed to keep my voice from betraying me by pretending I didn't know there were two meanings to nearly everything I said.

"I've learned many things about Margaret Chandler from her diary, her day-to-day life, her struggle with servants, her desire to have children, her pain at being separated from her family, and gradually, how she learned to love her husband— I suspect that it's possible that they had married out of respect and propriety, but never anticipated romantic attachment.

"I've also been learning about Madam Chandler's earlier life in England, and found some hints about her from how she approached life in provincial Massachusetts. She was going through a lot of difficulties settling into this new life: just married, uprooted from everything she was so well-suited to in England, and set down in a world in which she was the exotic, the suspect. I tried to imagine how the cosmopolitan Margaret would have been viewed by her neighbors, who might have been suspicious of her worldly ways, her Anglican religion, or her wealth and high station. It's abundantly clear to me that she had problems fitting in, she who would have been the ultimate social creature in England.

"But the most important lesson, the one I'll talk about today, has rather more dramatic overtones. I'm talking about one particular incident, but a crucial one that fills the pages of the diary I've been studying here at Shrewsbury. It has to do with a murder and a set of falsely leading circumstances."

I let that sink in a moment. With the lights down, except for the low-powered spots pointed at me, I couldn't see the audience very well, but could hear them buzzing and shifting in their seats. The coincidence of what was going on at the library was lost on no one.

"Madam Chandler wrote to her cousin, 'I count it as a

dear lesson, that the truth is more than a sum of facts.' Although that lesson almost cost her life, she was correct then, and her words still bear remarking today. Things are not always what they seem, the obvious choice is not always the right one. Occam's razor can cut too deeply, too deliberately, and it nearly was Margaret's undoing.

"We know from court records and a few antiquarian biographies about Judge Chandler's life and career, and in none of those is there anything referencing his actually presiding over a case in which his wife, Margaret Chandler, was a defendant, accused of murder. Now, not every court record survives, and the ones that do don't always tell the whole story. In this case, it seems that the records of this were lost or suppressed, possibly sealed. Our best description is pieced together from oblique scattered references and the diary itself. Perhaps I'll find more as my work continues, but for now, we know these facts from her own hand.

"Margaret was newly come to Stone Harbor, Massachusetts. She was a woman used to a fairly sophisticated life in England, and so perhaps it was no surprise that she should have spent a good deal of time in the company of the Reverend Lemuel Blanchard, one of the leading ministers of that seaport community, and a well-educated man. Madam Chandler wrote of how she had problems with her new neighbors, who probably weren't as cultivated as she was. Think of it as a clash of cultures. The Reverend, however, had been raised in England, had had a small parish in London, and was known to enjoy the pleasures of the table, perhaps a little more than was strictly appropriate for a minister in those puritanical days. In fact, Margaret herself wrote, 'Reverend Blanchard to tea today. He so thoroughly enjoyed the venison pasty that the Judge must eat cold beef pie for his supper as there was not a crumb of it left.' "

A small titter rippled through the audience, and that reassured me that I had relaxed them enough after my discomforting remarks before. I carried on, building the scenery a little more, and although I could only see her silhouette now, I noticed that Detective Kobrinski was standing to one side paying rapt attention, not to me, but to scanning the crowd.

"So maybe it was no surprise that she enjoyed his company. This congenial situation did not last, however. Reverend Blanchard had been ill, at first mildly, then much more seriously. He quickly deteriorated, dying within a space of three weeks. It did nothing for Madam Chandler's popularity that a well-loved minister collapsed at a party that she was giving, dying at her feet."

Audible shock in the audience this time; I gave the whispering a moment to die down.

"It is about this time that the majority of the entries in her diary are written in code—entries that I've only recently decoded. The substance of the journal now is this: Because his demise was so violent and so quick, it apparently didn't take much time for the rumor to start that Madam Chandler, who had been giving him tonics as soon as she knew of his discomfort, had poisoned him. That gave birth to speculation in several forms, one rumor that she was murdering him to cover up his knowledge of her sexual misconduct. The other rumor, one that seems to show up wherever you find historical rumors of women, sex, and/or poisoning, was that she was a witch."

A small gasp ran through the audience; this was much stronger meat than they had been expecting. I thought it was pretty juicy myself, and looked forward to having the same shocking effect on professional audiences later on. If I survived my little performance today.

"The distinction between poisoning and witchcraft were often confused in theology and popular concept, then as now, and particularly where women are concerned. Fortunately, Justice Chandler was able to employ the lessons learned from the witchcraft horror in nearby Salem, Massachusetts, in 1692, and was able to keep the trial focused on the charges of murder by poison. Still not very appetizing for a man who's just learning that he's in love with his wife."

I gave them that last uneasy laugh, knowing I once again was leading them into turbulent waters.

"Look at it this way. Margaret Chandler was a stranger newly come to a community. She came from a wealthy background, and her aristocratic ways must have seemed out of place, even alien, in what was essentially a provincial village. Her personality—by her own admission 'proud and stubborn'—probably rubbed people the wrong way, making it easy for them to malign her. I'm sure she was probably struggling with her recent separation from her old life in England—from everything she knew—and maybe she did ruffle feathers. I know from reading her diary that she had a hard time settling in and that she was a distinctly opinionated woman, even haughty, at times. If these are qualities that still can nettle today, imagine how they might have been received in a world that was organized on the superior-subordinate relationship of man to woman, a microcosm with a densely woven web of personal interaction governed by strict rules, rife with gossip and self-righteousness."

Here I paused, waiting to see who was getting it. There was an air of tension in the room, like the smell of ozone before a thunderstorm, but try as I might with the lights in my eyes, I couldn't see anyone reacting. All I could see was the detective sergeant, who seemed to be staring in particular at one corner. I couldn't stop to try and discern the source of her interest. I had to plow on.

"She was probably a 'difficult' woman, with all the freight that word implies, but I also know, from my intimate acquaintance with her—through her diary, of course—that Margaret had a strong sense of her role in life and was determined to carry it out. As a woman of rank, she took her duties seriously, helping the poor, tending the sick, sometimes even arbitrating neighborhood squabbles. She taught her servants to read and pray, she ran her household strictly but fairly, even generously, for the times. And in her own words, she 'took to regulating the habits of Mr. Chandler,' meaning that she reminded him to eat his meals, dress tidily, and become involved in the community on a social as well as judicial level. She describes with pride and affection how people remarked on these positive changes in Matthew after their marriage and her arrival.

"But all of this was forgotten when someone pointed out that it was shortly after her arrival in America, after her frequent visits, that the Reverend Blanchard fell ill and died. All that was remembered then was that she was a stranger. That distracted people from examining what had really happened, that the reverend was murdered, but by someone else, for reasons that I still don't know. I don't know, but I have my suspicions."

I couldn't help myself, I didn't mean to be dramatic, but I was dying of thirst and I paused to take a sip of water. You could have heard a pin drop in that room.

"A few conjectures? My impressions are, based on the documents that describe the situation obliquely, the diary and the records that do survive, that it was someone close to the reverend, possibly even in his household. As far as motive, I don't know for sure, but I get the impression from some of her hints that the reverend saw something he shouldn't have. Perhaps it was town politics.

"Perhaps"—I was reaching here, leaving my prepared text but following as the thought occurred to me—"he had something someone else wanted—position, security, wealth? Something that provoked his murderer to speedy, vicious action."

I was really working the nerves of the audience now, and I noticed Pam shaking her head. I was pushing it. I had to bring it back to my research.

"All I know for certain—now—is that Margaret Chandler knew who the guilty party was and ultimately convinced Matthew Chandler to look in the right place for the real murderer. But because she left her *diary*"—I stressed that word emphatically—"as a clue, we are that much closer to learning the truth of what happened the day she believed she would be hanged. We know that she was acquitted, but I am still hot on the trail of why.

"Dr. Maya Angelou once wrote that we, all of us, owe a tremendous debt to the past, that we must make an account of ourselves to those who came before us and struggled to make us what we are, what we can be. In this case, she was referring to our own personal antecedents, but I think that as archaeologists, historians, and others interested in the past, that idea holds a special message for us. It is an adjuration to look beyond the obvious, the easy, the comfortable, to consider all of the possibilities. In the case of Madam Chandler, there was simply a confluence of unrelated events that led to one innocent person being unjustly accused.

"Margaret Chandler was right, things aren't always what they seem, even when the facts are fitted into a sensible pattern. As the evidence accumulates, we are liberated to think the unthinkable, in the name of justice. We owe it to the past to learn the lesson that Margaret Chandler lived and taught, that the truth is more than a sum of facts. We must dedicate ourselves to that notion if we are to do good history, because that simple statement, a simple remark made in a private document, inexorably moves us to truth. Thank you."

There was a slight delay before the audience applauded, and there was something subdued about their response. I couldn't blame them, I was feeling a little wrung out myself. Luckily Harry was there to rescue me.

"I'm sure that Dr. Fielding would be happy to answer any questions you might have."

I didn't know about happy, but after a moment, a few

brave souls stuck their hands up and hazarded questions about my proposed archaeological work, a few about the role of women in the eighteenth century. Knowing that a good lecture begets good questions, I was able to calm myself down as I settled in and answered them.

With a decent pause after the last hand was raised, Harry thanked everyone, and the room started to empty out, save for the folks who wanted to shake my hand, touch the hand that touched the hand, so to speak, in a private audience. I saw that the director, Evert Whitlow, left in a hurry, his lips pursed and his eyes narrowed. Seeing this, Harry excused himself, wanting to speak to me but obviously pressed for time. "Be in tomorrow?" he mouthed.

I nodded and turned back to the last woman in line, who was explaining how much land her important Revolutionary-period ancestors had. After what seemed like an eternity, she left, and I was alone in the room, save for Detective Kobrinski, who was talking to Sasha, and Mr. Constantino, who, surprisingly, was waiting for me.

"I don't know what kind of game you are playing here, but I think we'd all be much happier if you left Shrewsbury immediately." It was clear that *he* was not happy, his temper controlled by the slimmest of margins. I swear I saw him trembling in the half light.

I kept my voice calm. "I'm not leaving. I haven't done anything."

"You've been nothing but trouble since you came here, and now, this . . . *garbage*. In front of an audience. Board members, even. This is going to stop, right now."

"It's going to take more than your wishing, for me to leave," I said. "If you're that concerned about it, take it up with the board. Let them ask me to leave. If you'll excuse me . . ."

I quite deliberately turned my back on him and started to pack up my slides and notes.

"This isn't over, not yet," Constantino growled.

"You're right about that," I said, watching him march out of the auditorium.

The other two women were still in conversation as I started to leave. "Ms. Fielding, I'll stop back by the house on my way out," Pam Kobrinski called, interrupting her conversation with Sasha.

I was so jazzed with adrenaline and the thought of what I'd just tried to do that it took me nearly the entire walk home to calm down. The cold air outside the house must have made me particularly sensitive, because the moment I opened the front door of the residence, the smell hit me. Something was burning. The smell increased in intensity as I quickly moved into the foyer, and I realized that now I could hear crackling coming from the residence's library.

I hurried in and saw that there was a small fire in the fireplace, and that whoever had started it hadn't properly opened the flue, for smoke was slowly accumulating near the ceiling. Coughing and cursing, I cranked the flue all the way open, but when I looked down, I saw that there was a book burning in the fireplace.

My heart stopped. Not the journal. It couldn't be Madam Chandler's journal . . .

I lost another precious moment fumbling with the fire screen, but finally wrenched the doors apart. Grabbing the poker, I tried to knock the burning book out of the fireplace and only succeeded in bouncing it against the inside of the screen, sending up a shower of sparks. I swore and threw the poker aside.

There was nothing else to do. I reached in and grabbed the corner that seemed least touched by the tongues of flame and flung the book onto the hearth. I faltered and lost another precious second when I dropped it again, before I seized it once more, determined to rescue it. I felt the heat of the fire on the tender skin between the top of my leather gloves and the hems of my coat sleeves. Finally I whipped off my gloves and began beating the book with them, until I began to believe I would be able to save it.

Although I now recognized that the book was in fact not Madam Chandler's journal, I still worked feverishly to extinguish the blaze. I slapped at it repeatedly, glad my gloves seemed to be holding out against the fire, for I now recognized that I was trying to rescue Faith's missing diary.

Chapter 19

MY FACE WAS GETTING HOT FROM MY PROXIMITY TO the fire and the added fear that I might be too late to save Faith's diary. There were smuts of burning paper flying up around me as I slapped at the flames consuming the diary, and I had to trust that they were not igniting the carpet when they fell. By the time I'd completely extinguished the small blaze, my leather gloves were a lost cause. I coughed as I determined whether anything had been preserved of the diary.

There was almost nothing left but a handful of feathery soot and tatters of burnt paper that clung delicately to the brittle bound spine of the notebook. The cardboard cover was virtually destroyed, as were most of the pages. Painstakingly, I removed the fragments that were completely burnt. Every time I moved the diary more of it disintegrated, but eventually I reached a thin core of pages that had partially survived. They were stuck together with soot around the edges, and I realized that Faith had not completely filled up her journal: a number of the lined pages were blank at their unburned centers. Suppressing all impatience, I worked back from the unburned parts, trying not to disturb those that were more badly damaged. Finally, I bent one of the blank sheets over, and pried off a scrap of a page with some writing on it. By getting so close that my nose was practically touching the sheet, I could make out handwriting, faintly seen through the scorch marks.

It was the last page of the diary and the only one that was still partially legible. What I saw were partial lines at the center of the page, and as I read, I struggled to re-create the complete sentence that would have encapsulated the surviving phrases:

> *e might become an engaging obsessi*
> *possessed by such a grand one himself. Who'*
> *ere such demons behind that mask, so d*
> *ious. Which will prevail when I tel*
> *know all his secrets? I think I can trust the*
> *y control in this. Such a wee sleekit c*
> *ut a diversion until*
> *ust choose between them b*

The smoke and ash irritated my throat as I puzzled over the words. They were the last words, perhaps, that Faith had ever written in her journal, for the entry, such as it was, ended halfway down the remnant page. A shiver crawled across my back, and I hunched closer over the scrap. She had a mind like a razor and the soul to match; her words chilled me. The way she calculated her emotions was inhuman. It seemed to me that Faith wrote about confronting someone, a man—obsessed by something—with her knowledge of him. Faith seemed to have been trying to decide how long to amuse herself before she had to decide about . . . what?

Whoever this man was, she obviously believed she was in control of the situation. Ultimately, the candidate for her obsession must have surprised her. I recognized a line from

Burns: "Wee, sleekit, cow'rin, tim'rous, beastie." Had the mousie turned on Faith to bite? And had he been the one to steal, and then immolate, the diary?

I phoned the library, but the guard told me that the detective had already left. I got up slowly, and tried to decide what to do with the remaining fragment of the notebook. It was much too fragile to move, and I didn't want to just leave it lying around, so I put it into the cabinet by the fireplace, just in case someone decided to get curious about my room again. I went upstairs, kicked off my pumps and changed into jeans and sneakers, swapping my wool coat for a thick fisherman's sweater. The weather was warmer today with more teasing hints of spring to come, but I felt a cold no number of layers could thaw.

I followed the road back to the library, figuring to catch Kobrinski on her way to see me. I didn't like where all of this was leading, I thought grimly, namely, straight to Michael's doorstep. He had more of a mask than almost anyone I knew and all that attitude had to be covering something. The only thing that kept me from just going up to my room and hiding under my blankets was the fact that it wasn't up to me to decide. I was glad of that, because it just didn't feel right to me—I didn't want to like someone who was a killer—but with such damning evidence, I had to tell Pam Kobrinski.

I'd almost reached the library when I stopped. Hairs prickled down the back of my neck. Not knowing why I did so, I turned around just in time to see the flapping tails of a dark overcoat disappear into the woods. I moved a few steps farther, wondering what in hell Michael, a purely urban creature, was doing walking off the road, much less heading into the woods. After all, the trees would certainly impair any dramatic entrance, I thought wryly, catching at that great billowing coat.

My heart caught in mid-beat and my blood seemed to freeze solid in my veins. Flapping. Billowing. *Billowing*.

Jack had described seeing Faith's jumper billowing, when it never could have.

Oh shit.

It was Michael out there, the night Faith was murdered, I thought, my stomach dropping away. And now Michael had tried to destroy the evidence that might connect him with her. Michael was the murderer.

"Oh. There you are."

The quiet voice at my shoulder startled me so violently that I pivoted around, throwing a perfectly focused, unthinking elbow strike to the speaker's head. It was the sort of reaction that my coach Nolan has been trying to coax out of me forever. The only problem was that Nolan has always urged me to know precisely what my target was. It wasn't until I'd swung around that I saw to my horror that it was Pam Kobrinski's head I was trying to knock off her shoulders.

I didn't have enough control to stop the strike, but my good luck loitered: My elbow whizzed past her, three inches shy of actual contact. She flinched backward, and deflected the blow as she went into a defensive stance. I stumbled, then froze as best I could, lest the good detective shoot me, just on principle.

We eyed each other warily for a second, me panting with panic at what I'd almost done, she watching to see what I'd do next. I put my hands over my mouth, then over my eyes, trying to figure out how to start apologizing.

"Hiding like that isn't a real good followup to an aggressive move. Makes you a real good target," Pam murmured, never taking her eyes off me as she slowly rose up from her crouch. She swallowed, licked her lips, then cracked her neck. "Makes me *want* to hit you."

I peeled my hands away from my face. "Oh God, you scared me . . . I am so sorry." Great; my two best strikes had come first when I was asleep, and then against someone on my side. On top of that, if Nolan ever found out that I'd backed off an attack, he'd nail my hide to the barn wall. Good job, Em.

"You jumpy for some good reason?" The detective finally relaxed, shaking out tensed muscles. The thoughts that had been engulfing me came flooding back.

"Just now, right now, it was . . . I saw Michael going into the woods," I stammered. I told her briefly about what Jack had said about billowy skirts and my discovery of the burning stolen diary. "He must have got panicked from my talk and tried to get rid of the evidence."

She suddenly was all business. "How far down?"

I pointed to the place, about a city block from where we stood.

She nodded briefly. "Here's what you do. First, you go to the library. You stay near people. You follow me and I swear to God, I'll shoot you myself." Her finger came within an inch of my nose. "I don't need any more heroics from you, Wonder Woman. *Capisce?*"

I nodded, my throat tightening. She didn't need heroics and I didn't need to be anywhere near this confrontation. Michael, how *could* you?

"Second"—she knelt down to check that her shoelaces were tied tightly—"You call every cop that Monroe's got. You tell them an officer needs assistance. Got that?"

"Got it," I said. "I go to the library, I call the cops. *You* be careful." Pam nodded and started running quietly along the verge, toward the point in the woods where I'd seen Michael disappear, moving with the confident grace of a big predator. I tried my cell phone: no signal. I went inside and headed for the security office. Locked tight. There was a phone in the hall near the library. Even when it occurred to me that Detective Kobrinski had to have a radio to call for backup, that she was trying to get me out of the way, I was more than happy to be gone and play the part of the chorus hollering for help. I was just digging a quarter out of my pocket when the library doors swung open.

Michael stood in the doorway, staring at me fixedly. Without thinking, I backed up a step or two. A brief flare of guilt—Michael, I've just betrayed you!—followed and was quenched by a strong flood of fear and anger that surged through me. I backed up, shaking my head, trying to understand what was happening.

Michael cleared his throat. "You've got to tell me, Emma."

I could barely think of what I should do, but settled for backing away another step. "What?"

"I'm not a bad-looking guy, am I?"

I blinked. "What?"

"I mean, if you shut off your overactive superego, you'd be on me in a heartbeat, right?"

"H—how did you get here?" I stuttered. My mind raced. He looked like he'd just woken up from my lecture, not like he'd been out tramping in the woods . . . there must be a back door. But I knew there was no back door from the room he'd emerged from.

"How did I get here?" He sighed heavily. "Okay, when a mommy and a daddy love each other *very* much, and *they're married*—somehow state approval's always required in these talks—" he muttered to himself.

"Michael! Where *were* you just now?" I demanded, closing the space between us. I was going to get some answers now, come hell or high water.

Michael paused, shaking his head, and backed away from me, now realizing that I was serious but not understanding why. "The library, trying to decide whether Sasha likes me. All those cute outfits, the little girlish confidences? She does, she wants me bad. And who can blame her, how can she even think of that bookworm geek when *I'm* in the

room? Oh, Harry's all right, but he's just too subdued for
me. More importantly, too subdued for Sasha. He's just dull,
quiet as a—"

" 'Wee, sleekit mousie,' " I finished, shaking my head disbelievingly. It couldn't be. But it suddenly made a whole
world of sense.

"Burns wrote 'beastie,' " Michael corrected. "But it
would be boring of me to point that out. I'm just thinking of
Sasha. She needs someone with a *life*. Harry's just got his
books. I like books too, but frankly, I bet Harry's got paper
cuts on his dick—"

"Michael, shut up for a second! Harry's the killer! I just
sent Pam Kobrinski after him, I thought it was you—"

"Me? Oh, Emma!" He sounded disappointed and disapproving. Then seeming to hear what I was saying, he took
the receiver out of my hand and dialed 911, without using
the coin I tried to press on him. "Don't need it for 911," he
said, impatiently.

"Right. Call the cops, tell them what's happened," I said,
backing down the hallway. "Tell them an officer needs assistance."

He covered the mouthpiece of the phone. "Where are you
going?"

"I'm going to warn Pam Kobrinski!" I called over my
shoulder, as I opened the door. "She's looking for *you*. She
won't expect Harry!"

"You can't go back out there! You'll be killed!" Michael's
fear was one of the few undisguised emotions I'd ever seen
him show.

"I can't take the chance that Harry will find her first!"

I'd sent Detective Kobrinski after the wrong person. That
thought repeated itself as I raced down the road. Oh God,
don't let me be too late! I thought about what she might be

running into, and moved even faster. What she'd said before didn't count; I couldn't stay put and do nothing. I headed into the woods, even though in every movie I've ever seen, the person who is told to stay put and then does not gets blown up or falls in the tiger trap or is eaten by the army of mummies. I got as far as a small clearing, fifty yards off the road, when I had to stop and catch my breath. I had to warn her, to make her look for—

I heard rustling in the dry leaves. Someone was coming toward the clearing, from the opposite direction of the path I'd followed.

Instinct insisted I not assume it was Pam Kobrinski. I dove behind a thorny bush and watched Harry Saunders enter the clearing. In one hand, he held a pistol. He was wearing the dark gray overcoat I'd seen him in when he got the Chandler letters for me. To my horror, I saw that there was blood smeared all over his hands. Oh no—Pam! But . . . but . . . surely I would have heard the gunshots . . . Though I now knew that Harry knew more than one way to kill, not all of them as loud as a pistol . . .

As Harry looked around, I could feel the hairs on the back of my neck standing up. He looked tired, but no worse than that. Did he know I knew he was the murderer? I didn't realize it myself until just a moment ago, and there was no way I could bluff my way past him. But he didn't look like someone who was being hunted; he looked like he was searching for someone himself.

There's a special thrill, even in the most innocent of situations, when you are watching someone who might be looking for you. The tension mounts as you wonder how long you can remain unseen. That sensation was nothing compared to this, blood pounding, every nerve twanging taut, adrenaline telling me to do something, anything, but quick. I thought I would black out from panic when his searching eyes seemed to stare right at me, and then felt the disorienting giddiness of rebirth when his gaze swept past me.

Anticipation mingled with desperation and sickness. I looked quickly around me, but no convenient stout branch or fist-sized rock offered itself to me as a weapon. I'd have to run for it, try to make a break for the road. With the possibility of Pam hurt or worse, I needed help.

Harry looked around the clearing again before he sat down on a stump and put his head into his hands, his back to me.

I gathered up my breath to make the dash. I had to run, I had to be as fast as I knew how. I had nothing I could use to stop him . . .

. . . Nothing but surprise.

I wasn't even aware that I'd decided to tackle Harry until I'd launched myself toward him. Probably better that way, but my decision startled me. I couldn't even make use of the microseconds of flight to form any solid plan or decide how best to land. I had time for only one thought:

Awww shit.

I knocked Harry from the stump, but things stopped going my way right after that. He was sprawled face-first into the leaves with his arm and the pistol underneath him. But my foot caught on the stump as I took him over, and so instead of landing right on top of Harry, I went skidding through the leaf duff next to him. At least I'd anticipated landing hard. By the time Harry had struggled up, I had a chance to roll up back onto one hip and launch a roundhouse kick at his hand, with every bit of rage I had in me.

It was a good kick—I landed it just above his wrist—and I knocked the gun away. The weapon bounced off a tree and fired as it deflected back into the clearing about ten feet from where we were tangled.

The explosion of the discharge, echoing through the forest, startled us both, and we each automatically covered our heads. Not for long. We lowered our arms and stared at each other, astonished. Harry looked so surprised, so much like the gentle, quiet man that I thought I knew, that instead of punching him square in the face, I hesitated after I scrambled to my knees. That was the worst kind of mistake.

He recovered one second faster than I did and lunged forward, slamming his fist into me. I twisted away as he approached and blocked with my left arm, so that instead of catching the blow in my stomach as he'd intended, it glanced off my arm and hit the back of my ribs. That hurt like hell, but not as badly as it could have. His next punch came quickly too, smashing into my shoulder and knocking me back over onto the carpet of dead leaves. My left arm went numb and my eyes filled on the jarring double impact; I couldn't see until I'd shaken my head clear. Only by good luck did my flailing foot trip him up, but that didn't slow him much. Harry began to scrabble toward the pistol, breathing hard with hitching breaths.

With an animal's noise, I flung myself on his legs as he tried to crawl away, and climbed up his back to slow him before he could get to the gun. Harry grunted and tried to roll over to get me off him. My breath was coming in gasps, tears streaming down my face as I tried to hang onto him, slow him down; he finally threw me aside, part of his coat tearing away in my hand. As he raised himself to his knees, I grabbed Harry's hair and yanked back as hard as I could. Harry screeched as my right fist crashed into his face; I felt the skin on my knuckles tear as they hit his glasses. He immediately swung his left arm up in a brutal uppercut that caught me square on the chin.

I saw stars as his punch slammed my jaw up into my skull, and I hit the ground again, stunned. Hot blood gushed like a searing river across loosened teeth, and I shook my head again and again, unable to clear my vision. Disoriented, I couldn't figure out where I was, where Harry was, or what was happening until I blurrily recognized his foot arcing toward my face.

I rolled to one side, trying to grab his foot, but wasn't entirely fast enough: Harry's toe connected with my left shoulder instead of my head. My arm, already throbbing, went dead to all sensation but blinding pain, so that instead of pulling him over as I'd hoped, he only stumbled. Then he surprised me. Instead of kicking me again, Harry staggered over and picked up the pistol.

I tried to get up and stumbled, a tearing sensation in my left shoulder sending electric sparks through my brain. That shoulder had already taken more than its fair share of abuse in my life and the sheer intensity of the pain now scared me. I backed up and got up very slowly as Harry lurched over, holding the pistol unsteadily before him.

"Don't . . . don't make me," he panted. Blood was streaming down the side of his face, and he kept shaking his head gently, as if I'd knocked something loose. I'd torn his overcoat nearly off his back, and dirt, pine needles, and the spines of leaves clung to what was left. "I don't want to, don't make—"

"Don't want to?" I said, my words like a moan. "What about Faith, Harry? And poor"—I struggled to catch my breath—"stupid Jack? What about Pam?"

"She didn't give me any choice!" Harry was adamant. "They didn't give me any choice, it was up to them, it was their decision . . ."

He drew closer, but still looked unsteady. I tried to muster the resources to get the gun away from him again, but I didn't think that I could move fast enough to surprise him. Giving myself the chance to catch my breath and catch him off guard, I tried words instead. Anything to keep him away.

"Why?" I asked as evenly as I could. My breath was still

coming in gasps, and I could feel my jaw beginning to swell. I could feel one or two of my teeth wiggling, loose in the back of my mouth, and the shocking, body-warm taste of blood sliding across my tongue. "Harry, what could ever make you—"

"Shut up! You don't understand, nobody understands!" he shouted. But instead of being overcome by what he'd done, as I'd hoped, he seemed to get angrier with me for reminding him. Harry stepped in quickly, grabbed the collar of my sweater, and practically lifted me to my feet. As I reached out to steady myself against him, he rapped my fingers away with the pistol. Reflex made me stick my bruised knuckle in my battered mouth—that did neither any good.

"Faith didn't give me any choice." Harry took a breath. "And Jack was always his own worst enemy," he continued more calmly. The blood and sweat were drying on his face like a gruesome mask, and one lens in his fancy tortoise shell glasses was cracked. He seemed to be recovering a lot faster than I was, though: He had a mission. "And now you've complicated things again, I need to consider my—"

I was bracing myself to drive my elbow into his stomach, when Harry suddenly whipped me around, slipping an arm across my neck. I saw why in a second: Detective Sergeant Kobrinski had crept up on us at the far edge of the clearing and had her pistol aimed at us. To my surprise, she looked unharmed.

I wasn't comforted, however. Harry tightened his grip on me and raised his gun to my head. "Options. I need options, Emma," he said. "And right now, you're all the options I have."

Chapter 20

"**P**UT THE GUN DOWN, HARRY," PAM ORDERED calmly. "Let Emma go."

"No, put *your* gun down, throw it away from you," Harry countered. "We're going to walk away and you're not going to do a damned thing about it. Not if you're smart."

"You okay, Emma?" Pam never broke eye contact with Harry.

"Uh . . . yeah," I said. But I could feel my jaw swelling and my neck was aching from the way that Harry was holding me. My feet hurt from spending so much time on tiptoe but that was nothing compared to the way my shoulder felt. I wished my arm would just fall off and be done with it. I could feel Harry's heart pounding, could smell the blood and fear from him. I wished that I could figure out what to do, but the last thing I wanted was to screw up any advantage that the detective might have.

"Harry, let go of Emma," she said. "You don't want to make this any worse than it is."

"And if you don't back off, you're going to have corpses here!"

As if "here" were the cue, a tremendous crashing was heard alongside of us. Several things happened, all too quickly. Harry tightened his grip across my neck. I clung to his arm, as much to steady myself as to try to keep him from accidentally strangling me, and tucked my chin to prevent that. I thought that I might have been able to get out of his grasp, but then there was the gun, and I had no idea what the detective might have in mind, and heavens knew, she was the expert here. Detective Kobrinski, not knowing what to expect, rapidly swung her pistol from us to the source of the disturbance, then back again. And Michael Glasscock skidded into the clearing, tripped over a log, and landed face-first in the leaves before us all.

"Goddamn trees," he muttered, picking himself up. Then noticing the tableau onto which he'd stumbled, Michael paused.

"Holy shit," he whispered in awe. He scrambled backward until he was alongside the detective, staring at Harry incredulously the whole time. "It *is* you!"

I could feel Harry relax slightly; Michael was no threat to him. "I don't think things have changed materially, Detective. Now there are just more innocent people to die. Lose your gun!"

She hesitated, with a scowl for Michael.

"Throw it away!" Harry screamed, jamming the muzzle of the pistol to my temple.

I felt the gun press into my head and squeezed my eyes shut. "Oh God!" I flinched, sending another spasm of pain through my jaw.

"Okay, Harry? Harry?" Pam's voice was urgent, attention-grabbing. "Harry. You're in charge." Detective Kobrinski tossed her weapon carefully on the ground behind her. "You're the one who can decide to end this right now."

Harry's gun pulled back, maybe a millimeter. I thought I

felt the pressure ease up, or maybe it was just what I was hoping.

My heart sank as she said, "We can work this out."

As much as I didn't like being caught between two gun barrels, this was even more alarming: I knew things were going to start happening now. Every fiber of my being was straining to be ready for whatever was going to come. I could only wait for the right moment—and when that moment came? Well, the only advice I could find to give myself was *Don't screw up*.

"How about a trade, Harry?" Pam offered. Her voice was so calm, so reasonable, I would have done it in a heartbeat. "Me for Emma."

"Not a chance." Harry swallowed, licked his lips. "Now here's what we're going to do—"

I don't think Harry realized he was shouting, another assault on my ears. I don't think he realized how tightly he was holding onto me, close to choking me.

"—We're going to leave here, and you're going to stay. If I see you near us, I'll shoot her."

Pam tried again. "Harry, you don't have to—"

He yanked me, ignoring her. "Move!" he bellowed in my ear.

I couldn't make my knees bend. I didn't want to leave. "Can't breathe," I gasped.

"You don't need to breathe, you need to move, now!" he screamed. A little fleck of foam flew out of his mouth past me.

I saw a tremor in the gun near my head and thought, Em, you've got to be better than this. You can't give him any reason to pull the trigger. Do what Pam is always saying, just start at the beginning, move from the known to the unknown. Just do what he says, just for a minute, and then we'll see. Break the problem into steps, deal with each one, and then we'll see.

The first step was the hardest to take, but I did it. After that it was easier; with that little bit of forward motion Harry began to practically drag me, and all I had to worry about was keeping my balance. Once I'd made the decision to move, it began to be easier to think beyond myself. To consider how I might survive this mess. Break it into steps, just like research, just take each big problem and break it into smaller ones. Stay focused and deal with every opportunity as it comes. Just don't screw up.

We lumbered awkwardly down the path toward the road that ran behind the library, off Shrewsbury land. The fence was chainlink here, and a large section of it was cut and bent back, creating an exit for us. An old dark Volvo station wagon was parked there. Harry opened the front passenger door and shoved me in.

"Get in," he ordered, shoving me over to the driver's seat. "You drive." He followed me and slammed the door shut behind him.

There was no way that I was going to make this *easy* for him. "I can't . . . my arm is . . . dislocated," I protested. My left arm felt horrible, but I didn't really know what was wrong with it. This was just the beginning of my plan, Step One: Don't be any more help than necessary.

"You'll manage. I have great faith in you." Harry got in the passenger's side, shut the door, and handed me the keys. "Don't try anything. I'm not a great shot—"

I thought back to the day at the historical center. Had it been him?

"—but even I can't miss from a foot away."

Don't try anything? That thought almost made me giggle. But giggling would have turned quickly to sobbing, and I couldn't afford that now. Don't try anything? That made Step Two clear: Don't inspire confidence in your abilities. I didn't even have to think about that one. Out of habit, I turned to fasten my seat belt, but then I reconsidered: I might want to make a hasty exit. Instead I probed at my shoulder, and didn't need to fake flinching; it hurt like hell. Step Three: Be patient and wait for your moment. But don't wait too long. And don't screw up, don't screw up, don't screw up . . .

Harry wiped at his face, seeming tired. "Now drive. Not too fast, not too slow. Nothing funny."

I pulled away, heading down the road that encircled the Shrewsbury compound until we were out on the road in front of the guard house, heading toward Monroe.

Harry was starting to shake a little now, a delayed reaction to the confrontation. He pushed the cigarette lighter in, and was talking breathlessly, almost animatedly. "Okay, now, you're the one who's going to decide how long you live, and the sooner you realize that, the better for both of us. So you try anything, there is absolutely nothing to keep me from getting rid of a little dead weight, right?"

I nodded, concentrated on driving and thinking hard. My arm and jaw both ached, throbbing out of synch.

"You sit there, you keep quiet, you don't get hurt."

I thought, "Too bad you can't say that in the library." I was surprised that I still had a sense of humor, and I clung to it. I needed anything that would help me think beyond my fear and pain right now.

We pulled down the road and I accelerated to about forty-five miles an hour.

When we were past the gate, I tried a question, testing the waters. "Where are we going?"

"The airport," he said after a second. "Head toward town. You may have a longer ride than I thought."

I didn't like the sound of that: too many variables. But the road to Monroe was very familiar to me and that led to a modicum of resolve. I eased up on the accelerator ever so slightly. "What about the books, Harry? Can you just leave them like this?"

Oddly, that question didn't bother him as I thought it might; I wondered what else might be going on here.

"The books are safe," he said confidently, rubbing at the still-bleeding cut on his hand. "They're where no one can hurt them. I can get them later." The cigarette lighter popped out, and he lit a cigarette from a crumpled package on the dash. It seemed to relax him. I wasn't sure whether that was a good thing.

I thought furiously. "It was all for the books, wasn't it, Harry?"

He shook his head in disbelief. "People don't realize how carelessly they destroy the past. You ought to be able to appreciate that."

I looked in the rearview and saw Pam Kobrinski's car following us, not too far back, but not too closely either. It might have been the sight of it that inspired me, having driven down this road twice before, expressly to see the detective. Suddenly, a plan sprang full-blown into my mind, but just the thought of it made my stomach turn.

Harry turned and saw the other car too. "Shit. Slow down." His moment of respite was over. "Let her see I've still got the gun pointed at you."

I slowed down even more, and the car fell back and matched our speed.

"Okay, pick it up again. C'mon." His hand was shaking with the gun in it.

I accelerated and the detective's car sped up too, never increasing or decreasing the distance between us. Harry was feeling crowded, I could tell, something that would only worsen if we started running into any more cops coming from Monroe. The mere thought of what might happen at a roadblock sickened me.

"*You* can understand, can't you Emma?" Harry almost pleaded; he needed a friend. "Why I had to do what I had to do? They were going to destroy history, and I had to stop them."

I stalled. "I . . . don't know," I said uncertainly. "It can't be worth human lives, can it, Harry?" Just talking hurt my mouth, but that was the least of my troubles. I had to keep him talking, I had to keep him distracted. "And what about Sasha?"

Harry's voice softened. "I love Sasha. I've never felt like that about anyone before, and what's more, I'm sure she loves me back. It's amazing." Then his face hardened again. "It wasn't until Faith began to threaten me that I had to think seriously about . . . keeping her quiet."

"Keeping her quiet." I thought I could simply repeat the words, but something in my voice goaded Harry.

"Faith brought that on herself! I couldn't have Sasha find out. I couldn't lose her. It's Faith's own fault she's dead."

I kept my mouth shut, thinking as hard as I could.

"I took the books. I never meant to hurt anyone." He nodded, inhaling deeply. "Hell, it seemed like no one would even miss them. It should have been no more than a puzzling loss, perhaps chalked up to poor management or petty theft.

"But don't get me wrong, Emma. When we're dead and dust, there's nothing left to speak for us. Nothing left of our thoughts. Books are the only legacy of our minds. The only way to touch the past. And they were treating them like they were baseball cards to be traded." He took an angry drag off his cigarette and coughed a little. "No, baseball cards get more respect."

"But you don't keep everything you buy, do you, Harry?" I reasoned carefully. "You decide what stays, what is exchanged for something more important." I couldn't afford to seem like I was challenging him, not with the gun, his frayed nerves, and that dangerous look in his eye. I needed to divert him, however, and continued as evenly as I could, following

Kobrinski's lead in letting him believe he had all the power, which was no real stretch for me.

While I spoke, my mind raced, trying to form my plan. I'd driven down this road often enough to pick my spot. The trick now was timing. The only problem was that the view I had admired so much before, the great drop to the next valley, now filled me with dread. If I misjudged the distance by so little as a couple of feet . . .

"That's right, *I* decide," Harry answered. "That's why Whitlow, the board, hired me. But they were starting to interfere with the process, with my work, my life, and so I had to act fast to save the books from those Philistines. The board wanted to sell some of the best things, the oddest things, because they didn't think they were as important as some of the first editions. So I began to move them."

I ventured a quick look. I could see the heightened color in his face, where the blood didn't cover it.

"But then Sasha came along. She . . . is special. I thought, maybe, one day, I could tell her. She might understand, and if not, she need never know." Harry continued, incensed. "But then Faith told me she knew, that she'd seen me heading through the woods one night. At first, she made me believe that she got it, that she could help, in fact. When I saw she was toying with me, she began to . . . make demands. She's vile, Emma, you have no idea. And when I finally balked, she threatened to tell Sasha. But I couldn't afford to let her do that."

He wasn't worried about losing his job or the police, I thought. He was worried about Sasha.

"Sasha changed the world for me. She was worth any number of Faiths. Emma, you . . . you *have* to understand."

I didn't like the tone in Harry's voice; it was harsh and insistent. "What about Jack? What about my room?" He was talking now, he wanted to talk, and I needed him to concentrate on that and not on me. I kept my eyes carefully on the road. "How could Jack have seen you carrying Faith to the stream? You can't see it from the house."

"Jack never saw me carrying Faith that night; he saw me carrying a tarp from the house—I didn't want to leave any traces of her in the car. I wasn't thinking clearly, I'd never . . . I should have just taken her into the woods. I thought that the water would help . . . disguise what had happened. When I saw Jack's note, it was a simple matter to invite him for a drink—drinks—later on. I didn't know if she'd given you her diary . . ."

"You pulled me off the stool." I kept my voice carefully neutral, inviting him to continue. "And burned the diary?" My humming nerves almost blotted out the pain in my jaw, made the rest of the world outside of the car recede. I had to struggle to keep my plan focused in my head.

Harry sounded defeated, confused. "I thought that I could implicate Michael by burning the diary at the residence. And I didn't mean to hurt you that day in the library; I was walking by and I saw you through the door. I just reached in and yanked—but I just wanted to scare you, to get you to leave, I never wanted to hurt you. Because I know you'll understand, I know you will. I had to do this. I've seen you at your work, you know what I'm saying."

It was so much worse than when Michael said I should know better, and I knew that Harry must have said the same thing to Faith. I shook my head and slowed the car imperceptibly. I needed a few more moments and took a chance. "Harry, my work is a big part of my life. You do know that, that's why I couldn't leave." I worked hard trying to think of something to distract him. "But it's only books, only work. I couldn't . . . do what you've done."

"Are you sure?" His voice was different now, not pleading. Scary. I heard a rustling and out of the corner of my eye, I saw Harry remove something from his shirt pocket.

" 'My dear Cousin,' " the librarian read. " 'I am delighted

to find myself alive, finally able to tell you that I am free . . . ' "

There was a sharp turn in the road, and navigating the curve in the fading daylight slowed down my recognition. I couldn't understand what Harry was saying.

" ' . . . My story is a remarkable one and had anyone described such a tale to me, I should have called him a liar.' "

Recognition dawned, and I turned and stared at Harry. "That's the beginning of Margaret's trial letter!"

"Watch the road!" Harry demanded, brandishing the pistol. He yanked sharply at the steering wheel.

We swerved suddenly, and fishtailing, the back end of the station wagon screeched, dragging against the guard rail before I straightened us out.

"You had it all along," I said shakily. There had been less than an inch of metal between us and the hundred foot drop on the other side of the rail, the view that I'd admired so much driving to Shrewsbury that first day.

"I wanted to see the look on your face when I was able to 'discover' it for you, one day." Harry's voice hardened. "What would you give to see the details of her trial, Emma? What does this scrap of paper mean to you?"

I stared straight ahead and said nothing.

It was getting darker and more and more difficult to see the road. I felt like shit, I couldn't think, not with everything that was happening, but more than anything, now, I needed to stay clear-headed. I knew what that letter meant, what it meant to me, what I'd sacrificed for my work. And now I didn't dare imagine what I had risked by staying to see Margaret's correspondence.

Suddenly, I smelled smoke. I looked across to the other seat in horror. Harry held a furled scrap of paper to his lit cigarette and it was catching fire. Slowly, then with increasing hunger, the flames consumed the fragment of paper that contained the answers to so many of my research questions.

"Jesus, no!" The car careened wildly as I lunged at Harry, trying to snatch the letter away from him. Again, he yanked the steering wheel back into position, keeping us from veering off the road.

"Watch the road, Goddamn it! Get your hands on the wheel!"

I was too late. Not much more than a scrap to begin with, the dry paper burned quickly. Harry let the last two inches of it curl and blacken, until there was nothing left but a wisp of smoke rising from the scrap and a smell of burning cotton thick in the air. He rolled down the window and threw the remainder out.

I gave him a look, full of malice and heartbreak, and turned to face the road again, gritting my teeth. Very soon now, Harry . . . I slowed the car again, ever so slightly.

Harry jammed the pistol in front of my face, emphasizing his words. "Just now you were willing to kill two people in order to save a letter, a sheet of paper, a *fragment*, written by a nobody, the wife of an insignificant provincial bureaucrat! Now tell me you don't understand how I feel!"

It was a long moment before I could choke out the words. "How could you? The way you feel?"

"It was a small price to pay to make my point, Emma." His reply was strained, tired and patient, as if he was trying to explain something very unfair to a small child. "I did this so you'll understand."

I glanced away from the road in front of me, as if considering this. I put aside mourning the loss of Margaret's letter to try and save my life. In the side mirror, I could see the headlights of the police car tailing us.

"Maybe I do, just a little, Harry." I ran my tongue around my teeth and tasted the warm slime of my own blood before I continued. "But you don't want to make this situation worse than it already is. If Sasha loves you, she'll love you no matter what. You need to—"

But I'd gone too far. "Nobody tells me what to do, Emma! Not the board, not Faith, and certainly not you!" He waved the gun again. "I'll be the one to decide what I'm going to do!"

I passed the mile marker I had been waiting for. It was time, now or never. I took a deep breath, said a short prayer to no one in particular and got ready.

"But not about me, Harry. I decide for me!"

And then I did what I knew I was going to have to do all along. I jerked the steering wheel sharply to the right, pulling as hard as I could.

For a moment, I thought I'd waited too long, that I was going to take us through the barrier and over the cliff into the valley below. I hit the brake and swerved into a stand of trees that stood off the soft shoulder of the road, a scenic lookout. After bumping off the road, the station wagon slammed into a tall pine, and the impact seemed to ripple through the heavy steel frame of the car. It was only the fact that I had been slowing down that kept us from going through the windshield entirely; I felt the steering wheel slam into my chest as my forehead smacked against the glass. All was black.

When I opened my eyes, it must have been only moments later, for the light outside hadn't changed. Harry was reaching over me and was trying to get the car to start again, to back the car away from the pine, but half the engine must have been embedded in the trunk. With the last ounce of sense I possessed, I surreptitiously reached for the door handle.

Harry was crying with frustration, screaming at the car to move, move you son of a bitch, when my hand slipped and the handle snapped back loudly into place. Harry quieted suddenly and then drew the pistol up, staring right at me. His face was even worse than after our fight, blood running down from his nose and forehead, where his glasses smashed in on the impact. He tore them off impatiently, blinking to see through the fresh veil of blood on his face.

"Get out of the car, Emma," he said quietly.

I couldn't understand what he was saying, and I stared at him. Harry's eyes looked like they did the day I told him I'd cracked Margaret's code, except now he looked utterly abandoned, bereft of hope and faith. My hand fell away from the door as I misunderstood his directions.

"No," he screamed, "Get out of the fucking car! Get out of the fucking car, or I will kill you, I'll shoot you here and now! Get out of the car, *now*!"

I found the handle and yanked it open. The door fell partly open with a resisting screech of crushed metal, and I had to throw my weight against it so that I could squeeze out. I thought I was going to pass out with the pain stabbing through my left side. "Harry, don't, you can't—!"

"Just once more, Emma. Just once more. Get out of the car, GET OUT—"

But even before I could squeeze myself through the partly opened door, Harry reached over and shoved me as hard as he could. I fell on to my left side and, expecting to feel the impact of a bullet through my head any second, tried to scurry away. I had just got myself to my feet when I heard the shot, loud and sharp, echoing forever in the cold dusk.

I flinched convulsively, clutching at myself. It had to have hit me in the shoulder, that's where all the pain was. But even as I looked down to see how bad the wound was, I realized the truth.

Harry hadn't followed me out of the car. He'd shot himself instead.

My relief at being left alive was only momentary, then the thought of what he'd done to me saturated my con-

sciousness. I staggered forward a foot or two, unable to believe what had just happened.

"No, no, no, no!" Rage consumed me, ate away even at
the agony in my shoulder. I couldn't believe that he'd burned
the letter and then taken away the last of Margaret's secrets
with him to the grave. I couldn't believe what he'd forced
me to do. What he'd forced me to see.

I spun around, picked up a branch lying near us and
swung it like a baseball bat at the windshield. It bounced off
uselessly, not even making another crack in the blood-
spattered glass. That only made me angrier, but the impact
had rendered my arm nearly useless again and I dropped the
stick numbly. I was kicking at the driver's side door with my
good hand, in a rage at Harry and the stupid, brutal things
he'd done, when Detective Kobrinski pulled up.

"This isn't what I wanted!" I screamed at her, pointing at
the car. "I didn't mean it! I just wanted him to stop!"

"Oh man," Detective Kobrinski whispered. "There's an
ambulance coming, but—"

"He's dead! He fucking shot himself . . . stupid, stupid!
He didn't have to . . . ! And now he's dead!" I started to kick
the car again, but the detective caught me.

"Oh God!" I wailed over her shoulder. "He told me to get
out! If I'd stayed he wouldn't have, if I hadn't . . . he
wouldn't have—"

"If you'd stayed in the car, he would have shot you too,"
she said quietly. "He would have shot himself anyway, there
was nothing left."

I struggled to free myself. "No, he wouldn't! No, he
wouldn't!" I tried to shove her away, but broke down entirely. "He made me decide!" I screamed. "I liked him! And
he's dead and I'm just like him and I killed him!"

"Emma, don't. You're not, you're nothing like—"

But I couldn't hear anything more of what she was telling
me. The horror of what I'd just been a part of was too much.

I stopped struggling, but sank to my knees, not minding the cold of the ground or the pain in my shoulder, but realizing that at some point, I would have to stop crying and figure out how to cope with what had just happened.

Pam Kobrinski held me as I sobbed, until the ambulance pulled up beside us.

Epilogue

Almost two weeks later, I swiveled around in my chair, staring at the books on the bookshelf. Outside the house that we lovingly call the Funny Farm, spring was happening and somewhere out there, Brian was fussing in the yard that was just recovering from its winter trauma. Although it was early still, he was planning what would go into the garden this year, his enthusiasm almost compensating for the still-weak sun. Like any new convert, he was attacking the chores with zeal if not finesse, a San Diegan intoxicated by the prospect of making something grow in this hostile climate. He was getting the hang of the seasons' changes around here, in terms of planting and home repairs, and I could see how happy all this was making him. I suppose, too, that raking and pruning allowed him to imagine that I really was working as I'd claimed I had to when he invited me to help.

Back in the woods, the blood on Harry's hands had been his own.

I took a drink. A quick look at the computer screen told me no surprises: I hadn't written a word since I sat down several hours ago. No matter. People were treading cautiously around me, put off I guess by the bruises that were still visible. "You'll feel better soon, just give yourself some time," was what they generally said, and I was dishonest enough to take the excuse they were offering me. I felt okay, I'm a fast healer. I didn't lose any teeth, my arm was feeling lots better, and all I'd needed was a couple of stitches where my head hit the windshield. Exceedingly small potatoes, considering that I could have been blown away at close range, but I felt as though I could never be carelessly happy again.

My real problem was that I was troubled with an excess of philosophy.

It had all been terribly simple. Harry had constructed a weatherproof hidey-hole in the ground in the woods near the library. Detective Kobrinski had found it and guessed that Harry had caught his hand on the heavy door that was covered with leaves. When she opened it and shone her flashlight inside, it was like looking at a separate wing of the library, she said. Harry had tripped the alarm a couple of times in figuring out his plan to remove the books, then tripped it periodically after that to throw the scent off himself. No one knew yet how many he might have moved away to some other location before he'd. . .

Outside, I heard the rhythmic rasp of a rake. Every once in a while, Brian would look toward the office to try and catch a glimpse of me, but I knew that he couldn't see me where I was sitting. At one point, he stopped altogether, chin resting thoughtfully on the wooden handle of the rake, and I could tell he was debating whether to come in and give me a good shake, figuratively speaking. I half wished he would, so that I could yell at him, tell him to leave me alone, make him feel guilty for making me upset after all I'd been through.

The raking started up again and I sighed. I took another

long, sour sip and tried not to think about thinking. A pile of
mail on the desk held no interest for me, and the only thing I
opened, from a gardening company in California, held a
packet of lily of the valley pips. I couldn't find a note with it,
but I assumed it was from Brian's mother and realized with a
heavy heart that I would have to call to thank her for thinking of me, sometime soon. Maybe Brian had told her what
had happened, and she was trying to cheer me up. I didn't
know, and couldn't bring myself to care; I didn't feel like
talking to anyone either.

I crumpled up a piece of paper and threw it for Minnie to
chase. She went after it with all the enthusiasm I lacked. As
Bucky had promised, she was a slender cat the color of cocoa powder dusted over black velvet, with fine little bones,
and dainty slipper feet. Her tail was like the short stroke of a
calligrapher's brush. It gave me no pleasure to watch her
gamboling.

The raking ceased and I heard the side door slam. Uh-oh,
I thought. Time for another round. I poured another half inch
of bourbon into my glass and braced myself when I heard
the inevitable knock on the door.

I took a sip and thought about it for a moment before I decided I could take it. "Yeah?"

As the door opened I deliberately swung around again so
that I was facing the computer screen, ostensibly busy at
work. "I'm sort of in the middle of something, sweetie—"

"I'll say, Auntie," said a familiar voice that wasn't Brian's.
"About halfway through that bottle, aren't you?"

"I didn't open it today, if that's what you're asking." I
turned around and saw Michael Glasscock pick up the bottle
of Maker's Mark from the desk. "What the hell are *you* doing here?" I asked.

Michael was dressed as he always was, the eternal overcoat shrouding dark clothing and an Anna Sui tie. There was

one significant difference, however. A bright turquoise silk scarf was tossed carelessly over one shoulder. A pinstripe suit and banker's brogues would have been less a surprise.

Michael arched one eyebrow in response to my unwelcoming tone and set the bottle back down. "My, my. A tribute to Jack? Why are you drinking that stuff? I had you favorably categorized as a single-malt girl."

"Bourbon's for working days. What do you *want*?"

"Ah, working days." He sauntered over to the bookshelf and began rifling through the titles. He picked out one book, read the back, frowned, and put it back. "A fine spring Saturday afternoon—for God's sake, even *I'm* out—and *you're* inside drinking and pretending to work. A bit Gothic, don't you think?"

I stared. "Excuse me, Mr. Sit-in-the-Dark-and-Mope? People who live in glass houses—"

"Shouldn't have sex," he finished, "unless they *both* are exhibitionists. Besides, I'm not brooding, I'm composing." Then squinting and sucking his teeth, oozing disbelief, he said, "And by the way, sitting in the dark is in my character, not yours."

Michael paused in front of a stack of CDs and scrutinized them. He looked around the room, his face troubled. "This isn't really the office I pictured for you. I had this very clear image of you when I was driving up here and this isn't it. The National Geo's are okay, but the science fiction? Real vinyl albums? An autographed photo of Ziggy Marley? Not you at all. It's a nice collection, real nice, but it's not you."

"It's not my office," I said dryly. "How did you get in?"

"Your husband out there—Brian, is it? He let me in. He said you'd be here, staring and flagellating yourself." Michael pulled a long face and pretended to knuckle away imaginary tears. "He's worried sick about you, you know—"

"Brian never said any such thing," I interrupted. Thinking

of my husband, I wrestled briefly with a small pang of guilt, then decided it was below the legal size limit and threw it back. I took another drink and offered the bottle to Michael.

He looked at the bottle askance, then shrugged. "When in the rural backwater," he murmured, raising the bottle to his lips. After a couple of glugs he grimaced. "Good God, that's sweet." He took another sip anyway. "No, of course, he did not say that. His words were, 'Em's in the downstairs office working. Stay for dinner.' From which I deduced the rest correctly."

I looked at him, doubtful.

Michael explained. "I'm sure he's evolved as hell, but he's a *guy*. And a guy does not admit to a comparative stranger that his wife is freaked out and drinking alone, pulling an Emily D."

I was starting to lose patience. "Michael—"

"And then something—I can only assume it was a small wolverine that was blown off course—began to growl at me from under the hedge. Biggest goddamned teeth I ever saw outside of a Spielberg dinosaur movie. I swear to God it was winking at me when it charged—"

"Quasimodo is a cat. *Felis domesticus*. And he only *has* one eye."

But Dr. Glasscock wasn't concerned with accuracy or details. "Anyway, I barely made it in here alive. I could feel the hot breath of hell searing my ankles as whatever-it-was snapped at me."

"And so it's a pity that you'll have to go past him on your way out," I said, rising. "Still, if Quasi didn't actually draw blood, he may just be playing. I'll get Brian to distract him while you—"

"I'm not going. Show me your office," he said unexpectedly.

I sighed. "If I do, will you leave me alone?"

He took another swig of my booze. "Nope. But I will tell you a secret."

"What secret?"

Michael only rolled his eyes back at my simple question. "Upstairs, I presume? C'mon, you can take your glass with you. I'm not one to stand in the way of someone else's party." He opened the door and bowed with a broad flourish.

Just to show him I didn't give a damn about his jibes, I took another big gulp and led the way up to the third floor. Minnie bounded along beside me, and then raced up ahead to check out this new territory. Bucky'd dropped her off a week ago, and she still hadn't been up there yet.

The door stuck a little as I opened it; it was the first time I'd been up there in the weeks since I'd been home. The air was warm and stale and familiar and I felt another pang of remorse and loss.

Michael pushed past me to stand in the middle of the room. "Now *this* is more like it. All these bookcases, with the glass doors, 1920s Arts and Crafts, right?"

"They belonged to my grandfather. Oscar. Some of the books are his, too. The rest went to Harvard when he died."

"Perfect," he replied. "You've got your overstuffed couch, your Oriental carpet, also Oscar-vintage, right? You've got your desk and chair and"—he paused to count—"three work tables. Filing cabinets. You've got your collection of little bits of rock and cultural shit over there, pictures of dirty children—"

"Those are graduate students. Field crews."

"—dirty children and postcards from exotic locales, lovely, good, more stacks of books on the floor, and papers, papers everywhere. A couple of color photographs of portraits of early 18th-century dead people, a couple of tasteful repros of Dutch genre paintings. This is much more like what I was thinking. Now what are we missing?"

Michael put his hands on his hips and tilted his head perkily and quizzically. I was starting to get tired of his antics, curious as I was. Minnie crawled under the couch and I could hear her sneeze; she backed out hastily, dust bunnies stuck to her whiskers. She glared at me with disgust, and then began to wash herself.

"Ah, that's right. Just as I suspected." He pranced over to the doorway and swung the door closed again. "Your diplomas. Hung up, but modestly, out of direct sight. Coolidge U., huh? I should have guessed. Classic archaeology background."

"Michael, what do you want from me?" I said tiredly. My carefully cultivated buzz was wearing off and that annoyed me.

"Nothing, nothing. I just wanted to see if I was right, that's all. And I was. I'm usually a very good judge of character."

I looked hard at Michael, giving a healthy dose of a skeptical eyebrow. "Yeah, right."

"Well, you know." He shrugged. "Apart from wives."

He walked over to a little glass-topped case where I had some of the earliest stuff I'd ever collected, things Oscar had given me—found out of context, of course. Without asking, Michael opened up the top and started picking up artifacts—my things—randomly, looking at them with no sign of interest, and putting them back any which way. I bristled.

"Give me that." I took a little burin out of his hand, replaced it, and shut the case firmly.

Michael peered at my bookshelves as if he'd never seen books before, then yawned. Apparently none of my reading impressed him. "You know, Emma, I have a truly world-class collection of comic books."

I should have been used to his nonsequitors, but I couldn't conceal my surprise this time. "What, comics like *Archie*?"

"Oh, well. I've got a few of those." He shrugged helplessly. "My mother thought they were nicer, say, than *Sergeant Rock* and *Ghost Tank*. But I kept right on collecting them, still do sometimes, started with *Superman*, *Batman*, and have you *seen* Miller's *The Dark Knight*? Unreal. I eventually moved into indies, of course, with *Fat Freddy's Cat* and *The Fabulous Furry Freak Brothers*, *Love and Rockets*, *Stray Toasters*, anything at all by Bill Sienkiewiedz, Japanese *manga*, *H-manga*—"

I had to interrupt Michael's monologue. "Aitch munga?"

"*H-manga*. Cartoon porn in books the size of small phone directories, really not to be confused with *Archie*," he explained impatiently, as if everyone else in the world but me knew about erotic Japanese comic books. "The reason I still keep the collection is because I got two things from comic books that made me what I am today."

I took another drink and mumbled, "I can't wait."

"The first was women. When I discovered Sue Richards—y'know, the Invisible Girl from *The Fantastic Four*?—it was the first time I was aware, really aware, of women. And that women had *breasts*—" he screwed up his face in near ecstasy, his hands reaching out as if to grab the items he was imagining. "When Sue appeared, I was in love; she was gutsy, she was gorgeous, she was powerful, and she was also a mom. She was perfect."

Michael's happy memory suddenly clouded over. "Well, shit. Now that I think of it, I seem to be running to type here. I never knew how profoundly the Invisible Girl affected me."

"Huh? But you just said—"

"Yes, yes. But Mrs. Reed Richards was a blonde brainy bombshell with large ta-tas. Ring any bells for you? Rang 'em four times for me—wedding bells, that is—and now . . ." He looked troubled for a moment, then shrugged it off. "Ah, fuck it. At least I'm consistent. Next. You ever read any comic books? Any at all?"

"No."

"Well, if you hadn't been raised in a tightly lidded cultural Mason jar, you might have known that at the end of every main story line, there's some sort of pious moralizing. Deathless prose like 'If only they had used their power for good, and not evil.' That was my first introduction to philosophy. I mean, if some alien race was trying to destroy Earth, but only to save their planet, was that really *evil?* It made me start to question things. And that led me to the glamorous, high-paying world of academic philosophy and its history."

"So?" Although I was still feigning indifference and had no idea where he was going with all this, I sensed it was terribly important that I listen to him. Nonsense and all.

"So. After many long years of studying the mystic arts, all histories, philosophies, and religions, living and dead, and by the way, drinking way too much strong coffee in ill-lit places with women in secondhand camouflage fatigues and berets, I finally came to a conclusion. And that was the *same* as what I'd learned from my comic books."

"Okay. I'll bite." I shrugged. "What was it?"

Michael took a deep breath. "With great power," he said, "comes great responsibility."

I don't know what I was expecting, but that surely was not it. "Jesus. I was an idiot to listen to you for this long," I said angrily. "Don't let the door hit you on the ass as you leave."

"Wait, wait!" he said. "You haven't heard my secret yet!"

"I don't care what your secret is! I've got better things to do with my life—"

"No, no you don't," he retorted. "You can't even decide whether your own life was worth saving."

His words were like a slap in the face. He was right, but I wasn't about to admit it. "Well, that was impolite."

Michael didn't know from impolite, apparently. "Pshaw, and similarly, horseshit."

Here it comes, I thought. A long pause settled on the room like a lead apron from the dentist office, an intensely physical presence that suddenly suggested danger. I slowly took a sip of the bourbon. "You're talking about cartoons, Michael—"

He looked pained. "Comic books, please. Graphic novels, in some instances."

"I—" I screwed up all my courage to say it out loud, reluctance overcome by a desire to preserve my protective self-pity. "I *killed* someone."

"And you really shouldn't do it again, unless you can't think of some other way that you won't die yourself. See," Michael wandered to the other side of the room, lecturing to himself. "See, I thought that you, having a nodding acquaintance with Darwin, you would have gone that route. Bump off a fellow species-member, successfully reproduce your own genetic material, and, eventually, die happy having fulfilled your biological imperative. Seems terribly simple to me, but then of course I haven't considered the high price of daycare—" He started to chew his lip. "That's something maybe I'd better start thinking about."

I couldn't believe him. "Jesus, Michael, are you listening to me? *I* killed Harry. I, me, *killed*—"

Michael batted his hand at me, all impatience. "I couldn't *not* hear you, you repeat yourself enough. Yes, yes, you killed Harry, you believe you're responsible. I've been thinking about that, and it sure sounds like agency, direct or indirect, to me. Even if you get around to believing you were the hand of God or something, you're still what did the deed. Of course, the cops, not being troubled with coming to some irrefutable philosophical conclusion, have called his death a suicide. That's not your problem, though—"

"It *is* my goddamn problem," I said furiously, but Michael began to laugh. I looked at him, disconcerted.

He sat down on my chair and pushed off, rolling across

the floor, shaking his head. "Oh shit, Emma. You really do think you are the center of the universe, don't you? First it's 'I can't leave, I'm involved in this,' all very martyr-ly and fatalistic. Now you're blaming yourself for the way everything turned out. A little internal consistency, puh-leeze!" Michael wiped his eyes, hauled himself out of the chair, and began to pace. "Sure, I could argue you're the center of the universe, plenty of evidence for it. But you gotta go one way or the other. If you are, then you don't have to worry about your actions—you are, after all, the prime mover. If you aren't, then it doesn't matter in the first place. You're just an insignificant bundle of water and nutrients on a wet little rock that's quickly getting overheated by a cold and dying star."

I felt a flash of adolescent impatience: He was totally missing the point. "Can't you see? I'm just like Harry. I am no better than he is . . . was." I walked over and looked out the window. Down below, Brian was inspecting the early daffodils critically. I rested my head against the glass and watched as he scraped cautiously at the dirt to see if the tips of green showing were really going to be tulips. I sighed. "When he burnt my . . . that letter, I *knew* what he was feeling—I nearly drove us both off the road to get at that letter." And, I thought, what about the rage I felt at the dean, that night he called up to prod me about my tenure review? It scared me to think how tightly I'd wound that phone cord around my hand, almost wishing it was his throat. I was capable of the same feelings as Harry. The same kind of passion. The same violence. And that scared me to death.

"Okay, that's where you're getting hung up." He gestured emphatically with both hands, framing the issue, rendering it moot. "Empathy is not the same thing as sympathy. When you did finally drive off the road, was it to save yourself or to punish Harry?"

I didn't really want to go back there, but I also wanted to

be convinced, so I told him. "I was just trying to get out of there alive—"

Michael threw his hands up, Q.E.D. "There you go. There's nothing wrong there. So, in simple terms, you're fretting about being angry that a bad person hurt you and might have done worse—to you and who knows what other innocent bystanders, if there are actually such things—and not thought twice about it. And you're upset that you were the force that stopped him from doing those things?"

I didn't answer.

He wasn't discouraged yet, and settled comfortably into searching out a rationalization that would work for me; rationalization on short order was a specialty of his. "Hmmm. Look, there are a thousand versions of the truth, I must have one that fits. Okay, how about this? What about vengeance? Jack and Faith, flawed as they were, didn't deserve to die. You made Harry belly up to the cosmic bar and pay his karmic tab, would you buy that?"

I shook my head, watching Brian pick up the rake and walk back toward the house.

Michael seemed to take all this as a challenge, trying to come up with every angle ever thought of. "Well . . . What if, by stopping Harry, giving him that one moment of realization of what he'd done, you've redeemed him?"

I turned and looked at him askance. "You don't believe in redemption."

He waggled his hand back and forth, mezzo-mezzo. "Jury's still out, as far as I'm concerned, but the real question is, did Harry?" Michael wagged a finger, sure he'd hit the answer, and began to pursue his point. "And, more important, do you? Every one of us has the capacity for evil or good. You had the power, you made the choice. All you have to do is make the decisions for the right reasons. And wasting your time worrying about why you're still alive is silly."

I walked over to the little glass-topped case and carefully reorganized the lithic and ceramic pieces that Michael had mixed up, moved out of order. I didn't feel a weight tumble off me, or anything dramatic like that. But I did feel as though a heavy, barred door had opened a crack, and that was enough.

I wondered about my attitude toward work too. Was I too dedicated? Was there such a thing, short of Harry's compulsion? Was it worth it? I'd tackled everything else in my life so ambitiously, what would it look like, what would happen, if I made the same time for myself? For me and Brian? The little puritan inside of me shuddered to think of the work ethic channeled for fun. For living. Something like anticipation kindled at the thought, and I carefully set it aside to consider later. I had a lot of thinking to do, but now, not all of it was grim.

"Are we done talking about you, now?" Michael sounded like a six-year-old pushed beyond all bounds of patience. "It's my turn, I want to tell you my secret."

I could manage almost half a grin. I shut the glass case and turned to him. "Okay, what's your secret?" I said like an indulgent parent.

But Michael wasn't smiling. Michael had suddenly turned serious. "Emma, I can't help myself," he said, wringing his hands. "I'm so in love."

My heart seized up in mid-thump and sat there immobile in my chest. "Ah, uh, that's, I—"

"I know it's sudden, but some good must come out of all this, don't you think?" He was begging me to agree with him.

I could barely think. My hands went cold as my face went hot, remembering his talk of brainy women who were well endowed; Bucky was always telling me that I took her share, in that department. "Sudden—ah, well, yes, as you say—"

"I think we should get married right away, and Sasha thinks so too."

"Sasha? *Sasha*?" I sounded like a confused parrot.

"What can Sasha—?" Then light dawned and, with a big, nearly audible *glug*, my heart started beating again. It felt like it does when you swallow too much all at once. I could tell by the warmth of my face that I hadn't finished blushing, though.

"Yes, what can Sasha be thinking, so soon after it turns out her boyfriend is—*was*—an evil, psycho madman who's just croaked himself?" Michael mused dramatically. "Even if poor Harry was a misguided fellow with an overweening sense of duty to the past, *I'm* thinking that Sasha's *vulnerable* now, and that gives me months, even *years*, before she learns to loathe me and becomes ex-wife Number Five."

I laughed out loud. "What were you just telling me about power and responsibility?"

"This is different," he shook his head and waved both hands, conveniently dismissing everything he just told me. "What do you say?"

"Well, maybe it *is* different," I mused. "Sasha won't be working in the same institution as you. And she's got a good head on her shoulders. Maybe she—"

"Hopping Hades, Emma, I'm not asking for your *blessing*, I'm asking you if you'll come to the wedding, if and when it happens! *Jesu Christo mio*, someone I know really *does* think she's the center of the universe," he muttered, shaking his head. "Is dinner soon? I'm starving. And where's the can? I've got a bourbon rental I've got to return."

Having directed Dr. Glasscock toward the bathroom, I went downstairs. I looked around, realizing the amount of work we'd put into the house, and it was so much better now that there was no comparison. I could ease up on myself, if I wanted to, give things a rest, to really enjoy what Brian and I had already. Bucky was right, and Margaret Chandler was right: fact and truth are different. The fact was that I'd felt overwhelmed, but in truth I could say I liked my life as it was now, and if I backed off on things that weren't so important, like the repairs, and the things that were soon to be out of my control, like my tenure review, I might have the chance to enjoy it all. Like I'd told Harry, I really did have the right to decide for myself. And I had a right to enjoy it, too.

In the kitchen, Brian looked up from his dinner preparations, expectantly, a question in his eyes.

I walked over to the sink, rinsed out my glass, then set it on the dish rack to dry before I nudged myself gently under Brian's free arm.

"Hey, sweetie," I said. "Want some help with those carrots?"

But he didn't even get a chance to answer me: the phone rang. Michael, of course, coming down the stairs, took it upon himself to answer it.

"No, it's not Brian, it's Michael, who's this? Kam? What? Someone named Marty is having a baby? Isn't that a guy's name? Okay, keep your shirt on, buddy, I'll make sure I tell them." He hung up and turned to me. "Hey Emma—?"

But I was reaching for my bag, tossing the car keys to Brian, who was already turning off the stove.

"Sorry, Michael, but you're on your own for dinner, I'm afraid. Sophia Asefi-Shah is on her way into the world, and there's no way I'm going to miss that."